T0072429

Praise for KAREN ESSEX *and*

Dracula in Love

"Dark, gothic, and utterly sensual. . . . The character of Mina Murray leaps from the pages in an extraordinary confession of what truly happened between her and Count Dracula. In this novel of forbidden desires and secrecy, purity is an overrated virtue."

—Michelle Moran, bestselling author of *Nefertiti*

"Beautifully written. . . . Romance and vampire fiction buffs will snap this up." —*Library Journal*

"*Dracula in Love* is a sensual fantasy feast, a flight of the imagination, a darkly rich pleasure."

—Margaret George, author of *The Memoirs of Cleopatra*

"Essex delves deeply into the lives and times of her characters . . . and her women characters are spirited and memorable."

—*The Times-Picayune* (New Orleans)

"Mina Harker is a heroine for the ages—bold, intrepid, and in love with one of the most dangerous, irresistible men in history. If you read only one more vampire novel, let it be this one."

—C. W. Gortner, author of *The Last Queen*

"In Essex's hands, Mina becomes a woman with unusual gifts and powers, and she must learn to use them." —*BookPage*

"Gorgeously written and erotically charged, the novel *Dracula in Love* is like its century-jumping central characters: deeply rooted in the past while pushing ageless mythology into strikingly current realms. Historical novels should have plenty of history, and this novel surely does. Romantic novels should have their share of sex and romance, and this novel delivers both. But its true revelation is its gripping sense of anticipation, heartache, discovery, and unflinching chill."

—Bruce Feiler, author of *Walking the Bible*

"Karen Essex [is] among the top historical novel writers of our day. Where will she go next? It most assuredly will involve a new slant on a woman with great passion from deep in the past."

—Bookreporter.com

"Karen Essex's historical novels give voice to women who flout traditional roles." —*Los Angeles Times*

"[*Dracula in Love*] is a haunting, feminist portrayal of eternal love, forbidden desires, and Victorian virtues. . . . A refreshing take on a classic that is sure to mesmerize readers." —*Fangoria*

Karen Essex

Dracula in Love

Karen Essex is the author of four acclaimed historical novels, including the international bestseller *Leonardo's Swans*. Her award-winning essays and articles have appeared in many periodicals, including *LA Weekly*, *Vogue*, and *Playboy*. She lives in Los Angeles and London.

www.karenessex.com

Also by Karen Essex

Dracula in Love

A NOVEL

Karen Essex

Anchor Books
A Division of Random House, Inc.
New York

FIRST ANCHOR BOOKS EDITION, JULY 2011

Copyright © 2010 by Karen Essex

All rights reserved. Published in the United States by Anchor Books,
a division of Random House, Inc., New York, and in Canada by Random House
of Canada Limited, Toronto. Originally published in hardcover in the United States
by Doubleday, a division of Random House, Inc., New York, in 2010.

Anchor Books and colophon are registered trademarks of Random House, Inc.

The Library of Congress has cataloged the Doubleday edition as follows:
Essex, Karen.
Dracula in love / by Karen Essex. — 1st ed.
p. cm.
I. Title.
PS3555.S682D73 2010
813'.54—dc22 2010005657

Anchor ISBN: 978-0-7679-3122-9

Author photograph © Lisa Rutledge
Book design by Maria Carella

www.anchorbooks.com

For Olivia Fox, brave and bold.

Look for the magic.

You must become who you are.

Friedrich Nietzsche

✢ Dracula in Love ✣

Prologue

*E*veryone has a secret life. Perhaps yours is merely a gossamer web of thoughts and fantasies woven in the hidden furrows of your mind. Or furtive deeds performed on the sly or betrayals large and small that, if revealed, would change how you are perceived.

Unlike most people whose lives remain private, my story has been written by another, sold for money, and offered to the public for entertainment. The author of the fiction claims to be above reproach because his records are "exactly contemporary." But these "records" are falsified documents, based on the lies of a cabal of murderers desperate to conceal their dark deeds.

The true story remains a secret—my secret—and with good reason. Reader, you are about to enter a world that exists simultaneous with your own. But be warned: in its realm, there are no rules, and there is certainly no neat formula to become—or to destroy—one who has risen above the human condition. That is wishful thinking. Despite what you have read in commercial fiction, in the supernatural world, science and religion are both ineffectual, and garlic, crosses, and holy water—no matter how many times it has been blessed and by whom—are equally useless and benign. The truth is deeper, darker, and stranger than you imagine. As Lord Byron wrote, "for truth is always strange; stranger than fiction: if it could be told, how much would novels gain by the exchange!" In the forthcoming pages, we shall see what is gained when truth is told.

At some risk to myself from mortals and immortals alike, I will now reveal to you what happened in that strange and seminal year of 1890, when I shed the cocoon of ordinary life, bursting through the membrane of prosaic earthly existence and into a world of preternatural magnificence. That is the world we learned as children to fear—the milieu of goblins, ghosts, spirits, and magic—when it is the tangible world that is rife with unimaginable horrors.

The truth is, we must fear monsters less and be warier of our own kind.

Mina Murray Harker, London, 1897

P. S. The astute reader will notice that I have employed herewith the same fictitious names used in the other tale, with the exception of Morris Quince, who in no way resembled the cowboy American stereotype Quincey P. Morris, and Dr. Von Helsinger, who was not a product of Amsterdam but of Germany, the world's leader in psychiatry during our century.

❧ Part One ☙

LONDON

Chapter One

In the beginning, there was the voice.

That was how it began on that first evening, with a masculine voice calling out to me in my sleep; a disembodied voice slithering into my dream, a voice of deep timbre and tones, of sensuous growls, and of low, hollow moans—a voice laden with promise and with love. It was as familiar to me as my own, and yet I knew not whether it came from inside my head, from outside me, or from somewhere not of this earth. Hushed like wind through a valley and smooth like velvet, it beckoned me, and I neither had, nor wanted, power against it. The voice was my master.

I have been looking for you, I said.

No, we have been looking for each other.

Then came hands, no, not exactly hands, but touch—the *essence* of touch, caressing my face, my neck, and my arms, making my skin tingle and awakening something long dormant inside me. Smooth lips gently kissed me and then pulled ever so slightly away. *Come, Mina,* the lips whispered, and I felt warm breath as the words came out. *You called to me, did you not?*

Eager to discover the owner of those lips, the giver of that touch,

I moved into the darkness, unaware where I was, or where I was being led, or by whom. But I knew that when we were finally united, it would be a homecoming. I felt as if my body were wrapped in warm skins and lifted into the air. Drifting through darkness and toward the unknown, I was not exactly flying but safely held aloft as I floated through nothingness. Something like fur tickled me beneath my chin and all around my neck and back.

After what seemed like a timeless journey, my bare feet touched mossy ground. Excited and intensely alive, my body was unfamiliar to me, except my heart, which beat with a new ferocity. The rest of me was some tingling mass of energy as I ran toward the hands and the lips with their promises of touch, of kisses, and of love. I saw nothing but felt hands come out of the darkness again and begin to stroke my hair and caress me with great tenderness.

But as I surrendered to the touch and the sensation, the sumptuous fur that had enveloped me dropped away, and the hands on my body turned rough. Suddenly I was clothed not in fur but in something wet. I began to shiver violently. Frigid air blasted my face, replacing sweet warmth. The dampness around me seeped through to my skin, chilling me to the bone. Someone—or *something*, could it be an animal?—pulled my garment up above my knees. A hand—yes, it was unmistakably a hand but not the hand that had touched me before—a hand so cold that it must belong to the dead crept up my leg, pushed my thighs apart, and found the only warm spot left on my body. I gasped and tried to scream but choked on my own voice as the icy fingers reached that inviolate place.

"Getting you ready is all." This voice was crass and mocking and not at all like the voice of devotion that had found me in my sleep.

I knew that I needed to resist, but I could not locate my limbs. I willed my legs to kick, my arms to rise, my fists to tighten, my muscles to gather their strength to fight this thing attacking me, but all the power in my body seemed to have disappeared. I wondered if I were dead and if this thing on top of me was the devil.

Yet I could not give up. Surely this mind that could think was still attached to a body. I opened my mouth to scream, but nothing escaped, not even a vibration. I took a breath, and a foul, sour smell shot up into my nostrils making me gag but letting me know that I was still alive. A warm, wet drop fell upon my eye, as if someone had spit on me.

I opened my eyes. I was not dreaming. No, the creature on top of me, reeking of stale beer and dripping his saliva onto my face, was all too real. But where was I? Who was this man, pushing my legs apart with his knees, this fiend with a coarse, unshaven face and bulbous eyes so red that I expected them to start bleeding? He pulled his icy finger out of me, shocking me as much with the withdrawal as he had with the insertion, and began to fumble with the buttons on his trousers. I rolled back and forth on the wet grass trying to get away, but with his free hand he gathered my nightdress at the neck, choking me.

"Stay put or you will be sorry you were ever born," he said.

I realized what was happening and I remember wondering what my fiancé would say when I told him—if I ever told him, if I lived to tell him—that I had been raped while wandering, insensible, in the middle of the night. In my mind, I saw Jonathan receive the news, his stricken face turning white, shying away from me in disgust. How could any man, even one as kind as Jonathan, look upon a woman the same way after this kind of shame? At that moment, I knew that I must free myself from my tormenter. My life, or more than my life—as I thought back in those more innocent days—was at stake.

I tried to scream, but the stranger's fingers were at my throat. He undid the last button on his trousers, and his manhood shot into freedom, red, stiff, and ugly. He took his hand from my neck and put it over my mouth, but I bit hard at it, harder than I thought I was capable of, as if I had grown new teeth. Cursing me, he withdrew his hand.

"Now you are really going to get it," he said, pulling my thighs apart. He stared and then looked at my face with his glowing red eyes. Mirth had replaced his anger and determination.

"What's this? A devil's mark?"

He meant the wine-colored birthmark on my inner thigh that rose in two points like angels' wings. I tried to clench my legs together, but he was the stronger. "You'll be a feisty one."

I started kicking and flailing with all my strength until my surroundings were a blur. I saw nothing but flashes of the smug look on his ugly face against a dark sky. I tried to find my voice, because I had remembered reading that a woman's best defense against an attacker was her shrill scream. At last and with persistent effort I felt a tremor rise inside my chest, snake through my throat, and find its way out of my mouth and into the cold night air.

"Get your filthy hands off me," I yelled, and then I screamed again.

"Shut up, little whore." The fiend hissed, raising his hand away from me to slap my face. I winced, my courage draining out of me like so much air as I shrank from him. But the blow did not come. Instead, I heard a heavy thud against my attacker's back, and something picked him up from behind and pulled him off me. I saw the shock and terror on his face as he was swiftly lifted away from me and thrown like a heap of rubbish on the ground.

I sat up. I could not see the face of my rescuer, but he wore the tall hat of a gentleman and a black evening cape lined in shimmery pale gray satin. In his hand was a walking stick, which he used to deliver blow after sickening blow to my assailant. It all happened very quickly, as if time had sped up. My rescuer was a whir of motion, a dervish, battering the attacker until he lay still on the ground.

The gentleman did not even stop to consider the limp thing he had beaten but suddenly faced me as I sat in wonder. Had I blinked and missed the act of his turning toward me? The thought crossing my mind was that I had been attacked by a fiend and saved by a phantom. The angle of the brim of his hat obscured his face, and his features were in shadow because the moonlight illuminated him from behind. Strangely, as if we were old friends, he opened his arms as if to welcome me. He was familiar to me, but I could not place him.

At that point, I could only imagine that he had the same ambition as the first attacker, and I gathered my nightdress around me and began to crawl away. The walking stick in his right hand bore the bulbous head of a golden dragon, mouth wide-open, baring long, pointy teeth. Slinking backward on my hands and knees, I waited for him to advance upon me, but he stood motionless, arms stretched out as if in surrender. He was a tall man, and, if posture may give away age, I would have to say that he had the lean physique of youth but the stance of a man of maturity. I thought for a moment that I should get hold of my senses and thank him, but the stories in the newspapers of girls being abducted in the night by well-dressed men were fresh in my mind. The potential danger in remaining vulnerable to him far outweighed my curiosity, and when I thought my legs would carry me, I stood up and ran away.

I soon realized that I was on the banks of the Thames, and that it must be minutes before dawn, that time when the world takes on an eerie color, like that of gray pearls; that strange time when the sky is a luminescent brew of moonlight and dawn. A cold air passed my face, and thunder shattered the silence. I felt drops of rain trickle upon me and I could not resist the urge to turn around to see if my savior had decided to pursue me. He had looked so benevolent with his arms stretched out to me, like the image of the Christ welcoming his flock. I wished, in part, that he had followed me so that I might find out who he was and how he came to be on the deserted riverbank at this hour. But the feral nature of his swift assault upon my attacker made me rethink my wishes.

I needn't have worried; he was no longer in the place I had left him. In the distance, I saw a shiny black coach with unlit lanterns and two strong black steeds to lead it. Thunder crashed again, and lightning darted through the open sky. The horses neighed, one rearing on its hind legs, while the other seemed to call out to the heavens. I tried to see if my savior was seated in the carriage, but its closed curtains guaranteed the privacy of whoever was inside. With no one I could see at the reins, an explosive round of thunder sent the horses bolting, and the huge coach, glimmering in the burgeoning light of dawn, sped away.

. . .

I did not know exactly where I was but knew that if I ran downriver I would soon be in the area of the school, where I worked as assistant headmistress, and safe in my living quarters. I had to remember how to breathe as I ran away from the scene of my potential disgrace. Though it was summer, the air was frigid, and the light rain that fell upon me only made me colder. Each breath chilled and choked me as I ran along the embankment until I saw a familiar landmark and turned abruptly toward the Strand.

I heard the wheels of a carriage behind me, but when I turned to see if I was being followed, the street was empty but for a few hansom cabs parked in front of the hotels. The cabmen huddled beneath the oilcloth coats that protected them from the drizzle, perhaps waiting to whisk clients off to catch early trains. A lone flower cart rolled past me on its way to market, the white lilies trembling in their pots, nodding to me as if to say good morning.

I calculated by the changing light in the sky that it was not yet five o'clock, when things would begin to stir both in town and at the school. I had to be in my room before that time. There would be no explanation short of a bout of madness that I could offer for arriving at the premises at this hour and in my nightdress that would satisfy Miss Hadley, the headmistress.

In truth, there was no explanation that I could possibly give, not even to myself, of how I came to wander out of doors in the middle of the night, only to have been nearly raped by a stranger on the banks of the river just before dawn and saved by either a saint or a demon in gentleman's evening clothes. How had either of those men found me? I recalled the earlier dream, and the contrast of the velvet voice and tender hands with the brutality of the man who had tried to violate me. Perhaps he was the punishment meted out for that wickedly sweet dream. A woman who would leave her bed, no matter how involuntarily, to pursue a seductive, disembodied voice would surely get what she was asking for. How could I have done that, considering that I was engaged to a wonderful man like Jonathan? The shame of it burned through me.

My thoughts were again interrupted by the unmistakable clatter of carriage wheels. I looked in all directions but did not see any vehicle coming toward me. The sound had emphatically been there, no mistake about it, but it was distant, as if it came from inside a crater. I attributed it to the way that sound carried in this city; conversations and noises from far away were carried into one's own parlor on random gusts of wind. Still, I could not shake the feeling that I was being followed.

Shivering, I slipped down the alley parallel to the old mansion that housed Miss Hadley's School for Young Ladies of Accomplishment, retracing the steps I must have taken earlier. The back door was unlocked; I must have left it so. I closed it with great care and quietly climbed the rear staircase, hoping not to disturb any of the boarding students in their dormitory beds or, worse yet, Headmistress. Mercifully, the cleaning and kitchen staff lived off the premises and did not arrive until 5:30 in the morning. After fifteen years living in the building, I knew every single spot where the stairs creaked, and, like a child playing a game of hopscotch, I sidestepped each telltale place as delicately as I could and reached the third story where I lived with barely a sound made.

As soon as I closed the door to my room, I heard the same sound of horses' hooves and carriage wheels outside. I knew the rhythms of the neighborhood as I knew the beating of my own heart. It was too early for any of the regular deliveries, and the intrusion of a vehicle at this hour was disconcerting. I went to the window, and through the milky glass, I saw the fog-bathed rear of the same gleaming black carriage as it receded from my view.

Pulse racing, I threw my wet nightdress into the drawer of my little chest and put on a fresh one. I leapt under the covers and shivered between cold sheets. I had had episodes of this mysterious and disturbing nature as a child, but it had been a full fifteen years or more since I had experienced one. I was twenty-two years old, and I was sure that I had fully outgrown them. But now the memories, vivid once more, came rushing back to me, playing out in my mind like little theatrical scenes.

I remembered being a very small child back in Ireland, playing behind my parents' cottage, where colored balls of light appeared and led me into the woods. There, I conversed with animals—squirrels, birds, foxes, even spiders and bees—and I was sure that they talked to me, though not in my language. I revealed this to my mother, who told me that animals did not have the ability to speak and that I must learn to control my imagination or it would lead to madness, or worse. Later that year, my great-uncle died, and my mother took me to the funeral. I was sitting quietly in the pew next to her, when the deceased man's spirit came to me and tickled my ribs. I squirmed, trying to suppress my laughter, and my mother angrily pinched my ear until the pain overrode the tickling, and my uncle disappeared. "What are you doing, you disrespectful little girl?" she asked. When I told her that the dead man had made me laugh, she shuddered, and from then on, treated me with suspicion.

Around this time I began to get out of bed at night and wander in my sleep. My parents found me in several different places—sitting in the garden, walking toward the river, or once, dancing under the moonlight and singing a song I had learned at church. My father, weary of my nocturnal adventures, took me by the shoulders and hair and dragged me inside and up the stairs. He threw me back onto my bed, locking the door behind him. I heard him yelling at my mother, using words about me that hurt my ears, so I put a pillow over my head and hummed to myself until they stopped and I could fall back asleep.

I learned to be very cautious in front of my parents, but one time I slipped and asked my father to be quiet because the angels were talking and I wanted to hear them. Over my mother's protests, my father locked me in my room without supper. My mother, despite her occasional feeble attempts to defend me, began to shun me for her own reasons. I often heard her private thoughts, but when I questioned her about them, she got very cross with me. She made the mistake of telling my father that I was a mind reader, and he demanded to know what evil entity was telling me what goes on in other people's minds. When I could not answer his question, he gave me a spanking.

After my father drowned in an accident, my mother packed a small black valise with my belongings and took me by train, ferry, and another train to Miss Hadley's School for Young Ladies of Accomplishment in London. I was seven years old. I was to be grateful because it was not a boarding school for bad girls, which is what I deserved, and it was not an asylum for the insane, which is where my father would have sent me—had he lived, she emphasized—and it was not a workhouse for girls whose families no longer could feed them but a place where girls were sent to learn to become young ladies. I was fortunate, she said, because we had suddenly come into some money for this, provided by my mother's late grandfather.

"You are just like your grandmother," my mother had said, "just the same sort of troubled creature. When she got older, she developed loose morals. She did not control herself or her urges. Do you want people to say that about you?"

I had no idea what she was talking about, but I shook my head violently so that my mother would know I did not intend to be that sort of person.

"And she came to a very bad end, so you must learn to control yourself and mind your behavior. If you learn to be good, then perhaps you will be allowed to come home."

And I *was* good. I became Miss Hadley's star pupil and pet. "I have never seen a girl with such a lovely complexion and compelling green eyes," she told my mother the day I arrived. I could tell that she was taken with me, and I foresaw that I could use that to my advantage. I listened attentively to whatever she had to say, both in the classroom and without. I assimilated her lessons with fervor unequaled by any other girl in the school. On the day of graduation, she said, "I have taught hundreds of girls, Wilhelmina, but none have I regarded as a daughter until I met you."

During my years as a student, my mother died. After I finished my education, Miss Hadley employed me to teach reading, etiquette, and decorum to girls between the ages of seven and seventeen.

Despite my rigidly conventional exterior, I knew that I was unusual. I knew that there was something wild and terrible and frightening inside me, something that I must continue to suppress at all costs. Headmistress did not know what I had been like as a child before I was sent away. She knew only the sweet and docile girl I had trained myself to be. I knew the truth. I knew that I was different from other girls, and I knew that the difference was not a good one.

. . .

I tried to rest before rising for the day, but I was terrified that I would fall asleep and once again hear the call of that voice. I got out of bed, washed, and dressed in the lace-collared brown linen uniform of the teachers. Our school motto was "Gentility Above All," and Headmistress insisted on a genteel familial atmosphere in which a girl's feminine and domestic attributes might be cultivated. Thus all teachers were addressed as "aunt," and the girls addressed me as Aunt Mina.

After last evening's lurid incident, the irony that most of this day was to be devoted to the study of etiquette and decorum was not lost on me. A full day was devoted to these subjects, while the other days of the week were divided into the study of drawing, simple mathematics, dancing, French, reading, and religion and morals. Because Headmistress considered herself an enlightened woman, she treated the pupils to occasional lectures by visiting scholars in the fields of history, geography, and science. The school had a splendid reputation, though it was criticized by suffragettes and lady reformers who, along with the right to vote, also campaigned for girls to be taught the same academic subjects, and with the same intensity, as boys.

Miss Hadley's School was home and family to me, and I did not receive criticism of it very well. I knew that it was my education in the feminine arts that had enabled me to attract my fiancé, a solicitor of great promise. His affections would have been unavailable to an Irish-born orphan with no family to protect me or vouch for me had I not learned to assimilate the qualities of a lady. Besides, it was common knowledge that too much education hampered girls in the marriage market. I was a realist. I knew that marriage to a man like Jonathan Harker, not voting in an election or reading Greek, would secure my life and improve my station. Moreover, as one who had little recollection of living in a family, I relished the domestic virtues I had learned at school, and I was eager to have a home and family of my own. Sometimes when teaching, I felt like a play actress, and I could not wait to be cast as mistress of a real house.

This morning I felt like even more of an imposter as I faced my young and innocent students, who looked like little angels, dressed in their crisp white pinafores with fluffy sleeves gathered at the shoulders. What would they think if they had seen me just hours before struggling beneath my attacker?

We began as we did every morning with the students wearing boards across their backs, their arms looped through straps at the shoulders to perfect their posture. All the girls complained about this until I asked them to observe my own erect carriage, and how it enhanced both my figure and ladylike demeanor. Some of the girls immediately took to the lesson, intent upon developing a sense of graciousness, while others fidgeted, complained, and fought against their harnesses.

"It is no use resisting the board, young ladies, for the board will always win. Aunt Mina has yet to meet the girl who could crack the plank with her shoulders," I said, eliciting giggles from the cooperative girls and sneers from the few angry ones.

"How ever does one get accustomed to being bridled like a horse, Aunt Mina?" A twelve-year-old looked at me with defiant eyes.

I did not answer her, and she thought that she had won a small victory over me. But my silence owed to a vision that came to me as I looked past her challenging face. I saw myself at seven years old, as Headmistress threaded my arms through rope loops. I remembered feeling humiliated, as if I were being put into the stocks. The board had jerked my shoulders back, and I hated the feeling of being harnessed and tamed. My temper rose, and the wild creature inside me wanted to run backward and crash myself into a wall to break the wood. I was about to try that very thing when I saw a man standing in the back of the room. He was tall and beautiful, with the long hair of a French dandy and the clothes to match, and he carried a walking stick with the head of a dragon. I remembered thinking that I knew him and that I was happy to see him. He smiled at me, slowly shaking one long, elegant finger at me. That calmed my spirits and inclined me to obey Headmistress so that she would let me speak with my visitor after the lesson.

"Be a good girl," he mouthed with his full and preternaturally red lips. I heard the whisper of his words, but no one else in the room acknowledged him. I relaxed, letting the yoke settle across my back, and I began to walk around the room, following the other girls. I wanted him to see how proud and ladylike I could be if I tried. But as soon as I turned the corner to pass him, I looked up and he was gone.

I had buried that memory for many years and now it came rushing back to me. Was it the same man, or had I imagined it? Had I imagined them both? Were the episodes that had troubled my childhood coming back to haunt me again? I could not afford this to happen, not now, when I was about to embark on a new life with Jonathan.

The girl who had asked the question was looking at me, waiting for an answer. It took me a few moments to collect myself before I could reply with the stock reply we gave to troublesome girls. "Girls sent home from boarding school are forever marked and usually end up spinsters," I said. "Let that be your incentive to cooperate with the lessons." The words sounded hollow and forced, but perhaps this girl would find, as I had, that once she succumbed to docility, it would suit her. She sulked— they all did, at least for a time—but then went through her paces around the room without further complaint; and for the remainder of the lesson, the ghosts of my past stayed safely tucked away.

Relieved, I was better able to concentrate during the lesson in elocution, a subject that I was especially suited to teach. The school was known throughout England for eradicating any evidence of a country accent, and Headmistress admitted that I, with my thick Irish brogue, had been one of her most challenging cases. "Nothing is more detrimental to one's marriage prospects than speech that gives away provincial origins," she would say to parents as she recruited their daughters. "It is a shame and a waste that a father spend a fortune for his daughter's dresses for the Season, but not a sou on polishing what comes out of her mouth."

With her diligent efforts, and nary a slap or a spanking that other girls had received, a soft, feminine, lilting voice eventually replaced the accent of my childhood. Headmistress often called me forth as an example to other girls, or to parents considering placing their daughters in the school. "Wilhelmina came to us sounding like a chambermaid and now has the voice of an English angel," she would say with pride. And then I would recite some lines of poetry and curtsy, and be rewarded with polite applause and gratuitous smiles.

After the elocution lesson, which passed without incident, we segued to the art of letter writing, so crucial to maintaining one's social connections and to running a household. That a lady must be eloquent both in speech and on the page was another of the school's tenets.

"Letters to tradesmen and other subordinates must be written strictly in the third person to maintain the proper distance between servant and mistress." I said. "However, one must not forget to be cordial at all times. When corresponding on a social basis, remember that there is a proper way to accept an invitation and a proper way to decline it. Never, never must a lady be condescending in rejecting an invitation, even when good taste prevents her from accepting it."

I set them to writing notes to imaginary staff, friends, relatives, and neighbors while I forced myself to remain awake until the teatime lesson, where we practiced how to pour tea, how to lift a teacup without rattling it (for no woman should rattle a man's nerves), how to lower oneself into a chair (where the lessons of the boards became most apparent), and how to lower eyes slowly and gracefully when speaking to a gentleman, rather than dart them away like some embarrassed servant girl.

"There is a precise moment to dilute the tea with boiling water, young ladies, and one should not be so distracted by idle parlor chatter as to miss it."

These banal lessons in decorum, repeated hundreds of times over the years, soothed me. I had not succumbed to this resurgence of what I thought of as my lower nature after all. I was still Aunt Mina Murray, who could preside over a roomful of girls, teaching them the ways of the drawing room that would net them the inevitable prize of a solid marriage.

At five o'clock in the afternoon, the day students went home, and the boarders and teachers took a light meal together at six. I was relieved when Jonathan sent a note of apology explaining that unforeseen business with a new client would keep him occupied until the next week's end. I finished my supper quickly, having a difficult time holding my eyes open, and fled to my room at the soonest possible moment that would not arouse suspicion.

To prevent another incident like the one the night before, I barricaded myself in my room by pushing a small chest in front of the door. I opened the drawer where I had thrown my nightdress, which was still damp, a fresh reminder of that horrible event. I rolled it up and put it back, hoping that I could wash out the grass stains before I had to explain them to the laundress or, worse yet, to Headmistress.

2 July 1890

Meanwhile, quotidian life went on. In addition to my teaching duties, I sometimes helped my old school chum Kate Reed, now a lady journalist, organize her notes and research. Kate's parents had sent their headstrong fifteen-year-old daughter to Miss Hadley's to polish her for the matrimonial market, but their efforts had an adverse effect, creating an even more insubordinate girl. After graduation, while her parents thought she was devoting herself to charity work, Kate apprenticed herself to Jacob Henry, a journalist she had met while surreptitiously attending a meeting of the Fabian Society. She followed him around for the better part of a year, organizing his notes and proofreading his stories.

Eventually he began to share authorship with her, and now she wrote stories both with him and on her own. She and Jacob were true comrades, she explained, meeting in the evenings to read the next day's papers fresh off the presses, often "over a smoke and a beer." Kate loved nothing more than to shock me, the teacher of etiquette and decorum, with her provocative new ways. She had tried once to include me in one of these evenings after she and Jacob had filed a lengthy story on crime against women. But I did not like Jacob's looks, what with his fingers stained with tobacco and ink, his chronically unshaven face, and his eyes that roamed over a woman's body without an ounce of respect.

I had been studying stenography and other office skills so that I might be useful to Jonathan in his law profession once we were married, and I had become fiendishly fast both at writing in shorthand and on the typewriter. With these skills, I had begun to help Kate, just as she had helped Jacob. A few days before the riverbank incident, I had gone with her to investigate some cheap tenements slapped up in the narrow, grimy streets of Bethnal Green and Whitechapel to accommodate factory workers.

Together we went into rooms of filth and misery, with no running water, where mothers and fathers were packed with eight and ten children in one room. Laundry, washed in the sewage-laden water of the Thames, hung everywhere, and stagnant privies sat in the yards. I have always been gifted, or cursed, with a keen olfactory sense, and I thought I would faint in the summer's miasma of human waste, diapers, cheap ham-bone stew, and perspiration. The wives we met were workers themselves—knitters, lace makers, seamstresses, or laundresses—still young but wrinkled and hardened, with crippled fingers like crabs' legs and callused skin. The women complained that no matter how hard they and their husbands worked, it was near impossible to meet the exorbitant rents.

Afterward, Kate worked our way into the landlords' fine offices using the feminine charms learned at Miss Hadley's. Eventually, however, her agenda emerged. "How do you expect these people to sustain their families if the rent consumes ninety percent of their salaries? You are enslaving them with low wages and high rents. Have you no sense of Christian charity?"

We had left the interview in a cloud of Kate's indignation, but I was beaming. "You gave those men a verbal lashing," I said. "I am proud of you."

Kate's eyes sparkled. "I love being at the *center* of things, not just observing on the periphery. I suspect that you love it too, though you will never admit it." Always dramatic, Kate selected the occasional word to single out for emphasis.

"Watching you work is like attending the theater," I said. "I observe, but I do not see the need to participate." And then I wondered if what I said was true.

Today, I walked through heavy summer rain to Kate's rooms off Fleet Street, passing newsboys hawking evening editions of the papers, their enthusiasm undiminished by the weather, and other street vendors selling their goods. She lived, to her parents' dismay, on the third floor of an eighteenth-century building that hadn't been renovated in fifty years and thus needed repairs. Her door was open, spilling soft yellow gaslight into the hallway, and I poked my head in. Sprigs of her dark blond hair escaped the haphazard bun at the nape of her neck, kept in place with a pencil. She held a burning matchstick in her bony fingers with which she had just lit a cigarette. She blew out the flame and waved the matchstick at me as if it were a magic wand, a big smile slashing her freckled face.

She hugged me with her long arms so that I could feel her wide shoulders begin to wrap round me. Tall and wiry, Kate had sharp-cut cheekbones and even sharper blue eyes. She was without a corset today, in keeping with her feminist principles.

"My editor is allowing me a full three thousand words for an article on the state of girls' education in Britain, the longest story of my career. Only you, Mina, have the organizational skills to help me sort through all this *data*," she said, gesturing to the pamphlets, magazines, and news-papers scattered about the room.

"You'd better make me some tea," I said, bracing myself for the task.

"Already going," she said, pointing to her steaming kettle.

"Lovely rug," I said. I had never seen the bright teal hooked rug, with its swirling abstract pattern of green, red, and yellow. Kate had made the room seem larger by hanging the bellows above the fireplace as a sort of sculptural relief. Three new wicker chairs sat around a wooden table with turned legs.

"Present from Father. He's venturing into machine-made rugs. He claims that the modern woman has a mania for home décor."

I surveyed the piles of papers. "What is your angle on the story?" I had assimilated some of Kate's journalistic jargon and had begun to freely use it.

"The task is to show the growing breadth of educational opportu-nities available to girls and the necessity for them to take advantage of them."

"Girls are already taking advantage," I said slyly. "Miss Hadley's School has no vacancies."

Kate gave me one of her sideways looks. "Did you know that the University of London is now offering all *degrees* to women, including one in medicine? Imagine someday being tended to by a lady doctor!"

Secretly, I used to fantasize about studying at a university, and I did feel envy that other girls were being given such opportunities.

She picked up a notebook and waved its pages at me. "Wait until you read my notes. Soon all children under the age of thirteen, girls included, will be mandated by law to attend schools—schools that give boys and girls the same sort of education in math, history, and the sciences. When that happens, you will have to say au revoir to Miss Hadley, in whatever language she considers a sign of good breeding. She will have to adapt or close." Kate blew a cloud of smoke into the air as if to emphasize her point.

"That will be a very sorry day for girls who want to become ladies," I said. "In any case, I think your predictions are wrong. The queen herself is against this sort of thing."

"It does not matter what an old woman thinks. Laws and people's minds are changing very quickly. Once we have the right to vote, things will change even faster."

I took an issue of *The Woman's World* from my bag and handed it to Kate, who had introduced me to the magazine. "That is what Mrs. Fawcett claims in her article on women's suffrage," I said. Kate and I shared copies of the magazine, which was published for "women of influence and position," and edited by Mr. Oscar Wilde. While I merely read the contents, Kate was trying feverishly to place an article within its pages.

"It's a very good essay, isn't it?" Kate said. "I wish I had written it."

"I found myself even more absorbed in the piece about weddings," I said. "After all, it won't be long now before I am Mrs. Harker."

Kate stubbed out her cigarette on a dainty porcelain saucer. "To be serious, Mina, you know that you have a way with words on the page. You should consider becoming a journalist yourself." Before I could object, she continued. "Mina, this is our *time*. I love you, my friend, and I see your gifts. Do not waste these opportunities never before given to those of our sex."

Her words surprised me. I was in awe of Kate's abilities but never dreamt that I possessed her talents. "Jonathan would never have it," I said.

"Then I should never have *Jonathan*!" Kate shook her head in little paroxysms as if the very thought of capitulating to a man's will would send her to the madhouse. Then she softened. "Oh, I know, he's handsome and intelligent and has a bright future, and you love him and he adores you. But does one really need a husband, lord, and master?" She looked at me with the same mischievous smile that I recognized from our adolescent days. "I think that the modern woman should only take *lovers*."

"Have you forgotten Lizzie Cornwall? She took a lover, and now she spends her time in the opium dens of Blue Gate Fields."

Lizzie Cornwall had taught at Miss Hadley's until one of the students' fathers turned his eye on her and convinced her to leave her employment. "He's going to set me up in beautiful rooms," Lizzie had told us, her dark eyes dancing.

"I always give her a little money when I see her," Kate said, sighing, "but she was a fool. We are not fools, Mina. We are women with intelligence and *gifts*."

"Lizzie had gifts, but now she walks up and down the Strand in a rented dress throwing herself at any man who passes. She's ruined! No one would hire her after he abandoned her. Discarded women are treated worse than animals!"

"Mina, how very dramatic you are. If you were not so concerned with preserving your sterling reputation, I should advise you to take to the *stage*." Kate put her lips together and rolled her eyes toward the sky. The face was so funny that I burst out laughing.

"You are as puzzling as a sphinx, Mina Murray," Kate said. "You speak one way, but sometimes your actions do not match your words."

"What do you mean?" I asked defensively.

Kate stood up, rearranging some paper Japanese lanterns she had stuck into an Oriental vase. "When Jonathan was away in Exeter last month, you leapt at the chance to go to the music hall to see those mashers. You do have a bit of daring in you."

It was true; I had accompanied Kate to see Kitty Butler and Nan King, two mashers who donned men's clothing and sang to each other as if they were sweethearts. "What would Jonathan think if had seen you in that place with girls drinking ginger beer and swooning over the performers?" Kate asked.

The girls in the audience—working-class girls for the most part—

seemed to be completely in love with the two singers, as if they did not understand that the two handsome "lads" were actually women. After the show, I pointed this out to Kate. "They have the beauty of a woman with the swagger of a man," she explained. "Why, I believe I love them too!" The two of us giggled so hard at this that people on the streets stopped to stare at us.

"I did enjoy that show," I admitted, "but what does that have to do with being daring?"

Kate put her hands on her hips. "The creature you call a *lady* would not be caught dead at such a performance, much less admit to enjoying it, if she weren't daring enough to test the limitations of society. I submit that you, 'neath your Miss Hadley's uniform and correct posture, are very much the *daring* sort. You just don't know it yet."

We worked together into the evening, and Kate suggested that she take us to supper at a nearby restaurant. The clientele were mostly journalists who stayed up late to meet the newspapers' deadlines or to read the early morning editions as they rolled off the presses. I thought that the establishment would have a ladies' dining room, which it did not, so that men, some of whom knew Kate, surrounded us. Mercifully, she declined their invitations to join them at their beer-soaked, newspaper-strewn tables.

As we quietly cut and chewed our capon, each lost in her own thoughts, a man in evening clothes came into the restaurant and scanned the room, his eyes landing on me. I stopped breathing until he removed his hat, revealing himself to be quite old and not at all resembling my mysterious savior.

I said, "Kate, do you ever have frightening dreams?"

"Of course, Mina. Everyone has *nightmares*."

"Have you ever confused being awake and being asleep? Or left your bed while you were still sleeping?" I was afraid to broach this subject with anyone as inquisitive and probing as Kate, but I had to know if others had had my experiences.

"No, but I have heard of such things. The condition is called *noctambulism*. A German scientist, I forget his name, did studies on it and concluded that it happened to people with overdeveloped sensory faculties."

I felt my stomach sink. "Of what sort? An overdeveloped sense of smell, perhaps?"

"Yes, or taste or hearing. Why do you ask, darling? Are you, of all people, taking part in *strange* activities while you are asleep?"

I was not ready to confess what had happened to me. I did not want to become the subject of one of Kate's investigations, professional or otherwise.

"No, not me. One of the girls at school leaves her bed at night and goes outdoors, but claims that she has no idea how she came to be there." I did not mind concocting this lie, as I knew that the two least likely people in London to ever have another conversation were Kate and Headmistress. "It leaves her feeling quite disturbed."

"The girl should be interviewed by a psychologist. These doctors are coming closer to understanding the workings of the mind in the dream state."

"I will pass your advice along to Headmistress," I said.

"That would really be something," Kate said. "Headmistress taking my advice."

"She knows that I am helping you with research," I said. "Despite that you were her least malleable student, she is always happy to hear news of you."

"Miss Hadley and her pupils are fortunate to have you, Mina. If you had been my teacher, perhaps I would have turned out differently," she said wryly.

"Oh, I doubt that," I said, and we both laughed.

Kate paid for supper out of her purse and escorted us through the dining room, tipping her little cap at the men as if she were just another of them. We walked to a cabstand, where she gave the cabman some money and instructed him to "take this lady to her destination straight-away." He nodded, not even casting a sideways glance at her being without a corset and without an escort at midnight. I kissed her good-bye, thanked her for her generosity, and got onto the seat, wondering if indeed the world was changing in her direction, and I, from my sheltered post at Miss Hadley's School, was unaware of the magnitude of the shift.

Chapter Two

*I*ntrepid reader, before I allow you to meet Jonathan Harker and proceed with our present story, I would like to briefly take you back in time one year to the spring of 1889, when Headmistress had decided to lease a floor of the house adjacent to the school to secure additional rooms for her boarders. She had called upon an old friend, Mr. Peter Hawkins, Esquire, who maintained offices in both London and Exeter. Hawkins had largely retired to Exeter, so he sent his young nephew and apprentice in the legal field who lived in London to advise on the transaction. That was how Jonathan entered our lives and entered Headmistress's rather fusty parlor, which was where I saw him for the first time.

The room had none of the new eclecticism of Kate Reed's flat, but had been decorated some fifty years ago by the elder Mrs. Hadley, from whom Headmistress had inherited the house. The furnishings were heavy and ornate, as was the style in the earlier part of our century. In keeping with its formal atmosphere, Headmistress used the parlor to receive prospective parents and their daughters, or her most special guests, serving them tea in bone china and using the linens from her grandmother's wedding chest, for which she personally supervised the starching, pressing, and folding. An antique Belgian point de gaze tablecloth of roses with raised petals covered the tea table, revealing only its lower legs, which looked as if they belonged on a colossal mahogany giant.

During their meeting, I had poked my head in the door to ask Headmistress a question, and Jonathan caught my eye. He looked quite boldly at me, making me blush. Before Headmistress could open her mouth, he had leapt to his feet requesting an introduction. One was dutifully provided, and I gave him a little nod, all the while assessing how tall and handsome he was, how white his collar, how starched his shirt, and how well-tailored his coat of subtle velour stripes. He had long hands so nicely shaped and so very clean that the white arc at the bottoms of his fingernails seemed to glow. I could not judge the color of his eyes. Hazel, perhaps, with a touch of amber. It appeared that he had had, that very morning, a haircut and a shave at his barber's. A hat, fashionable, but not ridiculous or unmanly, sat on the table. It looked new.

He inquired as to what subjects I taught, and was told that I instructed the girls in etiquette, decorum, and reading. He fumbled for words, making a feeble joke about being deficient in the first two areas, but considered himself rather well read for a solicitor. Headmistress dismissed me, but not before I looked him straight in the eye and smiled.

The next day Headmistress informed me that Mr. Harker had offered to lecture my reading class on the importance of developing strong literary tastes. He arrived a week later with notes in hand. He told the girls that as a student, he had read Goethe in translation and was so moved by the work that he decided to learn enough of the German language to enjoy the original. He had hoped that at least one girl present would develop that sort of serious literary sensibility. For those with more romantic tastes, he read a poem by Mr. Shelley, furtively glancing at me as he read, and blatantly staring at me as he explained its meaning. He looked very tired, as if he had been up the night before composing his lecture. At tea afterward, he confessed that that was exactly what he had done, and asked Headmistress's permission to call upon us again. She said, "If you mean to call upon Wilhelmina, then the answer is yes."

He stammered out a short sentence: "Yes, that is precisely what I meant." He then left in such a hurry that he had to return to collect his hat.

That was the beginning of our courtship: a year of fruitful visits, Sunday strolls and picnics, and lengthy conversations about similar interests over tea, culminating in a proposal of marriage put to Head-mistress just weeks ago, who accepted on my behalf with delight.

"It is the perfect culmination of every lesson I have taught you, Wil-helmina. You will be sorely missed here, but your success will be an inspi-ration to our pupils and a superb advertisement for the school. I am as happy as a mother that I had a hand in your good fortune, and even hap-pier that you did not need to marry beneath you."

We both knew that it had been a danger; girls with my ambiguous family background were usually left with the choice of marrying a man of even less status or spinsterhood. In fact, Mr. Hawkins, who had reared Jonathan after his parents died in an epidemic, did voice some conster-nation about me. I'm certain that he thought I was a fortune hunter. With Jonathan's good looks, education, and bright future, he had his pick of many girls from prominent families. But Jonathan explained to his uncle that we two orphans had found immediate kinship, in addition to romantic attraction. We understood the loneliness that only parentless children experience, and we both longed to create a family that would give us the sort of domestic life we had yearned for as children. After a long tea with Headmistress, and after interrogating me, Mr. Hawkins gave us his blessing. "Pardon my caution in this matter, Miss Murray," he said to me. "Jonathan is my liege, my kin, and my heir. I am thoroughly satisfied as to your character, and I am sure that you will be a lovely wife and a solid partner to him."

These days, when sitting with Jonathan, sipping tea and having a simple discussion, I was overtaken with gratitude for my good fortune. Unlike Kate, I was not "in the middle of things," where I might meet a compatible mate, nor did I have the family connections that would bring me a man of distinction. My dearest friend, Lucy, was a year younger than I and had already turned down a dozen offers of marriage from men she always tried to send my way. But after rejection by Lucy, those men simply pursued other heiresses of lesser beauty and wealth until they found one who accepted their offer.

Jonathan was above all that. He was good and kind and honorable, and he had an open mind and a broad way of thinking. He put love above fortune, and though he was manly and protective, he also encouraged me to read books and newspapers so that we might discuss literature, which I have always enjoyed, and also current events, which I must admit that between him and Kate, I had begun to find more interesting.

Today, he entered that same parlor, removing his hat with what I can only describe as flourish. He kissed me on the lips, an intimacy we had allowed since our engagement. "You will not regret the day you agreed to marry me, Miss Murray."

"I never believed I would, Mr. Harker," I replied, remaining on my tiptoes, hoping that he would kiss me again. I let my arm linger around his neck, enjoying the broadness of his shoulders.

"Truly, Mina, something extraordinary has happened. A count, a member of the Austrian nobility, has retained the firm to conduct a substantial real estate transaction in London. My uncle is consumed with settling two entailed country estates and has turned this affair entirely over to me."

Jonathan's eyes, today honey-brown, had a new sparkle. His skin was flushed with the early summer warmth and with his own enthusiasm. "After a lengthy correspondence, the Count was very specific that my uncle send me as his personal emissary. I leave in a few days for the duchy of Styria."

I wanted to share Jonathan's enthusiasm, but all I comprehended was that this business would take him out of the country and away from me.

"Don't you see, Mina? A substantial bonus will be coming to me. We will have a very tidy sum of money to begin our married life, enough to lease one of those little town houses you have set your heart on in Pimlico."

I slapped my hand to my mouth in surprise, a most unladylike gesture, but I could not help myself. "Do you mean it, Jonathan?" I asked. "You would not toy with me about so important a subject?" I had spent hours imagining Mr. and Mrs. Harker living in one of those brand-new houses with a cozy parlor, two bedrooms, a dining room, a kitchen, and a water closet.

Jonathan saw my happiness. He picked me up by the waist and twirled me around. "Mr. Harker! You forget yourself!" I teased.

"Oh, no, Mina, when I *finally* forget myself, it will be much more interesting than this!" Since our formal engagement, Jonathan had begun to hint at the excitement of the marriage bed, which of course, both thrilled and embarrassed me.

I poured our tea and sat down, and Jonathan sat in the chair next to me, pulling it close. "Of course I would not tease you, Mina. Seeing you happy makes me happy. I have sent for a brochure on the property. After my business with this count is concluded, I shall be more than ready to negotiate the lease. Our first home will have two bedrooms. Do you think that Quentin will mind sharing a room with little Maggie for the first few years of their lives?"

Jonathan and I had spent endless hours picturing the children we would have together, their names and characteristics, and the details of their early years.

"But little Maggie may arrive first. We will have to ask her if she would mind a baby brother invading her nursery."

"Maggie is a very generous child," Jonathan said, breaking into a broad smile at the thought of his future daughter. "She will be delighted to share her quarters with her brother, provided he respects the dollies that Father has given her. Do you know, Mina, that I have already bought her one."

"You bought Maggie a doll?" I asked.

Jonathan was blushing. "I went to the shops yesterday and found an entire department devoted to children's toys! Imagine! I bought a dolly for Maggie and a little wooden train for Quentin."

I squealed, wrapping my arms around myself at the thought of Jonathan's love for our future children. "I hope you don't think me foolish," he said.

"I think you are the most wonderful man I have ever met!" I said, and I leaned forward and kissed him delicately on his lips. He reached into his pocket and brought out a small jewelry box, handing it to me. I had been given so few gifts in my life that I was not sure how long I should wait to open it. "Well, go on," he said, smiling. "The box is not the gift, Mina."

I opened it slowly. Inside, resting on alpine green velvet, sat a gold filigree heart on a chain, with a small gold key attached as an amulet. Both the heart and the key were dotted with little amethysts. I took it out of the box and let it hang in the air. To me, the little stones were as dazzling as diamonds.

"It's the key to my heart, Mina, which you already possess." He took the necklace from me and fastened it around my neck.

"It is beautiful, Jonathan. I shall treasure it," I said. I pressed the necklace into my breastbone.

"I have wanted to give you something for a long time, but I did not know if it would be appropriate. Today, I could not help myself. I was carried away with buying gifts for my family." Jonathan reached into another pocket and retrieved a small leather-bound notebook. "I also purchased one of these for you and one for myself. I leave tomorrow on my journey, but let us record our every thought and experience so that when I return, reading the diaries will compensate for the time we spent apart."

"What a lovely idea," I said, running my hand over the smooth brown leather.

"There must be no secrets between a man and his wife. We must share our innermost thoughts. That is the way to keep a marriage vital and fresh." Jonathan had been reading marriage manuals since we announced our engagement.

Every woman intuitively knows to censor her thoughts when expressing them to a man, husband or otherwise. Undoubtedly men go through a similar process when speaking to women. But the sincerity of Jonathan's words touched me, so I thought I would try to confide at least a small part of my recent experience.

"Does sharing innermost thoughts also apply to one's dreams?" I asked.

He blushed. "Dreams are out of our control, Mina."

"I have had disturbing dreams of late," I said. "Frightening dreams, in which people are doing bad things to me, hurting me."

Again, he took my hand. "Dear Mina, who could possibly want to harm you, even in a dream?"

"I dreamt that I was being attacked by a man."

He waited, and then he dropped my hand. He took a sip of his tea. "I was afraid of this very sort of thing. Did you not tell me that Kate Reed took you into those terrible tenement houses in the worst part of the city, and then dragged you to the offices of the very men who built them, where she confronted them?"

"Yes, but—"

"Do you not think it dangerous for a woman to be running around the filthiest part of London, and then confronting the men who developed it?"

"Yes, of course I do, but it is Kate who confronts. I am as quiet as a mouse."

"But that neighborhood is rife with criminals. You might have been hurt. Don't you see, Mina? Venturing into these seedy worlds with Kate is giving you nightmares. The mind doctors now say that dreams are reflections of one's own fears. If you are exposed to frightening places and frightening men, then it follows logically that you will dream of being attacked." Jonathan considered himself a thoroughly modern man, following all the new trends in science, medicine, and industry and especially the explanations of Mr. Darwin about human evolution.

"But the dreams are upsetting," I said. "The actual experiences were not."

"Your unconscious mind gave you the dream to warn you against doing these things again." He took both my hands and kissed them. "When we are married, all bad dreams will disappear. I shall banish them from our kingdom, my princess!"

Jonathan's concern for my well-being always had the effect of salve on the wounds of my childhood. Had anyone ever cared for me so? Yet I did not want my activities with Kate prematurely curtailed.

"Let us strike a bargain," I said. "If I promise not to venture into dangerous situations, will you allow me to assist Kate until we are married? After that, I will be too busy making our home. Besides, I only learned stenography and typing to help you, and that is what I shall do, at least until our first child is born."

The tension melted from his jaw and relaxed into a big, boyish grin. "That sounds like my girl," he said.

"I love your smile, Mr. Harker, and I will do anything to keep it on your face," I said, touching his cheek.

"But no secrets between us, Mina? No matter what misadventures you are led into at the hands of Miss Kate Reed?"

"No, my darling, I promise," I said, wondering how I would keep my side of the bargain if I had another strange episode. "No secrets."

22 July 1890

Jonathan had been gone two weeks, and the school term was coming to an end, when Kate invited me to accompany her on an assignment. Godfrey and Louise Gummler, husband and wife spiritualists and photographers, had risen to popularity in recent years in London, thriving in a city where many who had claimed to photograph spirits had already been exposed and driven away. A newspaper photographer that Kate knew had examined their photographs of clients with spirits hovering in the background and had suspected that they used a sophisticated double-exposure technique to achieve the effect. A French spirit photographer using the same technique had just been put on trial and convicted in Paris. The Gummlers charged a good deal of money for their service, and Kate and Jacob, always keen to expose fraudulent activity, were anxious to get to the truth of the situation.

Kate had convinced her father to give her the money to purchase an elaborate mourning gown to play the part of a bereaved mother. "I suppose you can wear it again after I'm dead," he had said, handing over the money. "It will please your mother to see you so nicely turned out."

This evening, she was somberly beautiful in a swirl of black silk moiré. I suppose that she wanted the Gummlers to see that she was a woman of means, ripe to be swindled out of a goodly sum of money. Either that, or she secretly enjoyed wearing silk finery and could not admit it, considering her ideals. Jacob wore a dark suit, which he had purchased years before to cover funerals of important people for the newspapers. He did not look quite the equal of his "wife," but men of means often did not pay much attention to their dress. He had, however, found some way of bleaching his fingers clean of their perennial ink stains.

I came along as godmother of their fictitious deceased child. I did not own a mourning gown, but Kate assured me that the dark-colored dress I wore as a uniform would suffice. I put on a short cotton jacket to improve my style, but Kate said it brightened up the look too much and made me take it off. She threw a coarse black woolen shawl around my shoulders and stood back to look at me. I turned to look in the mirror.

"I look like your poor relation," I said.

"That is the *point*, Mina. You are to look as miserable as possible, and with your pretty face and perfect ivory skin that glows like a white rose in the moonlight, and the two emeralds that you call eyes, it is rather difficult."

The Gummlers' parlor was a study in fringe. Flowered Spanish shawls draped most of the furnishings. Madam Gummler herself was a middle-aged woman with red streaks of rouge caked on her cheeks and powder in the creases that ran from her nostrils to her mouth. Godfrey Gummler appeared to have taken all the hair from his head and applied it to his face. He was bald as a baby's behind, but wore the long, furry muttonchops and capacious beard made popular years ago after the Crimean War.

The centerpiece of the room was a boxlike camera, also draped with a Spanish shawl. Madam Gummler put her arm around Kate as she ushered us inside. "My dear, I was touched by your letter. Tragic! To find one's little infant dead in the crib! Taken from you without warning, without illness, for no foreseeable reason!" She called Jacob and myself angels of mercy, "flanking this lovely woman in her time of need. How fortunate she is to have two stalwarts such as you by her side." And then to the three of us: "Do sit down."

Kate sat quietly at the table as Madam Gummler poured three cups of tea, placing their saucers on little lace doilies to protect the shawl on the table.

"First, we shall call upon the spirit of your dear little son," Madam Gummler said. "After we establish a firm connection, my husband will take the photograph. As you can see by our walls, we have had great success in the past, reuniting the living and the dead."

The walls of the parlor were lined with framed photographs of the Gummlers' living subjects, all seated in this very room, each with a ghostly figure hovering in the background. The portraits covered the walls from the wainscot to the floral wallpaper trim bordering the ceiling. The ghosts varied; some were identical to the subject, which Madam Gummler explained meant that the camera had captured the subject's etheric body, or higher self, while other spirits were different entities entirely.

"Here is Sir Joseph Lansbury with his beloved mother," Godfrey said. Sir Joseph looked to be a dignified man in his forties; the ghost of his mother was a matron in a white cap and white dress with a lace collar. Others were photographed with baby ghosts wearing christening costumes, or older ghosts in antique garments. Some of the apparitions were angelic forms or, in some cases, mere swirls of light that one had to presume were spirits.

"The spirits themselves have told us how the photography comes into being," Godfrey explained. "They manifest themselves by merging our sphere with their own. This creates a mixed aura. When rays of light pass through this hybrid atmosphere, they are refracted, which causes their images to be projected on the plate."

"That is most interesting, and a fair scientific explanation," Jacob said.

"It is a mere veil that separates you from your child, Mrs. Reed. Just a thin membrane, invisible, made of vapor. Believe me, he is just on the other side. What is the little darling's name?"

Kate, who apparently should have had a life on the stage, produced a single teardrop and said, "Simon. After his grandfather." Jacob reached out and touched her hand. What players they were! For my part, I sat quietly sipping tea and trying to look as lugubrious as possible. Godfrey went about the room lighting candles. He lowered the gas lamps on either side of the fireplace.

"Simon. Lovely. Now we begin," Madam Gummler said.

"Should we all hold hands?" Jacob asked.

"No, none of that nonsense is necessary," she replied. She raised her hands to the ceiling and with eyes turned upward, she called out in a voice from deep within—octaves lower than her speaking voice. "I call upon the heavenly bodies and angels of high rank to deliver the spirit of the child Simon Reed! Simon Reed, your mother is calling to you! If little Simon has already made his transition and is sitting in heaven with God, then ask the Lord to allow us to borrow his spirit for a brief moment to comfort his bereaved mother. Let us borrow him from eternity! O Holy Ones—Michael; Jophiel; Uriel; Gabriel; and Afriel, protector of babies and children—hear my pleas and answer me!"

Her eyes were closed, and she swayed gently as she waited for a reply from the heavens. I looked about the room. Everyone's eyes were shut tight. Candles flickered, making the photographs on the walls doubly eerie. But nothing happened.

"Simon Reed, your mother, father, and godmother are calling out to you. O Spirit Mothers, free the infant to come to us, and we shall return him to you, where he may rest in your holy bosom for eternity."

Suddenly, the medium's breathing pattern changed, and she started to take short breaths, as if she was about to have an asthmatic attack. She threw herself back in her chair as if something had knocked the wind out of her.

"Another presence has entered the room," said Madam Gummler, opening her eyes and looking directly at me. "Is there anyone near and dear to you who might inhabit the spirit world?"

She looked convincingly afraid but excited at the same time. Either she was an actress with the skills of Ellen Terry, or she had genuinely felt something happen that had gone undetected by the rest of us.

I looked at her blankly.

"Anyone close to you who is deceased?" she asked.

"Why, everyone," I said. Jacob laughed. Kate opened her eyes and looked at me angrily. "Surely *we* are not dead, Wilhelmina."

"N-no, of course not," I stammered. "Perhaps my mother may be trying to contact me."

"No, it is emphatically a male who is attempting contact."

"I cannot think who it may be," I said, hoping that it was not my father. The last time I remembered seeing him, he beat me and yelled horrible things at me. I did not want him manifesting here in this parlor, intruding upon the new life I had created and saying things that would disturb Kate's opinion of me.

"Perhaps it is Simon," Kate offered.

"Yes, oh yes, I do feel little Simon as well. Yes, I do. Oh, what a sweet little darling. He has a message for you, Mrs. Reed." Madam Gummler closed her eyes tighter as if she were straining to hear someone. Then she spoke in a high, delicate voice, imitating a small child. "'I am here, Mama. I did not leave you. It's just that God wanted me by his side.'"

"Oh!" Kate exclaimed.

"Let us take the photograph while the child is with us," Godfrey said, rising from the table. He lit the two lamps on either side of the mantel, drowning out the softer light of the candles. "We must have enough light to take the photograph but not enough to frighten away the spirit," he said. "These are delicate balances that must be maintained." He placed a high-backed Jacobean-style chair in front of the fireplace and asked Kate to sit in it. "Now, Madam Gummler, if you please."

Madam Gummler rose from her chair, tossing the corner of her shawl that had drooped off her shoulder back around her neck. She walked to the camera and placed her hand above it. "This encourages the process," she said, swirling her hand over the camera.

"How should I pose?" Kate asked.

"Hold out your hands as if to receive your little boy," Godfrey said.

Kate did as she was told, sitting very still while Godfrey took the picture.

Madam Gummler put her hand over her chest and took a deep breath, looking as if she were about to swoon. She turned to me. "Someone is trying to contact you, and he is being most persistent. Would you like a photograph, dear?"

I shook my head violently.

"Please do not reject the spirits who have come to see you. It insults them," she said. "I work to keep my parlor a hospitable environment for those on the other side. Do not destroy my efforts with your skepticism."

"I am not skeptical," I replied, trying to keep my voice calm. "I simply cannot afford your fee."

"Why, Wilhelmina, we will pay for the photograph," Kate said magnanimously. "Perhaps little Simon wants a picture with his *Aunt Mina*," she said, taunting me with the moniker my students used for me.

"Yes, Wilhelmina, please allow us to get this for you," Jacob said. I supposed that he and Kate wanted to gather more evidence for their story.

"But Mr. Gummler has already taken the camera away," I said. He had indeed left the room with the camera immediately after Kate had been photographed.

"Ah, but I have returned." For how long he had been standing at the parlor door I did not know. "I unloaded the exposed plate in the darkroom, and I have placed a fresh plate in the camera," he said, attaching the instrument to its tripod. "If you please," he said to me, pointing to the antique chair, which suddenly looked to my mind like it had been used in the Inquisition.

I did not see how I could refuse. I took Kate's place in the chair and, sitting very still and very glum, allowed myself to be photographed.

"I understand from other clients of yours that you allowed them to witness the development process," Jacob said. "May we be afforded that privilege?"

"My pleasure," Godfrey said, "if you can spare the time."

We entered a small darkroom, foul with the odor of the chemicals of Godfrey's trade. The room was stuffy and lit with a single lantern, its glass darkened with red-black paint. "It only takes a minute or two to develop the negative plates," Godfrey said as he brushed both sides of the plate with a little camel-haired brush to remove the dust. "High-contrast pictures must be developed quickly, and in these cases, the contrast between the living subject and the spirit provides a veritable chiaroscuro of dark and light." He placed the first negative in a pan and mixed a solution that smelled like ammonia in a large cup. After stirring it like a sorcerer with a glass rod, Godfrey poured the solution over the negative and swished the dish from side to side.

"Remarkable!" he said. "Mother, come look at this."

Madam Gummler lowered her head over the dish. "Why look, there is the little babe," she exclaimed. "There is your Simon, come to see his dear mother."

The three of us looked over her shoulder. On the plate, as if it had come straight out of the ether, a wispy image of a bundle appeared lying in Kate's lap. The face was indistinguishable, but the image did look like a baby swaddled in a pretty lace blanket.

Kate looked at the image, and then looked at Jacob.

Madam Gummler asked Kate if she needed to sit down, or if she thought she might faint, as was usual with women who make communication with their deceased children. Kate answered without emotion. "Will we be able to take a finished photograph with us when we leave?"

"Why yes," Godfrey said. "Though I would prefer if you left it with us to dry. We could send it tomorrow."

"No, we are set to leave for the country tomorrow to visit our relations. We must take the photograph with us," Kate said.

I was surprised at Kate's restraint in not exposing her true mission, but I supposed that she had to carry the ruse straight through to obtain her evidence. I began to have difficulty breathing, what with the acrid chemical odors and the heat in the tiny, cramped room generated by five bodies and no ventilation. I said as much, and Madam Gummler offered to make tea for us in the parlor while her husband developed the other negative and made prints of the pictures.

"You must be very excited," Madam Gummler said to Kate as she poured tea for us.

"You have no *idea* how very much," Kate said.

"Perhaps your photograph will show you who is trying to contact you, dear," the woman said to me. "Sometimes the spirits are shy, but this is someone of power. I felt him here," she said, pointing to her heart.

Kate snickered, and I was afraid that she was about to give us away, but she busied her mouth with sipping tea. After seeing the image of Kate's nonexistent dead baby, we all knew that the Gummlers were running a fraudulent operation, but I was still curious about what Madam Gummler was saying. I wanted to question her, but I also did not want to alert Kate as to my recent disturbing incident. Not inquisitive, disparaging Kate.

Jacob walked over to the fireplace, which was not lit, it being summertime, and stared into it as if flames were there keeping his attention. Madam Gummler took a Spanish shawl from the back of one of her chairs and draped it over Kate's shoulders. "It's best to keep the body warm when one goes into shock from having contact with the dead."

I wished she would have put the thing around me. I felt a draft sweep through the room and past my face, though no one else seemed to notice it. My body, which had been so hot in the darkroom, now felt as if a piece of ice were slithering down my spine. I wrapped my hands around the warm teacup and brought it to my stomach. It did not help the inexplicable coldness that was sweeping over me, and my hands started to shake. I put the cup down, hoping that no one would notice.

Madam Gummler was about to offer more tea, when Godfrey entered the room. He spoke to his wife. "Mother, I need your assistance."

She excused herself and followed her husband back to the darkroom. Kate looked at me. "Are you well, Mina? You look positively *stricken*."

"I'm just a bit cold," I said.

"Do not worry. We will soon be out of here," she said.

"Quiet, darling," Jacob said. "The spirits might be listening." They both giggled. I did not know if he called her darling because he was pretending to be her husband, or if they were, in fact, lovers and Kate had declined to tell me.

The Gummlers entered the room slowly, Madam Gummler leading her husband as if the two were in a solemn procession. Each held a still-damp print with two fingers.

"We have a rather startling surprise," Madam Gummler said. Godfrey went to give me the photograph, but his wife snapped at him. "One at a time, dear."

She gave one of the photographs to Kate. Jacob and I rose to look at it.

"There he is, little Simon, so lovely in his mother's arms," Mrs. Gummler said.

"What do you think of little Simon, Mr. Reed?" she asked, handing the photograph to him.

"I think we have everything we require," Jacob said.

"Require for what purpose?" Godfrey asked. His eyes, already hooded by heavy lids, narrowed into suspicious little gashes.

"We are journalists and colleagues, sir. We are not married, and neither of us has a child, either alive or dead."

"We told you our story before we arrived," Kate said in the familiar tone she had used with the tenement landlords. "You tampered with the plate before taking the photograph. You have deceived many people and defrauded them of money, but it won't continue."

Rather than succumb to humiliation or back down, Madam Gummler replied calmly. "Journalists, you say? Who came here with a lie? I ask you, who are the real frauds here? I submit it is the two of you."

Godfrey looked at me. "The real question is, who is this woman?"

"Me?" I put my hand to my chest. What did I have to do with anything?

"She is our apprentice," Kate said.

"I suspect she is more than that," Madam Gummler said. "I think she must be a sorcerer's apprentice." She held the photograph out to me. "Do you know this person?"

I looked at the image of myself sitting in the chair looking placid, uninterested, and a little bit afraid. Behind me, however, stood a man in elegant evening clothes. He wore a tall hat and a cape and carried a walking stick, which he held beneath the knob, exposing the golden dragon's head atop it. Unlike the picture of the swaddled babe in the first photograph, his body was not a swirling and indistinguishable mass of ghostly light but nearly as fully formed as my own. His deep-set, haunted eyes stared directly at me. Long hair flowed about his shoulders. I did not have time to scrutinize the image because I recognized him instantly. As soon as I did, the icy feeling again crawled up my spine, all the way through my head and into my eyes. Blackness welled up, obscuring my vision, and I felt my body go weak. Before I could break my fall, I hit the floor and lost consciousness.

. . .

When I came to, Kate was insisting that Madam Gummler call a physician, whereas Jacob was insisting that they take me away from the place as soon as possible. I sided with Jacob, who went outside and found us a hansom cab. Madam Gummler handed me the photograph of—

what could I call him?—the spirit of my mysterious savior—but her husband wanted to keep it to study.

"It belongs to us," Kate said, grabbing it from them. I suppose she wanted to have it as evidence. I did not argue with her, nor did the Gummlers, and with photographs in hand, we left their parlor. On the way home, Jacob asked what had caused me to faint so suddenly, and I made an excuse that I had been feeling ill all day and probably should not have attended such a sensational event.

"Clearly, they tamper with every negative plate. I'll wager that fifty women in England are in possession of a photograph with that handsome ghost standing behind them." Kate turned to Jacob. "I wish you had waited to disclose our identities. They would have spun a fabulous tale about Mina's ghost that we might have used in our story."

"I was bored," he answered. "We knew they were frauds, and we exposed them as such. Not exactly a challenge. Besides, why should some bereaved mother not believe that her child is hovering about in heaven?"

Kate had initiated the investigation into the Gummlers, and I could see that she was taking Jacob's lack of enthusiasm as a personal attack. Fortunately, this took the emphasis off what had happened to me, and all the way home, they argued over the merits of publishing the article.

I left the photograph in their possession. I was terrified of certainty; if I never looked at it again, I would not have to confirm what I saw. I would be able to tell myself that the ghostly image was a photographer's trick. As Jonathan had explained, it was a manifestation of my fears. In time, I would realize that my mind, upset by recent events, had attributed the features of my savior to this figure, and I could eventually put the incident to rest. Once safely married to Jonathan, these strange occurrences would dissipate into thin air. I would be so busy keeping our house and preparing to start our family that I would not have time for mysterious forays into the unknown. Just as enrollment in Miss Hadley's school had made my early experiences with the supernatural disappear, so marriage to Jonathan would force normalcy upon me and once again obliterate these inexplicable elements.

But that very night, something happened in my dream that I could not put off to a rational explanation, an experience thrust upon me on some astral plane where I was not in control but subject to the specters that prowl the ethers. In this dream—though it felt more vivid than an ordinary dream—a man was on top of me and inside me, and I wanted him to be there. I held him in place, digging my fingernails deep into his back, clutching him to me, urging him to move deeper and deeper into me. Wicked and desperate, my desire was unbounded. I was frantically reaching for something, but what it was I did not know. My lust was like a ladder that must be climbed one rung at a time, but I could never reach the top.

I woke in the middle of this experience, body quivering, drenched in my own sweat, and still frantic to reach the unknown destination to which only the lover could deliver me. I was alone in the room, but the presence was still deep inside me, filling that dark cavity. I lay quietly for a long time, taking in my surroundings and reassuring myself with the familiar details of the room—the little chest of drawers, the single straight-backed chair, the washstand with a bowl and pitcher on top and the small wood-framed oval mirror above it. I named the furnishings out loud, hoping that the addressed items would somehow acknowledge me too and let me know that I was indeed in my room and not still dreaming. But was I? I was alone and yet I could still feel the man, or some presence, inside me.

The naming did not make the sensation go away. I had never touched myself in that place, so I did not know what it should feel like inside. I slid my nightdress up and my hand down. Cautiously, as if I were touching someone other than myself, I let my fingers slide past my navel; down my stomach; through the hair; and to the moist, hidden part of me. What a mystery it was, this part of my body, more secretive than a heart or lung, for I had seen pictures of those organs. I heard a noise outside my door and retracted my hand, but soon realized it was only the wind coming through the hall and rattling the doors. I wanted to go back to sleep again and forget all this, but I could not ignore the full feeling inside me. Something was literally filling me up. Had some ghost come in the night and violated me? If so, I had been his desperate and willing victim. I reached again between my legs, spreading them wider. Using my middle finger, I located the small entrance, and carefully slid my finger inside. It felt like nothing I had ever felt before, soft and smooth, and empty and full at the same time, a moist cushion of a cave. Something inside me contracted around my finger, resurrecting the familiar throb of my dream. Where had my lover come from, and where had he gone? I felt nothing but the wet, creamy, hot walls of my own body. Something made me want to linger and to explore, but the more I enjoyed the sensations, the more I knew that I should stop the journey along this dark path. I retracted my finger slowly and brought it into the cool, night air, and it carried with it the heavy, salty scent of the inside of that secretive grotto. Once I pulled my finger out, the full feeling subsided, as if no one had ever been inside me.

. . .

The next morning, I received a letter from Lucy Westenra, my dearest friend from school days, who was on summer holiday with her mother at the seaside resort of Whitby. "I am lonely for a female companion with whom to share the contents of my heart and mind, not to mention some interesting news on a subject dear to us both," she wrote, enclosing a train ticket. Lucy knew that Jonathan was away and that Miss Hadley's closed every August. The students and staff went to their families, and Headmistress traveled to see her sister in Derbyshire, so that I, with no relatives to visit, would spend a solitary month reading books, walking about London, and supervising the maintenance of the school property. I went through the daily mechanics of living, but with the abject loneliness of one who has no familial destination such as one was supposed to have in the summertime.

I had not received a letter from Jonathan in the weeks that he had been away, which also set my nerves on edge. Was he safe? Was he thinking about me? I attributed the lack of correspondence to the inefficiency of the post, so I sent him a letter with Lucy's address in Whitby, asking him to write to me there.

In truth, I was anxious to have this interval with Lucy who, unlike Kate, would delight in the details of my impending wedding plans. Lucy had an ardent admirer in Arthur Holmwood, the future Lord Godalming, whom I had yet to meet. If Lucy had news to share, it must be that Arthur had asked the question he had been wanting to pose to her, and that she, who never seemed to be in love with him but had accepted that it was her fate to marry a member of the peerage, had answered in the affirmative. Lucy would not trouble me with Kate's questioning of what the trajectory of female life should, or could, be in some utopian world that would never exist. It would be a relief to spend time in Lucy's exuberant company, where we might share excitement about our destinies as brides.

Part Two

WHITBY, ON

THE YORKSHIRE COAST

Chapter Three

The train to York pulled out of the station on a sluggish summer morning just before dawn. I sat very still as it made its way through London and her outskirts, as if I were anticipating being grabbed by some unknown party and held back from leaving the city's narrow streets and confines. As soon as the train cleared the city's smoky skies and morning mist, I felt as if I had been set free. The sun broke through dark clouds, transforming wet fields into endless expanses of shimmering green. Golden bales of hay, rolled up tight into spools, glimmered on the fields looking magical, like Rapunzel's spun hair. Lazy horses and sheep turned their noses up to the sun to take in its warmth. Farm boys in tall boots trudged through pastures muddy from summer rains, but the same life-giving sun that shone upon them shone through the window and upon my face. As the train creaked along, warm air wafted into the open window, perhaps bringing soot from the engine with it, but I did not care. Other ladies held handkerchiefs to their faces, but the air was fresher than anything I had felt against my skin in a long time.

Many hours later, when we reached York, I transferred to a coach that would take me over miles and miles of moors and into Whitby. The flat landscape now gave way to rolling hills, the coursing over which began to make me feel queasy. The sun, my constant companion on the train, suddenly disappeared behind dark clouds. Flocks of white birds scattered as we rode along, flying away to take cover against whatever the dim skies would spit down upon them. We stopped briefly at Malton to pick up new passengers, and I asked the coachman whether the time on the clock tower was correct. It was not possible that it was just twelve o'clock noon.

"The old clock stopped at midnight years and years ago, but no clock-maker in England has been able to repair it," he replied, shaking his head.

I refreshed myself with an egg sandwich and a cup of tea purchased at the station, and soon we were back in the coach and climbing into the moors. The gloom became more intense as increasingly dark clouds gathered, bringing with them the sensation of twilight, though it was just four o'clock in the afternoon. I looked out the dusty window to see that the skies behind us remained bright blue, as if the clouds were following the coach into the moors. A silly thought, of course, but I suddenly felt as if the harrowing experiences of the recent past would not be left behind at all but would follow me even on my holiday. I tried to focus on the heather, its lovely deep violet color muted by the gray daylight. But it bloomed only in places; instead of lush blankets of purple, lonely expanses of low vegetation and coarse, dull grass, dominated the scene.

The coach passed a big stone cross at the side of the road upon which hung a dried wreath of ivy, undoubtedly a memorial to a roadside death. A woman sitting opposite me made the sign of the cross and waited for me to follow her example, but I looked away and out the window at the bleak landscape and the ominous horizon. A brewing tempest was hardly unusual for an English summer, but I could not escape the portentous feeling that something was following me from London—something I would prefer to have left behind. The first sight of the sea should have heartened me, but as I watched the tide roll out, it seemed that the receding breakers threatened to suck me with them into the roiling water.

Because of my evening arrival, Lucy's mother had hired a man to meet me at the station. He had been given a thorough description of me and took my bag from my hand as soon as I stepped out of the carriage. In my fearful state, I wrongly assumed that he was a thief preying upon visitors until he identified himself. Embarrassed, I apologized several times, which he received with a good laugh.

Lucy greeted me in the parlor of the rooms they had taken on the second floor of a huge guesthouse in East Cliff, sitting high above the sea and overlooking the red roofs of the town, the beach, and the double lighthouses that welcomed vessels coming into the harbor. She was thinner than the last time I had seen her, but her golden hair floated like waves around her shoulders. She had tied part of it back with a silky pink ribbon that matched her day dress. Her skin, always pale, had more color, and the light sprinkle of freckles that had covered her nose and upper cheeks since I had met her thirteen years ago were more prominent.

"I have been riding a bicycle," she said by way of explaining her heightened color. "Mother is furious that I've let my skin get dark, but I don't care a fig."

"You, riding a bicycle? Like a common woman? Lucy, I am surprised at you!"

But I was not surprised.

At school, Lucy, with her pretty blond hair and innocent blue eyes, looked like the perfect angel but was secretly an unruly child who stole sweets from Miss Hadley's personal trove of goodies and enacted elaborate schemes for which she never got caught. One morning, however, as Miss Hadley marched us to the park in a weekly outing, Lucy diverted the two of us from the pack of girls and revealed her latest plan. We would approach perfect strangers, explaining that we were collecting money for the blind, but we would use the money to buy candies.

I was petrified, but I went along with her, walking up to ladies in bonnets and men with whiskers freshly groomed by their barbers, allowing Lucy to tell her story and nodding my head in agreement. When we had collected two handfuls of pence, we caught up with Miss Hadley and slipped back into the group. But later, one of the older ladies who had given us money came up to Miss Hadley, congratulating her on the philanthropic nature that she had instilled in young girls. Miss Hadley listened attentively, then with one hand yanking Lucy by the ear and the other pulling my braid, she made us confess our story.

"But we were going to give the money to the blind!" Lucy insisted. She told the story that her mother had taken to doing good deeds for the needy, which so inspired Lucy that she wanted to impress her mother with her own charity.

"Henceforth I suggest you help your mother with her work, rather than do these things on your own."

Miss Hadley demanded the return of the coins, gave the money to a one-eyed beggar sitting by a park bench, and let the matter drop. Another girl would have been spanked and sent to bed without dinner.

Such was Lucy's talent for escaping her crimes unscathed.

"Mina, you are the most old-fashioned person I know," Lucy said, in answer to my qualms over ladies riding bicycles. I supposed that she still got away with doing anything she wanted to do. "My mother would be so very pleased if you were her daughter instead of me."

"I do not care what you say. I cannot imagine mounting such a thing and still comporting myself with any dignity whatsoever."

"Perhaps you have not seen the new safety bicycles, but they are very popular in resort towns. A little stand keeps them in place while one mounts and dismounts, with hardly an upset to one's skirts at all. A little fresh air and exercise is beneficial for females too!" Lucy's big blue eyes were almost wild with excitement as she expressed this idea.

"Has Mr. Holmwood been taking you on these bicycling adventures?" I asked.

"No, no, not Arthur. Someone else, a friend of his from their Oxford days, an American named Morris Quince. He is occupying my time while Arthur is away on family business," she said, turning from me. She called for tea and sandwiches, which were served by their locally acquired maid, Hilda, who informed us that Mrs. Westenra had already gone to bed with a headache.

"She is always ill nowadays," Lucy said. "Her health has never been good, but since Father died, she has deteriorated. The doctor thought that the sea air would invigorate her heart, but I'm afraid the opposite has happened."

Lucy looked forlorn. She had been close to her father, who had died the year before.

"Nonsense. One more month of sea air and you'll see improvement," I said, patting her hand. "Your letter sounded as if you had news to share." I wanted to distract her from her woes, but Lucy shook her head. "No, dear one, you first. I want to hear all about your Jonathan."

I took my sketchbook out of my satchel and opened it to the page where I'd sketched a white wedding gown. "It's taken from designs I saw in *The Woman's World*, with a few of my own additions and alterations," I said. "I am going to have it made in Exeter, where the seamstresses work for a fraction of what is charged in London. Do you like the wreath? It is made of orange blossoms."

"Why, Mina, it's a variation on the gown you sketched when you were a girl of thirteen and secretly designing your wedding dress in the evenings before bedtime," Lucy said. "You even said that you would wear white too like the queen."

I had not remembered my girlhood vision of a wedding dress, though I did recall hiding the sketches under my bed. "How strange. This design is the very latest fashion. How could I have known what that would be nine years ago?"

"Perhaps you are a visionary! I always thought that, of the three of us friends, you were the most intelligent. Don't tell Kate I said that."

"Well, it isn't true," I said. "Kate's intelligence is now a part of the public record. She has been writing long and thoughtful pieces of journalism for all London to consume, while I am still teaching girls how to sit and to pour tea."

"Tell me everything about your wedding," Lucy said excitedly. "Will it take place in Exeter?"

"Yes!" I answered, feeling pleasure at being able to share my plans with a friend. "Mr. Hawkins and his sister have offered to host a party after the ceremony."

Many months prior, chaperoned by Jonathan's aunt, I had spent a weekend at the Exeter home with Jonathan and his uncle. As soon as I saw the Cathedral Church of St. Peter, I knew that I wanted to be married in it. I was awed by its size, by the immense flying buttresses, and by the fading colors on its once brightly painted façade.

"Will I be invited?" Lucy asked coyly.

"You are my family, Lucy," I said. "I have none but you and Kate and Headmistress, who is mother and father to me. You will attend me in a silvery gown that will bring out your blue eyes," I said, producing an article on planning a wedding. Lucy eagerly snatched it from my hand.

"I tore it out of our copy of *The Woman's World* before Kate had a chance to read it, and I do not feel the least bit of remorse about it," I said. "Surely she would not want to defile her sensibilities with these *bourgeois* ideas." My imitation of Kate made Lucy squeal with laughter. "But everything in the article is true. Marriage for a woman means that every aspect of her life changes. She enters a new home, takes a new name, and takes on new duties. Marriage means that a man has sought a woman out and placed her above all women, choosing her to cherish and to protect. It is an exalted position."

"Your wedding day will be glorious," Lucy said. "You are marrying someone you love. Nothing can harm you now." She looked away from me as if she heard a noise outside the window, but I could hear nothing but the sea, which crashed loudly against the Whitby cliffs. I recall having heard that no matter where one stood in Whitby, the sea was a constant audible companion.

"And your news? Are there to be two weddings in the near future?"

"I have accepted Mr. Holmwood's kind offer of marriage," she said quietly.

"Congratulations, dear friend," I said, taking both her hands, which were cold, and kissing her cheek, which was hot. "He will make a fine husband, and you will make a lovely bride and mistress of the manor."

Waverley Manor, his family estate in Surrey, was known to be one of the finest homes in southern England.

Lucy's smile looked like a fresh knife cut across her pretty face. "Oh, yes, the sheer size of it is rather intimidating. But Arthur says that his only desire in life is to make me happy. What more could I ask for?"

I started to give my heartfelt agreement, but she interrupted me. "I think it's time for bed. We are sharing a room. Won't that be fun? This is our last opportunity to be together before we are old married ladies."

The Westenra house in Hampstead was of formidable size and elegance, and whenever I had slept there, I had my own room with an enveloping feather bed. Still, on most nights, Lucy climbed into bed with me, and we talked until dawn. I was disappointed to call our evening to an end so soon, but I voiced no displeasure, washing my face and hands and changing into my nightdress while Lucy did the same.

The bedroom window faced an old churchyard with gravestones that seemed haphazardly placed as if they might topple against one another in a strong gust of wind. Behind it I could see the ruins of Whitby Abbey, stark against the night sky. We were in bed before ten o'clock with the lights out and the window open so that the roar of the sea might lull us to sleep. I could hear the voices of people walking down Henrietta Street to the harbor, but I must have been more tired than I recognized because in a few moments, I slipped into a dreamless sleep. Not long thereafter, though, I was awakened by a noise. I opened my eyes to see Lucy tiptoeing out of the room.

"Lucy? Is anything the matter?" I asked.

"No dear, I just want to peek in on Mother to make sure she has taken all her medicines. I will stay the night with her if she asks me to. Go back to sleep." She blew me a kiss and walked out the door, and in moments, I fell back asleep.

. . .

The next morning at the breakfast table, Lucy received a note from Morris Quince, Arthur Holmwood's American friend. The note announced that Quince would be away for a few days, and Mrs. Westenra expressed her delight that he would not be gracing her parlor. "The Quince family is absolutely scandalous, Mina, and the scion is no better," she said. Lucy rolled her eyes.

For as long as I had known her, Mrs. Westenra had always appreciated a good gossip session, and she spared no detail about the infamous Quinces. "Oh, the father is wealthy," she said, slathering butter on her toast and then covering it with runny blackberry jam. "But he began his career as a circus performer! When the American Civil War broke out, he began to smuggle goods over enemy lines, and, apparently, had no compunction about selling stolen battle plans to either side, or that is the rumor. They also say that the man is actually a Jew, which of course would have abetted his journey into banking and finance. That, dear Mina, is where he made his second fortune."

Though Mrs. Westenra had looked pale and ill at the start of breakfast, talking of Morris Quince's unscrupulous father brought a good deal of color to her cheeks. Lucy, on the other hand, looked tired. Little purple veins had crept out beneath her eyes, which were red at the inside corners.

Mrs. Westenra continued, "It is a well-known fact that the senior Quince keeps a showgirl as his mistress, but they say that Mrs. Quince does not mind because—Mina, dear, forgive me for what I am about to say. I pass this along to you because I want you to be armed with the realities of this man's background, should he try to charm you. As I was saying, Mrs. Quince pays no mind to her husband's indiscretions because she is reputedly engaged in a sapphic relationship."

Mrs. Westenra picked up another piece of toast, methodically smearing it with the contents of the condiment tray.

"I am sorry, Mrs. Westenra, I do not follow," I said. "Is Mrs. Quince a poet?"

"Dear Mina, dear, dear Mina. You must keep up with modern terminology. Dr. Seward—you have not met him, but you will. He was crazy over our Lucy, but, of course, she could not turn down the future Lord Godalming for a poorly paid mad doctor, now could she?"

Lucy had never mentioned a doctor who had been one of her suitors. She merely shrugged, pouring herself more tea.

"At any rate, when I told this very story to Dr. Seward, he informed me that 'sapphism' is the medical term for the disease in which women fall in love with other women, transferring to them the same feelings that normal women have for men."

"Mother, you must stop telling everyone these awful stories," Lucy said. "You are merely repeating idle gossip. How will Mina be able to look Mr. Quince in the eye when she meets him?"

"He is very handsome, dear. It is quite the pleasure to look him in the eye," Mrs. Westenra said. "I thought our Mina should be warned about him. He might try to charm her away from Mr. Harker."

"Mother!" Lucy threw her toast on her plate in exasperation. "Mina is solidly in love with Mr. Harker. No one may taint her character; she would not allow it."

"You are both naïve young ladies," said Mrs. Westenra. "It is my duty to prevent you from falling prey to men's schemes. Mr. Quince has a certain raw American charm but has no solid plans. The man paints! What sort of a man paints? A man who likes to see ladies without their clothing—that is who paints!"

Small beads of sweat appeared above her quivering lip. She patted her mouth dry with a napkin, then picked up her fan and fluttered it rapidly. "Mina does not have a mother's guidance and welcomes my insights. Is that not correct, Mina?"

Headmistress always stressed the importance of deferring to one's elders, though Mrs. Westenra's warning did little but increase my desire to see this terrible man.

"Did you sleep well last night?" I asked her, attempting to change the subject.

"No, Mina, I did not. I tossed about all night."

"I am so sorry," I said, "but that explains the pallor in Lucy's cheeks. I suppose you were kept awake too?" I looked at Lucy, whose face froze, but she put her hand over her mother's. "I looked in on you at midnight,

Mother. I sat in your room for a long time, but I suppose you don't remember."

"You must not let my condition ruin your good health," Mrs. Westenra said. "I will speak to Dr. Seward about giving you medication to help you sleep."

"I won't take it," Lucy said in a very argumentative tone. "Someone in this family must remain alert."

"That is what servants are for! You vex me, my child. If your father were here, he would tell you to do as I say!" She shook her head furiously, the slack skin on her cheeks vibrating to and fro. "Oh dear, I hope Mina is spared the horrible sight of one of my paroxysms. They come on so suddenly, not like heart palpitations at all. The angina is a separate condition, I have learned. The attack comes on swiftly, beginning with a sharp pain here in the breastbone."

She pointed to the place with her finger. She began to take quiet, slow breaths, making circular motions in front of her chest. "It is terrifying to feel as if one's heart were about to collapse, Mina. An indescribable dread comes over me, and my skin becomes like ice, as if the very blood has stopped flowing in my veins. My poor heart gasps for its vital fluid, and I feel as if I am dying. It must be terrible to die! Oh, my poor husband." The memory of Mr. Westenra overtook her, and she started to cry, dabbing at the corners of her eyes with her napkin.

Lucy remained indifferent during her mother's presentation, sipping her tea as if she were the only person in the room. Later, when she and I were alone, I said, "If you did not have a mother, perhaps you would appreciate a mother's concern."

She looked at me as if I had betrayed her.

"I only mean to say that I wish I had a mother to help me navigate through life's passages and into womanhood."

"Perhaps you are fortunate," she said. "You are free to navigate for yourself, and in a girl's life, that is a privilege."

. . .

Lucy decided to nap after breakfast, and I welcomed the time alone. The sun was not exactly shining, but it was apparent beneath a thin film of cloud cover. I wanted to explore and to find a place where I might write in my journal. I had been told that the best view of Whitby was from the old churchyard cemetery that overlooked the village, the harbor, and the sea. I climbed the one hundred ninety-nine steps to St. Mary's Church, obeying the local superstition that each step must be counted or bad luck would befall the climber. I stopped to admire a large ancient-looking Celtic cross at the entrance to the churchyard, then peeked inside the small church, dark but for the light that shone through the stained-glass triptych behind the altar, illuminating at the center the body of the Christ hanging upon the cross. A few dark-clad women prayed fervently in the shadows. I lit a candle for the dead, dropped a coin in the offerings box, and went outside.

All the benches in the yard were taken, but I did not want to give up my mission. A solitary old man occupied the bench that sat furthest out on the promontory with the best view of the sea. He looked as if he had once been husky, but the decades had shrunken him to the size of an old woman. His clothes probably fit him well some twenty years ago, but hung in folds now on his bony frame. His skin was as brown and shriveled as a roasted peanut and covered with dark spots and moles.

"Would you mind if I joined you?" I asked.

He acquiesced to my request in a thick Yorkshire accent, the sort that we worked hard at Miss Hadley's to remove.

"I won't disturb your tranquility," I said, opening my journal and removing the cap from my pen.

"I'll have all the tranquility I need soon enough," he said, swallowing his vowels, as they were wont to do in the area. I was not sure what he meant, until he nodded his head toward the gravestones. I smiled, and then looked out to the sea to collect my thoughts. I started to write in my journal, but the old man, short of company, I suppose, began to talk to me about his life.

He was the last survivor of the men who had once "addled a living" in the whaling industry. "Whitby ships were known to be the strongest vessels in the water," he said, explaining that all the great sailors of the last century including Captain Cook himself preferred ships made by Whitby shipbuilders.

"The vessels had to be strong to withstand the winds that rise up in these frigid waters, and the men had to be strong to face the sea and the prey and the privateers. I was a young man on one of the last of the great whaling ships, the *Esk*."

I knew I was in for a long-winded tale, so I took a deep breath and donned a look of interest.

"We were coming home, were not thirty miles from the harbor, struggling all day against a southerly breeze, when of a sudden, violence in the air like you have never seen came squalling in from the east. Our sails were shortened, so we were not prepared for the likes of that storm, and were caught against the leeward shore." The more he talked, the more animated and younger he sounded. "I felt the *Esk* hit the reef and I knew she were grounded. She broke up, she did, spitting out every man on board into the sea, like we were no better than seeds from a piece of fruit. I was near six and twenty, and strong as an ox. I hung on to two men trying to keep them above the water, but in the end, only three of us survived.

"After that, I turned to herring to addle me living. Imagine, one day chasing the biggest fish in the sea and then being reduced to catching the smallest!"

I expressed my condolences for the shipmates he had lost. "They are all here, the ones who were found," he said, waving his arm around the churchyard. "I visit them every day, keeping them up on the news of the town. They appreciate it, they do."

"How do you know that, sir?" I asked.

"Because they thank me. The dead speak to us if only we have the patience to listen. The others that were lost to the sea, eaten up by the very fish we catch for our own dinners, they speak too, not in words but in terrible howling cries. And who can blame them? Young men losing their lives in their prime? One day, strong and brave, like young gods, then at the whim of the winds, they become food for the fishes. Strange, if you think on it. They have made cannibals of us, those fish."

I did not want to think too long on that gruesome image, nor about communications from the dead. I had come to Whitby to escape that. I gave him my name and inquired of his. He told me that he was known as the whaler. I was about to bid my new acquaintance good day when he invited me to see the very place where he had washed to shore.

"On some days, you can still hear the cries of the sailors," he whispered, and something bade me to accompany him back down the steps and toward the shore.

The day was cloudy and not warm. A few bathers gathered at the shoreline, but none braved the water. Optimists had rented big umbrellas and chairs, sitting under blankets against the wind. The sea was boisterous, crashing relentlessly against the cliffs in the distance, spewing waves onto the beach and forcing the bathers to move their chairs away from the encroaching waters. I hiked up my skirt as far as I dared as we strolled along in the sand. Vendors selling tea, lemonade, and cakes had set up stands along the beach. Suddenly, the old man pulled me aside, guiding me by the arm to hide behind the tea stand.

A tall man with a large physique and ginger-colored hair sticking out of a cap walked brusquely on the beach, the legs of his pants rolled up to his knees, revealing powerful-looking calves. As he walked, he roared at the sea, as if he were trying to scare it away from the rockbound shore. "That man appears to be in an oratory competition with the sea," I said, pulling my shawl close against the wind.

"Aye, best to avoid him. He'll nark me till I'm mithered."

"Has he tried to harm you?" I asked. The man did, indeed, look insane and somewhat dangerous, either exercising his arms or waving them at some unseen thing as he yelled into the waves.

The whaler laughed. "Harm me? No, he'll fill me with pints and make me tell him my stories. He'll take me off to a place where we cannot take a young lady and pour ale into me until I cannot walk."

The old man explained that the fellow was a writer who managed a theater. He had come to Whitby chasing stories of monsters and ghosts, looking for a play to write for a famous London actor. "What is his name?" I asked.

"The redheaded man?"

"No, sir, the actor. I enjoy the London theater when I am able to attend."

The old man had been told the name as if he should know it as well as he knew his own, but, as he had never heard it before, he had promptly forgotten it. "Along with most of what was in my brain," he added. "But I remember all the stories of the haunted and the dead, and that is what that fellow likes to hear. Claims my stories are worth sheer gold, but he only offers me the pints. What are my stories worth to you, young lady?"

I explained that I was but a poor schoolteacher with no money to spare.

"Then your beauty will be my reward for the tales I tell you," he said. "I'll not be fuggled out of what's due me till I get me eyes full of you and your coal-black hair."

With the other man long down the shore, the old whaler and I resumed our walk. He showed me the place where he had swum to shore after the shipwreck, and where the bodies of his shipmates had been found. I did not comment. I did not want to be thought without compassion for the dead, but I did not want to linger. What was once a lovely shoreline now seemed like a massive graveyard, each rock on the beach a headstone.

He stopped walking, cocking his ear toward the waves. "Can ye hear her?"

I listened but only heard the sound of the water relentlessly rolling onto the shore. "Hear who?" I asked.

"Mirabelle! Oh, she was a good girl, but she lost her head to a bad man, as women are wont to do. Some devilish seaman, used the poor girl up and then admitted that he was leaving her to go back to his wife and seven kiddies."

I was about to tell him that I did not want to hear two sad stories in one afternoon when I thought I heard a woman's voice roll onto the shore with one of the waves. I stopped in my tracks.

"You heard it," he said, matter-of-factly.

"I did hear something," I said. "I cannot be sure what it was."

"My lady, it was Mirabelle. Listen to my tale and then judge for yourself. From the day the sailor went away, Mirabelle walked along the sea, longing for him, hoping to see his ship sail back into the harbor. She knew in her heart that he would miss her and come back to her."

"And did he?" I asked, anxious to hear a happy ending.

"Of course not. And the poor girl, by calling out to him, was playing a dangerous game. Too many sailors have lost their lives to these waters over the many years, and being young and virile men, they did not want to die. No, miss, they resented God for taking their lives and so they make bargains with the devil.

"The spirits know that by stealing the blood of a young woman, they can bring themselves back to life! That is the truth of it. The spirit of a handsome young man came to Mirabelle at twilight and kept her in his company until dawn. He made love to her and at the same time drained her of as much blood as he could take from her, and from that blood, he made himself stronger. She could not resist him, for such passion makes an addict of a young woman. He had a strange power over her, and his kisses that were killing her also made her swoon with pleasure!

"The girl's parents were innkeepers who expected her to put in an honest day's work, but soon she had no life in her to hold a broom, and she fell asleep as she tried to do her chores. The parents thought she was sick and called for a doctor, but he was helpless to name the disease that was wasting her away. Every night, she sneaked out of the inn and met her lover, who was getting more powerful with each meeting, while Mirabelle, once a beauty like you, became so pale and thin that she was almost invisible. She refused food and could never sleep. Then, one morning, she was found dead at the hearth, a broom in her hand. Her poor body had given out. And just as her mother found her daughter's body crumpled at the hearth, she heard the father welcoming in a loud and happy voice a guest at the inn. He was a young sailor who had been given up for drowned some ten years before, and there he was, looking no older than the day that he had disappeared.

"You see, Miss Mina, the air is thick with the spirits of the young sailors and fishermen who died in the sea. They still yearn for the love and touch of beautiful women, young men that they were when they were forced to leave their bodies and earthly pleasure behind. I tell you this to warn you, beauty that you are with your jet-colored hair and your lovely skin more pure and delicious than the top of the cream, and those eyes of yours that stole their green from a sultan's emerald. Beware when you walk this shore. Pay no heed to the blether of the boggarts. In death, they possess silvery tongues that can charm a maiden. If the spirits of the dead call out to you, swaddle yourself tight with your shawl, make the sign of the cross for protection, and walk away."

Chapter Four

*T*he Austrian count has a beautiful daughter with a spectacular inheritance and renowned social standing, and Jonathan has fallen madly in love with her." I looked into the mirror, noting that a deep crevice had snaked its way between my eyebrows, bifurcating my forehead and making me look older than my years.

"What an imagination, Mina," Lucy said. "Jonathan loves only you."

I had not heard a word from my fiancé in the five weeks since he had left London. At first, I feared for his safety, but bad news travels quicker than the good, so if something had befallen him, I would have already received word of it. Now I worried that he had met someone better suited to be his wife. The miracle of his love had always seemed like a fairy-tale gift to me, an orphan with nothing but good skin and nice eyes to recommend herself. Perhaps he was more ambitious than I had judged, and he had found someone whose connections could abet those ambitions.

"It is possible to love one person until a truer love comes along," I said. "That is what the novels tell us. That is what history tells us. Guinevere loved Arthur until she met Lancelot. Do you not agree that it is possible to love one person but encounter another whose very soul speaks to you?"

Lucy picked up a fan from the dressing table, waving it in front of her face, though it was not warm in the bedroom. She had become thinner in the last two weeks. Her peach-colored moiré dress threatened to slip from her shoulders, but she still had good color in her cheeks, and her spirits were generally high.

"You are not answering me because you know that I am correct," I said. "It is entirely possible that Jonathan has either met someone he considers more appropriate to be his wife, or that he has reconsidered his feelings for me."

"Don't be a goose, Mina," she said, making light of my fears. "Now put on your pretty smile and help me receive Mr. Holmwood and his friends."

Holmwood and his school friends, the infamous Morris Quince and Dr. John Seward, were waiting in the parlor when Lucy and I entered the room, but Mrs. Westenra shuttled us to the dining room so quickly that I barely had time to put a face to each name. When we sat down, she apologized ad nauseam for the humbleness of the table and of the fare, regretting that she had not brought the proper china from Hampstead and that she had allowed the cook to go visit her family rather than accompany the Westenras to Whitby. "But my health is to blame. I just do not think of things as I did when I was well."

She dominated the conversation with this topic all the way through the soup course, when Holmwood, who was seated next to her, finally put an end to it. "I will send my man to fetch everything from your Hampstead pantry and kidnap the cook from her mother's cottage if it will make you feel more at ease, madam."

I found Holmwood to be charming in a dutiful way. His sharp nose was just the right size for his face, which was long and angular, and the right proportion to sit above his lips, which were not full, but neither were they thin and reptilian, as with so many unfortunate men. He had a gangly masculinity, and it was easy to envision him succeeding at the leisure activities for which he was known to have passion—riding, hunting, and sailing. Despite these sports, his hands were slender and effeminate. His coloring matched Lucy's, but his hair was slightly darker and thinner. I suspected that the few curls that dangled about his scalp would soon desert him.

He paid lavish attention to Mrs. Westenra, whose health once again bloomed under his gaze. She did her best to ignore the much-discussed Morris Quince, who sat next to me, whereas I was the unrelenting object of the eyes of Dr. John Seward, who sat opposite me. The three men had planned to set off on a pleasure sail in the morning to Scarborough, but Quince had arrived with his right arm in a sling, owing to falling off his horse in an early morning canter along the shore.

"The animal stumbled over a rock and tossed me off his back," he said in an accent I'd never before heard. It was not the flat American accent I was accustomed to. When I had asked him where in America he resided, he cocked his head and answered, "New York," as if there were no alternative locations in his country. He pronounced certain words as if he were English, and I wondered if he had picked up an accent at Oxford, or if this was a peculiar way that wealthy people in America spoke. Quince said that he would not be joining his friends for the sail because his arm would render him useless. "I would be a liability," he said. "Dead weight."

I suppose that he could be described as dashing. One could see him galloping along the violent Yorkshire coast, pushing his steed through the crashing waves. What one could not envision was him losing control of a horse and falling off. He was Arthur's height but had a more substantial frame. His neck did not want to be contained by his collar. His hands, which were large, with long elegant fingers and nails cut razor straight, fascinated me. Though they were perhaps the most manicured male hands I had ever seen, they seemed to have great power. The wineglass almost disappeared in his palm as he picked it up. While

Arthur's hair hung about his face like curled fringe on a shawl, Quince's was of a single unit, a great, beautiful flow of thick walnut that operated as one organism.

He had big gleaming teeth and an easy smile, though he did not smile often. By Mrs. Westenra's cautious description, I had expected someone entirely different, some American rogue whose character was easy to read. Morris Quince was not that man. With a painter's intense gaze, he stared at everything through large, brown, guileless eyes. It didn't seem to matter whether he was looking at his roast beef; at the color of the wine as it was poured; or at Lucy, whose face he studied as she answered a question posed by Dr. Seward. All the while, he—Quince, that is—was carrying on a conversation with Arthur, predicting the velocity of the morning winds. Mrs. Westenra pretended to listen to that conversation, but she too was fixated on Lucy and on the plates of her guests, gauging, I thought, whether our hearty consumption indicated approval of the food.

Dr. Seward, on the other hand, had finished his supper and was staring at me. He had tried to make conversation with me several times, though I did not know what to say to him. When we were introduced, he had taken my hand and looked me over hungrily as if I were his dinner, and he, a starving man. Though he was the only one of the three friends who was not wealthy—he was a doctor at a private asylum—he had a regal brow, as if the cliché of the intelligent having larger brains were true.

For one brief moment, all casual chatter subsided, and Mrs. Westenra filled the space. "Dr. Seward, I must ask your opinion on the subject of angina."

Arthur turned all his attention to this conversation, leaving Morris Quince and Lucy to sit in uncomfortable silence next to each other. Lucy pushed her peas to and fro as if watching their journey from one side of the plate to the next was interesting, but she did not eat. Perhaps she could not imagine what to say to Quince, but she was usually at ease in any conversation, particularly with men. Yet she sat there as if he did not exist. I was yanked out of my reverie by the sound of Quince's voice directed toward me. "Miss Lucy tells us that you are affianced, Miss Mina, but your gentleman is not present. Does that mean that the good doctor might have a chance at your affection?"

"Mr. Quince!" Mrs. Westenra affected a face of great mortification, but not so genuine as that of Dr. Seward, who blushed purple.

"I know I should apologize, but I am not sorry," Quince said, his toothy grin in full form splashed across his face like a half moon risen in the night sky. "I am a brash son of a brash denizen of a brash city. John is my great friend, and I just want to know if this Mr. Harker is good enough for you, Miss Mina."

Arthur stood up. "Dear God, Quince, have you learned nothing in my company?" He turned to me. "Miss Murray, he's an insensitive and ill-bred American oaf upon whom I have taken pity and befriended. Can you forgive him?"

No one seemed more entertained than Lucy, who showed the first sign of life this evening. "Mina is not so delicate as she seems. She manages classrooms filled with little girls who are more unruly than you men."

I mustered my courage and turned to Quince. "I must inform you that Mr. Harker exceeds all expectations." I cast my eyes downward as Headmistress taught me to do when in the company of men.

Soon thereafter, Arthur gathered his friends to leave, allowing that they were to set sail very early in the morning. "Sure you won't change your mind?" he asked Quince, who lifted his injured arm up as an answer.

"Best that I stay dry."

John Seward took my elbow and moved me aside. He looked at me with watery eyes that had seemed to go very dark. "I am pained to have been the cause of your embarrassment, Miss Mina," he said. "How can I make amends?"

He was handsome in his way. His voice was both authoritative and soothing, which I imagined made his patients feel at ease. Its low register imbued him with more masculinity than his thin frame suggested.

And there was a bright intelligence in his gray eyes, which were trying to understand me, or read my thoughts. Or perhaps diagnose me.

"There is nothing to apologize for, Dr. Seward. Your friend is prankish. It's rather charming," I said, casting my eyes downward again, hoping that the conversation would end.

"I shall have to be satisfied with that," he said. He dropped my hand, but not until he held it for longer than was comfortable to me.

With that they began to take their leave, and I noticed that the final and most heartfelt good-byes of the evening were between Arthur and Mrs. Westenra.

After everyone left, Mrs. Westenra said, "Why, Mina, you seemed to have captured our Dr. Seward. He was crazy about Lucy, but of course he did not really expect to conquer a girl with her fortune. On the other hand, were you not affianced to Mr. Harker, he might have made a fine match for you."

I did not take her words as an insult because they merely bespoke the truth. In fact, I went to bed thinking of Dr. Seward's attention. If Jonathan abandoned me, could I learn to love the doctor?

After we changed into our nightclothes and climbed into bed, I tried to make conversation with Lucy, but she pleaded exhaustion and shut her eyes tight against my words. Disappointed, I rolled over on my side and soon slipped into a dream.

. . .

I lay on a divan in an unfamiliar parlor. Morris Quince, Arthur Holmwood, and Mrs. Westenra were standing above me with grave faces, watching as Dr. Seward's hands pressed firmly into my stomach. He closed his eyes, feeling his way along the crevice below my ribs. I was without a corset, wearing a thin dressing gown. The tips of his fingers worked their way downward and along my pelvic bone, igniting all my nerves. Blood rose to my face, and I shut my eyes, turning away from the others' gazes. Seward and I breathed in unison, our heavy inhalations the only sound in the room. I wanted him to continue to move his hands lower to where my body was stirring. I started to move my hips involuntarily, aware that I was being watched but unable to control my movements. I fought with my own desires, trying to steel my legs against parting, but my body would not cooperate with me. Horrified, I began to sweat and wriggle as the doctor's hands massaged the soft part of my belly, thrilling me, only now they were not Seward's hands but the big, beautiful, powerful hands of Morris Quince. I arched my back, so that the palms pressed into me, and I started to murmur, no longer caring what the spectators thought of me, only desiring the man's touch.

I moaned so loudly that I woke myself up and found that I was alone in Lucy's bed. The linens on her side were cold. She'd apparently been gone for some time, and I was relieved, knowing that she had not witnessed the writhing and moaning I'd been doing in my dream. I assumed that she had spent the night once more in her mother's room. I tiptoed across the room and stepped into the hall to see the time on the clock—three thirty in the morning. I heard the front door creak and then close, followed by light footsteps that seemed to be coming toward me. Could it be an intruder? Tourists visiting the area were warned to lock their doors against thieves who were ready to take advantage of the relaxed mood of those on holiday. I slipped back into the bedroom, getting ready to scream loud enough to alert our neighbors. I held my breath and then peeked down the hall.

What came toward me, one hand holding her shoes, the other hiking up her skirt, was Lucy. Her hair was bedraggled—ripped from its pins and ornaments, and frizzed by the damp sea air. I left the door ajar and jumped into bed, trying to pretend that I was asleep, but she was in the room before I could settle myself. When she realized I was awake, her eyes darted around the room as if she thought someone else might be there. She stared at me, looking like some wild-eyed Medusa.

"Why are you spying on me? Did my mother put you up to this?"

"I would think that you should be explaining, not asking questions. I had a bad dream and woke a few moments ago to find you gone."

Lucy collapsed on the bed. Her collarbones jutted out, emphasizing her thinness. She looked strange and stark but somehow also luminous.

"Can you not guess? I would think it as plain as the nose on my face. Oh, it is so difficult to hide being in love. Mina, I am bursting with it. My love for him is in every pore of my skin, trying to express itself to the world. I can no longer hide it from my best girlfriend."

"In love?" I had seen no evidence of this great passion at dinner. "You have been with Mr. Holmwood?"

"Dear God, no, not him! I despise him, except that he brought my true love to me, and for that I love him. But for that alone. How marvelous that we have deceived you! That should mean that my mother and the rest do not know either."

"Oh, Lucy, no." In my mind's eye, I saw those powerful hands and knew that they were the ones that had removed the pins from Lucy's hair and tousled her golden mane.

"Mina, do you know what love is? How it feels? Do you know what it is like to be in the arms of a man of passion?" Lucy sat up and put her face uncomfortably close to mine. "I went to his studio. He has been making a secret portrait of me in the nude! Can you believe that I have agreed to this? It is a measure of my love for him. I was to sit for him tonight, but he took off my clothes and lay me on a table and tickled every inch of my body with his softest paintbrush until I begged for mercy."

I thought she must be mad, saying these things. I recalled how Lucy and Morris seemed to have nothing to say to each other at dinner and now realized that they were acting out a performance of indifference to hide their secret.

"How can he paint with his injured arm?" I asked.

"Oh, that is but a brilliant ruse so that Arthur would go sailing without him!"

"Lucy!" I was mortified at the way the two of them so casually deceived others.

Lucy took me by the shoulders. "Mina, if you do not feel this exquisite way about Jonathan, you should not marry him. Everything we are told is a lie—that the love between two people should be some polite arrangement when in truth it is . . ." Lucy paused to find the right words. "It is an opera!"

"The ladies come to a bad end in operas," I said quietly.

"I should have known better than to tell you. You are the voice of reason, whereas I am speaking from the depths of my soul," she said far too loudly.

"Please be quieter," I said. "You will wake your mother."

"No, I won't. I mixed her sleeping draft myself."

"Lucy! You are not a doctor. You might have harmed her!"

Lucy settled on the bed. "I forgive you, Mina. If someone had tried to explain these feelings to me before I experienced them, I would have had the same response. But you are engaged to a man. Have you never felt thrilled by his proximity or by his touch? Are you so very cold, Mina?"

Lucy's face contorted into a frown. "Perhaps good women like you do not experience these sorts of feelings. What is it like, Mina, to never have committed a transgression?"

"I am not without sin," I said.

I let the words slide out of my mouth and into the world. I too had kept in my secrets and longed to confess to someone. Lucy's features lifted again. She sat up straight.

"I have dreams," I began. "Dreams in which strangers visit me. But the experiences are too vivid to be mere dreams." I told her about hearing voices in my sleep and being lured out of doors and about the night I awoke to find myself being attacked by a madman with red eyes and a hideous odor, and of the elegant stranger who both saved me and terrified me. I told her about the dreams that followed in which I had done terrible things—lurid things that no woman should do. I did not tell her of tonight's dream in which Dr. Seward was caressing me with Morris Quince's hands. In that dream, I could put a name to my delicious tormentors, and that made it impossible for me to confess.

"I know that there is something dark and inexplicable in my character that is causing these episodes, but it is beyond my control to stop it," I said.

Lucy patted my hand as if I were a child. "Mina, you are one who walks in her sleep. My father suffered the same affliction, and you must be careful, because it led to his demise. He walked out of doors in the middle of a damp and frigid winter night and caught pneumonia. As you recall, he never recovered." Lucy spoke tenderly as she always did when she talked about her father.

I had not known the circumstances under which he had contracted the lung disease that had killed him. I started to tremble.

"Mina, darling, you are not wicked. You had the misfortune to be a beautiful girl walking alone in London. The man who attacked you probably thought you were one of the ladies of the night. You were defenseless. The mysterious one who stopped the attack was probably just a man about town who had spent the evening with friends at his club and was doing a good deed."

Could it be that simple? I wanted to accept Lucy's rational explanation. Though she was swept up in her own passion, she seemed sure that what was happening to me was not out of the ordinary.

"Jonathan says that according to the mind doctors, dreams are reflections of one's own fears. He believes that my adventures into London's dark byways with Kate are responsible for these nightmares," I said.

"We could inquire of Dr. Seward," Lucy suggested. "I am sure that he would enjoy interpreting your dreams." Her eyes shone with mischief.

"I could not speak of these things to him," I said. "It would not be proper."

"That is my Mina, always concerned with propriety. What must you think of your Lucy now?"

"I fear for you," I said. "What will become of you, Lucy? You are engaged to another man."

"Morris has a plan. He says he will lay down his life before he allows me to marry Arthur, or any man other than himself."

"What is stopping you from marrying him now? This is not the fifteenth century. The unification of kingdoms is not at stake. Why did you accept Arthur's proposal when you love someone else?"

"I would marry Morris Quince tomorrow if he would allow it. His father has cut him off because he refused to enter the family business, choosing to paint instead. My mother controls my fortune and she despises him and loves Arthur. I have told Morris that I would run away with him, that I don't need money as long as I have his love, but he won't have it. He insists that I deserve better than poverty."

"At least he is correct about that!" I said. "You are not a girl accustomed to hardship. A woman has to be smart, Lucy. Are you not afraid that Mr. Quince is toying with you?"

Lucy struck back quickly. "No! No, he is not toying with me. I hoped you would understand. Now I am sorry that I told you at all. You'll probably go running to my mother and spill out everything and make her have one of her angina attacks."

I assured Lucy that her secret was safe with me, and asked for her assurance that what I had told her would remain between us. "Of course I will respect your wishes," she said, "but I hardly see how some bad dreams compare with a passionate love affair that is happening in our real lives."

I helped Lucy with her clothes and her corset, noticing that above the slash marks of the stays, other marks had appeared on her back and chest—red and blue, like bruised roses. I did not mention them. We kissed each other good night, but I was left with the feeling that Lucy wanted to retain some sort of superiority over me, not a moral superiority but rather its opposite—descent into passion—which for her transcended every good thing we had been taught to believe.

. . .

Though Whitby Abbey was just steps from the churchyard, which I visited daily while Lucy napped, I had studiously avoided its grounds. While I actually enjoyed whiling away hours in the churchyard cemetery, staring at ancient tombstones and reading the maudlin inscriptions, there was something about the old ruin that depressed my spirit. In those days, with no word from Jonathan, the deteriorated majesty of Whitby Abbey, surrounded by mist and fog, stood like a monument to my own loneliness.

Today, however, the sun shone brightly, turning the abbey's bleak walls into gleaming white bones upon which a vivid imagination might reconstruct the building at its highest glory. I sat on my usual bench in the churchyard and took out the little leather-bound journal. I had started to write down some of the old whaler's ghoulish stories, thinking that upon Jonathan's return, they might amuse him. I had been learning about the abbey's history, so I began to jot down some of the facts:

> Whitby Abbey, an immense roofless ruin that had once been home to prosperous Benedictine monks, was abandoned when Henry VIII decided to rid the nation of Catholics and their monasteries. Now it is a pile of rubble and stone, with only its magnificent bones still standing, stubbornly resisting time and weather. It is the centerpiece of the headland, and its property must have been vast hundreds of years ago when it was built in the days of knights and Crusaders. But they say that years of bashing by the sea have considerably diminished the size of the promontory. I wonder if, in the future, the sea will gobble up the ruin, with its walls of tiered Gothic arches that diminish in size as they ascend toward the sky.

"Well, well, miss, if you're not the busy blue fly."

I looked up to see my elderly friend smiling at me with his eyes, which were sometimes the only part of him that still seemed alive. His cheeks looked like Whitby's big, pockmarked, wave-battered cliffs and his arms, gnarled and twisted driftwood, but his eyes were sea blue and watery. It was as if he had assumed the characteristics of the topography he had observed over a long lifetime. He was nearly ninety years old, he claimed, though the record of his birth had been lost in a fire, and no one who had witnessed it was still alive. He had long ago forgotten his birthday, and so had his daughter, now a woman of seventy years old. "We've a half memory between us," he had said. "I only remember the stories I have told and retold."

Still, he got along well on his severely bowed and crooked legs, and seemed livelier to me than the two napping women with whom I was presently staying.

"Do you never take a nap in the daytime, sir?" I asked.

"I'll sleep when I'm dead," he said, sitting down. "I'll enjoy the company of a pretty girl with warm hands and pink cheeks while I may."

I told him that I was writing down some of Whitby's history for my fiancé to enjoy, and that I intended to include the stories he had been telling me.

"Surely you have heard the legend of St. Hild?" he asked.

It was impossible to spend any time at all in Whitby without learning St. Hild's story. I told him what I knew—that she had been the abbess of the monastery in the very old days, when Oswy of Northumbria was king, and that she had presided over a community of men and women who devoted their lives to praising God and meditating upon His Word. He suggested that we take a walk around the abbey's grounds so that he could tell me more of the story, "but not at the crackin' pace you would take with a younger fellow."

We strolled across the field, where others, taking advantage of a rare cloudless sky and warmth, had spread colorful quilts and were picnicking on lunches of sliced chicken, bread, fruit, cheese, homemade pies, bottles of wine, and pints of beer.

He saw me looking at the food. "Listen, miss, for this may be the last time I ever tell the tale, so I am going to tell it long and true."

He took a wheezy breath to gather his energy. "Hild was a royal woman, a princess, and might have been a queen, what with her beauty and her lands. She was a relation to the good king, who vowed that if he was victorious in defeating the pagans, he would give up his newborn daughter to the church. Now, at this very time, Hild was bearing witness to the wickedness of the pagans who would not surrender to the One True God, and she made a promise to devote her life to changing this. After the king won his battle, Hild gave up her worldly possessions, took charge of the king's infant daughter, and founded this monastery. It was said that men and women alike bowed to her wisdom and her powers. The bishops of England were so enchanted by her that they chose this spot for their meeting place."

The old man's eyes turned rheumy as he squinted against the sun. He was looking up at the façade of the abbey. "Though she died many hundreds of years ago, she is still here." With some effort, he raised his arms high in the air to show her omnipotence.

"I see the look of wonder on your face," he said. "You should have more respect than to doubt the words of an old man who is to meet his Maker soon enough to make a truth teller of him. On these very grounds where we stand, Lucifer sent a plague of vipers—horrible creatures full of poisonous venom—to defeat St. Hild and to destroy her good works. The devil did not want to give up the Yorkshire coast to God," he said. "And look about you at the beauty. No one could blame him.

"But St. Hild was not one to give in to the devil. Nothing scared her because she had the Lord on her side. She drove the snakes to the edge of the cliffs, cracking a long whip to drive them over the side and into the sea. But some of those creatures of Satan refused to jump, and those she killed by snapping off their heads with a lash of the whip. Others, she turned to stone."

"That is a remarkable story," I said politely.

"'Tis true, girl. Don't you keep looking at me that way, with the doubting face that young people turn on their elders. Someday, after I'm gone, you'll be walking these grounds, or on the shore beneath them, and you'll stumble over a rock with the face of a snake. You will look at his beady eyes and his tongue lying flat against his lips, and you will think of your old friend."

"I will not require a relic to remember you," I said, much to his delight. He laughed, and I noticed that, despite a few missing front teeth, all his back teeth were still firmly set in his gums, a rarity for anyone his age.

"If you come here on a moonlit night, and you look into the windows of the abbey, you can see her going about her business. She still presides here, so help me God, she does."

The sun grew stronger, and I felt perspiration trickle down the front of my corset. My nonagenarian companion seemed less fatigued than I, and, as ashamed as I was by this fact, I did not have a parasol with me, and I was getting overheated in the glaring sun. I apologized to him for taking my leave.

"But I have not yet finished the story," he said. His voice turned to a whisper. "There is a wicked spirit on this very ground, battling Hild for the abbey. You'll want to know about her, won't you?"

Despite the old man's disappointment, I bid him good afternoon and returned to our rooms, where I found Lucy and her mother still napping. I checked the basket where Hilda—one of the town's many who had been named after the saint—left any mail that had arrived, but there was no letter from Jonathan. Disappointed, I loosened my stays and slipped into bed next to Lucy, falling into a dreamless sleep.

20 August 1890

The weather turned miserable and stayed so for days, with rain pouring down upon the stacked red roofs of Whitby, sliding into the narrow streets and flooding them, and keeping us indoors. The sea-born tempests swept inland so violently that the rain came sideways, like little knives slashing the air. At night, crashing thunder overwhelmed the ubiquitous roar of the sea that continued to throw itself incessantly against the cliffs. I was not sure which sound was more disquieting, though there was an exquisite excitement in the sky's rumbles. Sometimes I sat by a lamp, trying to read while imagining that gods and Titans were wrestling in the heavens over one mythical siren or another.

The dramatic weather prevented Lucy from leaving to meet her lover. He managed to have notes delivered to her, sent under fictitious names, which brought fresh color to her face as she read them. The strain of separation was demonstrated by her fidgety demeanor and especially in her dissipating flesh. At meals, she tried to hide one serving of food beneath another to allay her mother's fears about her obvious weight loss. I too begged her to take a little food, even some fruit or a sandwich at teatime.

"Clearly you have never been passionately in love!" she said to me, watching me eat another pastry doused with cream. "You have not heard from Mr. Harker, and yet you eat like a cormorant! It is unseemly, Mina. It is I who should be criticizing you and not the other way around."

"I do not see how starving myself will bring word from Jonathan," I said. "Anyway, I am certain that he did not receive the letter I sent giving him this address. When I return to London, I will have a pile of letters from Austria." At least I had been comforting myself with that thought.

After days of rain, on Saturday evening, the twenty-third day of August, the sun announced itself just at the time it was meant to be setting, raising the temperature and sweeping a balmy breeze over the town. That bright golden ball sank slowly into the horizon, illuminating the hilly terrain as it fell. We watched twilight's grand show from the cliffs above the town, so happy to see the sun, as if it were a long lost friend whose homecoming we welcomed, even though its visit was brief. We heard that entertainment was to be had on the pier that evening, and we expressed our desire to attend. Mrs. Westenra surprised us by wanting to join us.

It seemed that the entire town had come out to hear the band, which played popular songs. As we passed the bandstand, a man playing a beautifully curved cornet of brass and silver boldly winked at me, and I could not help but smile at him before I turned my head away. We three ladies bought ice creams and took a small table where we could listen to the music without being trampled by the coarser people who were drinking beer and those couples who wanted to dance.

Lucy was distracted to the point of silence, scanning the crowd for a sign, I supposed, of her beloved, while Mrs. Westenra was content to sit quietly and tap her foot to the music. I occupied myself watching the passersby. Everyone was caught up in the magical combination of the clement weather and the lively rhythm. Men walked spryly, and the women on their arms swayed to the tunes. Some fathers waltzed along to the music with little girls standing on their feet, while one family— a father, mother, brother, and two sisters—held hands doing a kind of group polka, the mother leading the movements. She hopped to one side, and then to the next, with the others trying to keep up with her until the little boy tripped on her skirt and fell to the ground crying. A few of the spectators gave him a rousing hand of applause, which both embarrassed him and made him proud as his father carried him off to the lemonade line. I imagined that in years to come, Jonathan and I would be that family, dancing merrily on our holiday, a family of doting parents and children secure in their love.

It was then that I saw the red-haired writer watching me. He was strolling with a woman I assumed was his wife, a dark-haired, strikingly beautiful woman in the sort of detailed white lace and linen dress that fashionable London women wore to holiday places. A boy with soft blond hair who wore a crisply starched sailor suit, the sort of thematic clothing that a doting grandmother would purchase for a boy's holiday to a seafaring community, walked between them. The lady was pointing a graceful arm toward the lighthouse, telling the boy something about it, or so it appeared. She looked regal, with her swan neck wrapped in white netting and her back as straight as a queen's. I remember wishing that I could train my students to carry just a small portion of that gracefulness.

The red-haired man, I now saw, had a huge bump on his forehead that looked like a tumor, which prevented him from being called handsome. He had a closely trimmed beard that was just a shade lighter than his hair, which he wore parted on the side. It was thinning, forming a valley of scalp on the left side of his large brow. He was, however—due to his size, stature, and penetrating gray eyes that were staring directly at me—an imposing figure. I suppose that Lucy and I were worthy of the male gaze, what with her pale blond beauty shown off nicely in a peach summer frock, in contrast to my black hair set against light skin. Tonight I wore my favorite dress of pale green linen, which everyone said complemented my eyes, and a cotton bolero jacket perfect for a summer evening. In retrospect, he might have been staring at us only because we were two pretty young women, and he was taking advantage of his wife's momentary distraction with their son. The more sinister implications of his engrossment came much later.

The band began to play a French song about cicadas that I knew, and I sang along, if only to have something to do while the man scrutinized me.

"'Les cigales, les cigalons, chantent mieux que les violons.'"

"What a charming song," said Mrs. Westenra. "What does it mean?"

I sang the jolly lyrics in English, but the last stanza was not as cheerful as its predecessors. "Now all is dead, nothing sounds anymore but them, the frenzied ones, filling in the spaces between some remote Angelus."

"What odd lyrics," she said.

"Mina has to sing all sorts of nonsense to her pupils," Lucy said, her first words of the evening.

I looked at the man to see if he was still watching me. When he caught my eye, he quickly turned away and became involved in whatever his wife and son were studying in the sea.

Suddenly I felt the temperature drop. The air was no longer balmy, as if the weather had pulled a prank on us while we were distracted by the music. The wind had picked up sharply in a matter of seconds, making the little awnings over the food stalls flap rowdily. Paper food wrappers flew off tables, skittering past our feet. Ladies held their coiffures in place with their hands.

"What a chill!" Mrs. Westenra exclaimed. "When will I learn to take my shawl with me? We should have gone to Italy. That is what Mr. West-enra would have wanted to do. I am lost without him, lost!"

"It is not so cold yet, Mother," Lucy said. "Mina will give you her lit-tle jacket."

I started to take off my bolero, but Mrs. Westenra stopped me. "I will never fit into that little thing you call a jacket. We must go."

"No, not yet," Lucy said. "The band is still playing."

Thunder crackled in the sky, not once, but twice, and the band stopped in the middle of a song. The musicians looked up before put-ting their heads together in a forum on whether to continue. People around us slid their chairs back and stood, and parents dragged reluc-tant children away to try to beat the coming storm.

"No, Papa, no!" a little boy insisted, wriggling in his father's arms.

Lucy joined the chorus of protesting children. "I believe the sky will clear soon enough. This will pass." As if to make a liar of her, clouds of white mist drifted in from the sea, settling all around us.

I looked behind us where the red-haired man had been standing with his wife and son, but now a crowd had gathered around them, and I could no longer see them. Everyone was staring out to sea and pointing.

"I am going to see what's happening," I said.

"Mina, don't go. We will all catch our deaths in this weather," Mrs. Westenra said, looking frantic now. Lucy too darted her wild eyes back and forth. "Let her go, Mother. She won't be long. We can wait here."

"Don't worry over me," I said. "I will just go see what the fuss is about and I will meet you at home shortly if you decide to leave."

"Don't be long, Mina. This isn't the sort of weather to take lightly," the older lady warned.

Lucy started a second round of protestation, and I left them to their argument. I ran to where people were gathered, standing on tiptoes to see over one another. Men from the coast guard had joined them, push-ing their way to the front of the crowd, where waves thick with foam crashed against the pier. I followed their gaze into the distance. Beyond the harbor, a large sailing ship bobbed up and down in the upsurge. I snaked my way deeper into the crowd so that I could hear what the coastguardsmen were saying.

"She's going to hit the reef," said one man to the other.

"Why does the captain not head for the mouth of the harbor?" The red-haired man asked the question in a deep voice tinged with an Irish accent. I recognized it because it sounded like my own when I was lax in my speech—from the west coast of Ireland, but mostly lost after many years in London.

"He's got his hands full with that crosswind. It came from nowhere," one of the men answered.

"It came from the bowels of hell," said another. "Though the captain at the helm is steering like a drunk."

The wife of the red-haired man had her son by the hand now and was dragging him away, but the father remained engrossed by the vessel bobbing up and down in the brutal waves like a prop in a puppet show. Behind us on the East Cliff, a crew turned on the searchlight, sending a bright, bluish beam out to sea.

"That will guide her safely into the harbor," a coastguardsman said.

"Only if she avoids the reef," said another.

The light skimmed over the peaks of water as they convulsed into the sky. I saw a glimpse of the illuminated vessel before a large wave broke over the pier, sending us reeling backward into one another as we tried to avoid it. I fell backward and into strange arms that caught me in a strong, sure grip.

"Miss Mina!"

Morris Quince had me by the arms. He put me upright. "Let's get you out of this storm."

I was not surprised to see him; throughout the evening, I had guessed that he was the hoped-for object of Lucy's searching eyes.

"I want to see what happens," I said.

I turned back to the sea and the unfolding drama. More people crowded onto the pier despite the crashing waves that threatened our safety. I did not want to leave, though I had always been one to avert my eyes from the sight of a disaster. I would walk out of my way to avoid watching the aftermath of an overturned carriage or a collision of carts. I had no stomach for such things, and yet I wanted to stay on the pier and find out the fate of the crew and passengers of the ship even if it meant being drenched to the bone in my favorite frock.

"Please don't be stubborn, Miss Mina, or I'll have to throw you over my shoulder. Americans have no compunction about these things. We are the savages that people claim we are."

I had no doubt that this outrageous man would do precisely as he threatened, though I could not help but smile at his self-mockery. Still, I had an aversion to him because of what he was doing to jeopardize Lucy's future. "Have you seen Lucy and Mrs. Westenra?" I asked.

"I paid a man with an umbrella to take them up to the inn at the top of the hill. They're waiting for us where it's nice and dry."

Another wave convulsed out of the sea, crashing over the pier, but we were able to duck the worst of it. Morris laughed, as if he were a boy playing a sport and had just scored a winning point. The searchlight swept over our heads and again found the vessel, which had moved closer to us, two of its sails battered and torn. The yard of one mast dangled in the water, while another fraying sail, puffed and straining, sped the boat along its deadly path. The ship was almost on its side as the waves— great foam beasts climbing their way to shore—navigated what looked like a potentially fatal outcome for the vessel and its crew. The light revealed the name of the vessel, the *Valkyrie*.

"She's a charter boat out of Rotterdam, carries cargo for whoever can pay the price. The captain knows his way into this harbor," said the coast-guardsman. "Why does he allow the sea to have its way with the boat?"

The searchlight clearly showed the path into the harbor's mouth, but the captain ignored it, allowing his boat to continue to list helplessly toward the shore. It appeared that the catastrophic accident of seventy years ago described by the old whaler would be reenacted right before my eyes.

A wave like the gargantuan arm of Poseidon shot up from deep within the sea, slapping the starboard side of the ship.

"Looks like she's hit the reef," yelled one of the coastguardsmen.

"Great gods!" Morris said, his attention now fully engaged. Without taking his eyes off the water, he opened his cloak and put it over my shoulders. I could have objected, but I appreciated the protection and warmth it gave my skin, now wet with seawater and cold from the fierce wind. Lightning flashed across the sky with such ferocity it made me cower. Instinctively, I leaned closer to Morris, hating myself for being a skittish woman who so required the protection of a man that she would depend upon a dastardly one such as this. Yet I would not be dragged away from this awful but majestic performance put on by nature.

The wind shifted without warning, enhancing the sheer wild and random power of the sea. As easily as it had slammed the boat against the reef, it rose at an even greater velocity and freed it, throwing the boat helplessly toward the pier. Now the boat and we spectators were entirely at the mercy of the sea. The water made swooping curls, like the snarling lips of a monster, ringing the vessel in a watery prison. At this point, the sea was dictating its path with an encircling chain of turbulent waves.

As if changing its mind and granting a reprieve, the waves tossed the vessel upward again, veritably throwing it into the mouth of the harbor. The crowd let out a little cheer, until we collectively realized that the boat was headed directly toward us and would slam straight into the foundations of the pier.

I thought we should run away, but there were too many people behind us, and most of us were in too much awe of the spectacle to move. Morris must have figured as much because he tightened his grip around me, bracing us for whatever happened. But at the last moment, as if it were actually ruled by tempestuous Neptune, the fickle sea changed the direction of its waves, and the boat slid straight into the sandy pit of soil and gravel that jutted from under the cliffs.

Many of the people on the pier hurried down the steps to the shore to help the rescue party or perhaps to welcome the heroic survivors or maybe just to gawk at the potential dead. The searchlight grazed the ship's deck, as a rescue crew, all too familiar with the aftermath of a shipwreck, rushed forward with planks to make a gangway for whomever was onboard.

They waited, but no one and nothing stirred from that vessel. The searchlight stopped abruptly, illuminating the sailor at the helm, presumably the vessel's captain, whose head drooped over the wheel. The grotesque scene came into focus slowly, bringing with it a long moment of eerie silence in which neither thunder nor lightning nor wind disturbed the quiet of the night. No one on the pier, not even the coastguardsmen, spoke a word. It was as if the light had stopped time, freezing both man and nature in that moment.

The men on the shore, who had been poised to rush the ship, stood still, gazing at the macabre sight before them. A sailor's body slumped over the helm, his hands tied to the wheel's spokes with figure eight knots, distanced just enough to enable him to handle the big wheel. A dark rivulet of blood streamed from his neck. He looked almost as if he had been crucified.

"Saints preserve us, the captain is lashed to the helm!" The red-haired man cried out to the coastguardsman, who, without looking away from the ship, confirmed what he said with a nod. "Looks to me like it's a bloody corpse that brought in the vessel."

"The ship was sailed by a dead man." As people grasped this reality, they put their hands to their mouths or shouted shrieks of disbelief or raised their palms to the sky as if to ask God how this could have happened.

"Fucking hell," Morris Quince whispered softly.

A clap of vicious thunder broke our quiet moment of astonishment. As if awakened from a dream, the rescue crew began to move slowly toward the *Valkyrie*. Suddenly, the men jumped back again as a huge dog, a giant beast of an animal lit up like a streak of silver by the searchlight, leapt from the vessel and onto the shore. Though everyone cowered from it, the dog ignored them, taking its own path up the East Cliff and heading in the direction of the cemetery as if it knew exactly where it was going, and why.

Chapter Five

*I*s he not the most handsome, extraordinary man you have ever met, Mina?"

Lucy and I were undressing for bed, or rather I was, and Lucy watched me. She had no interest in discussing the shipwreck or speculating on the mystery of the dead captain but preferred to reminisce about the thrill of seeing Morris. I rinsed my mouth slowly and closed my jar of toothpaste, checking my teeth in the mirror, while I decided whether to challenge Lucy. As her friend, I felt I owed it to her to point out the ramifications of her actions.

"But, Lucy, he is Arthur's friend. Surely this will not come to a good end."

"Oh, Arthur is not a true friend. He simply thinks it's daring to have a friend from a scandalous American family. He speaks badly of Morris behind his back."

"Perhaps he is speaking the truth," I said. "Perhaps you should take heed."

"You are supposed to be my best friend, Mina, and yet you have not tried at all to understand!"

"I only understand what I see. Look at yourself." I pulled Lucy off the bed and stood her in front of the oval cheval mirror. She crossed her arms in protest, but she did not look away. "You are wasting away to skin and bones. You do not eat. You do not sleep. And all day long, you are as nervous as an alley cat. Your sweet temper has become sharp. When you talk about your love, you look like Lizzie Cornwall, sick and dizzy from smoking opium but craving it nonetheless."

"I do crave his love. It has replaced every other appetite." Lucy's eyes danced in the sockets in the strange way they did when she thought of Morris Quince. She pulled a note out of her bodice. "He slipped this to me when no one was looking. I am going to meet him!"

"Lucy! The weather!"

She went to the window and opened the shutters. "Look. It has cleared. God himself is smiling upon my love."

The rain had stopped and the mist had lifted. A cool breeze wafted in. I looked out the window and traced the seven brightly burning stars comprising the Starry Plow, so vivid that it looked as if I could reach up and use it to scoop water out of a well. The single good memory I had of my father was when he had me in his arms one night and pointed it out in the sky.

"Morris would not let me come to him in the rain, Mina," she said, thrusting the note into my hand.

If the weather clears, meet me after midnight. If it is raining, don't dare risk the health of the one I hold dearer to me than my own life. I am racked with anguish being so near to you and not being able to touch you.

Soon, my love, soon,

M.

"These are just words, Lucy. Any man can write words on a page if it costs him nothing," I said.

"Apparently not Jonathan Harker. How long has it been since you have had words on a page from him?"

"Lucy, how unkind!" Her words made my own fears come roaring back. Jonathan did not love me. Jonathan had met someone more suitable to be his wife. I was to be a spinster schoolteacher for the rest of my days. These fears had overtaken me a few days prior, and I had written to Mr. Hawkins to ask if he had had word from Jonathan, but I had received no reply.

Lucy took my hands in hers, which were cold. Her skin, once so enviable, looked as thin as tracing paper. A network of blue veins formed a spider's web on her left shoulder. The tendons at the bottom of her neck stuck out like claws. "Forgive me, Mina. Let us be the good friends we have been to each other since we were girls. We are both in love. One day, you will marry Jonathan, and you will come to visit Morris and me in America."

"America?"

"He says that he will go to his father and beg forgiveness. Once he is back in the family fold, we will be married and we will live in New York."

"You are not thinking of Arthur's feelings at all?"

"No, I am not! He knows I do not love him. He spent one year seducing my mother so that she would insist on the marriage. He knows that she controls my fortune and I must do as she says. That is an underhanded way for a gentleman to behave."

I wanted to remind her that seducing a friend's fiancée, such as Morris had done, was also an underhanded way to behave, but it was apparent that my arguments held no sway against her passions.

Lucy waited until she was certain that her mother was asleep. Then, tucking me in as if I were a child, she extracted another promise of discretion, turned out the light, and slipped out to meet her lover, while I fell asleep to disquieting thoughts about the mistake she was making.

.   .   .

I dreamt that I was somewhere warm, safe, and enveloping, like a womb. I was floating, wondering if I were a baby about to be born, when all my senses exploded, throwing my body into chaos. All at once, I was everywhere and nowhere, as if I had burst outside myself. I felt as if my skin were being flayed, making way for something that crawled onto the surface of my flesh. I stuck my neck out long in front of me, and my hind legs pulled in the opposite direction, as if I were elongating my body. Pushed on by a tingling sensation I tumbled and tumbled, and found myself suddenly on grass, where I lunged forward like an animal onto all fours. Crouching, I felt balance and a sense of strength and power. I looked at my hands, which had become something else, some other appendage, covered in pale fur, with five sharp black claws all pointing forward, and black webbing between each toe. I stretched them wide, knowing that I could curl them around an object—the head of a small bird, the soft belly of a mouse—if I wanted to. And I did want this very much. I was ravenous and driven to prowl.

In that same instant, all thoughts disappeared from my mind, lost in an avalanche of sensations that eviscerated things like words and ideas. Out of my mouth came sounds and cries, but I had lost all ability to form words, or even to know the meaning of words. My sight became less and more at the same time. All colors turned to black, brown, and gray, yet images became sharper and more defined. I could see into the shadows, where the very blades of grass and the leaves and buds of plants were sharply defined though it was a dark night. I was acutely aware of my ears, hot, pulsing, and humming. Now fragrance took command, and I was struck with the scents of the evening. Unable to resist, I rolled on the ground, breathing in the wet tang of dewy grass and the musk of the mud in which it grew. I glided my muzzle through the blades, letting each soft edge tickle my nose. When I lifted it, I caught the delicate fragrance of wildflowers and the powdery sweetness of red clover. The aromas permeated my body as if I could smell with my eyes, my toes, and my tail. I detected the essence of living fowl on the feathers of a fallen bird, but was quickly distracted by the blood-warm effluvia of rabbits and voles wafting up from a small hole in the ground.

The air carried the scent of wet leaves after a forest rain. My senses were torn in two, with one thing calling my attention into the air and another, even more compelling, back down to the earth. The miasma of fetid earth, God's creatures, and the aromatic night air swirled in my head and through my body, competing with a cacophony of noises that grow louder and louder. The muffled sound of my paws as they made contact with the ground resonated in my ears. I felt in my body the vibration of all things touching the earth—animals small and large, as they interacted with the same soil that I was treading. The rustle of leaves in the trees, the screech of the wind blowing the hairs on my face, the fluttering of bees' wings, the distant cry of an owl—I heard each as a distinct, sharp sound. My senses were in control of my body. I was a living machine that processed sights, smells, and sounds.

Submit.

The command came from nowhere and from nothing but was put forcefully into my head. Confused, I looked around, sticking my muzzle into the air. Something crept up behind me, tackling me, pushing me to the ground. Soon, this creature was on top of me, not hurting me but rubbing its fur against mine and rolling me over on my back. Ah, how I recognized its scent—the salty iron of its blood mixing with the vital juices of its last kill and the pungency of the woods hanging from its slick fur. Its familiarity allayed the fear in me as I was jostled to and fro. A huge, soft tongue licked my belly, paralyzing me with pleasure. I stretched out long and could feel every inch of my spine against the earth, which was cool, compared to the tongue that worked its way up to my neck. The great nose of the beast rubbed and caressed the length of my long wolf neck, imprinting itself on me.

Yes. I am returning to you.

The words broke the spell of night's aromas and sounds and the pleasures brought by this animal that held me captive on the ground.

Do you remember who you are?

The voice was familiar and male, but the mouth I stared into was not human. The creature bared its teeth. Four sharp fangs, pairs from above and below, jutted toward me, threatening to tear into the my belly-soft flesh, while the little bits and pieces of me would be shredded more slowly by the small, straight teeth between the fangs. The great red tongue that had given me pleasure hung between those feral canines, as if anticipating the savory taste of my muscle and bone. I rolled to my side, trying to escape, but the beast growled at me, threatening me again with its gaping jaws.

I went limp, succumbing to my fate. The world around me turned to black as I anticipated the agony of the canines ripping into my flesh. I waited for a very long time in darkness, all sound, sight, and smell obliterated by fear and anxiety. But nothing happened. It was hard to tell what was more frightening: the fear of being eviscerated by the larger beast or the utter terror of his absence.

Do you remember, Mina? Do you remember?

I woke up surprised to find that I was still Mina, and not a young dog or wolf or fox or whatever form I had taken in my dream. Nothing about my body had been transformed, though my senses remained heightened. Not as acute as in the dream but sharper than they had been before I went to sleep.

But I was not in my bed. I was sitting on the grass in the moonlit shadow of the ruins of Whitby Abbey, and I had a companion. At first I thought I might still be dreaming as I looked into his midnight blue eyes. He stared at me without blinking or making a move toward me. He did not look dangerous, but how could he not be, with his size and the sinister V-shaped mane that began at his muzzle, rising above his eyes and around his taut ears? His coat was silvery gray. His paws had to be six inches wide. He was larger than a wolf, perhaps was a wolf—I did not know. He had frightened every spectator when he had leapt from the ship, but here he seemed to be standing guard over me, letting me take in his features.

But the most disarming thing about the creature was the intelligence in his eyes. There are ways that men look at women—with desire, with hunger, with respect, with disdain, with confusion. This creature looked at me as if he knew me. There was something noble, even regal, about him, as if he was bred to protect a king, or as if he were a king. Yes, I could see him sleeping beside a throne or commanding from one. His coat glittered like armor in the moonlight. I could see why he had looked like a silver streak when he jumped from the vessel. He did not look like an animal that had been long at sea but like a perfectly groomed prize of an indulgent owner or a lordly creature of the forest that presided over lesser beasts. With his gleaming coat and sinewy musculature and poise, he looked well fed, exercised, and cared for by standards that would make most children envious. Perhaps he was the beloved companion of the captain who had arrived inexplicably lashed to the helm. Whoever had done such a horrible thing to the man had clearly not harmed the animal.

But was he the animal from my dream? After witnessing his dramatic disembarkation from the vessel, had I dreamt that I was this creature and now, by coincidence, was encountering him? Would I soon be looking into his gaping jaws but this time not in a dream world, where I could simply open my eyes and find safety?

I was breathless, but the profound serenity of the beast staring at me without malice settled my nerves. The memory of soft fur nuzzling my neck made me want to reach out and stroke his coat. Secure that he would not attack, and bolstered by the crazy idea that he had given me that very promise with his eyes, I sat up straight, ignoring the leaves and grass that clung to my sleeves. I was afraid to move, but he came to me. He stared at me with his intelligent eyes, and I felt all fear and resistance leave me. He sniffed my arm and then nuzzled my chest with his head. I let him rub his warm fur against my neck all the while taking in his familiar scent, the same one from my dream. I was reveling in this exchange when, without warning, the animal turned and ran away. I watched his thick haunches retreat. His legs sprang from the earth with a kind of preternatural buoyancy that I had previously not witnessed in man or beast. It was as if some unseen power were pushing him from below, giving additional spring to his gait. He jumped over a pile of rubble, random stones that had fallen from the abbey's central tower. Leaping through one of the lower windows, he disappeared into the shell of the abbey.

I tried to get my bearings. I knew exactly where I was—the abbey is a rather conspicuous landmark—but the question of whom and what I was became harder to answer. I shuddered, hugging myself tight. The fog that had disappeared earlier settled once more over the promontory. It seemed darker now as the mist thickened, and I heard a hollow moan sweeping through the interior of the abbey's shell. It's only the wind, I told myself. I knew I should get back to the rooms, but without my animal companion watching over me, I was afraid.

I wanted to follow him into the abbey, but even by day, I found the building's hulk too foreboding. The arched windows stood like dark open mouths waiting to spill secrets, mysteries from a past better left undisturbed. But this had been a holy place, not some medieval torture chamber where dark spirits wandered, seeking revenge for horrific acts committed against them. This had been the home of saints and of the saintly, of God's chosen. There was nothing to fear. I had had a strange dream. I had walked in my sleep, and I had encountered the animal that had come over on the wrecked vessel. It was a simple story.

Looking up at the abbey wall, I started to rise. I would take one peek inside to see if I could catch a glimpse of the animal. But before I could take a step, a shadow glided across one of the windows—not a dark shadow but something white, something not quite whole—and I dropped back to my knees. As it passed, I heard a whooshing sound, like the winter wind that rushed through Miss Hadley's halls on the coldest evenings. From somewhere within the abbey, the wolf dog howled, sending great spiraling wails into the night. Had the animal also seen the apparition? I could have sworn that it was the outline of a female form, but I credited the old whaler's story of the long-dead abbess with that thought. I hoped that my eyes were playing tricks on me as eyes often do in the dark. The fog and the moonlight and my sleepwalking had conspired to make me see strange things. The animal was merely responding to the sound of the wind. Yet the calm I had felt while with the wolf dog was now gone, and I was aware of every nerve in my body.

The night grew colder and darker as the moonlight dissolved into the fog. I knew I had to make a move, though I also felt safe in my inertia. Finally, it was the dampness of the earth seeping through my clothes that forced me to rise. I turned toward the churchyard but was stopped dead by what I saw before me.

I tried to take a breath, but my lungs failed and my knees grew weak. Was he a man or an apparition? He was not dressed in evening clothes, but it was unmistakably my savior from the riverbank, the man who had somehow made his way into the Gummlers' photograph. How had he found me in the middle of the night on the Yorkshire coast? He looked illuminated, like a figure on stained glass, not by moonlight but by his perfectly ivory skin, which turned the mist surrounding him into a halo. I backed away, stumbling on a rock, but he did not move.

"Whoever you are, please go away," I said. My voice was full of fear, with nothing in it that might inspire him to obey me. He was not transparent but was solidly before me, wearing a long, tailored waistcoat, the kind a gentleman would wear for a country walk.

"Why are you following me?" I asked, my voice trembling.

You know why.

He did not speak, but I heard his voice in my head and recognized it as the voice from my dream. The accent was vague in origins but aristocratic. The words were pronounced with care to each letter and syllable. The tone was deep, almost bottomless, authoritative. I did not know how to respond, or if I should respond. My heart pounded in my chest. As long as I did not move, and he did not move, I would not be harmed—or that was the flawed logic that guided me at that moment. I put my face in my hands to avoid his stare.

"What do you want with me? Why are you doing this to me?"

You know why.

"I don't know why! I don't know anything!" I started sobbing and did not stop until my hands were wet with my own tears. I had no idea how long I stood there crying, but when I looked up, he was not there. I waited, convincing myself that he had been an apparition after all. When I felt safe again, I turned to run away, but he was again in front of me, standing statue still.

"Who are you? What are you?" I screamed the words, angry now that this being was taunting me, following me so that there was no relief and no escape.

Your servant and your master.

"Please leave me alone." The insistent tone disguised the fact that my words were actually prayers meant to play upon his pity. He had saved me once; perhaps he would not harm me if I begged for my life.

The power is yours, Mina. I come to you when you call to me, when I feel your need or desire.

"Quit following me," I said, turning and walking away from him. I hugged myself tightly as I walked toward the cemetery. After a few moments, out of curiosity, I turned around. He was no longer there but had disappeared into the fog, leaving me alone and shivering, my hands still wet with tears.

I did not need my eyes to witness the absence; I felt it in my very being. Disappointment washed over me. Where had he gone? I found myself wanting to find him, to track him down as he was tracking me, and to demand an explanation. I was shocked at my own courage in even thinking this way, but something drove me on. I was sick of the weak person I had been. I wanted to yank her out of my body and stamp on her, making myself strong and brave.

"Come back to me," I demanded, but nothing happened.

My pulse calmed, and I was able to breathe again. The winds seeped through my damp clothes, chilling me clean to the bone. I was so cold and tired that I thought my spine might crack if I did not get to a warm place.

Suddenly something came out of the mist and enveloped me, like the cocoon that had earlier wrapped me and brought me into the night. It was not anything that I could see or feel, but an energy, a vibration, an invisible shell that cosseted me.

You are cold. Come inside.

The only structure I could see was the hollow shell of Whitby Abbey.

Will you come with me?

I did not have to say anything. My body submitted for me. I felt myself moving through space, though I did not know where I was going. Either my eyes were closed or I was in total darkness. I felt like some winged creature soaring over unknown territory, being steered by something outside myself, but knowing that I was not lost. Lights like stars whirled past me from out of the darkness, and when I opened my eyes, I was lying on a bed covered in rich tapestry and piled high with pillows. The room was lit by candles in colossal iron holders that flickered on the walls. A great fire was ablaze in the hearth. I recognized the triptych of slender, arched windows, though I was seeing them for the first time from the inside. No longer empty, they were fitted with glass through which I could make out some of the stars that hovered over Whitby on a clear night.

We were inside the abbey, though apparently outside time. The room was warm and the roof intact, and he was lying beside me.

Every moment that has ever existed in time is still here, Mina—every thought, every memory, and every experience.

Now that I saw him in the candlelight, he was more beautiful than I had imagined. Skin marble white, paler than mine and glowing, and hair like the night sea's glossy waves. His face was long and angular with a strong brow, like the artists' renderings I had of the Arthurian knights. With his midnight blue wolf eyes, he stared at me, taking me in.

"Who are you?" I asked, my voice timid and feeble.

You and I have gone by many names. It does not matter what we call each other. What matters is that you remember. Do you remember, Mina?

His lips did not move, and yet I heard every word that he said. I wanted to ask a thousand questions, but one long and slender finger reached out and touched my lips. Locking eyes with me, he slid my nightdress from my shoulder. Shock waves rippled through my body as his finger followed the curve under my neck, dusting my chin, and slowly sliding to the other ear. Surely just one finger could not create this bedlam inside me.

Ah, so you do remember.

My heart palpitated wildly, but I was not afraid. Something familiar about him prevented me from fearing him, though I had witnessed how dangerous he could be on the banks of the Thames when he had thrashed my attacker.

"Yes, yes, I remember," I said. I would have said anything to keep his hand on me, to wallow in the wild energy he brought to my body, and to stare into the infinite violet blue of his eyes. Though I said nothing else, every nerve in my body begged him to keep touching me.

What is your desire?

I did not have the audacity to say the words aloud, but this being knew me and knew my thoughts. Our eyes were locked, and our minds were linked. I felt connected to him in a way that I had not known with another person. We were not one, but we were in harmony, as if we were both parts of the same symphony. With eerie slowness, his finger moved down my neck to the breastbone and across my chest until it reached my nipple. Then something extraordinary happened. He held it there, barely moving but sending a wild sensation through my breast that resonated in every curve and turn of me. My body was like a musical instrument that only he knew how to play. I tried to breathe while he moved at the same deliberate pace to the other breast, all the while staring into my eyes. I was electrified, fierce currents dancing through my veins. I gasped for breath, which only heightened my arousal. I had no idea how long I lingered in this blissful place. It might have been minutes or hours, but I rode the wave of it, letting it wash me through with excitement.

You are mine again, Mina. I have waited for you and watched over you since you were a little girl. Do you remember those times?

He stopped touching me. He looked into my eyes, waiting for me to answer. But my thoughts took another direction. Here was the phantom that had been luring me out into the night since I was a child. Could it be that he was responsible for my father's disdain and my mother's rejection? Excitement slowly turned to anger. As much as I did not want to leave the blissful place, I could not help myself, and he read my thoughts.

I came to you to help you, Mina. You were in danger. You needed me.

I began shrieking at him. "Yes, I remember everything. I am Mina Murray, whose parents sent her away from home because she was a strange and frightening child. I have made my own way to a good life, a respectable life, and a life over which I have control. I am a teacher at a school for girls, and I am engaged to be married to a man who loves me."

I knew that I was sabotaging my own pleasure and perhaps so much more by rebelling against him and whatever memories he wanted me to have. I knew I was fighting against the very ecstasy he evoked from my body. But just as I could not earlier resist submitting to him, I could not combat the hostility I felt now. He was asking me to remember the very things I had spent my life trying to forget.

Do you want me to go, Mina?

"Yes, go!" I cried aloud. "Leave me in peace before you wreck my life again." I curled up like a fetus and began to cry. Soon, my body was racked with sobs and grief. I cried for a long time, until every tear was wrung from my eyes. Cold began to seep in again through my clothes. I uncurled myself and opened my eyes. My mysterious stranger was gone, and I was lying on the grass inside the stark ruin of the abbey in my nightdress, looking up at the stars.

. . .

I climbed through the empty window of the abbey and walked to the churchyard, where low lamplight flickered on the headstones. A cemetery at night may frighten some, but after my experience this evening, the familiarity of the place comforted me. I paused at the grave of a child, resting my hand on the wing of an angel so that I could wipe off the grit that was irritating the bottoms of my feet, when I saw two figures on the bench where the old whaler and I sat by day looking out over the sea. An unmistakably familiar wavy blond mane cascaded over the back of the bench, while a man's form loomed over her, his face buried in her neck.

I had wandered into this scene involuntarily and should have run away as quickly as possible, but I was riveted by the sight of his mouth consuming her neck, her cheeks, her shoulders, sliding luxuriously back up to her ear and lingering there. He opened her shirt, exposing her bosom, and lifted one breast out of her corset. Then he picked her up and put her on his lap so that she straddled him, and I watched them in profile as he took her breast into his mouth, licking and biting her nipple. I was close enough to see his slick tongue lapping at her, and my own lust, so recently aroused, began to stir. The feeling was so vivid that I could imagine that it was not Lucy on that bench but me, with Morris Quince's well-formed lips on my nipple and his huge powerful hands all over me. I stood still, relishing the feeling, when he looked up and saw me. His shoulders dropped, and he said something to Lucy, whose head jerked around.

"Mina!" Her voice was full of admonition. She jumped off Morris's lap and stood up, taking big strides over to me. Her hands made two fists, which swung back and forth like a toy soldier's. "Why are you following me?"

Her blouse was open, and I stared at the white skin of her breasts, which were still of considerable size considering her weight loss. The bruiselike marks I had seen earlier were more plentiful now and deeper in color.

"I am n-not following you," I stammered. The cold night air, the strange events, and the shock of seeing Lucy, caught up with me. "I—I don't know how I got here. I was walking in my sleep again."

"Mina?" Morris was taking off his linen jacket and putting it over my shoulders. I am sure he was embarrassed to see me in my transparent nightdress. "You are all wet and you have no shoes! We must get you indoors."

Everyone looked at my bare feet, which were stark white. My toes grabbed at the ground as if I were trying to hold myself to the earth.

"I cannot allow a lady to walk barefoot," Morris said, looking around as if a pair of shoes would miraculously pop out from one of the graves. He looked helplessly at Lucy, waiting for her to suggest something. "I will carry her," he said.

Lucy's impatient expression said that she did not sanction the idea. "What would happen if we are seen, with you making such a spectacle?"

"I can walk in bare feet. I have done it many times," I said. I wanted to disappear into the ether just as my phantom had done.

"But you look ill, Miss Mina. Your teeth are chattering. You look as if you've seen a ghost." Morris's eyebrows were squeezed tightly together, forming one long hedge across his strong brow.

"I—I have bad dreams," I said, torn between taking comfort in his concern and Lucy's annoyance at having been interrupted. Morris Quince's kindness felt like a rope thrown to save me from drowning, but Lucy was not allowing me to hold on to it.

"We had better just go," Lucy said. She nodded her head at the jacket around my shoulders. "You can't take that with you."

"But she is half naked and has had a shock."

"My mother will see it," Lucy said with finality, and I took the jacket off and handed it back to Morris. "I'll give her my shawl." She untied the shawl, which she'd looped around her waist, and draped it on my shoulders. "We must part ways here," she said to him, leaving him looking forlorn as he watched us walk away.

Lucy was silent for a while. She put her arm around me and pulled me close to her. "My, you are cold, Mina." I snuggled closer to her, slipping my arm around her. I could feel the top of her hip bone jutting through her skirt. Despite her thinness, her body gave off immense heat.

"You are playing a very dangerous game, Lucy," I said. "Half the town is probably still awake, what with the shipwreck."

"He was walking me home when we decided to go to the churchyard to look out over the view. We had no intention of carrying on like that out in the open, Mina, but we are so much in love."

The sky was mottled with shifting gray clouds that parted, revealing one bright, shining star. We walked for a few blocks, and when we turned the corner, Lucy stopped dead, her hand tightening around my shoulder, holding me back.

"I'm freezing—" I said, but Lucy interrupted me, pointing up the hill to the rooms. Fiery yellow light blazed in the bank of windows lining the two parlors, as if Mrs. Westenra was hosting a party in the middle of the night.

"She's found me out!" Lucy wrapped her arms around her stomach as if her entrails were about to fall out. She bent over, gasping for air. I thought she might vomit on the pavement. "I cannot go in there," she said.

"The lights may be on because your mother took ill," I offered. That was the first thought that came to my mind. "Someone may have called for a doctor. Hilda, or a neighbor."

"Yes. That is undoubtedly what has happened," Lucy said, running her fingers through her snarly hair. "Oh dear, poor mother!"

Then her face took on the wild-eyed look that had become familiar to me. She took my hands in hers. "Oh, I am a terrible person. I am more worried that my affair has been found out than I am about my mother's health; more concerned with it than with my poor friend, awakening alone in a strange place!"

Lucy's eyes were wide and glassy, floating in the sockets above her gaunt cheeks. I was very cold and I knew by the burning lights above that the evening's drama was not over. "We had better see what the trouble is inside."

Lucy smoothed her clothes and checked her buttons. She brushed her skirt with quick little gestures, her hands like feathers. "Do I look composed?"

"More than I," I said. "At least you are clothed. But you had better hide those marks on your neck and chest. I am assuming that Mr. Quince put them there?"

Lucy took the shawl from me and wrapped it around herself. "No matter what is said, or what questions are asked, leave the talking to me," she said in a tone that was a far cry from the impassioned love victim of moments ago.

I had no choice but to believe in her. At school, while Kate liked to think of herself as the rebel, Lucy was the one whose quick tongue and blithe way of doing whatever she wanted put her above the rules. Kate was defiant, always making a spectacle of her disobedience, whereas Lucy felt entitled to do as she pleased and never expected anyone to stop her. I hoped she was still the girl who could get away with collecting money for candy and saying it was for the blind.

We walked up the stairs to the rooms and opened the door. The parlor was lit for company. A tea service sat on a pedestal table but the chairs flanking it were empty, as were the two divans that faced each other over a small, low table. The room looked like a theatrical set before the actors had arrived to begin the play. We ventured deeper into the parlor, where we heard voices from the hall. Mrs. Westenra appeared, a pink-and-white striped nightcap framing her face. She was followed by a night watchman in uniform.

"Merciful heavens," she cried. "They are safe!"

"As I assured you, madam," the policeman said. "During the summer months, young ladies like to stroll at night. No harm done, eh?"

"No harm? I nearly died from fright! What can you girls have meant by disappearing in the middle of the night? Lucy, are you trying to murder your poor mother? And Mina?"

The policeman stood behind the lady, his eyes averted. I suppose he was trying not to look at me in my nightdress.

Mrs. Westenra took a lap robe from the back of a chair and put it around me. "What is the meaning of wandering about in this unseemly condition?"

Lucy did not wait for me to answer but struck out on a defensive attack. "Mother, please calm yourself. Mina and I have been through our own nightmares this evening. Why is there a police officer here?"

"Why?" The lady looked in disbelief at the officer. Upon closer inspection, I saw that he was very young. His swallow-tailed coat with gleaming silver buttons, wide leather belt, and polished boots endowed him with authority that he did not yet own. I felt sorry for him having to deal with a distraught middle-aged woman prone to histrionics.

"Why?" Mrs. Westenra continued. "Because I woke in the middle of the night feeling poorly. I went into the bedroom to ask you to attend to me, Lucy, and I discovered an empty bed. At two o'clock in the morning! I did not know what to do. Hilda is spending the night at home, I was alone, and my heart—well, my poor heart. I thought I would die, it was pounding so loudly in my chest. I went to the window and screamed for help. I was shrieking like a madwoman. A kind gentleman sent word to the chief constable, who sent out a watchman—this delightful young man here—who has comforted a frightened woman. I might have succumbed to a full attack of angina had it not been for him. Why, he even mixed my medication for me. And perfectly so, I might add." She smiled at him.

"You have been very brave, madam," he said, adjusting the chin strap of his police helmet under his strong, square jaw.

Lucy stood tall, taking over the situation. "I cannot thank you enough, sir, for attending to my mother. Her condition causes her to become overemotional."

Mrs. Westenra started to protest, but Lucy interrupted her. "It is all very simply explained. Mina suffers from the same sleepwalking malady as Father did. She has had some dreadful incidents recently in London, which she told me about the evening she arrived here. Isn't that right, Mina?"

True to my promise, I nodded but kept silent, letting Lucy tell her story.

"I woke up and saw that she was not in the bed. From what she told me of her previous episodes, I knew that she could venture quite far, so I rushed outside. I should have left a note for you, Mother. I am very sorry, indeed. But I was desperate to find Mina before she came to any harm."

"And are you quite all right now, miss?" the officer asked me. "Had you wandered very far?"

"Yes, to the churchyard," I answered. "I go there every day because the view is so lovely. I suppose that my body simply led me there out of habit."

"All the while in your sleep?" He looked suspicious now.

"Oh yes," Mrs. Westenra said. "My late husband suffered the same illness. We used to discover him in the most unusual places. Sometimes he did not return at all but was found wandering the heath near our home in London."

"Strange, indeed, madam. But I have heard of such things. My gran says that the spirits like to call out to us when we are asleep." He smiled weakly, as if he did not know whether to believe his grandmother's superstitions or not.

"Your gran must come for tea sometime when our friend Dr. Seward is here. He will set her straight on these matters," said Mrs. Westenra, assuming the learned air I'd seen before when she had mentioned her discussions of medical affairs with John Seward. "It is the mind that imagines such things, the unconscious mind, which is a very different organ from the conscious mind. If you read up on the latest findings of medical doctors, you will see that I am correct."

"I shall do that, madam," he said politely, but smiling at Lucy. Because of his young age, I suspected that he wanted to win her good opinion, not her mother's.

"Might we let this good man leave now so that we all can get some sleep?" Lucy's technique for getting herself out of trouble had not diminished. She had lied to her mother and to the night watchman and was getting away with it. The officer was already taking steps toward the door.

"Lucy, dear, take the lamp to the top of the stairs so that our guest will have some light," said the mother.

"Not necessary," said the officer. But Lucy already had the lamp in her hand. When she turned around, her shawl fell from her shoulders, and the light illuminated the pattern of purple bruises and wound marks stippled against the cream white of her neck and chest. Against the bright lamplight, they were like roses flowering in the sun. Rings of tooth marks sat at the base of her neck, like red-rimmed eyes staring out at the world.

The officer squinted his eyes at Lucy's neck. "Miss, were you attacked by someone?"

Lucy put the lamp down, but her mother picked it up, holding it up to her daughter's face. The marks were even more awful in the brighter light offered by the proximity of the lamp.

Lucy put her hand to her throat. "What? No, of course not."

Mrs. Westenra said nothing, but stared at her daughter's neck. Rather roughly, she took Lucy to the mirror on the wall and turned her toward it, holding the lamp so close to Lucy's neck that she jerked her face aside to avoid the heat of it. Lucy looked at her own reflection, and then shied away from it.

"You certainly look as if you have been attacked," Mrs. Westenra said.

"Miss, if someone has hurt you, it will do you no good to protect him." The officer now assumed the authority he had earlier lacked. "This is a peaceful place, and we do not take kindly to the sort of violence committed in London. If a lady is harmed in these parts, we find the culprit right away. We do not let him haunt our streets to commit more mayhem. You can be sure of that."

"Lucy?" Mrs. Westenra seemed to be challenging her daughter. I was grateful that Lucy had made me promise to keep quiet. I was fearful for her, but at the same time I was curious to see how she would get out of this predicament.

She did not disappoint. Rather than turn red with shame, as she should have done, Lucy stood as defiant as a war goddess, her bruised neck held high. She asked her mother to sit down. "I wanted to spare you the details of the horror that befell me," she said, putting a hand on her mother's shoulder. "I was afraid that the shock would bring on an attack, and then, what would I do? I did not want to be responsible for causing that, Mother."

I stepped into the shadows to hide my astonished face as Lucy unfurled an amazing story. I soon realized that she was purloining my own experience on the banks of the Thames and placing herself in the roll of victim. She illustrated in detail the madman I had described, using my own words and images. "Red eyes like a monster!" she said, explaining how she had been in the churchyard looking for me when a man jumped out of nowhere—"was he man or fiend?"—and fell upon her, biting her and sucking at her neck and throat and bosom while he held her hands and legs down with his limbs.

The watchman took a small pad from his pocket and began to scribble furiously as Lucy spoke, occasionally stopping her to clarify a detail. "And you say he smelled of drink?"

"I suppose so. Though it was so acrid and horrible that I wondered if he was a corpse escaped from the grave!" Her eyes were huge now and gleaming in the lamplight. The watchman sat on the divan next to Mrs. Westenra so that he could put his pad on the little table and write faster. I could see little prickly light-colored hairs sprouting above his pouty crimson lips, not thick enough to grow a proper mustache. His acorn-brown eyes were fixed alternately upon Lucy and his notes, his head bobbing up and down trying to keep up with her words. The deeper Lucy got into her story, the more convincing she sounded, her confidence and dramatic inflection rising parallel to the interest of the watchman.

Mrs. Westenra sat terribly calm through all this. I would have thought that any mother, let alone one with a nervous condition, would have shown more emotion listening to the details of an attack on her daughter, but Mrs. Westenra took in the story with uncharacteristic serenity. "However did you evade this monster, Lucy?" she asked.

"It was Mina who saved me," Lucy said, gesturing to me with her arm as if I were being presented onstage like a performer.

All eyes turned upon me, leaning against the fireplace mantel, hugging the lap robe tight around my shoulders, thankful to have been forgotten until this moment. I knew that Lucy wanted me to play a part, but I was frozen.

Lucy rescued me from responding. "Before the madman could do any, well, any irrevocable harm, Mina wandered into the cemetery and saw us. Her screams frightened him, and he ran away like a coward!"

The night watchman pressed Lucy for more details, but she claimed that shock prevented her from getting a good look at the attacker. He explained that he might have to return with further questions if the chief constable was not satisfied with his report. "We will do everything possible to find this vermin and bring him to justice," he assured us.

When he left, Mrs. Westenra ordered me to wash my face and my feet and go to bed. I was surprised at the commanding tone in her voice. "Lucy will be along shortly, Mina."

I did as she said, pulling the curtains tight against the breaking dawn, and climbed into the bed, stretching out on the cool linens, eager for sleep, but I heard Lucy and her mother arguing.

"I have told the truth," Lucy said, to which I heard Mrs. Westenra groan.

"I was a married woman!" she said. "Why does every generation believe it is the discoverer of pleasure? Your father was a spectacular lover." Even through the wall, I could hear the triumph in her voice.

From Lucy's mouth came a groan that matched her mother's. "I am going to bed," she said as if it were a proclamation. When I heard her footsteps approach, I turned my back toward the door so that when she entered the room, she would think I was already asleep.

Chapter Six

onster, Murderer, or Madman in Whitby?'"

Lucy flashed the *Whitby Gazette* at me and then continued to read from it. "'Miss Lucy Westenra of London was the victim of a mysterious attacker so horrible in appearance and odor that the terrified young lady mistook him for a corpse risen from his grave in St. Mary's Church cemetery, a popular setting of many of Whitby's infamous ghost stories. The monster left the young lady bruised about the neck and shoulders. Fortunately, the brutal attack was interrupted when Miss Mina Murray, a schoolteacher, also of London, wandered into St. Mary's churchyard.'"

The article went on to caution ladies to refrain from venturing out of doors unescorted. "'We who wish for the continuation of the peaceful and secure atmosphere of our idyllic seaside community must remind our readers that the Whitechapel butcher who so terrified the capital city was never apprehended. If he has come to our locale, he will have found the sort of female of ill repute upon whom he preys in short supply in Whitby, and may be casting his evil intent toward genteel ladies such as Miss Westenra. We urge an attitude of vigilance and prudence from residents and visitors.'"

"Who reported this to the papers?" Lucy asked, looking at me as if I had committed the deed.

"Kate says that reporters get most of their leads from the police," I said.

"This is sure to bring Arthur Holmwood here! I don't want to see him!" Lucy said when her mother was out of earshot.

We passed the rest of Monday without incident, but on Tuesday morning, we heard a rap at the door. Lucy jumped out of her seat.

Hilda answered the door, and Dr. John Seward walked in with his medical bag. He tipped his hat to both of us before removing it. Mrs. Westenra rushed into the parlor.

"I came as quickly as I could," he said to Mrs. Westenra, who greeted him extravagantly. She was not surprised to see him.

"Look at our girl, Dr. Seward," she said to him, taking Lucy by the arm and presenting her. "Pallid and thinner than ever before! And look at these bruises. I daresay they have faded since the attack, but they are ugly reminders of her ordeal."

Seward lifted Lucy's chin so that he could examine her neck. "I imagine that her psyche is more bruised than her body. That is what happens in cases of violation."

"I was not violated!" Lucy protested.

"When a lady is physically accosted, she feels mentally violated. Your sense of safety has been shattered. But do not worry; I am here to treat you. Your good mother sent a telegram to Arthur in Scarborough, and he insisted we come immediately. He is finding us rooms and will be arriving soon." He gave her a broad smile. "See there? All shall be well. Now, if you don't mind, would you please lie down, either on the divan or on a bed, so that I can examine you?"

Lucy looked irritated. "I am not ill. I am as well as I have ever been. John Seward, you are wasting your time. Surely there are lunatics in London who need you."

"Lucy! The doctor has inconvenienced himself for your sake!" Mrs. Westenra was outraged. "You are insulting not only Dr. Seward but Arthur as well!"

Dr. Seward put a hand up to Mrs. Westenra, politely silencing her. He spoke patiently to Lucy. "Dear Miss Lucy, this sort of hysteria is a common response to what you have endured. The first thing we must do is to settle those nerves."

He opened his satchel, releasing a whiff of something bitter, some chemical odor that I had to turn away from, as he sorted through bottles of medication.

"My nerves are settled!" Lucy said in a shrill voice that contradicted her words. Seward ignored her and asked Hilda to bring him a spoon and glass.

He poured two spoonfuls of liquid from a bottle into the glass and filled it with water from a pitcher, making a cloudy potion. He handed it to Lucy. "Now be a good girl and take your medicine. Then I will examine you so that I might fully assess the state of your health."

Lucy looked exasperated. "But I am not nervous. I do not have a condition! I merely wish to be left alone. Tell them that I am well, Mina!"

I remembered what Mrs. Westenra had said about Seward's infatuation with Lucy. It did not seem appropriate to have such a man as one's doctor. "I think Lucy is mending," I said. "She was very calm yesterday and she slept well last night."

"Mina, are you trained in the medical arts?" Mrs. Westenra asked, barking her words at me. She looked quite hostile. "If you are not a doctor, then you must leave the medical decisions to Dr. Seward." She turned to Seward. "Perhaps you should have a look at Mina as well, John. These incidents of noctambulism can be very dangerous. One such incident was the death of my dear late husband."

My body went cold thinking of submitting to an examination by

John Seward. But seeing how Lucy's defiance was not helping her situation, I remained calm.

"I appreciate your concern, Mrs. Westenra, but I have had only two episodes. When I return to London, I will see Dr. Farmer, Miss Hadley's physician, who has cared for me since I was a child." I was not sure that Dr. Farmer was still alive, but hoped that the mention of another physician would divert the attention from me.

"Both you and Miss Lucy have the constitution of a lady, Miss Mina, and therefore are more susceptible to nervous conditions," Dr. Seward said. "A strapping girl from the working classes may survive the sort of attack made on Miss Lucy, or may wander about in the night air half asleep and remain unscathed. But ladies like the two of you with refined sensibilities must but be looked after carefully," he said.

"Lucinda, I am your mother and guardian, and I am morally and legally responsible for you. If you are as well as you claim to be, I suggest you do what the doctor says and allow him to confirm it," said Mrs. Westenra.

"You must do it for your mother, Miss Lucy," Seward said. "You don't want her worries over you to provoke another attack of angina."

"Well, then, I will cooperate, if only so that you may discover for all your troubles that I am in perfect health!" Lucy said. She picked up the glass containing the concoction Seward had mixed and swallowed it down theatrically, arching her back and raising the glass high into the air so that her neck was long and her curls dipped down the length of her backbone. She reminded me of a poster I had once seen of an actress playing Lady Macbeth. Then she turned to me and spoke in a perfectly controlled voice. "Mina, will you help me undress and get into a dressing gown?"

I followed her into the bedroom, whereupon she closed the door and sprang on the bed like a panther. "You must go to Morris and tell him what is happening," she said, hushed and hissing. "Tell him that I will meet him at some arranged place tonight, and we will go off together where no one will find us."

"Lucy, be rational." I sat with her on the bed and stroked her arm. "Do you really want to give Morris Quince control over your life? You will be at the mercy of his feelings, and men's feelings are not to be trusted."

"This is no time to remind me of your old-fashioned doctrine of love, Mina."

Before I could put reply, we heard men's voices outside. Lucy jumped up and looked out the window, and I followed, looking over her shoulder. Standing on the pavement below, Seward was conversing with the red-haired man, whom we had seen on the night of the shipwreck. He was holding a copy of the *Whitby Gazette* and demanding an audience with Lucy.

"It's that theater manager from London," I said.

"Why does he want to see me?" Lucy asked.

I put my finger up to silence her so that we could hear their conversation.

"No, you may not see her. I am a doctor, she is my patient, and she has suffered a trauma. She is in no condition to answer your questions." Seward spoke not harshly but in no uncertain terms.

From our vantage point above, the man's hair was like a thicket of ginger-colored hen's feathers. He spoke softly, and his back was to us so that we could not hear what he was saying. But we could hear Seward's reply. "Yes, I am familiar with the good reputation of your theater, but that does not alter my patient's condition. She is sedated, and I will not allow her to receive company."

"How dare John Seward decide who I can and cannot speak with!" Lucy was indignant. "I shall give him a piece of my mind," she said, turning toward the door. But I grabbed her arm.

"Do you really want to tell your tale to a stranger, Lucy? The man is a writer looking for ghoulish stories to put on the stage. He might make any use of whatever you tell him."

The red-haired man spoke again, but his words were carried away from us on the wind, whereas Seward's rose into the window.

"The lady is in a state of hysteria, sir. Do you actually believe that a corpse broke through its coffin and attacked her? I might add that there is no reason to believe that her attacker should be identified with Jack the Ripper. That is a newspaper's way of selling copies. I am sure you are aware of their tactics."

The red-haired man shrugged his broad shoulders and said something else, and Dr. Seward took a card from his pocket. "I would be delighted to help you in your research," he said, extending his hand to the other fellow, who shook it firmly. "Send me a note with an appointed time, and I will see you at the asylum in Purfleet."

Distraught, Lucy turned away from the window. "That man outside—I do not trust him. What if he is a reporter? What if he starts investigating and finds out that I am a liar?"

Lucy leaned against the bedpost, taking little bird breaths through her mouth. It seemed that the medication was taking effect.

"I know someone who is acquainted with him. I will get more information about him to put your mind at ease. Now you must rest, Lucy. Let me help you out of your clothes. After John Seward takes a look at you, you can go to sleep."

"Please, Mina, go to Morris. Tell him that we must leave tonight. Tell him what they are saying about me. I am not hysterical! I am a woman in love, and I cannot have my love, and that is what makes me act this way."

I helped Lucy into a satin gown the color of pink champagne, with a wide collar of white lace and tiny pearl buttons. She had worn it a year ago when I visited her, and I remembered how the pink blush reflected the color of her cheeks and made her skin, already radiant, rich with rosy hues. Now it had the opposite effect and seemed to drain what vestige of color was left in her pallor and highlighted the marks on her neck. Her eyes were heavy with the medication. She placed one hand upon her chest as if she wanted evidence of her continuing heartbeat. I did not want to leave her looking so helpless, but she would be under the care of her mother and a doctor. Who was I to interfere with their authority?

"Rest well, my darling Lucy. Things will look better when you wake up."

. . .

He lived in precisely the sort of dwelling one would have expected, a weatherworn stone cottage by the sea built for a fisherman and repaired haphazardly by his own hand through the many decades of his occupancy. It was protected from the inhospitable rock-strewn beach by a roughly built low wall that looked as if the stones had leapt from the shore and tossed themselves one atop the other. I rapped on the door and, receiving no response, knocked on a window, noticing the few flecks of paint that remained on the otherwise worm-eaten wood of the windowsill.

An old woman came to the door. More stooped than her father, her spine bent sharply like the tip of a crochet hook. She stuck her head out and up like a tortoise stretching from its shell. I told her that I was an acquaintance of her father's and that I had missed him today at the churchyard.

"Oh, he is there," she said. I saw by the little random pickets that stuck out of her mouth that she had retained the same amount of teeth in the same pattern of loss as her father. "He won't be leaving the churchyard again. There is no stone up as yet, but we put him in the ground yesterday."

"I am so sorry," I said while she looked me up and down "How did he die?"

"Don't be joking with me, young lady. How did he die? He was a few years shy of the century mark. The good Lord got tired of turning him away. He left us on the night of the shipwreck, as was fitting, him being an old man of the sea."

She beckoned me inside, and it took a while for my eyes to adjust to the dark room from the stark light of the afternoon. She bade me sit on a rickety chair pulled up to a solid pine table.

"That was his chair," she said. She poured me a cup of lukewarm tea and gave me a piece of cold toast slathered with honey. "He would be pleased to see you sitting in it. He talked of you, miss, of your green eyes and hair like jet. He said that had you known him as a young man you would have fancied him."

I smiled at the thought.

"Though seeing you now, I don't agree. You are a fine lady from the city, and, even in his youth, he carried the stench of the fishing boats." She did not sit but leaned on the other chair while she talked.

I saw his pipe resting on the mantel and my eyes started to well up, knowing that I would not see him again. "I hope he did not suffer," I said.

"That day, he took to his bed after his breakfast and would not get out of it, even to sup, but once the storm started, I heard him go outside. I found him facing the sea, screaming into the waves. I tried to coax him back into the house, but he said that his friends who had died at sea had come for him. They were standing on the shore talking to him, and he was calling them by name."

"Yes, he told me that he imagined that sort of thing," I said.

"Imagined? There is no imagining, miss, when voices call to you from the sea. If you heard them just one time, you know that they are as real as this table." She thumped her fist on it to make her point, rattling my teacup in its saucer. "Did I imagine it when, as a little girl, Pap and me walked to the abbey at night, much against the wishes of my mother— God rest her soul—and we listened to the cries of Constance."

"Constance? He only told me of St. Hild." I remembered that sunny day when I was too hot to let him finish his tale.

The whaler's daughter sat down on the chair opposite me, wrapping her teacup in her bony hands. She had short fingers with prominent joints that reminded me of the talons of birds of prey. "Constance of Beverley was a wicked nun who forsook her vows to take up with a lover, a French knight with a bad reputation. As penance, she was buried alive in the walls of the convent. Some nights, you can still hear her scream for release. But St. Hild keeps her there as a warning to women who might succumb to temptation."

I shuddered, remembering my own experience at Whitby Abbey.

"You weren't the only fancy Londoner who enjoyed my father's tales," the old lady offered with considerable pride.

"Is that so?" Kate always said that if you allowed someone to talk enough, they would tell you everything you needed to know.

"Another fellow, a very important personage of the theater, sat here in this very room listening to old Father's stories."

Pleased that I did not have to find a way to bring up the subject of the red-haired man, I tried to sound as if my interest in him was casual. "Oh, yes, he pointed that fellow out to me once. Do you know his name?"

"I knew it, but, as old Pap used to say, I forgot it as soon as I remembered it." She laughed at her own construct of words. "But he could not get enough of the old man's tales. You see, miss, he is a writer come to Whitby for inspiration. For we have here a most interesting population of spirits, ready to show themselves to whoever is looking in their direction. This fellow said that all London was still living under the terrible threat of the Ripper and that he wanted to make up a similar sort of character, but have him be even more atrocious, something more terrifying than a man, something akin to Mr. Spring-Heeled Jack. For, as he said, who is to prove that those Whitechapel women were not murdered by something more monster than human?"

A few times I had caught some of my students reading the outlandish tales of Spring-Heeled Jack, the monster who wore gentleman's clothes, but had great batlike wings, pointy ears, red eyes, and the ability to leap great lengths. Inevitably, there was one girl in each class who had inherited a copy from an older brother and used it to frighten the smaller girls.

"And such a monster may indeed have come here to plague us, as if we need more unnatural creatures on this shore!" She picked up a copy of the *Whitby Gazette* and waved it at me. "You have seen this?"

"Yes, I have," I said, standing up. "You are quite certain that the man with the red hair is an artistic sort of person and not a newspaperman?"

"The fellow said he was here to collect stories to put in books and on the stage. He already wrote two books that no one paid much attention to, poor fellow, but he believed that after all the murders committed by the butcher of London, the town was ripe for the appearance of a fresh monster, and that Whitby was just the place to find such a creature in our store of goblins and ghosts."

I said good-bye to the whaler's daughter and left the cottage with mixed emotions. While I realized that Lucy's future was not mine to decide, I did not want to be the one to deliver her into the hands of Morris Quincel.

I located the building that housed his painting studio and rang the bell. An older woman with gray curls escaping her white house cap opened the door.

"I am looking for Mr. Morris Quince, the American painter?" I said politely. She looked at me with suspicious eyes. Of course, she had seen Lucy at the apartments and must have thought that I was just another of Morris's conquests.

"Well, you're too late," she said with a look of mean satisfaction.

"How is that, madam?" I asked politely.

"He left yesterday. Packed up his things and went back to America. Now I have a vacancy during the high season, and it's too late to advertise."

I supposed that the shock registered on my face.

"So, he surprised you too, did he? Well, you are not the only young lady to come round. But you are the prettiest, if that gives you any consolation. The last one was as brittle as a bird and a bit too eager."

I gathered that she meant Lucy. "Did he leave a forwarding address or a message of any sort for a Miss Westenra?"

"He left nothing behind but soiled sheets, the dirt from his boots, and a couple of empty canvasses," she said bitterly, closing the door in my face.

A light sprinkle began to fall on me, but I was in no hurry to deliver the grim news to Lucy, who was probably still sleeping off her sedative. The sky was darkening ever quicker as the end of summer approached. The sun had gone into hiding behind an ominous steel-gray cloud that hung above like a big flatiron. The air felt decidedly different from yesterday—cooler, sharper. Autumn was on its way.

With a heavy heart, I walked up the steps to the churchyard. I raised the hood of my cape and opened my umbrella. Headmistress had given it to me for my twenty-first birthday, knowing how fond I was of the purple foxglove that bloomed in the park. When open, the underside revealed in each of the panels a spray of painted stems, lush with lavender bells. "No matter how bad the weather, you will always be able to look up and see something that will cheer you," she had said, knowing that my quiet moods often concealed an orphan's melancholy.

Sheltered, I walked the cemetery to look for the old whaler's grave, but gave up what with the rain pouring down around me. Hot tears began to roll down my cheeks. All good things ended. Lucy had been ecstatic when she was with her lover. She had been so certain of his love, as certain as I had been of Jonathan's feelings for me and of his intention to marry me. I walked to the bench where the old whaler had told me his stories, trying not to let the actions of Morris Quince bring up my fear that Jonathan had deserted me; tried to push out of my mind the vision of returning to my room at the school and seeing my mail basket empty.

The rain beat down in staccato on my umbrella. I tilted it back to see a large black vulture flying overhead in defiance of the weather. The creature had an immense wingspan, circling and soaring above me. I watched his performance, wondering if he was stalking a small animal in the vicinity—dead or living—upon which he would prey. Finally he flew away, disappearing into the clouds.

I looked out to sea where the ruined vessel, the *Valkyrie*, its cargo hold emptied and its shredded sails down, sat heavily in the sand. The newspaper reported that the mystery of the captain's condition had remained unsolved. The members of the coast guard, who disentangled the body, declared that someone had tied the captain to the helm, negating the assumption that he had bound himself to the wheel to prevent storm winds and waves from carrying him into the sea. The seamen stated that it was impossible for a man to have tied such elaborate, expert knots on himself. The county coroner declared that the gash in his throat was a new wound, leading to the logical but implausible theory that someone had tied the captain to the helm, slit his throat, and jumped overboard in the midst of a brutal storm. The locals—and I am sure that the old whaler would have led this chorus—asserted that the deed had been carried out by the sailors who had drowned in the angry waters off Whitby's shore.

A controversy had arisen over whether to repair the ship or to destroy it. According to the newspapers, an anonymous individual had chartered the boat in Rotterdam. This person was supposed to have been a passenger on the vessel, but neither he nor his body had been found. The entire cargo of fifty large crates was his property and would be shipped to the location determined before the storm. The escaped dog was being sought by members of the Royal Society for the Prevention of Cruelty to Animals.

The abandoned boat slumped against the shoreline like some lone convict awaiting sentencing. *Abandoned, abandoned.* I could not get the word out of my head. I turned to walk back toward the steps that would take me into town and toward my unhappy task of informing Lucy of the betrayal when I stumbled on a rock, losing my balance. I leaned down to see what it was that had caused this mishap and picked up a stone. The markings on it looked like a little girl's plait wrapped tightly into a bun, or the curled tail of a seahorse. I turned it over, exposing the face of a serpent with an open mouth revealing two tiny fangs and a long flat tongue. The stone fit neatly into the palm of my gloved hand. It was beyond a doubt the coiled body of a snake, or, at the very least, it had once been one.

Chapter Seven

 returned to a quiet house. Lucy was still sleeping in her bed, her blond hair splayed across the pillow. Her mouth was open, and a tiny stream of saliva had dried up into little white flakes in its corner. I was trying to close the bedroom door as quietly as possible when she began to stir. Her eyelids fluttered a few times as she whispered my name.

The room was growing dark so I struck a match and lit a bedside lamp. Lucy squinted against the light, shading her eyes with her hand. I sat on the bed next to her, blocking the light for her while her eyes adjusted.

"Oh, I cannot move," she said, closing her eyes again. I thought for a moment that she would fall back asleep and that I would have a reprieve. But she opened her eyes again, and this time, with an anxious look.

"Well? Did you speak with him?" Despite the lethargy in her body, her eyes peered at me as if she were the predator and I the prey.

"Lucy, my darling, there is no gentle or nice way to say what I must say." I put my hand over hers, but she drew it away.

I told her the truth: I had gone to speak with Morris Quince, but he had left to go back to America. She did not react as I anticipated, with tears or self-recrimination. She leapt from the bed and tore off her night-dress. She pulled the dress I had laid on the back of a chair over her head. "I don't believe you," she said when her head popped out of the top.

"What are you doing?" I asked. "You are making too much noise. Your mother is asleep. You'll wake her."

"I am going to see for myself. Mina, you have been in league with my mother since you have been here in Whitby. I should never have trusted you."

She slipped her shoes on but did not bother to lace them and raced to the front door, where she was met with a shock. John Seward and Arthur Holmwood were standing there, Holmwood's hand raised as if to knock.

"There she is," Arthur said, kissing Lucy's forehead. The men entered the room, and Seward put down his black bag. "Miss Lucy, you really should not be out of bed, what with all you have been through."

Hearing the men's voices, Mrs. Westenra came rushing in. "Ah, our knights have arrived!"

The men came deeper into the parlor, removing their hats. Everyone stood awkwardly until Mrs. Westenra called for Hilda to make tea.

I will never forget the way that Lucy composed herself at that moment to get the information she so desperately sought. She took a breath and broke into a smile. I knew the smile was utterly false, but I think that the men did not see it. She graciously invited them to sit down. "Mr. Holmwood, I hope you did not upset your holiday in Scarborough for my sake, for as you can see, I am very well."

"You look as lovely as ever, Miss Lucy," he said formally. "But I think we should let the good doctor here be the judge of your health."

"Of course," Lucy said, looking around the room as if something were missing. "But where there are two, there are usually three. Where is Mr. Quince?"

She astonished me with her innocent tone. Her mother stiffened.

"Why, I have no idea," Holmwood replied. "He was to travel by land and meet me in Scarborough, but the wretch did not. His voice was inflected with the sort of affection men reserve for their irascible friends. He turned to Seward. "John, have you heard from Quince?"

Seward scrunched his shoulders in a shrug. "He is our friend, but we allow him to be socially unreliable, as Americans tend to be."

Holmwood spoke slowly, considering his words. "An interesting breed, but they do not have an English gentleman's sense of honor, or of the sanctity of his word. He is probably off on an adventure, as per usual. Probably involving one young lady or another." Holmwood winked at Seward.

"Miss Lucy, you look a little peaked. I would like to check your vital signs," Dr. Seward said.

But Lucy had reached the limit of her acting skills. "I am not ill. I am well!" Lucy stood, raising her hands into the air like a dancer and then letting her fingers glide down the length of her body as if to emphasize its state of well-being. "I am all *too* well! Now please excuse me." She threw her head back and walked into her bedroom.

"I apologize on my daughter's behalf," Mrs. Westenra said. "She is not herself since the incident."

"It's a typical response from a female who has been attacked, Arthur," Dr. Seward said. "One must not blame the patient."

Both Seward and Mrs. Westenra searched Holmwood's face, looking for signals of his mood.

"Why don't I go check on Lucy?" I said. I started to make my way to Lucy's room when Holmwood stopped me. He had yet to comment on Lucy's outburst, but his face was wrenched into an uneasy frown. "Miss Mina, would you please take a message to Miss Lucy?"

Mrs. Westenra put her hand on Holmwood's sleeve. "Now, Arthur, please do not take any drastic measures. Lucy has had an upset, but she will recover and she will again be the Lucy you proposed to."

Holmwood look appalled at the lady's little speech. "Madam, you misinterpret. I would never abandon Lucy in her hour of need." He looked truly insulted. "Please tell Miss Lucy that whatever unfortunate

thing has happened, it will not cause me to love her less. In fact, I—I—"
he stammered, looking to Seward as if for inspiration or permission, "In
fact, tell her that I wish to expedite the day of our marriage. Tell her that
I desire nothing more than to care for her as a husband must care for his
wife, and that I shall set an immediate date for our wedding."

"Mr. Holmwood, I am overwhelmed!" exclaimed Mrs. Westenra, as
if it were she who would marry him the sooner.

"That should go a long way to speeding up Lucy's recovery," I said
politely, though I knew the opposite to be true. I excused myself, with
the three of them watching me as I walked away. I found Lucy in the
bedroom sitting at the vanity brushing her hair and examining her face
in the mirror.

"Mina, I know you think me a fool, but my heart beats with the certainty that Morris would not have abandoned me to Arthur of his own
volition."

"Let us put aside Morris Quince for a moment Lucy—"

She stopped me, holding the hairbrush in front of her like a shield
against my words. "I will never put Morris Quince aside. If you knew
anything about love, you would not advise me to do so," Lucy said.

I intended to give an impassioned speech about the wisdom of marrying Arthur Holmwood and becoming mistress of Waverley Manor,
when we heard the light rap of Hilda's knuckles at the door.

"Miss Murray?"

I opened the door, and Hilda handed me a letter. "This just came
for you by messenger."

"Thank you, Hilda," I said. The envelope of high-quality laid paper
with a teardrop flap and a dragon seal was addressed to Miss Mina
Murray. The script was extravagant, with large letters finely formed. I tore
open the envelope and read the note given in the same penmanship:

*You will find Mr. Jonathan Harker in a hospital operated by the Daughters of
Charity of St. Vincent de Paul in the city of Graz. You may trust that this*

information is true and is brought to you by one who cares only for you. You will be protected on your voyage, should you choose to go to him. I remain—

Your servant and your master

I tucked the note into my pocket and tried to regain my composure. Even in her mad state, Lucy could see that I was in shock. "What's the matter?"

"Jonathan's been found," I said. I could not disclose how I had received the information, and indeed, I did not know how this all-knowing, ubiquitous creature who called himself my servant and my master had found me in Whitby or how he knew Jonathan's location.

. . .

Two days later, in answer to a telegram that John Seward suggested I send to the hospital, a letter came back that Jonathan was indeed on the list of patients. He was recovering from a case of brain fever, and it was advisable for a relation to come to his aid. Seward translated the letter and assured me that Graz was renowned for its hospitals, owing to the excellent medical school in the city.

"My, but it is useful to have one friend from university who did not waste his tenure at drinking and sport," said Arthur Holmwood. The two men were holding vigil every day at Henrietta Street, pestering Lucy over her condition. She spent most of her time in bed, feigning headaches just to avoid them, all the while certain that word from Morris would arrive at any moment.

Seward smiled at the compliment, but a worried look came over his face. "Brain fever is a blanket diagnosis for a variety of illnesses, Miss Mina," he said. "When you return to England, if you do not find him fully recovered, I will have Dr. Von Helsinger examine him. He was my mentor in Germany at medical school and, I am happy to say, now my colleague at the asylum. His theories on the interaction of blood, brain, body, and spirit are considered radical, and yet I believe him to be a man decades ahead of his time."

"Then I am certain that Mr. Harker would like to meet him, for he too is a very modern thinker," I replied. I wanted to emphasize to Seward that I was engaged to a man of substance.

I sent a telegram to Mr. Hawkins, Jonathan's uncle, that he was in Graz and that I would go to him immediately. He replied with apologies for the illness that prevented him from taking the trip in my stead but wired ample funds to a bank in Whitby to pay for my journey and any medical costs that Jonathan had incurred.

I had never traveled out of the country, much less traveled alone, and long dialogues were held about my safety and the best and most expedient route I should take. I allowed these matters to be decided for me, as I had no knowledge that might help form a strong opinion one way or another. I sent a note to Headmistress explaining why I would not be present at the start of classes, and allowed John Seward, who knew German and some of the Slavic languages that were also spoken in Styria, to coach me in the pronunciation of a few key words. Arthur Holmwood used his family connections to have a passport issued to me in haste.

At the Whitby station, Seward reviewed my itinerary with me once more. "I envy Mr. Harker his malady if it means that such a beautiful woman is willing to travel so many miles to see to him." He stole a furtive glance at Lucy, and I had the firm impression that in addition to flattering me, he was trying to make her jealous.

I took Lucy aside to say good-bye. I clutched her hands in mine and kissed both her cheeks. "I beg of you to be wise, Lucy. Your future depends upon it." I whispered these words into her ear, but when I drew back and looked at her face, I saw that she had no intention of obeying me.

With an uncomfortable feeling in my belly for the welfare of my friend, I thanked the two men for all that they had done for me and I turned my thoughts to the future. Tonight I would be in the city of Hull, where I would catch the boat to Rotterdam, and then travel by train to Vienna, and then on to Graz.

Part Three

GRAZ, IN THE
DUCHY OF STYRIA

Chapter Eight

I arrived in Graz in the rain, thicker than our English showers, and falling from a disconsolate gray sky. Though it was afternoon, dark clouds entrapped the town, making it look as if night had fallen. The foliage had just begun to turn colors, with gold, brown, and burnished patches intruding upon the lush green landscape. I had been trying fruitlessly to find the hospital for about an hour. My nerves were prickly from the long journey, and every doubting voice chattered in my head. The language here, harsh, guttural, and incomprehensible to me, fell upon my ears like an assault, much like the rain that beat down on my hood. I saw nothing like the sort of English tearoom in which I would have taken shelter back home, warming myself and asking directions that would be delivered back to me in the language I spoke. Those words would fall now upon my ears like a mother's nursery rhyme, bringing feelings of safety and comfort. How much we take for granted in familiar surroundings.

The fog that drifted from the mountains in great clusters of white glided over the city like ghostly watchmen. One such mass escaped from the crevice of a mountain and headed my way. I could not help but recall the eerie images of spirits in the Gummlers' photographs. I had the disconcerting feeling that I was no longer alone, that perhaps the being that had informed me of Jonathan's whereabouts had followed me here, as he had been following me everywhere else.

Sometimes, faithful reader, we are called upon to reconcile and live with mystery. Prior to the note he sent, I had been able to convince myself, albeit halfheartedly, that my savior was a figment of my imagination. But the note, with its accurate information, now made that impossible. He was real; he read my thoughts; he could find me wherever I traveled; and, apparently, he was omniscient. Moreover, though I feared him, he thrilled and fascinated me. And now, after having had his sorcerer's hands upon me, giving me pleasure, I had to face my beloved fiancé, who was lying ill in a hospital in a foreign country.

I walked quickly along the quay of the river Mur, which wound its way through the town, its waters rushing past in foamy crowns. In the middle of the city sat the Schlossburg, a hill topped by a red brick ruin of an early medieval fortress with an adjacent clock tower. Though I had no idea where I was, I had the river, the fortress, and the tall onion-domed steeples shooting up from the town's many churches as my landmarks. I asked each passerby, reluctant to stop in the rain, for directions to the hospital, which I am sure I pronounced dreadfully despite Seward's careful tutelage. A man pointed me one way, which led to a dead end, where a lady pointed me back in the direction from which I had just come. I went through this exercise twice more with mounting frustration until a kindly gentleman walked me to the entrance of the hospital, which was tucked away (like many things in Graz, I later found out) off an Italian-style courtyard hidden from the street.

An attending sister wearing the white sail-like headdress of her order and a starched apron over her heavy black habit greeted me in the hospital lobby. Every word that Seward had taught me went flying out of my head in the face of her stern demeanor. Stammering, I took the telegram out of my pocket and thrust it at her. She read it with her lips moving slowly over the words. Then she nodded and led me through a hallway where stately sisters in the same habit glided silently like ships on a calm sea, their hands tucked in pockets beneath their aprons. We came to a small ward with beds separated by heavy unbleached muslin curtains for privacy. I attempted to ask her about Jonathan's condition, but she answered me in her language, which I did not understand.

She pulled back a curtain revealing a thin man with a white streak like a lightning bolt through his brown hair and a lost, hollow look in his eyes. Only when the sister addressed him did I recognize my fiancé.

"Mina! Can it be?" He leaned forward, but as soon as I approached the bed, he withdrew. "Or are you some apparition come to toy with me?"

I was afraid to startle this haunted-looking person by coming too near, so I sat on the bed by his feet, which he quickly pulled toward his chest. He mumbled something in German. His eyes, always changeable, were now almost black, as if the irises had taken over the pupils.

"Jonathan, darling, it is your Mina. I have come all this way to see you and to take you home," I said.

The sister whisked the curtain around the bed and went away. I could hear the quick march of her hard heels on the wooden floor as she left the ward. I was afraid to be left alone with this stranger who was inhabiting Jonathan's body, this fearful man who had aged at least ten years in the eight weeks since I had seen him, and who looked dubiously at me.

"Is it really you, Mina? Come closer so that I may touch your hand and look into your eyes." His voice returned to nearer his normal way of sounding. I slid closer to him and gently put my hand out, palm down, as one might do to a strange dog. He took my hand in his, which was terribly hot. He spoke in a confidential tone. "Forgive me, Mina, but I must be careful. Very careful."

I explained to him that I had traveled for days and days from the Yorkshire coast all the way to Graz to find him. He looked at me as if I were a riddle he needed to figure out. He beckoned me closer with his index finger and he whispered, "Women can change. They are not always as they seem."

What brought on these ideas, I did not know. "I have not changed, Jonathan. I am as you left me."

"I must be assured that you are not one of them," he said. "They always feign innocence, just as you are doing now." He leaned back against his pillow assessing me.

"Who feigns innocence? Remember when we said that we would keep no secrets from each other? Please tell me what happened to you."

"I have been deceived, but I will not succumb again," he said. "If you really are my Mina, then you will help me get far away from this place."

I wanted to pursue this idea, but Jonathan was in no condition to speak rationally about whatever had befallen him. I needed to find his doctor. Perhaps confusion and paranoia were symptomatic of the disease. If only I had asked Dr. Seward more questions about brain fever, but I had been in such a hurry to come to Jonathan. Now I worried that I had arrived unprepared.

I kissed him gently on the cheek, which he allowed, and told him that I was going to find his doctor and make arrangements to take him home. But I could not find a doctor—or anyone for that matter—who spoke my language. Finally, the staff produced a petite, French-speaking nun from Alsace, Soeur Marie Ancilla. I asked her to speak slowly because I was not accustomed to speaking with French people, who generally spoke rapidly.

With great patience, the sister explained to me that Jonathan had been found wandering the countryside in Styria. Some peasant women who harvested pumpkin seeds for oil found him one morning as he walked out of the forest and into their field, calling out names. He did not seem to know where he was or who he was, and he was shaking, either from the chilly morning air or because he was in shock. One of the women gave him a mixture of herbs to drink to calm him and asked a farmer coming to market to drive him in his cart to the hospital in Graz. Groggy from the sedative, he slept, fevered and delusional, for several days. The staff doctor examined and observed him, and diagnosed him with brain fever. Finally, Jonathan woke and started to cooperate, taking food and drink and the prescribed medication. But it took him a week before he remembered his name.

"Did he ask for Mina?" I asked.

"No," she said. "That name does not sound familiar." She explained that no one understood Jonathan's babbling. At first the sisters thought that he was praying, but they soon realized that he was having delusions. His body showed the signs of wickedness, she said, which let the sisters know that his rants were of an obscene nature. The nuns prayed for him, knowing that he was in the grip of the devil. In the past few days, however, he had been quiet and passive.

I questioned the sister on the use of the word *obscène*. She crossed herself and said that she was quite certain she was using the correct word.

"What do you mean that his body showed the signs of wickedness?" I thought she would deliver some superstitious nonsense, but she spoke with candor. "I grew up on a farm. The patient was like a bull in a meadow of cows."

I knew what she meant, of course. Who had put him in this state of arousal? All my fears of his infidelity came rushing back. "If he was not crying out for me, was he crying out for someone else?" I asked.

She shrugged, declining to be specific, perhaps in the interest of discretion. "The imaginations of men can be terrible," she said to me. "And fevers confuse the mind, making it easier for the devil to plant his seeds." I wanted to ask her more questions, but I could tell that she was too uncomfortable to elaborate. Before she left I asked her to find Jonathan's doctor and ask permission to bring Jonathan home.

I returned to the ward, where other visitors had come to see the patients. Conversations in languages I did not understand came from inside the curtained cells. I stood on the other side of the drape from Jonathan and his bed. It was quiet inside. I slid the drape open gently so as not to make a sound. Jonathan had dozed off. His skin glowed from the fever. His mouth was slightly open, and if not for the gray streak that had taken residence in his hair, he would have looked like my Jonathan having a nap. But then his brow furrowed, his breathing quickened, and his head began to move from side to side so rapidly that I thought he might injure his neck. Little moans escaped his lips as if someone were hurting him. Suddenly he grabbed the bed rail and thrust his hips upward, his manhood creating a tent in the middle of the blanket.

I stood very still, not knowing what to do and too embarrassed to call for help. I watched him in fascination and horror as he shoved his pelvis at the air. Chatter and laughter from the other patients' cubicles drowned out his moaning. I threw the curtain closed behind me so that no one else could see inside and I waited and watched until Jonathan's frenzy came to an end with a few loud moans of either agony or ecstasy, I could not be sure. Exhausted, he settled back on the bed.

I sat by his feet, not wanting to disturb him. When his eyes opened and he saw me, he hugged himself protectively. "They have been here," he said. "They have come back."

"I think that your fever is causing you to have bad dreams," I said, though after my conversation with the nun and what I had just witnessed, I was sure of nothing.

I put my hand on his forehead as Headmistress had taught me to check the girls for fever. Jonathan's skin was cool to the touch. "The fever has already broken. I will soon be able to take you home."

"Oh, Mina, I thought I was lost forever. Thank God you have come." He opened his arms to me and I went to him and let him hold me tight.

A doctor interrupted us. He was youngish, just a bit older than Dr. Seward, with dark hair slicked back with some sort of oil. He had a thick, impeccably combed mustache, and wore a somber, tight black jacket and vest with a skinny tie in a bow at the neck. His manner was formal and his English was hesitating but easily comprehended. He explained to me that he could not give permission to someone who was not a relation to move a patient who was not quite ready to be discharged.

Jonathan objected. "No, I must go home. I must get away from here, Mina. Bad things will happen if we do not leave here at once."

"You are very safe here, Mr. Harker," the doctor said. "Have the sisters not taken good care of you?" He turned to me. "Miss Murray, can you stay with us in Graz for a few more weeks while we treat Mr. Harker?"

Before I could answer, Jonathan spoke up. "Mina, if we marry here in Graz, then we can leave at once." The doctor and I both looked at him, and then at each other, surprised. "Is that not correct, Herr Doctor? If Mina is my wife, then on what authority might you demand that I remain in this hospital?" I was astonished at the change. If I closed my eyes, I would think that I was listening to a barrister in a courtroom, when moments ago, he had seemed so confused.

"Yes, I suppose that if Miss Murray is your wife, and she wishes to take you home, I will not have the authority to keep you here. But I wish you would heed my advice and wait."

"Perhaps we should listen to the doctor, Jonathan," I said sweetly. "Why don't we wait until we are certain of your recovery?"

Jonathan's arms were folded across his chest, but he reached out with one hand to take mine. "Please, Mina. If you love me and if you came here to help me, you will marry me as soon as possible. If you do not get me away from this place, there will be no recovery."

. . .

A few hours later, I left the hospital to find an inn to freshen myself and to get something to eat. I was walking through the courtyard when I heard someone call out from behind me. "Fräulein!"

I turned around to see the nun who had greeted me upon my arrival hurrying toward me. She took me by the arm. "Let us walk together," she said.

"Why didn't you say that you spoke English?" I asked. I was both embarrassed and offended that she had earlier left me to flounder, stammering in mispronounced German, when she might have helped me.

"I did not want to speak to you. But I went to the chapel and prayed upon the matter, and I feel that I must. It is my duty before God."

She introduced herself as Schwester Gertrude and told me that she was born in the Styrian countryside just south of Graz. Her father was a winemaker who had many daughters. "By the time I was ten years old, my six older sisters were married, and the money for dowries had run dry. That is when I came here to the convent. I know this country and its people. I know its secrets too, the things that people do not like to speak of."

We walked out of the courtyard and onto the wide street. The sky was clear and the town seemed cheerful to me, with many ornate and gilded medallions on the buildings' façades. Colorful coats of arms and statues of Baroque ladies dressed as pagan goddesses graced the grander structures, and complex wrought-iron arches decorated the doorways. We walked through a narrow alley where all the light seemed to drain from the city and, at its end, found ourselves in front of a grand cathedral.

"Come with me into the house of God," she said. I was too curious to resist her. The entrance was adjacent to a mausoleum for some Holy Roman Emperor, where angels—tall soldiers of God—holding olive wreaths guarded the door to his tomb. I found it ironic that symbols of victory adorned a mausoleum; no one, including the emperor inside, achieved victory over death.

The sister led me into the dark and chilly church, lit only by two dim lamps flanking the altar and a small table of candles for offerings. Schwester Gertrude dipped her hand into a marble urn of holy water at the rear of the church crossing herself extravagantly, and I followed her as she genuflected before the altar with great piousness and then entered the back pew, where we sat down.

"Now you must listen carefully. I am telling you this before God. My immortal soul depends upon telling the truth." Dread rose in me as she began to speak in portentous tones. "I come from the hills where Herr Harker was found wandering. It is a land inhabited by beings, some who are human and some who are not. Herr Harker shows all the signs of being touched, so you must take great care in seeing to his recovery. It is not just his body but also his soul that must be tended. You must pray; pray for him and with him."

"What do you mean by beings who are not human?" I asked.

She continued: "There are creatures in these mountains that are in partnership with evil. They know things about men, and that is why they are able to tempt even the pious into sin. By making pacts with the devil, they can cure a man of disease or make him rich. Child, there are women in those hills who can make flowers bloom in the dead of winter. They promise old men that they will be young again, and ambitious young men that they will be wealthy."

"Why do you think that Jonathan has had anything to do with these creatures?"

"He is not the first, nor will he be the last. The women who found him said that he was crying with great desperation for his lover. We have seen these victims before and have heard tales from our mothers and grandmothers of the young men who have been seduced by these witches. The men of the Church tried for hundreds of years to rid our countryside of them, but they persist. The devil helps them to survive even the flames. They appear to burn to ashes, but somehow they live to haunt the hills of Styria."

"I do not believe that any of this applies to Mr. Harker," I said. Why did old people feel the need to spread these kinds of tales? "My fiancé has been diagnosed with a fever of the brain by a doctor of medicine. I wish you would not try to frighten me with these stories!"

I stood up to leave, but she grabbed my arm, pulling me back down. "The explanation for what happened to Herr Harker is not in the medical books. It makes no sense to an educated lady like you, but there are many things in this world that are beyond the understanding of men. Marriage, a holy sacrament, to a righteous woman, will help Herr Harker to recover. You must trust in God and be patient. I am praying to St. Gertrude for his soul and for you."

She stood up and left the pew, crossing herself and genuflecting again before the altar. Without looking back at me, she left the church.

I sat back and took a deep breath. I had never entered a Catholic church in London. In truth, I was Catholic by birth and by baptism, but when my mother sent me away, she advised me to adopt the Church of England as my religion and never mention my Catholic roots. "Your suffering will be greatly diminished if you do this," she said. I remember asking her what I had to do to be Anglican, and she said, "It is all the same, Mina. Only some of the words used are different. Just keep your mouth closed in these matters and pretend piety."

It seemed easier to let my eyes flow over the cathedral's ornate magnificence than to absorb what the nun had said. I must admit that something stirred in me as I looked over the blinding glimmer of the gilded pulpit and opulent chandeliers, the golden statues of saints and cherubs, and the marble sculptural relief above the altar, crowned with an exquisite representation of Mary. I was either moved or awed or both. I needed to take comfort in *something*, and I looked up to see God's angels above me, blowing golden trumpets. Above them, the statue of a benevolent, bearded saint raised his hand in a gesture of peace. I stared up at him, anxious to receive his proffered comfort, but soon realized that he was not going to provide any answers to the many questions darting about in my mind.

Outside the cathedral, I stopped to look at a mural painted when the city was suffering under a trio of plagues—the Black Death, a Turkish invasion, and locusts destroying the crops. In the scenes below, the townspeople shrank from this multiplicity of horrors, watching as their loved ones were carted off in coffins. Enthroned above were the pope, the clergy, and the saints, presumably those who would intercede with God and save them.

How nice it would be if a deus ex machina would swoop down from above and save us all from the chaos and woes of human life. I was desperate for some being with superior knowledge to explain the strange chain of events that had begun this past summer and did not seem to be ending. Now Jonathan, who I thought would be my salvation, was being subsumed into the mystery.

As I walked through the streets, I passed a wedding party standing outside a municipal building under a sculpture of the Roman Lady of Justice. The bride wore a simple dress, but her face was radiant as her handsome groom toasted her with a flute of rosy red wine. I walked quickly past them, the scene only reminding me that Jonathan's demand that we marry immediately meant that my dreams of an Exeter wedding would never come to fruition. Feeling terribly sorry for myself, I decided to make the climb up to the top of the mountain to see the ruins and to gather my thoughts.

The climb up the stone steps to the Schlossberg must have taken twenty or thirty minutes of labored breathing. My thighs burned with the effort, but it kept me from ruminating on my troubles. Reaching the top, I paused to look out over the great expanse of the city with its tiled roofs and the mountains beyond that rolled out like curved, slumbering bodies. An elderly gentleman with a scarf of crimson wool and a jaunty cap nodded to me as he passed by, reminding me of the old whaler, but I did not smile back. I had heard enough stories today. I found a bench and sat down, though the rain was about to fall. My stomach began to convulse as if I were going to be sick. The awful feeling rumbled up through my chest and into my throat, finally combusting behind my eyes and spilling out in a stream of tears.

What was I to do about all the strange things that were happening? Yes, I had found Jonathan, and yes, he still wanted to marry me. But how I came to discover his whereabouts was as puzzling and frightening as the state in which he was found. I looked up to the heavens. "This is not fair. I have worked so hard, *so hard*, to try to make a good life for myself. Why are you doing this to me?"

I had no idea who I was accusing. Did I really believe that I was God's victim? If we give thanks to God for whatever good comes our way, then why should we not blame Him when our carefully formed hopes and dreams are dashed?

Despite the ominous clouds, rain did not fall. I looked up to see a tiny ray of sunlight begin to split the sky, a knife slicing through the pervasive gloom. And then, as if the sky were nothing but an artist's canvas and the rays of the sun were drawing me a picture, the purple clouds dipped and then rose again, forming a creature with great wings and a long tail. In a few moments, it looked as if a dragon was hovering over me to protect me beneath his majestic span.

I felt a growing sense of calm, as if all were well in the world, as if nothing could harm me, no matter what my present circumstance. My mind settled, and I began to think clearly. I saw that if I took things one small step at a time—marrying Jonathan, getting us home, helping him get back to work—I could navigate us out of these troubles and back into the life we had planned to live together.

The gentlest rain began to fall, a drop here and there. The wind picked up, rattling the trees and shaking clusters of leaves into the air. The mighty beast above lost its shape, its wings now simply the clouds that would soon pour more rain upon the town. I put my shawl over my head for protection and began the walk back down the steep incline.

Chapter Nine

The hospital in Graz was in a former mansion built in the Italianate style for a Venetian merchant. The attached family chapel was still intact, and the sisters used it for their daily worship. They kindly offered it to us for our wedding. With our passports for identity, we procured a license, and within a week, I found myself trading my long-held dreams of a proper wedding for being married in a ceremony in Latin in a strange country, with an inexpensive lace mantilla covering my hair, and wearing a dress I had owned for three years. Rather than Lucy in a gown of silver, two nuns in black served as my witnesses.

Jonathan had been released from the hospital, and we spent our wedding night at the inn. After a small, quiet supper together, we retired to the room. I had no idea what to expect. I changed into a nightdress and lay quietly beside him in the bed. I watched the candle's flame make quivering shadows on the wall, waiting for him to undress me, because that was what I had heard that men did. I had tried to gather information for this occasion. I wanted to please my husband, and I wanted our marital life to begin properly. When we were courting, I yearned for his touch and the pleasure that would come to us through intimacy. Though he had been sick, I still expected that he would want what all men wanted from their wives once the marriage has been celebrated. I thought that the light in the room might be inhibiting him—that he was concerned for my modesty or for his—so I asked him if he would like me to blow out the candle.

"No," he said. "I do not care for the dark."

I wondered if the brain fever had taken away his ability to engage in the act, and then I remembered watching him in his sleep as he made love to someone in his dream. But I also knew that I had to be patient. He had been through some kind of ordeal, which I still did not fully understand, and had contracted a disease from which he was not yet entirely recovered.

"Darling, I want you to know that I love you, and I know that when you return to familiar surroundings, you will quickly recover, and we will be the happiest couple in all England," I said. I rolled over and kissed his cheek, caressing the other cheek with my fingers. His warm body felt good against mine, and I put my hand on his chest, letting it rest there.

He turned to face me, scooping me into his arms and pressing me hard against his body. I lifted my face, and he kissed me, at first tenderly and then harder, until I let my lips open. I felt a thrill as his tongue passed my lips and entered my mouth for the first time. He tightened his hold, and I wrapped my leg around his hip as if it was the most natural thing in the world for me to do. Comfortable and snug around him, I began to relax, giving in to the pleasure. Though I had given up my dream wedding, I loved the feeling of finally being married and in my husband's arms. I was less nervous than I had anticipated and eager to experience what was to come. He put his hand under my nightdress, running it up my thigh, over my hip, and to my breast. A little murmur escaped my lips. Then, without warning, he let go of me and turned away, giving me his back. "It's no use," he said.

"Jonathan?" I asked. "What is it?"

"I have waited for this moment since I first saw you. I have dreamt of it every day, looked forward to it, lived for it. And now it is ruined, and it is because of me and my weakness. I have wronged you, Mina. I must confess my sins to you or they will eat me alive and drive me to utter madness!" Unable to face me, he said all this to the wall.

I had feared Jonathan's infidelity ever since those long weeks in Whitby when I had had no word from him. I knew that this confession would be a tremendous relief to him but a burden to me. Such information, once shared, can never be retracted. I wanted to tell him to keep his secrets to himself, but when he finally turned to look at me, I saw in his pained eyes that the admission of guilt was necessary if he was to mend. Very calmly, I said, "I am your wife now. We must have no secrets."

He breathed uneasily, trying to stanch the flow of tears. He began at the beginning of his tale, when he arrived at the Count's castle in the Carinthian mountains. He was received in splendor, with a kind of lavishness to which he was unaccustomed. "I was blinded by their opulent living, Mina. Food and drink such as you have never seen, the quality and quantity overwhelming. The Count imported wines and ingredients from Italy and France, spices from the Far East, and plate and crystal from the finest makers in the world. In this manner was I greeted and entertained by him and his household."

Jonathan completed the business transactions with the Count in a few weeks, whereupon the Count left him in the castle to see to his affairs abroad. "He invited me to remain in his abode if I wished. I had been entertained in the evenings by his nieces who lived with him, ladies who could sing and dance and play instruments and recite poetry. I admit to you, with some shame, that they dazzled me from the start, one in particular who gave me all her attention.

"I was taken in by this foreign siren, Mina. I had no intention of betraying you. But after the Count departed, in the course of one evening of feasting and drinking wine and watching these women perform their exotic dances, I succumbed to what were the most overt advances. I am not proud of myself, but I daresay that any man would have lost control under the circumstances."

I saw through his strategy of simultaneously apologizing while making excuses for himself. I laughed to myself at Schwester Gertude's story that my husband had been enchanted by a witch, when like any other philanderer, he had simply had an affair behind my back. "How many men have used the language of enchantment to excuse their indiscretions?" I asked. "Is this not what all men say? 'I fell under her spell'?" I sat up, pulling the covers to my neck. "And so you succumbed to her charms. Whyever did you leave? Did you tire of her so quickly?"

He put his head down, shaking it slowly. "I don't know what happened."

I had to exercise control to not scream. "But you were there, Jonathan. What do you mean?"

"I mean that one moment I was in the throes of seduction and pleasure, and the next, I found myself wandering through fields and orchards. I was alone and lost, with only my clothes on my back and a small rucksack. They turned me out, or I escaped—I cannot be certain. I had money in my pocketbook and my identification papers, but my memory of those last few days was gone. I wandered, but for how long I do not know. The rows of plants in those fields were a labyrinth to my addled brain. The light in the valley was so soft, as if someone had draped a veil over it. It seemed like some magical place. I remember staring into a pond at my own face and not recognizing myself. I had no idea where I was or who I was. I walked and walked, and I stumbled into the field where women were picking the seeds out of split pumpkins. I stood there, watching their quick hands dip into the fruit and gather up the seeds. Something about the way the slime dripped from their hands sickened me and I started yelling things. I am not even certain what I was saying. That is when I was given a mixture to drink, which obliterated me. The next thing I knew, I was waking up in a hospital with a German-speaking nun standing over me asking me questions."

He leaned back on the pillow as if this confession had exhausted him. His lips were dry, and he kept licking them and biting his upper lip with his lower teeth. He looked altogether distraught.

"Jonathan, you began by telling me of an infidelity. But you speak of the women in the plural. Did you bed all of them?"

He looked straight ahead, refusing to meet my eyes. "I am ashamed to admit this to you, Mina, but they shared me among them."

My body went cold, but he turned to me with a look of ferocity. "You must understand. They were not like ordinary women. I have never known women devoid of the simple principles of goodness. I am the most wretched of men, but I felt as if I had no choice in the matter, that my will was entirely suppressed. I was innocent until they got hold of me."

He put his head in his hands. What could I say? This was beyond anything I dreamt I would ever hear. My Jonathan, whom I loved and trusted, and upon whom I pinned all hope, had participated in orgiastic play with strange women.

"I am not worthy of you, Mina," he said. "I cannot even meet your eyes."

He rolled over on his side, again giving me his back. I lay watching the shadows on the wall until the candle burned itself out. Soon, I heard a gentle rumbling from Jonathan, a sign that he had purged his conscience enough to retreat into his dreams, probably aided by the chloral that the doctor had given him for sleep. I, on the other hand, knew that my night would be spent reviewing everything that he had confessed. I slipped out of the bed and opened Jonathan's valise, extracting the medication. I mixed a small amount into a glass, which I filled with water from the pitcher on the nightstand, and drank the bitter liquid down. I climbed back into bed and fell asleep to the sound of Jonathan's rhythmic breathing, trying to forget the many sweet fantasies I'd had for my perfect wedding, yearning for the exquisite touch I had anticipated from the man I loved, and wondering if I would ever have it.

. . .

I was lying on a soft bed of fallen leaves, their crunch unmistakable beneath me as I twisted and writhed. The air was cool, but he was beside me, keeping me warm. He was as familiar to me as my own breathing, yet I was aware that his was not a simple human touch. His presence was less dense than the human body's but more powerful and able to engulf me. I took in the ambrosia of his hot scent—wood, leather, and ancient spices—earthy, in contrast to the feel of his being. I opened my eyes and saw that we were lying in a grove of trees with golden leaves beneath unfamiliar stars that blazed across an immense velvet sky. The wind tossed about a single glistening leaf, which rose and fell at the air's will. I watched it dance with the breeze as my lover flooded my senses. Eventually, it fluttered beside us and fell to the earth.

"Where are we?" I asked.

"We are nowhere, Mina. You have met me in the river of time. It flows backward and forward, and we are adrift in it. We can meet here anytime, if you are willing."

"Tonight is my wedding night. I must be with my husband."

"There are many ways to be married. You and I have done it a dozen times."

"But now I am married to Jonathan," I said.

"Not in this realm but only on the temporal plane. Here, you are mine. I have followed you through decades, centuries, trying to lose your scent and the memory of you, but I cannot do it. Can you not look into a mirror, or into your own bank of memories, and remember who you are? Who we are together?"

His voice was rich, full of the promise that I have dreamt of a dozen times. Though he was barely touching me, his mere proximity thrilled me. It was as if our spirits were entwined, dancing together, though our bodies were not joined.

"But who am I?"

"You are the woman with viridian eyes, the color of a rare stone worn by the immortals. I have not seen such eyes in one hundred years. Are you ready for me, Mina? I have waited a long time for you to be ready. It is only fitting that your true husband makes love to you on your wedding night."

He kissed me with agonizing languor, and I quivered with anticipation of what was to come.

"Yes, I am ready," I said, eager for whatever bliss he would bring. Between his lush kisses, he whispered to me, his words tumbling into my open mouth:

> By the ravenous teeth that have smitten
> Through the kisses that blossom and bud,
> By the lips intertwisted and bitten
> Till the foam has a savor of blood.

"Blood is the true love potion. Remember?" He twisted my long black hair around his hand, sweeping it from the curve of my neck, where he buried his face. His lips worked their way up to my ear. "There is no going back, Mina, not this time. I am answering your call. And you have answered mine."

"No," I said. "No going back."

I knew what he was going to do because he had done it before. My body remembered the sensation of it, and my every nerve heightened with expectation. I knew the danger and the pleasure, but there was no turning back now.

"What will I taste like?" I asked.

He inhaled deeply at the base of my throat. "Sweet and pure," he answered, "like white lilacs." With the intensity of a wolf tracking its prey, he began to explore my body. I felt the electricity of his mouth on my skin as his teeth searched for their point of entry. I waited, breathless, anticipating this thing that I both feared and longed for.

"You are sure, Mina?"

"Yes, I am sure. Please, please do it." He waited until I asked again and then once more, teasing me until I was begging. Finally and with haste, he bit deep into my neck, breaking the skin in a single clamp of his jaw and attaching himself to me. I cried out in exquisite pain. I was his host, feeding him with my very essence, with my life force. I was no longer a body at all but a vehicle to serve him, to make him stronger, and to make me a part of him.

But that was only the beginning. He pulled my hair tighter until my ear met his mouth again. "Wherever there is pulse, Mina, that is where I want to be. I want to drink in the very life of you. I want to feel and know the throb of your body." He let go of my hair, unwinding it from his hand, freeing me, but all I wanted was to be his captive. He read my thoughts and he answered me with his mind.

I am not finished with you.

He lifted my arm to his mouth and nipped at the inner part of my elbow and my wrist. At each pulse point, he broke my skin, and I felt bits of my essence flow from me and into his mouth. With my heart pounding inside my chest and my legs quivering, he ran his lips down the side of my body, where his beautiful and treacherous mouth bit slowly into one side of my groin and then the other, sucking to his pleasure, taking mouthfuls of me. Each time my insides tensed and then exploded with ecstasy. He turned me over so that my face was in the soft pile of leaves, and I breathed in their earthy aroma as he broke the skin at the backs of my knees. I cried out, but he paid no attention and slithered down my legs, biting me behind my ankles. I howled, arching my back in a blinding fit of rapture.

"The sounds of your pulses are like celestial music, Mina. The body sings. Can you hear it?"

I heard nothing because nothing outside him or outside this experience existed for me. I was in communion with him, giving myself over to him, letting my essence drain into him, and I thought that nothing of me was going to survive except what had gone into his body. Kneeling over me, he pulled my hair again, arching me toward him, and he bent down and lunged into the other side of my neck, taking his fill. I exploded inside, pounding with the bliss of immolation.

"I am dying," I said, the words staggering out of my mouth.

"No, you are dying into me. And if you die into me again and again, I promise you will live forever. Do you want to live forever?"

"I do, my love, I do. I want to be with you forever."

"You will not turn me away again? You will not sentence me to enduring your cycles of birth and death while I wait for you to remember who and what you are?"

"No, my love, I am yours."

"We are wedded, Mina. You must leave the rest behind."

Suddenly, I felt as if I were being torn in two. All went black, and for some time I was lost, and I was sure that I must have ceased to exist. Then, in a flash, I was floating above my body. Looking back, I saw my mortal form on a bed of gold leaves, tiny rivulets of blood breaking the monochrome of the snow-white skin on my naked body.

. . .

The next morning, I was surprised to wake to the sound of doves cooing outside the window and the smell of the fire burning in the parlor of the inn. Morning light streamed through the lace curtains, dappling the walls. I fully expected that when I rolled over, I would see my dream lover instead of my husband. But Jonathan was lying next to me on his side. His big hazel-brown deer eyes looked as startled to see me as I was to find him in the bed.

We could barely look at each other as we dressed, gathered our belongings, and walked to the train station. I had asked Jonathan if he wanted to stay at the inn for a few days to regain his strength, but he wanted to go home. His mood improved as the morning wore on. The color in his face was good, and he walked with energy and confidence, carrying my valise, opening doors for me, and helping me into the train, probably doing these small things to show that he intended to compensate for his infidelity. For my part, I was grappling with the bizarre dream of the night before. I tried not to think of it, but the delicious memories crept into my mind, titillating me to the core. At those moments, I felt myself blushing against my will and I had to turn my face away from my husband.

The rolling hills we traveled through were lined with rows of crisscrossed crops—apple and pear trees, vines of grapes, and maize—creating bafflingly precise geometries. In the forested areas, the branches on the trees drooped lugubriously like the long sleeves of Druid priests.

Jonathan pointed to the curved roads that cut through the hillsides and valleys. "Forged by Romans, Mina!" he said. "So many civilizations have come and gone on this land—Celts, Romans, Normans, Mongols, French. Who knows how many more?" He smiled at me, but I turned away, wondering if he had learned the region's history from his Styrian lovers. Had his sordid tale inspired my dream?

"My world would be immeasurably better if we could look each other in the eye," he said. He took my chin with his hand and turned my face around to meet his. "I want you to know that I love you, and that my love for you is far above these horrible and decadent acts in which I have participated. I can be a good and faithful husband if only you will give me the chance. Men can be tempted, Mina—that is why we must have the love of a good woman. Otherwise, it is too easy for us to get lost."

I turned away from him, looking out the window at the rows of crops on the hillsides in lines so perfectly straight. Humans were capable of goodness and perfection, but our behavior seldom matched those qualities. Was it our destiny to sling stinging betrayals at each other? I thought of Lucy and wondered if she had lost her mind and confessed her sins to Arthur. Lucy had seemed possessed by the same passions that had consumed Jonathan and left him howling in the fields of Styria. How could that be love? And what about me? A man had made dark, unnatural, earth-shattering love to me in my dreams on my wedding night, but he was not my husband. What bizarre part of my psyche continued to invite these scenes?

Mr. Darwin demonstrated that we—male and female alike—were descended from wild animals. Women, held high in men's esteem and given the task of living up to a higher moral standard, seemed as capable as men of bestial behavior. Jonathan claimed that the women seduced him. It made sense, I suppose. It wasn't as if men evolved from beasts and women evolved from angels. But if women too gave free rein to our base wants, as I did in my dreams, what would happen to our society? There would be no order in the world. And I craved order. That is what marriage, particularly ours, was supposed to provide—blissful, predictable order against the chaotic and unpredictable nature of human life.

"You must give me time," I said. "In time I believe I will be able to forgive you. After all, you are my husband."

Time. What was time? *Time is a river that flows both forward and backward.* How could that be true?

He took my hand. "Your response is more generous than I deserve, Mina. I need time too. I am not worthy of you. I must find a way to purify myself."

We both must purify ourselves, I wanted to say. But I did not think that I could carry through with an explanation.

Part Four

EXETER AND LONDON

Chapter Ten

*D*earest Mina,

How I wish you were here with me, though you will be edified to
know that in the past weeks, your commonsense voice has been
ringing in my ears. Unlike you, I was one of Miss Hadley's worst
students. I did not listen to her wisdom, or to yours, and now I
regret what a fool I have been, though it appears that I have an opportunity to
remedy the wrongs I have committed.

I have been a horrid creature to Mr. Holmwood. His father passed away
just after you left us at Whitby. Arthur went home to tend to business, and when
we reunited in London at the beginning of this month, he returned to me as Lord
Godalming. Lord Godalming! This is the individual whom I have treated so
badly, whose gentle affection I ignored in favor of the bolder stroke of crude lust.
He arrived at the house in Hampstead with a gift for my mother and a corsage of
orchids for me. He asked to be alone with me in the garden and presented me with
his grandmother's diamond ring, which is absolutely dazzling. On one knee, he
asked me to make him the happiest man in England and then gave me a lovely
note from his mother, expressing the hope that we would immediately set a date
for our wedding. "I am eager to have you as my daughter and to instruct you in
the duties that accompany the title of Lady Godalming and the many joys and
responsibilities of life at Waverley Manor."

Any sane woman would have sunk to her knees in happiness, but I did the opposite. I told him that I was in love with Morris Quince and waiting to hear from him. Arthur smiled a very sad and knowing little smile, and at first I thought he was smirking at me. But he took my hand and said, "Miss Lucy, you are not Quince's first victim. He has seduced many a pretty and chaste girl, and for some reason—perhaps to overcome his inferiority as an American—he always sets his sights on the women I most admire. I hold you blameless. But if you are waiting for Morris Quince, you will see your hair turn gray and your life pass you by before you hear from him."

Mina, he said this with such tenderness and understanding that it melted my heart. You were correct: Morris played me for a fool. Arthur told me that Morris came to him before he left England and taunted him with our affair! How could I have been so blind? You saw through the man, but I was entirely caught up in his wicked web of deceit. I would have bet my life—and almost did—on Morris Quince's love for me. What fools we mortals be!

I am the most fortunate of women. Unlike our poor lost Lizzie Cornwall, I will not be cast out into the streets but will become Lady Godalming. We are to be married immediately. How I wish you could be present as we always dreamt, but I know that you are with Jonathan. I do not love Arthur, not yet, but my mother says that any woman can learn to love a man who is good to her, and Arthur is certainly that.

Thank you for all your wise words, Mina, and for your patience with me. Your good counsel has helped me to get on the right path. Love is a terrible, terrible thing. I still dream of Morris and long for his touch, but I know that with Arthur's help, I can move past these feelings.

Your affectionate friend forever,
Lucy

P. S. I will not insist that you address me as Lady Godalming!

Exeter, 20 September 1890

I received Lucy's letter in Exeter, where Headmistress had forwarded it to me. Jonathan and I had settled into Mr. Hawkins's home, and I had written to my employer that I would not be returning to my job, that Jonathan and I had hurriedly married in Graz, and that with his illness, he required my full attention and care. I apologized profusely, knowing that my absence would put Headmistress back into the classroom, which, at her age, she would not relish, but I had no choice.

I had worried over Lucy in the weeks I was away, and I was greatly relieved to know of her turnabout with Arthur. I supposed they were married by now, and perhaps even away on a honeymoon voyage. I vowed to send her a note congratulating her and relating the news of my marriage as soon as I had the time.

In the interim, I was busy caring for Jonathan, who suffered a relapse upon our arrival when he discovered that Mr. Hawkins was ill. After years of enduring painful ailments brought on by severe ulcers, the old man had been diagnosed with chronic gastric catarrh. He complained of a sour mouth and stomach that made eating most undesirable, turning away his meals and losing much of his body weight. His doctor advised me that the condition often caused neurasthenia in the patient, which only worsened the disease.

I found myself nursing both men, aided by Sadie, Mr. Hawkins's longtime housekeeper, but she too was getting up in age and relied upon my stamina. Sadie prepared the main meals, but I visited the markets to purchase our supplies. Both Jonathan and Mr. Hawkins called for me constantly, and I rushed from sickroom to sickroom with medicines, teas, elixirs, and compresses. Mr. Hawkins required ten to fifteen drops of arsenic every two hours, accompanied by soothing conversation and a specially prepared poultice to put on his stomach. Jonathan was always hungry and asking for food, and at the same time, apologizing to me for putting me through the trouble of caring for him.

I encouraged each man to take a midday meal in the dining room, mostly so that I could sit in that lovely room and eat, rather than perch at the kitchen table with Sadie, gobbling down food between my errands. I also thought that the men might provide each other with some cheer. But Mr. Hawkins had given Jonathan the assignment in Styria with the highest intentions to advance his career and supplement his income; Jonathan's resulting illness depressed the old man's health and humor more than his own ailment. Jonathan too was downhearted over his uncle's failing health, so that I was living with two melancholy people. I slept alone on a small daybed in the library. I had tried to lie next to Jonathan, but he cried out all night in his sleep, tossing and turning like some tortured thing.

I took refuge in my daily walks in the town. As soon as I walked out of the door, the crisp autumnal air, so fresh and clean, hit my face, cleansing away the heaviness that lurked inside. I strolled down the street, looking over at the red brick houses on the hills and the rolling green of the surrounding countryside. I liked to walk past the old mill with screeching seagulls circling the water below, then on to the high street, where Mr. Hawkins kept an office, in addition to the one in London. I stopped to purchase whatever goods we needed from the markets and shops, and then turned around and repeated my steps, heading for home before the patients woke from their naps, which usually coincided with the ringing of the city's old curfew bell at five o'clock.

It was a pleasant enough daily diversion, though I could not control my sadness when passing the cathedral in which I had dreamt of marrying, reminding me of lost dreams and dashed plans. With the coming of autumn, I missed the school and the rooms full of giggling girls and the structure of the daily lessons. I had wanted relief from all that. Now I wondered if I had failed to appreciate the small and uncomplicated happiness that it had provided me for so many years.

After weeks of wretched pain, Mr. Hawkins passed away one Monday morning at dawn. Though I was very fond of him, I was not sorry to see the end of his terrible suffering. He had left his home and his business to Jonathan, dividing his money between Jonathan and his aunt, so that we found ourselves in a sudden position of affluence. At the funeral, Mr. Hawkins's friends and clients offered condolences to us and assured Jonathan that they would continue to be represented by the firm—meaning Jonathan—in all legal matters. After the services, when we were drinking tea in the garden, he looked up at the sky. "Mina, our lives should be beginning, but there are moments when I fear that mine has already ended."

"Darling, we have everything to look forward to," I answered. "You are free of the fever, and with the resources that Mr. Hawkins left, we can make every dream we spoke of in Miss Hadley's parlor come to fruition."

"I will try to be that man for you, Mina. I owe you that. You are truly an angel of mercy and forgiveness. But sometimes I fear that the man who envisioned that life with you is no longer here. Some monster with whom I am not yet well acquainted, some rogue with a propensity for doing the unthinkable, has taken his place. Can you be patient with me? It is more than I deserve, but I am asking it anyway. I would not blame you if you refused."

I promised Jonathan that I would stand by him. True, he had betrayed me, but he also suffered terribly for it. I wondered if he had not already been ill and beside himself with fever when he committed those acts, so unlike a man with his character. I should have asked his doctor, but I was too ashamed of the infidelity to speak of it. Besides, I loved him, and I saw enough glimpses of the uncorrupted Jonathan of the past to believe that with time and with love, he would return.

The weather turned colder. By day, Jonathan went into his office to tend to business matters, but at home, though he was affectionate, I often caught him staring into the dancing flames in the fireplace looking forlorn. One evening, about a week after we buried Mr. Hawkins, Jonathan mixed some drops of a sedative into his brandy and retired early. I stayed up late staring into that same fire, wondering if it might give me some answers, until it burned to embers. I fell asleep on the divan in the parlor, and woke early covered by a blanket that Sadie must have placed over me sometime during the night. Then news arrived that morning in two hastily written letters—one from Kate Reed and another from Headmistress—that would distract me from Jonathan's angst and forever change the course our lives were to take.

Lucy was neither at Waverley Manor nor on her honeymoon. Both she and her mother were dead.

London, 10 October 1890

A light rain fell from the low ceiling of omnipresent gray outside the entrance to Highgate Cemetery, drizzling upon the parade of black umbrellas in the funeral cortege. We descended from the mourning coaches that Arthur Holmwood had hired to follow the garland-draped hearse, drawn by six onyx-coated ponies. A canopy of ostrich feathers covered the hearse, decorated with gold and brass emblems. Little page boys wearing formal livery attended the coachman. Through the glass panes, I could see Lucy's coffin covered in rich, dark velvet. The pallbearers—John Seward and others whom I did not know—slid the casket out of the back of the hearse with careful black-gloved hands. It was completely unreal to me that my friend was inside.

"It looks like it's carrying a princess," said one lady who reached beneath her veil to dab her eyes with a handkerchief.

"Madam, I assure you that it is," said Holmwood as he took his place at the head of the procession to walk Lucy to her crypt.

I opened my umbrella, though I was self-conscious that the spray of purple foxglove on the underside might peek through and interrupt the ubiquitous black, but I knew that Lucy would have loved to see that burst of color. I tripped over my hem, upsetting the somber promenade of people in front of me. My dress of coal black parramatta silk trimmed in stiff crape was borrowed from Mr. Hawkins's sister from the wardrobe of mourning clothes she had ordered for us. The dress had arrived in that larger lady's size, so that I had to alter it as best I could, but it was still too big and too long for me.

We followed Lucy's coffin through a leafy, overgrown path toward her final resting place. The rest of the cortege—the procession leader with his baton and attendants, the servants from Lucy's household, and the professional mourners and mutes who had walked in the parade from the church—fell in line behind us. Kate, leaning on Jacob's arm, walked in front of me, wearing the intricate ebony gown she had purchased for her ruse with the Gummlers.

How nice it would be to have a man at my side today, when I felt limp with shock and grief. Jonathan had offered to come with me, but he was very busy with the work neglected by Mr. Hawkins during his illness, and, besides, I was afraid that exposure to travel and tragedy would bring about another relapse.

I had traveled in mourning clothes to London. Kate and Jacob met me at the train station, and we hired a cab to take us to the church where the service was being held. On the way, I had asked about the deaths of both Lucy and her mother.

"Mrs. Westenra died of heart failure just a few days after Lucy's wedding. The poor girl had no chance to celebrate her marriage."

Kate had not been in touch with Lucy but had gathered this information from people she had talked to at Lucy's wake. "I tried to contact Lucy after I saw her mother's obituary in the newspaper, but she did not answer my notes. The service for Mrs. Westenra was private. I thought that Lucy might even be away on her honeymoon."

"I cannot imagine that Lucy is dead! I saw her just six weeks ago."

"Her husband said that the cause of death was acute anemia brought on by refusal to eat and melancholia. She died in a private asylum, Mina. Apparently, her condition was advanced enough for her to be committed."

"But she wrote me a letter dated a little over a month ago that she was about to be married. She sounded so happy. What could have happened?"

"I don't know. The young Lord Godalming is beside himself with grief," said Kate. By this time, we had arrived at the church and were standing outside. "You should have seen the Westenra's house last night, Mina. Arthur had hundreds of candles burning in the rooms and wreaths of white roses and gardenias on all the doors. It was positively transcendent. I am so sorry that you did not see our girl all dressed in white tulle, with the most delicate pearls in the netting. I have never seen a sight so beautiful except—"

Kate stopped, choking on her words. "Except Lucy when she used to smile."

She broke down, bending over in tears, and Jacob took her in his arms and rocked her gently, whispering things into her ear that I could not hear. In that moment, I knew beyond a doubt that she and Jacob were lovers. I remember how morally superior I had felt to her just a few months before, but now I envied that she had the love of a strong man who would hold and comfort her.

Arthur Holmwood, with his mother on his arm, had overheard this. He took me aside, and with frantic eyes, said, "Mina, you've no idea what we have been through. Lucy, my poor Lucy! I should have buried her in black. She was still in mourning for her mother, and I for my father. But I could not bear to see an angel go to Heaven in black!" He turned to his mother. "Was I wrong, Mother?"

I could not see the lady's face beneath her heavy veil. I remembered that her husband had died not two months earlier. She clutched her son's arm and with a very tired voice said, "Come, Arthur, help the mourners out of their carriages."

"She should be in our family tomb," he said. "I have done everything wrong!"

"She should be beside her parents," said his mother. "She was theirs much longer than she was ours."

I sat numb through the service, staring at Lucy's coffin. I thought of Jonathan, of Lucy, of myself—of all the hopes we had harbored. How could the fabric of our lives have disintegrated so quickly? And, of course, I thought of Morris Quince, who was absent but who may have been responsible for Lucy's demise. If she had never met him, she would have quietly married Arthur and learned to love him, as many a woman before her had done. It was Quince who had made her sick with love. It was Quince who had killed her. I sat in the pew with my fists clenched.

I wanted him to pay for what he had done, but he had escaped to America unscathed and probably already had another naïve girl under his spell. After the service, I got into one of the funereal carriages as quickly as possible and was silent on the drive to the cemetery. I was too angry to participate in the predictable postfuneral lamentations.

Now we walked down the wooded path to the mournful tune of the pipes and drums that Arthur had commissioned, past ornate marble monuments topped with delicate angels, crosses, and other sculptures. Thick with chestnut and maple trees that blocked out the skies, Highgate seemed more forest than graveyard. The Westenra crypt was in the Circle of Lebanon, a cluster of tombs beneath a magnificent centuries-old cedar of Lebanon that gave it its name. We passed through the entrance, an Egyptian style arch flanked by two ancient-looking columns and two tall obelisks, where the path began to slope gently to a semi-circular arrangement of tombs with Roman-style doorways.

The procession stopped, and we gathered ourselves around the entry, where the pallbearers stood with Lucy's coffin. My hands began to shake, and I looked for someone who might help steady my nerves when John Seward's deep-set eyes met mine. I cannot explain his look, a mixture of fear and sadness. He seemed to need even more comfort than I. Kate told me that Lucy had died in his care while he and his colleagues heroically attempted desperate measures to save her, and that she thought he felt responsible for Lucy's demise.

The minister began to recite prayers, and everyone bowed their heads. Kate had instigated a scheme that I would read a poem that Lucy had liked in the days when the three of us had become enthralled with the poetry of Christina Rossetti. Headmistress believed that such maudlin literature would thwart the sunny temperaments natural to young ladies and diminish our enthusiasm for accomplishment. Naturally, Kate and Lucy had smuggled it into our dormitory, reading it by moonlight after everyone else had gone to sleep.

"Don't you remember, Mina? Lucy said that she wanted the poem to be read at her gravesite," Kate had said, thrusting a copy of it into my hands.

"She was fifteen at the time, Kate. I think she would have changed her mind."

"Perhaps she had a premonition that she would die young," Kate said.

"Perhaps you have spent too much time investigating mediums," I replied. "Besides, if you feel so strongly about this, you should read the poem yourself."

"You were Lucy's closest friend and you are the *elocution* instructor. I sound like a shrill harridan in comparison."

Objectively speaking, it was true. My voice was gentle and melodic.

Arthur Holmwood was all for the idea. "If that is what my darling would have wanted, then we must make sure that it is done," he had said.

Now I heard his voice at the end of the minister's prayers.

"Miss Mina Murray—oh, I am sorry, Mrs. Jonathan Harker, that is—will now read a poem that Lucy had admired when she was a student at Miss Hadley's School for Young Ladies of Accomplishment."

Everyone looked up, following Arthur's eyes, to rest upon me. My heart started to pound in my chest, and I tried to smile, but not too much for the solemn occasion. Shaking, I walked forward to the casket. It was difficult to retrieve the poem from my pocket, what with my gloved, trembling hands. Arthur gave me an encouraging smile as he took my umbrella and held it over my head.

I began slowly, for there is nothing less eloquent than allowing nervousness to speed us through important moments. "When we were just girls at school, Lucy told us that she wished to have this poem read at the site of her burial. I had hoped that I would be a very old woman delivering these words, if at all, for it would have been my fondest wish to have had my companion for many more decades, and even more, that I would have passed before her. This is for Lucy." I read:

O Earth, lie heavily upon her eyes;
Seal her sweet eyes weary of watching, Earth;

Lie close around her; leave no room for mirth
With its harsh laughter, nor for sound of sighs.
She hath no questions, she hath no replies,
Hush'd in and curtain'd with a bless'd dearth
Of all that irk'd her from the hour of birth;
With stillness that is almost Paradise.
Darkness more clear than noonday holdeth her,
Silence more musical than any song;
Even her very heart has ceased to stir:
Until the morning of Eternity
Her rest shall not begin nor end, but be;
And when she wakes she will not think it long.

I got through the delivery of the poem, even smiling at one point when I remembered Lucy, her young face bright with revelation, exclaiming, "Imagine, death is a place where all cares disappear!"

We watched the pallbearers place Lucy's casket in the vault with her parents, whose coffins sat on the first and second shelves of the tomb. The men slid Lucy's casket onto the third shelf, hitting the wall of the vault with such finality that it made me shudder.

John Seward came out of the vault and met my eyes. He walked to me, and we stared at each other. His ever-questioning eyes, full of sadness and longing, searched mine. The rain had stopped. "Let me take that for you," he said. He shook out my wet umbrella.

We were both silent again. I put out my gloved hand, and he took it and kissed it. Then he cupped it, using the opportunity to link arms with me. "Shall I escort you back to the carriages?" he asked.

We walked together to the entrance of the cemetery. "I have not spoken with you since your travels," Seward said. "Is Mr. Harker recuperated from his illness?"

I was groping for a discreet answer to his question when I saw a man standing beside a familiar gleaming black carriage with two restless black horses. He was dressed in a handsome suit of thick velour, with a dark green vest and a black shirt. A silk cravat pinned with a silver dragon covered his neck. The beast had emeralds for eyes, which seemed to be staring directly at me, as did the man from beneath his low-brimmed hat. He held open the door to the carriage.

Come, Mina. Let us be on our way.

Dr. Seward did not seem to see my savior standing there, much less that he was holding the door open for me. Seward continued to talk as we walked right past the carriage, even though my savior held my gaze.

There is nothing for you here, Mina. Come with me.

No one else seemed to notice him, which was strange, considering his formidable presence would surely command anyone's attention. Was everyone so caught up in mourning the passing of a young life, or was I hallucinating? I wanted to run into the arms of my mysterious stranger, just to see if he was real. But Dr. Seward was already helping me into one of the carriages in the cortege.

"You seem very distraught," he said to me. "You must tell me what is the matter."

Dazed, I took my seat in the carriage, and he sat next to me. "What is it?" he asked. His liquid gray eyes were full of concern. The carriage began to move, and I looked out the window, where my mysterious stranger still stood, staring at me as we drove away.

I turned around, running directly into Dr. Seward's questioning eyes. "It's a rather difficult subject," I began slowly.

"I am a doctor. You may confide in me," he said.

"Thank you for inquiring about my husband. I believe that he needs help," I said, though I knew in the back of my mind that the person who also needed help was me.

. . .

I unburdened myself to Dr. Seward as much as I dared. I did not disclose Jonathan's infidelity, only that he had suffered a shock before contracting the fever. The doctor urged me to bring Jonathan to the asylum, where he and his colleague might observe and treat him. He assured me that Dr. Von Helsinger was a pioneer in understanding the complexities of the mind, and that if anyone could usher Jonathan out of melancholia, it was he. I did not know if Seward was looking for an excuse to spend more time with me, or if he was genuinely interested in helping Jonathan. I knew only that I had to take action. If Jonathan regained his strength, he could put behind him whatever he had done in Styria and be a husband to me. And that, dear reader, was what I believed would put an end to my own bizarre dreams, yearnings, and visions. Please do not think me naïve; I was merely—how shall we say?—uninformed. It is easy to judge the actions of another, but at the time, I completely believed my own simple logic.

I had arranged to spend the night in my old room at the school. Headmistress explained to me that it would be my last opportunity, as she had found a replacement for me who was arriving in two days. "Of course, no one will ever replace you, Wilhelmina. But I am too old to teach. Young girls these days are allowed to act just like little boys at home, and then their parents send them to us to sort them out. I do believe that if these lax and indulgent parents are not careful, girls will be entirely spoiled, and no one will want to marry them."

Headmistress had passed her sixtieth birthday. Her hair was silver gray, swept up into a French-style knot that added to her considerable grandeur. While many private schools kept their students in mean conditions, denying them heat and well-cooked meals, Headmistress charged a high fee and warned parents that if they could not pay their daughters would be sent home immediately. She had explained to me over the years that she could either be harsh with the few whose parents tried to take advantage of her, or she could tolerate lack of payment, which would make life less luxurious for all the girls in her care.

We sat in the parlor, each with our impeccable posture and manners. I had spent much of my life imitating this woman, whose graceful hand lifted a teacup and brought it to her lips as if it were part of a ballet.

"Tell me, Wilhelmina, why did you and Mr. Harker marry so suddenly? I thought you had your heart set on an Exeter wedding."

I told her what I had told everyone else, a condensed and sanitized version of the truth. "Jonathan contracted a fever of the brain while he was in Styria, and I went there to help him. He did not think it would be proper for us to travel together if we were not married."

"That was very sensible," she said, and she patted my arm.

She reached into a drawer and produced two envelopes, which she handed to me. They were addressed to me in Lucy's handwriting. "These arrived at the time that I was searching madly for a teacher to replace you. I just found them earlier today under a stack of papers. I hope that whatever she wrote to you gives you some comfort for the loss of her."

I held the letters tight to my bosom. Headmistress kissed my forehead and went upstairs, while I remained in the parlor. A few embers burned in the fireplace, but the room was chilly. I retrieved Headmistress's shawl from the back of her chair and wrapped it around me. It smelled of the rosewater that she put on her neck after a bath. I breathed it in deeply, remembering all the times that the scent had given me comfort and strength and had staved off the ever-present loneliness that lurked just outside the perimeter of my life, and I started to read.

25 September 1890

My dearest Mina,

Has there ever been a reversal of fortune as dramatic as mine? I will try to elaborate in as much detail as I have time to gather here on the page, for my devoted Hilda, whom mother and I took back to London with us, has promised to sneak this letter out and get it into the post. I am sending it to Headmistress, who I know will faithfully forward it to you wherever you are. I dream that you are fulfilling the plan that you and Jonathan had of letting one of the little Pimlico houses, and that you are there now and will come to see your Lucy as soon as you receive this missive.

Mina, I am a prisoner in my own home, and my jailer is supposed to be my protector. Just three days after Arthur and I were married at Waverley Manor, as we were packing for our honeymoon tour, we received word that my poor mother had died. After all the years that I silently mocked her, skeptical at times that her ailment was real, she had an attack of angina in the night and was found in her bed, reaching for the servants' bell. The death of a loved one is always a shocking thing, especially to me, an only child, who has no other living relations. But the most shocking news was yet to come. After we buried my mother, Arthur and I visited the solicitor, who read us the will. I then discovered that before her death, my mother changed the terms of succession.

The considerable fortune left by my father is passing directly to Arthur rather than to me. My mother's words, included in the document, were that I was a flighty girl of uneven temper and I required Lord Godalming's sober mind to ensure the continuance of the trust. She added that her medical condition would undoubtedly lead to her untimely death, but she could go to her grave in peace, knowing that she had done a mother's duty by seeing her daughter married to a man of distinction. Her final request was that if we had a daughter, we would name it after her.

Now you might not think this news to be egregious. However, in my short stay at Waverley Manor, I gathered very interesting information. Arthur inherits a title and vast lands but has no money to speak of. He requires my fortune to support us in the style to which we are both accustomed and to renovate the manor house, which, though grand, has not seen improvements this century.

No sooner had the solicitor read the words than I saw at last the plan that had undoubtedly been made between Arthur and my mother. Outraged, I turned to my husband and accused him of marrying me for my fortune. "That is why you professed love even after learning that my heart belonged to another. Your motive all along was to gain control of my money!"

"Don't be ridiculous, Lucy," Arthur said. But I was not assuaged. I asked the solicitor, Mr. Lymon, when had my mother made these changes. "Immediately upon returning from Whitby," he said.

"You made changing the will a condition of marrying me, did you not?" I demanded of Arthur. He did not answer, but put his arm around me and explained to the solicitor that I had suffered an assault in Whitby, and, combined with the shock of my mother's death, I had not yet recovered my senses. I begged Mr. Lymon, who had been a friend of my father, to help me. "My father would not want this!" I said. "My father would have wanted me to be protected." I held on to the man's desk, screaming these words as Arthur tried to take me away. I am certain that I did appear to be mad, but I was in such a state of shock that I could not control myself. "Please allow Lord Godalming to take care of you," Mr. Lymon said, with a look of great pity in his eyes for me, as if I were the madwoman Arthur claimed me to be. "Lord Godalming knows what is best for you."

I thought of Morris, of what true love had felt like, and that I would never again have that feeling. My husband had married me for my money, had successfully gotten control of it, and now may do with me as he pleased. I saw the obsequious manner with which Mr. Lymon treated Arthur, and I realized that those four all-important letters before his name, l-o-r-d, meant that no one would question his word against mine. I had to find another tactic.

I let Arthur take me back to the house in Hampstead, which was supposed to be mine but is now his. I begged him to make a settlement with me so that I could live in my father's house alone and in peace. I told him that he could have the money as long as he paid me a stipend to live on. "I beg of you as a gentleman and a peer. You know that you do not love me and never did. I will be satisfied with a small portion of my inheritance. We need never see each other again. I merely want my freedom."

He turned to me with a flash of anger such as I have never seen and said, "That is correct: I may do as I please. And it pleases me to tell you that if you do not begin to obey me as a wife should, I will have to resort to less gentle measures."

I had no idea what he meant by this and I was much too afraid to ask. Behind my back, he immediately sent for John Seward, who arrived with his sinister black bag. He mixed me a sedative, which I at first refused, but I was upset and confused and in shock. Craving some semblance of peace of mind, I swallowed it and I slept.

When I awoke, Seward was still there. He has assumed total authority over me, Mina! And he has done so with a sort of self-satisfaction that I find disconcerting. I attribute it to the fact that he once confessed his feelings to me, and when I told my mother, she insulted him. She asked him how he thought a man with his lack of income and standing might woo and win a girl such as myself. He said to me later, "I am not so poor nor so poorly paid as your mother might think!" She had wounded his pride, but at the same time, she did not want to see me the wife of a man whose residence was a madhouse. I would never have been so unfeeling as she in my treatment of him, though I confess that I never had an ounce of affection for him.

The next morning, my former suitor and now physician announced that I was to have more of the dreaded medicine for my breakfast. They have taken to giving it to me all the day long. I have devised a way to make them think that I am drinking it, but as soon as I am out of their sight, I vomit it into one of the window boxes. Still, some of it gets into my body and I feel quite delirious much of the time. John Seward sits by my bedside, and, under his doctor's guise, he asks the most intrusive personal questions, Mina, about my monthlies! When I told him, blushing and looking away from his face, that they did not arrive on the same day every month and that oftentimes, I skipped a month altogether, he acted alarmed. "I was afraid of that, Your Ladyship," which is what he has taken to calling me with the most ironical tone in his voice. I wish I could describe it to you. The undertone is that, though I now have a title, the balance of power between us has shifted, and he has the control over me. He convinced Arthur to hire a nurse to attend me, and she examines my menstrual blood and reports back to him on its characteristics and volume. I do not know what this has to do with making me well. But the more I protest that I am healthy, the more I am told that the protestation of well-being is a symptom of hysteria.

Seward has proposed that I be taken to the asylum, Lindenwood, where I will be observed and treated by his colleague from Germany, a Dr. Von Helsinger. I have made it plain that I do not intend to comply with his wishes, but the more that I assert my will, the more he and Arthur insist that I am suffering from some sort of hysteria and require treatments only available in an asylum. I wonder if it is best to acquiesce to their demands so that I may be proven sane and left alone.

I hate to burden you with these affairs. But, Mina, I am desperate. Perhaps

Mr. Harker, as he is a solicitor, will be able to suggest a course of action that will
rescue me from my present situation and give me my freedom from Arthur
without becoming destitute.

I await your response. Make haste, darling Mina!

Your despondent and unfortunate friend,

—Lucy

What grief settled over me. Here was Lucy, my dearest friend, begging for help from me, and I had been caught up in my own troubles with Jonathan and unaware of her woes. Now she was in her grave and it was too late. I slowly opened the second envelope, hoping it contained better news. But how could it?

4 October 1890

Dear Mina,

I am writing to you from inside Lindenwood, John Seward's asylum on the
river at Purfleet. Hilda has stolen some paper from Seward's office and a pen. We
patients are not supposed to have such instruments in our possession for fear of
what dark uses we will make of them. I must confess that if I thought I would be
successful, I would stab myself with this pen and end my life.

I must be brief, for if I am caught writing to you, my "treatments" will
become ever harsher, and I will be restrained again. Yes, you have read that
correctly. Your Lucy, who you know to be of sound mind, has had her wrists
and ankles shackled to a bed for having a "disobedient nature." But I must not
dwell on those inconsequential details, though I believe it would give me some
comfort to know that someone has knowledge of what I have been subjected to
within these walls.

I was examined by Dr. Von Helsinger, who has prescribed a series of
treatments that I fear is killing me. He is a most terrifying and bizarre man,
though John Seward holds him in the highest esteem and believes that his
unorthodox methods carry the seeds of genius and the answers to many perplexing
medical problems. Arthur has now joined in this admiration, so there is no one to

advocate for me against him. Von Helsinger explained to me that he has been performing experiments on women by transferring the blood of men, who he believes are stronger, more moral, healthier, and more rational, into women. Mina, you should see this man's eyes as he talks about his work. He has the look of one of the insane who wander the streets, talking to invisible entities! John Seward and Arthur were at his side, listening to his madness as if it were the most brilliant lecture delivered by an Oxford don. They paid no attention to my look of disbelief.

Now I must relate the horrible details of what they are doing to me. Remember, Mina, this is after other treatments that I thought I would not be able to endure—freezing cold baths, force-feeding—oh, it was all too horrendous, but I mustn't linger on all that. I must get to the point, and my mind wanders these days as a result of the sedation and from the new treatments, which have weakened and sickened me so that I am no longer the Lucy you knew but some shadow self, who only exists in those moments when I conjure up a shred of hope that I will be released from this place.

I know you will think this bizarre, but, believe me, I am not hallucinating. The two younger men take turns emptying their blood into me. I am drugged in advance so that I cannot resist. While he waits for the medicine to take effect, Von Helsinger asks me if the men do not deserve a little affection for their troubles. Too weak to resist, I say nothing. Whichever man is giving the blood—Arthur or John Seward—is encouraged to caress my body and kiss me. "There, little miss, is that not what you like?" Von Helsinger asks. "Oh yes, she likes this. Don't you, Lucy? You liked it when Morris Quince touched your body, didn't you?" Arthur taunts me with this, Mina. I never should have confessed my affair.

Von Helsinger watches these acts with great fascination, even directing the men how to touch me, and even though it is plain that it is humiliating and repulsive to me. "If she pines for you, her body will accept the blood!" he says. Mina, the glint in his eyes as he instructs the men to have their way with me is truly frightening. The two younger men are enthralled by his every word. When Arthur isn't taunting me, they are completely silent as they stroke and kiss me all over my body. I can hear their heavy breaths breaking the awful silence in the room. I cannot tell you the state of self-disgust this invokes in me. When Von

Helsinger feels that my body is ready, he takes my naked arm and makes an incision into which he inserts a tube with a central rubber bulb for pumping. Then he rolls up the sleeve of my donor, tying a cord around the upper arm and rubbing the rest of the arm, stroking its muscles, looking for the right vein. After much examination, when he finds his target, he makes a similar incision in the arm of the man and inserts the other side of the tube.

They have performed this operation two times. Each time, I feel weaker. I cannot take food, my sight is blurry, and I have little strength. In fact, I must close soon because this exercise has left me exhausted.

I am trapped here. Arthur is my husband and therefore my guardian, and if he can persuade a doctor that I am mad, I can be committed here indefinitely. Seward and Von Helsinger are free to keep me here as a subject of their laboratory experiments, imprisoning me to aid their strange studies and to accommodate Arthur's wishes to have me out of the way so that he may do whatever he likes with my father's fortune. My fortune.

Mina, time is of the essence. How I wish that I could send word to Morris. I know that you hold the lowest opinion of him, but I am also certain that there was some feeling in his heart for me, despite his having abandoned me, and that he would come to my rescue if he knew how desperate and acute my situation. Please present my letters to your dear husband and beg of him to think of a means of getting me released from this place. Oh, this horrible place! I feel it packed with the spirits of those who have died here! Sometimes I think I hear them moaning in the night. Time is crucial. I will not last long if they continue to administer the treatments. I cannot eat and I am shaking with fever.

Your desperate friend,
Lucy

. . .

Kate's ink-stained fingers gripped Lucy's letters tightly, turning her nails and knuckles white with tension. No longer clad in black, she was back to the loose-fitting clothes she wore when working, but I could still see her chest move as she took short, audible breaths.

We sat in the Cheshire Cheese off Fleet Street, where Bohemian artists and newspaper people fought over the table at which Doctor Johnson himself had once sat and held court. Kate ate lunch here so often that, without needing to order, a waiter had placed two plates with steaming rump steaks in front of us. They sat untouched.

"What do you make of this, Kate? Did they kill Lucy? Should we go to the police?" I hadn't been able to go to sleep after reading Lucy's letters, and now my eyes were burning, my back ached, and my mind was a jumble of ruminations that had slammed against the walls of my brain all night long.

"And present the letters of a 'madwoman' against the word of *Lord* Godalming? That would not be wise, Mina. You must try to think like a crime investigator. These letters do not prove a thing. Many doctors are experimenting with the transfusion of blood from one patient to another, sometimes with positive results. Some use the blood of lambs and claim it has revived dying patients entirely. Lucy had a very vivid imagination. You yourself have told me the story of how she imagined that the American was in love with her."

"She had quite a bit of help from that gentleman, who told her so."

"Nonetheless, she had a vivid and often prurient imagination. She thought all the boys were in love with her."

"And they were, if I recall," I countered. I detected a little strain of the old jealousy that Kate had for the prettier and more flirtatious Lucy. "But those letters, Kate. We cannot just drop the matter. Lucy lost her life! She did not belong in an asylum and she was not sick."

"That is not exactly true." She picked up her utensils and began to slice the meat. "You said that she had lost weight, and that she seemed quite out of her mind over this Morris Quince, and then even more disturbed over the loss of him. Perhaps she *was* completely mad by the time she wrote those letters." Kate waved her fork at no one in particular. "On the other hand, madwomen are subjected to terrible things in the name of curing them. Oh poor Lucy. She should have just married the *lord* and *kept* the lover."

"I am afraid I may have made a pact with the devil," I confessed. "I made arrangements with John Seward to take my husband to the asylum."

Kate had speared a chunk of steak with her fork but stopped short of putting it in her mouth. "Did you?"

I explained to Kate that Jonathan had not been himself since he had contracted brain fever in Styria, and that when I told Seward of his condition, he offered to examine and treat him. I did not reveal the extraneous details of Jonathan's infidelity, nor did I reveal the incidents that were leading me to believe that I too needed a doctor's care. "Obviously, I would not want Jonathan to have the sort of treatments Lucy described. On the other hand, he does need help, solid medical help."

Kate chewed her steak while she pondered this. She held her empty fork in the air as if it were one of the pointing sticks I used in the classroom. "Mina, an exposé on the treatments in some of these asylums would make a gripping *newspaper* story. Really, the mad doctors do the most barbaric things, from what I have heard. Strange, perverse things—as horrible as what Lucy described and even worse—all in the name of science and medicine. Oh, it would be a gruesome story, but the readership would eat it up, I assure you."

"Kate Reed, you have been on Fleet Street too long!" I could not believe what my ears were hearing. Had she gone mad too? "Perhaps you could have yourself committed to do the research," I said. "It won't take much to convince John Seward, or any other man, that you are mad."

"Mina, it is not like you to be sarcastic," she said. I believe I had actually hurt her feelings. "I am a journalist. It is my duty to expose practices that may be *harmful*. And if it is mostly women who are being harmed—as it inevitably is—then I am especially interested and obliged."

"I apologize if I insulted you. But we must think about Lucy and Jonathan, not some article that might be written."

"You must keep up with me, Mina. We *are* thinking of them. The mad doctors in private asylums are not supervised and are free to do what they wish. Oh, some of these places are mere resorts for the wealthy who need a rest from society after the Season. That is the sort of place where someone like Mrs. Westenra would go. Remember that ridiculous woman? I know I should be saying 'God rest her soul,' but I cannot be a hypocrite."

"Kate!"

"Mina, will you never tire of being *nice*? I hear that these asylums hold some of their patients for life and turn them into veritable *slaves*. I have thought to write on this before, but Jacob said that for centuries, the Church tried to stop medical men from dissecting human corpses, which delayed scientific discovery. He thinks that we should not interfere with medical experimentation, even if we find the methods gruesome."

"I am not interested in writing a story, Kate. I am only interested in helping my husband and in getting to the bottom of how Lucy died."

All around us people were carving, chewing, and swallowing their food while laughing and talking. Some picked up chops by the bone, tearing the meat off with their teeth. For some reason, it reminded me of the way Lucy said that her body had been handled and abused, and I had to turn my eyes away.

"On the other hand, if something terrible did happen to Lucy within those walls, and you found out about it, your story would be a great tribute to her memory."

"You cannot expect me to subject Jonathan to these sorts of vile treatments that Lucy described?"

"Oh, they will not do those things to a *man*. Not against *his* will. And you will be there to supervise." Kate was smiling now as the idea took hold. As we finished our meals, she continued to talk as if I had already agreed to her plan. "One of the great benefits of being a *lady* journalist is that no one thinks that you have a brain at all. People will reveal to you the most amazing things. It won't take long for Dr. Seward to tell all about Lucy's demise. Especially to you, pretty Mina with your dazzling eyes and *ladylike* comportment. Society women love to volunteer at the asylums. You might convince Dr. Seward that you are just another do-gooder."

Each time Kate emphasized a word, she leaned forward with her lips like a woman about to take a bite out of her veil. "Mina, you know you want to do this. Just *admit* it."

In fact, the part of myself that had always been intrigued with Kate's journalistic activities was quickly being drawn into the plan. "I am interested in learning about the last days of Lucy's life. I cannot promise that I will gather enough material for a newspaper story," I said.

"Oh, but you will, Mina. I have no doubt. You always play the goody-goody with me, but that is only because you want to act as my foil."

She wiped her mouth clean with a napkin. "Now listen carefully and I will quickly instruct you in the art of gathering information. You will find that the *feminine* habit of interrupting silences with meaningless chatter will not serve you. I have discovered that if I sit in silence, the subject will begin to blurt out things that would have gone unspoken if I had started chattering."

"I have never seen you silent, Kate. You are a very aggressive interviewer."

She considered this. "Normally, I interrogate vigorously. But it is not in your nature to do that, so you must use this other tactic, which I assure you will produce results. Pretend innocence and ignorance. Smile sweetly, as you do anyway, and let them do the talking. If talk ceases, just sit there. Out of the *discomfort* of silence, the most interesting *information* is revealed."

Part Five

LINDENWOOD ASYLUM,
PURFLEET

Chapter Eleven

16 October 1890

We drove toward Lindenwood as the sun was setting. The desolation along the Thames at Purfleet, downriver from London, was broken up by industrial buildings—bone mills, gristmills, soap factories, tanneries—whose chimneys shot great clouds of smoke into the sky. The rays of the setting sun infiltrated the black atmosphere, burnishing the sky. As we drove along the road that followed the river, I saw pockets of scum and debris floating on its surface. The water, an unsavory grayish brown, rushed past as if in a hurry to leave this grim landscape.

Lindenwood itself was protected from these views. The grounds were secluded by thick stone walls made black with soot and age, and by the growth of ancient trees twisting together, locking out the modern world of manufacturing and machinery that had sprung up along the river. The old mansion, with its grand façade of limestone bricks, narrow lancets, and four colossal turrets at its corners, sat at the end of a long drive. Dr. Seward had told me that the eccentric aristocrat who had built it in the latter part of the last century had donated it to serve as an asylum at the time of his death. It looked more castle than manor house, what with its feudal architecture. Over the clatter of the carriage wheels, I heard the tall, wrought-iron gates creak as they closed behind us, and

I looked back to see two men fastening them shut with thick chains. I did not like the idea of being locked inside, but I calmed myself by remembering that within this walled environment, I would find help for my husband; the truth of what happened to my best friend; and, if I was lucky, relief from the strange things that had been happening to me. Little did I suspect that I would soon discover so much more.

Jonathan had been more than amenable to the visit, even excited at the prospect. "You deserve a strong husband, Mina," he had said. "I am determined to be that man for you. Besides, I am fascinated by the new theories on the complexities of the unconscious. I welcome an opportunity to become acquainted with experts who will discuss the subject with me."

A hospitable woman in a bright blue apron and cap greeted us at Lindenwood's massive and foreboding door, introducing herself as Mrs. Snead. She appeared to be somewhere in her forties with a crooked smile and a strange way of looking just to the side of whomever she was speaking to. Thick, dark-stained paneling covered the walls of the reception hall that was hung with portraits of old gentlemen, each seeming to follow us with his sober gaze. The atmosphere was elegant but heavy—with what, I did not know.

"Dinner will be served at seven," Mrs. Snead said. "Would you like to have tea in the parlor, or would you like to be escorted to your quarters?"

We opted for tea in the parlor, sitting in chairs with serpentine legs and tall backs that reflected the shape of the pointed-arched windows. A young woman wearing the same blue uniform rolled in a tea cart and served us piping-hot tea with fresh cream and slices of ginger cake. Another member of the staff stacked logs in the great stone fireplace and lit lamps, illuminating the opulent surroundings.

But as the light infiltrated the room, I saw that the upholstery was frayed and the stuffing of the divan opposite us sagged almost to the floor.

"This is not what I expected," Jonathan said, relaxing in his chair. "One feels more guest than patient."

"I agree," I said. But unlike him, I found the discrepancy disquieting.

The bedroom was no less ornate. Carved hooded medieval monks supported the heavy wooden ceiling, again giving me the feeling that I was being watched. The bed's canopy of sharp spires reached almost to the ceiling. Panels of blood-scarlet brocade threaded with gold curtained the thick velour-covered mattress. I sat on it to test its comfort, wondering if Jonathan would at last consummate our marriage on its soft, inviting plane. He gave no indication that he was thinking any such thoughts. He took off his coat, splashed water on his face, and sank into an armchair, instantly engrossed in an old book he had picked up on the side table.

At six forty-five in the evening, Mrs. Snead fetched us for dinner and escorted us to the candlelit dining room, where we sat like children dwarfed by the high ceiling. John Seward arrived a few minutes later with a stout older man whose wild gray beard eventually came to a point at chest level. Grizzly eyebrows sat like mats of twisted yarn above his dark eyes. He wore a rumpled suit that was probably expensive when it was purchased in some other decade. He bowed to me in the old-fashioned way and kissed my hand. He gripped Jonathan's hand and did not let it go as he said his name. "Herr Harker. Yes, Herr Harker. Yes, I see. I do see." He studied Jonathan as if he were a specimen under a microscope until Seward said, "Dr. Von Helsinger, you have met our other guests?"

So this was the famous doctor. I had thought that we might have had our first glimpse of a patient, what with his disheveled clothes and hawkish stare. He wore a monocle on a tarnished, diamond-cut silver chain around his neck. His protruding eye sockets wrapped so far around his face that they looked as if they might slide right off.

The dining table seated fifteen, and some nearby residents of Essex had joined us. "An institution such as this must keep good relations with its neighbors," Seward whispered in my ear as everyone was seated. Two serving girls poured wine as the doctor and his neighbors made polite conversation about local politics. Jonathan sipped the wine and proclaimed it to be as fine a claret as he had ever tasted. When the first course, turtle soup, was served, I noticed that Von Helsinger examined it with his monocle before he tasted it, but I found it to be sublime. I said as much to Dr. Seward.

"The recipe was brought to us by a former patient. She was a friend of the lord mayor, and this is from his very kitchen. It takes the cooks two days to prepare and it is made, I assure you, from real turtle meat."

Seward, away from the more illustrious shadow of Arthur Holmwood, was a changed man. The lids over his gray eyes did not seem so heavy, and his fraught look was gone. This was clearly his kingdom, and it seemed that he ruled it well.

"Is it common for a patient to bring recipes to your kitchen, Dr. Seward?" I asked.

"This was a very special case, Mrs. Harker," he said, addressing me by my married name for the first time. "The patient in question came to us after months of neglecting all domestic duties. She had a kitchen staff, but she refused to plan menus or to attend to any household concerns whatsoever. She left her children in the care of a governess, while she shut herself in her study, reading books and writing letters to politicians in the Liberal party with whom she was obsessed."

Dr. Von Helsinger picked up his bowl, drained the last of the turtle soup, and released a heavy sigh of contentment. "It stands to reason that in these times of ladies infiltrating the masculine domains of thought and intellectual inquiry, they become victims of brain strain. If left untreated, the result is melancholia or, in worse cases, hysteria. This lady was fortunate. She came to us in time for us to help her."

"I hypothesized that if she were made to do domestic labor as treatment, she would recover her natural propensity toward it," Seward said. "She worked in the kitchen, preparing food and serving it. At first, she was rebellious, but gradually she came to enjoy it, even introducing her favorite recipes to our humble kitchen."

Dr. Seward rang a bell, and the serving girls brought in platters of beefsteak and winter vegetables, which they held for each guest to take a portion. Jonathan complimented Seward on the politeness and efficiency of his staff. My husband's handsome features, softened by the candlelight, had returned, and he looked like the affable man I had wanted to marry. He was enough changed that I worried that the doctors were wondering why I had brought him to the asylum.

One of the lady guests agreed with Jonathan's assessment of the staff. "I declare, Dr. Seward, I must have you interview servants for me."

"My wife's taste in servants tends toward the lazy and the dishonest," said her husband, and everyone laughed.

"Thank you for the compliments," said Dr. Seward. "Most everyone on our staff is also a patient, or a former patient."

This news stunned me. I wanted to turn around and look at the girls who had served the food to see if I could detect any traces of mental illness on their faces.

"Work has been the cure for so many of our patients," Seward said. "And it is good economy too. We provide the most advanced modern treatments, but they take time and are administered at great cost, especially the labor."

I saw a way into my purpose and spoke up. "Dr. Seward, before my husband and I married, we agreed that I would devote a goodly amount of my time to charitable works. While Jonathan and I are your guests, I would very much like to volunteer my time to help you in any way that I can."

The doctor did not seem receptive to my idea. "That is a very noble wish, Mrs. Harker. Ladies often have the best intentions, but patients do not exactly mind their social graces. I would not want you to suffer any insults at their hands."

I wondered if he had something to hide and I became more determined.

"I doubt that your patients could be any worse than some of the little girls I have taught." Everyone laughed at that.

"What do you think, Dr. Von Helsinger?" I asked.

The gentleman turned his wide, insect stare on me. His mouth was set in a smile, but the rest of his face remained sober. "If Herr Harker would postpone our meeting tomorrow, I would be happy to spend the day escorting the beautiful lady through the asylum. It would be a pleasure greater than any I expect at my age."

Something about the way he looked at me made me shrink back in my chair, though I tried to maintain my smile. Jonathan must have seen it too.

"I cannot postpone our business together, sir. I have important matters in both London and Exeter that must be attended to," he said sternly, which gave me a little thrill. I had not seen him play the protector since before he left for Styria.

"Then it is up to me to satisfy you, Mrs. Harker," said Dr. Seward, smiling.

. . .

All night long, I heard moaning sounds. I slept fitfully, awaking several times and sitting up in bed. But then, the noise would stop. I must have been having nightmares, but I could not recall their substance. I woke with a headache.

At an early hour, an attendant delivered a breakfast tray to our room, and then, at eight o'clock, as no one was allowed to wander the asylum unescorted, a man came to take Jonathan to see Dr. Von Helsinger. Fifteen minutes later, Mrs. Snead came for me. I wondered if she too had once been a patient. She spoke clearly, but her face twitched almost imperceptibly, as if she intended to wink but could not complete the action. We walked down the wide staircase together, and as we reached the set of stairs nearest the ground floor, I heard the same voices I had heard in my sleep. I stopped to listen. It sounded as if the very walls were moaning.

The sounds escalated as we walked across the reception hall. Mrs. Snead took a ring of keys out of her apron pocket and opened a pair of tall double doors. The groaning assaulted my ears—grunts, whimpers, cries, moans—and came together in a cacophonous song of collective misery. Some sounded guttural, others were high-pitched. All sounded female, and I inquired as to why this might be so. "This is the women's ward," Mrs. Snead explained. "The men's ward is separate."

Mrs. Snead paid no mind to the din and walked ahead of me down a corridor with many doors, some with peepholes and some with bars. Whereas the private part of the mansion where we were quartered had a faint scent of dry wood and dust common to old houses, this wing smelled of iron and rust, and the air itself was damp. We climbed another stairwell, narrower and darker than the one that served the main house, and arrived at the door of Dr. Seward's attic office.

He was sitting at a desk in a room with a pitched ceiling and tiny windows, speaking into a phonograph in an oak box on a little wrought-iron stand. He heard us enter and turned around. "Good morning, Mrs. Harker," he said. "I was just recording my physician's notes into the phonograph. Such a convenient contraption. You are familiar with them?"

"Why, no," I said. I remembered Kate's admonition to feign ignorance. "Do you record everything that happens here in the asylum?"

"Everything important," he replied. "It is a superb record-keeping tool." He tried to interest me in a cup of tea, but I assured him that I was all too eager to begin our tour of the facility.

"Very well, then." He picked up a stack of charts and led me back down the stairs and into the hall, where we passed two women in blue aprons who nodded politely. "A moment, please," he said. "This is Mrs. Harker, who is visiting us and will be volunteering her time." He introduced the two severe-looking women as Mrs. Kranz and Mrs. Vogt, hall supervisors. "Most of our patients are quite peaceful, but these ladies are on duty in case of an incident," he said before dismissing them.

"I wish you would dispense with these formalities," I said, smiling at him. "I would be delighted if you would simply call me Mina."

"Then you must call me John," he said. "But we mustn't let the patients—and others—know of this little intimacy."

"Of course not, *Doctor* Seward," I said. I knew that it was wrong to flirt with him, but I sensed great longing in him, and I was not above exploiting that to gather information.

He opened double doors to a small library with a tall paneled ceiling and a lazy fire in the fireplace. Two elderly women playing cards occupied a game table, while a young girl lay on the divan, mumbling to herself and rubbing her breasts. The two old women paid her no attention but wordlessly flipped cards onto the table.

The doctor and I stood in the doorway. No one looked up. "That is Mary," he said, gesturing to the girl. "I admitted her three months ago. She is fifteen. Her parents brought her to us when the commencement of puberty incited a mental illness. Would you like to see her chart?" He handed it to me.

Written in thick blue ink and a scratchy penmanship, I read it with some difficulty:

> Facts Indicating Insanity: Causeless laughter alternating with obstinate silence. She is wicked and excitable in the company of gentlemen. Her parents were alerted to the disturbance when she turned cartwheels on the lawn in full view of observers of both sexes. The family doctor was brought in to examine her, but she refused to comply with him and would not stick out her tongue for the examination.

I scanned the page to read what Seward had written after his last visit with her a few days prior:

> She takes but little food and sits for hours with her eyes closed, patting her breasts. Water cure, isolation, etc. completely ineffective. Vaginal lavage with potassium bromide to calm the excited tissue give only temporary relief. She is particularly excitable in the menstrual state, but at other times can be made docile with medication.

"I am not going to interrupt her," he said, taking the chart from me and making a note on it. "She appears to be calm enough."

One of the older ladies slapped the last card in her hand on the table. Her shock of long hair was like marble, stiff and white with caramel streaks. She might have been sixty or eighty—I could not tell. She caught me looking at her, and I was struck by the color and vivacity of her eyes—vivid green and as bright as a baby's. Her eyes looked as if they belonged on another face, a face that still had many years left in this lifetime. Her body, however, looked brittle with age.

"That woman is staring at me," I whispered to Seward.

"Vivienne has been here for many years. I cannot introduce you to her in front of her card partner, Lady Grayson. She thinks that Vivienne is the queen, and it upsets her terribly to hear otherwise."

We walked down the hall, with him at a faster pace and me trying to keep up, to a door with a small opening slashed by two iron bars. I could not see inside because the doctor blocked my view. The asylum's ambient moaning filled the hall, but none seemed to be coming from inside this particular room. He put a large key in the lock and left it there as he spoke.

"Jemima, who you are about to meet, suffers from an emotional insanity." He opened Jemima's chart and read: "'She is lively, cheerful, and very talkative, but at times becomes insensible and will take no nourishment. At these times, force-feeding is recommended.'"

"Force-feeding?" Lucy said she had been force-fed.

"Yes, the tube is put down the throat and a healthful concoction of milk, eggs, and cod-liver oil goes through the tube to nourish the patient."

"I see." I tried to imagine a tube being pushed down my throat.

"I know what you are thinking, Mina, but when a patient tries to destroy herself by not taking in food, what else can we do to save her? And it is so common with young women to refuse to eat." He continued to read from the chart. "'She has irregular menstrual periods and a peculiar nervous system, but her flow of animal spirits is abundant. If the menstrual cycle could be regulated, she would be able to be sent home.' I do apologize for the indelicate nature of these details."

A perfunctory apology, if I have ever heard one. I believe he was enjoying subjecting me to topics that in a social situation would have been strictly forbidden.

"Please don't apologize, John," I replied. "If I am to volunteer here,

I want a complete picture of the patients. It will help me to interact with them."

"Jemima came to us with fluttering, nervous hands, which aggravate the confused mind even more. The first step was to settle the hands." He turned the key and opened the door, leading us into a long room, where about a dozen women of different ages sat at tables doing embroidery, needlepoint, knitting, and sewing at machines. All hands were busy making scarves, draperies, pillow slips, doilies, caps, and mittens. The colors of the fabrics and yarns were a jumble of brightness against the plain white walls and the gray asylum uniform worn by the patients.

A woman in the blue apron indicating that she was on the staff sat in the corner. Seward nodded to her. No one else looked up.

"The patients come to us distracted, their minds dizzy with all sorts of worries, phobias, and concerns, and we settle them by having them work with their hands," the doctor said. "In turn, we sell the goods they make to raise funds for the asylum. We even fulfill personal orders from our neighbors. And the uniforms of the staff and the patients are all made in this room from donated cloth."

"Impressive," I said. "Very efficient."

"Jemima?"

A young raven-haired woman looked up. When she saw Seward, she put down her embroidery frame and ran to him. Her creamy skin and bright eyes distracted from the drab gray dress hanging loosely around her frame and the fact that her nails were bitten to nothing, the surrounding cuticles and skin gnawed red. She tried to put her arms around the doctor for an embrace, but he held her at a distance. "There now, that will do," he said, embarrassed, taking her by the wrist and placing her arm by her side. "Jemima, how are you feeling today? Well, from the looks of it."

"Yes, Doctor, I am well. Very, very well."

"Your chart says that you have been eating your meals. This is Mrs. Harker," he said. "She might be bringing you your lunch tomorrow."

The girl gave a little curtsy, though she was just a few years younger than I.

"If you continue to take your food and work steadily, you will be able to go home soon," he said.

The girl took two steps back, firmly planting her feet in a show of protest. "No! I don't want to go home," she shrieked. "I'm not well at all. Not well, I tell you!"

The outburst was so sudden that I took a few steps back, in case she tried to attack us. The attendant rose from her seat, but the doctor motioned for her to sit back down. "There, there, Jemima. I did not mean to upset you. Of course, you won't be sent home until you are ready."

That seemed to settle her down. "Be a good girl and go back to your sewing." She thrust her shoulder forward and rolled her head back in a sort of dance hall girl pose, and Seward escorted me out of the room.

"Do you see how changeable they are, Mina?" His eyes drooped at the corners. I knew that he wanted me to feel pity for him, but it occurred to me that the girl Jemima was probably in love with him, and that is why she wanted to remain in the institution. I even wondered if something might be going on between them.

"She has been with us for six months." He fumbled through the charts and produced one with her name. He put the others in my hand while he read from hers.

" 'Facts Indicating Insanity: The patient left the family house for three days and nights during which time she claims that she married a railway policeman, though she cannot say where it was or recall his name. She ran away repeatedly to try to return to the policeman, whom the family says does not exist. At home, she displays herself in a window wearing a dressing gown without modesty.'

"The family physician committing her wrote: 'She has lost all mental control in consequence of morbid sensual desires.' She has attempted to escape Lindenwood by shattering windows and has subsequently been restrained."

"Restrained?" I asked, smiling pleasantly, remembering Lucy's letter and Kate's instructions.

"In the most humane manner, I assure you," Seward said. "Would you like to see the restraining instruments?"

"Oh yes!" I said with the enthusiasm of a child who had been offered candy.

Seward led me further down the hall to a mezzanine area, where we turned a corner. With a key, he opened a door, and we entered a room. Light streamed in through the single source of a small arched window. The room smelled of chemicals. He must have heard my little sniff. "It's the ammonia used to clean the leathers. We sterilize them after every use. We are very modern here."

Leather cuffs and straps of many sizes hung in bundles on hooks on the wall. He opened a closet, taking out a heavy linen garment with long sleeves that ended in mitts and a complex system of tie strings that dangled chaotically.

"Whatever is that used for?" I asked.

"We use the jackets in the more difficult cases to prevent the patients from harming themselves and others. In less severe cases, we use them to pacify."

I cocked my head. "Pacify?"

"With male patients, we use them to control violent behavior. But with female patients, we have found that confinement of the arms and hands soothes the nerves. So many things cause ladies to become overexcited. You are such sensitive creatures. Prayer, which settles the male conscience and soothes his soul, has the opposite effect on ladies. We do not know why this is. Reading novels can have the same effect. We call these jackets camisoles because they calm a lady's nerves in the same way that putting on a lovely garment might."

"How does it accomplish that?" I asked, assuming a guileless face. I wished that Kate could be there to see me.

"I will show you," he said. He walked behind me, reaching around and holding the jacket in front of me. I could feel his body, or some kind of kinetic energy, coming from it, though inches separated us. "Hold out your arms."

I reached forward, and he slipped the sleeves over my arms. "It's a bit too large for you," he said. He tugged on the sleeves, pulling me backward so that I rested my back on his chest. He took a deep breath, and I felt his chest expanding against my shoulders. He worked the sleeves all the way up my arms, first one and then the other, until my hands were in the mitts. "There we are," he said. "All snug." He crossed my arms over my chest turning me into a mummy, and for a moment—just a moment—he stopped, wrapping me into his embrace. I shivered. If the garment was meant to settle nerves, it was having the opposite effect on me. I felt a stretch across my shoulders and forearms as he laced the strings hanging from the mitts of the garment behind my back, imprisoning my hands and arms and making me immobile. I thought I might panic, but I fought the urge. He rubbed his hands on my upper arms. "How does that feel?"

Though I was ashamed of the thought, I did not want him to stop touching me through the coarse linen. I was afraid, and yet I did not want the moment to end. I wanted to feel him, but not see him.

"Mina." He said my name softly, letting the sound float past my ear and into the dark, damp room. I faced the wall of restraints, a jungle of buckles and straps.

"I feel helpless," I said. "The more that I know I cannot move, the more I want to move. It's a little frightening."

"There is nothing to be frightened of," he whispered in my ear. "Would I ever let anything happen to you?"

He guided me to a straight-backed chair and sat me down, kneeling in front of me. "Doesn't that make you feel at peace?" he asked, his gray eyes looking up into mine, questioning me. To have said no would have shattered him.

"The goal is to make the patient feel secure," he said. He reached around and tugged at something on the back of the jacket. "Feel these loops?"

His cheek was so close to mine. I had not taken a breath in some time. My throat and lungs seemed to have shut down. Unable to make myself speak, I nodded. He stood, walking over to the wall and returned with a long leather strap.

"If the patient continues to struggle, we attach the strap to the jacket and hook it to the wall. That way we may calm the patient without confining her to a bed. I want you to know how humane our treatments are. No one is hurt in our care."

He took another leather strap off the wall, and then came behind me, and I felt two little tugs at my shoulders as he clipped the straps to the jacket. My arms were going numb inside the garment, but the beating of my heart overrode the feeling. He yanked the straps tight, pulling my back straight against the chair, correcting my already impeccable posture. I had the image of using this contraption on my pupils; they would never complain about the backboards again. He hooked the straps to the wall and came round to look at me and admire his work. I was rigid and completely imprisoned.

"Now that doesn't hurt a bit, does it?" he asked, his voice as smooth as warm butter. "It can't be any worse than a corset. In fact, my theory is that women are accustomed to submitting to the corset, so it predisposes them to the straitjacket."

Still struggling to take more than the shallowest of breaths, I could not quite speak. Nothing was smothering me, or physically hindering my breathing, but the feeling of being helpless overwhelmed me. He could do anything he liked to me, and I would be powerless to stop him.

Seward knelt in front of me again. "You are struggling, Mina, but in reality, you are swaddled like a baby in the safety of its cradle. Struggle heightens the very hysteria we try to cure. Don't struggle, Mina. Submit."

Submit. Where had I heard that command before?

"I—I want to submit, John, but my body wants to struggle."

"It's not the body that is struggling but the mind." He put his finger under my chin. "Relax, Mina. Relax. Let the sound of my voice relax you."

He went back to the wall, returning with two black leather cuffs. "When the jacket is not enough—which is rare—we confine the feet. It helps, as you will see." He knelt, buckling a cuff around each of my ankles, and then hooked them together. He scooped a chain from under the chair and attached it to the buckle that united the cuffs. I could barely move my feet at all.

Seward was on his knees now, staring up at me like a suppliant praying to a saint. He looked at me with the sort of adoration and excitement that he claimed prayer aroused in women. I was afraid, desperate at being denied the use of my hands, arms, feet, legs, but at the same time, I suddenly felt powerful, as if I could demand anything and not be refused.

"How beautiful you are, Mina," he said, his eyes grazing every inch of my face. "How your skin glows. And your eyes, well, they are devastating." He let out a loud sigh and moved closer to me. His eyes were focused on my lips, and I was sure he was about to kiss me. I was afraid of what he would do if I tried to stop him, but I knew that I must.

"Was Lucy confined this way?" I blurted it out on hot, fast breath, and he jumped back as if he had been kicked in the stomach, bending over so that I saw the top of his head, and the funny way that his hair was parted on a diagonal, like an incision across the scalp.

"Lucy." He said her name, looking at me with emotions I could not identify—pride? loss? humiliation? weariness? anger? "No, not like this."

He did not meet my eye but began to unfasten the buckles and ties that bound me. Once loosened, I slipped the jacket off and handed it to him. "Rub your arms to bring back the circulation," he said.

I did as he instructed, and the blood flowed back into my arms.

"I do not think it wise to speak on a subject that will undoubtedly cause pain," he said.

I did not know if he meant to me or to himself.

"She was my dearest friend. I thought that knowing about her final days would help. I need some satisfaction, John, or my grief will go on and on." My eyes began to well up with tears.

He handed me a monogrammed handkerchief, but he did not look at me. "I must finish my morning rounds with the patients. I think it best if you rest before lunch."

Sniffling, I followed him out of the room, where he handed me over to a hall supervisor, who escorted me back to my quarters, where Jonathan was in good spirits after his first examination by Dr. Von Helsinger. "I believe he can help, Mina. I believe he can get to the bottom of what happened to me, and why the experience has left me in this weakened and melancholic condition. He uses the method called hypnosis to lull the patient into a relaxed condition where memories return and are easily related."

"Has he given you any medication?" I asked. "Or any treatments?"

"Nothing of the sort," he replied. "We talk, that is all. Unburdening myself to him leaves me feeling uplifted and more hopeful, though when it is all over, I barely recall what I have said."

I satisfied myself with this offer of hope, remaining confident that I had done the right thing in bringing him to the asylum. At least Von Helsinger did not seem to be harming him.

I sent a note to John Seward asking him again to allow me to volunteer in some way, and he sent a note back suggesting that I might read to the more lucid, calm patients. I was happy with this idea; I thought that if I could be alone with some of the patients, I could question them about Lucy.

. . .

The following morning, Mrs. Snead came to fetch me, and I accompanied her on her rounds to deliver breakfast trays to the patients. The wealthier patients, I had learned, had private rooms, while the others slept in dormitories, "where they fight like dogs, madam, sometimes tearing the hair out of each other's heads. The medicines calm them, though, so most sleep like babes."

I tried to inure myself to the pervasive moans, screams, and shrieks filling the atmosphere, but each loud cry released a fresh burst of pain or anger into the air, rattling my nerves. "Why are they screaming?" I asked.

She looked at me as if I were the crazy one. "Because they are out of their heads, madam. The worst ones are shackled to the beds and they do not like it." Yet Seward declared that he calmed patients without strapping them to their beds. What else was he lying about?

"Do you remember the patient Lucy Westenra?" I asked.

"I do, indeed. The poor thing was as thin as a rail and refused to eat. They did what they could for her, madam. Tended to her day and night. The doctors did it all themselves. No, none of us was good enough to touch Miss Lucy. Broke the young doctor's heart when she passed. The old doctor's too. And the young gentleman who was her husband, all of them sat up with her for so long. Didn't want to give up the body. 'Twere all so sad."

I wanted to ask her more questions, but she was fumbling with her great ring of keys. She found the right one and opened a door, gesturing for me to go into the room where a lone woman sat, face upturned and lips moving, talking into the air. I had seen this lady, Vivienne, playing cards the day before, and something about the way that she had held my gaze with her deep green eyes had intrigued me.

"Mrs. Harker is going to visit you and read to you, Vivienne," Mrs. Snead said. "Be a good girl, now."

"You finished your porridge, I see," I said, looking at the empty bowl on her tray as Mrs. Snead whisked it away. She shut the door, locking it behind us. The openings with bars on them ensured that a cry for help would be heard immediately. Nonetheless, I did not like the sound of the key twisting in the lock. But looking at the elderly lady wrapped in an old shawl with moth holes, I could not see a reason to be afraid.

Vivienne waited until she heard Mrs. Snead's footsteps recede. "I always take every scrap of my meal," she replied. "I must be strong when he comes for me. He is going to take me away." She smiled like a little girl with a secret.

Seward had said that Vivienne had been in the asylum for many years. Was she actually being released? "Who is coming for you?"

She motioned for me to come closer. She whispered. "I am Vivienne."

"Yes, I know. Vivienne is a beautiful name," I said. Something in her voice triggered a memory in me. "You're Irish!" I said. "I am Irish too, but I have lived in England for a long time."

"Irish, you say? Well then, kinswoman, you are familiar with their ways." She sat back, assessing me, a brick of silence.

"Whose 'ways' are you talking about?" I asked.

She retreated from me even more. "Oh no. I know your tricks. They sent you to run him off when he comes."

"No one sent me, Vivienne. I came here to help the patients. I had a friend who was here for a little while. Her name was Lucy. She was very pretty with long golden hair. Did you see her?"

She sat up a little straighter. "Maybe I did," she said. She looked as if she was reaching back in her memory, and my heart began to race, thinking that I might have another witness to Lucy's last days. I patiently told Vivienne a little more about Lucy.

"Was she one of *them?*"

"Who are *they?*" I asked very quietly, trying to look profoundly curious. I thought that if I imitated her secretive tone, she would be more receptive to me.

"Who are they? They are listening to us right now, so we best be careful what we say and do not insult them. They are the Sidhe." She pronounced it *shee.* "They are also called the Gentry. They go by many names when they walk among us."

"I have heard of the Sidhe," I said. It must have existed somewhere latent in my memory because it did sound familiar. "They are the fairies. Is that right?"

She looked at me with disdain. "Yes, the fairies, but not the little sprites and sylphs that live in the forest. The Sidhe are royalty. They are the windborne spirits who can make their bodies as solid as yours or mine if they want to have truck with us. I have been among them. I have seen their *queen*," she said, her voice and body animating with a new energy. "She sits on a throne, surrounded by a fire of shining light, the light from which they all emerge and to which they return to rejuvenate themselves!"

I sat back discouraged. I was not going to get any information about Lucy; I was going to once again be the captive of an elderly person's fanciful stories.

"I think I may have heard these legends when I was a child," I said.

"It is no legend. They are the elder race, child, the original people, the dreamers who dreamt up the world. They formed themselves out of the swirl of life that flows through all things."

With her remarkable eyes that locked tight on mine as she spoke, her long still-beautiful hands that gesticulated with her words, and her singsong Celtic voice, she began to captivate me. Perhaps it was my destiny to be a companion to half-mad elders. "How do you know these things?" I asked.

"It started on midsummer's eve, when I was just a girl of seventeen. I had joined the followers of Áine, the fairy goddess who still walks among us in disguise."

I knew that superstitious women in Ireland still called upon the old goddesses.

"I heard others tell the stories of her power and her magic. Áine can turn herself into whatever form she would like to take—a mare, a dog, a wolf, or a bird. She can help a woman to get with child or make a bad crop grow strong. She is irresistible to men, and has her way with kings and gods alike. If she desires a man, she will turn herself into an animal of prey to make him chase after her, and the hunter soon finds himself in her lair. She mates and bears children, but she tires of men and she abandons them. She once bit off the ear of a king when he tried to overpower her and left him lying in his blood. You can hear her discarded lovers howling in the woods after she has had them and disappeared."

At this, Vivienne cackled, and I thought of Jonathan, wandering the fields of Styria after his affair. I supposed that these old tales were metaphors for what happened when men succumbed to lust.

"Áine's followers imitated her ways, and it was whispered that she gifted some of them with her powers, so I sought to join their circle. Midsummer's eve is her holiest day, the day of the year when the veil that separates the two worlds is thinnest. I slipped out of my bedroom window at the eleventh hour and met my sisters in the woods. They had already lit a fire, and we decorated our hair with roses and began to chant her name, Áine, Áine, Áine. The moon was as pregnant a one as I had ever seen, and the light of it illuminated our young faces. Our skin was shimmering like we were creatures of heaven as we danced around the fire, and our voices sounded like a choir of angels. It is no small wonder we attracted them to us."

Vivienne's eyes radiated with a peculiar light as she spoke. I did not want to interrupt this reverie, which, as with the old whaler, brought the poor aged thing so much pleasure in the telling. "Now remember, the Sidhe can take whatever form suits them, and if they fancy you, they will turn themselves into whatever will seduce you. On that eve, they came to us as men. It was the most remarkable thing. We heard winds rupture upon winds as they broke through the veil. The atmosphere cracked open, letting through beams of light, brighter than the sun. The thunderous noise died down, and we heard their music, tinkling silver bells and celestial harps. Then we saw them riding out of the light, skin shining with the electrical fires of the Great Cosmos.

"So here they were, a small army of them, some marching, some on horse, straight from heaven—tall, stately, magical creatures with luminous hair of gold. They bore the features of mortal men, only more beautiful, more radiant. Some of the sisters passed out cold on the ground, while others screamed as the Sidhe warriors swept alongside them and carried them off on their horses. In spite of all the chaos around us, he and I locked eyes as he rode toward me on his steed, with his flowing hair and red cape and his enormous dog bigger than a wolf at his side."

"What color was his dog?" I asked, ever more drawn into her tale.

"Silver!" she said. "And feral!"

I had to wonder if I had been in the company of one of these creatures at Whitby Abbey.

"Soon he whisked me upon the back of his horse, and he took me to his kingdom. It was just a leap to the other side of the veil, child. I am telling you, no sooner had the horse jumped a fence than we were in a place not of this earth."

"You were in the fairy kingdom?" I asked. "But where is it?"

"It is right here," Vivienne replied, opening her arms out to encompass the space around us. "It exists alongside us, though we cannot see it. If you are ever lying in your bed late at night when all the lights are extinguished, just reach up into the darkness, and a creature from the other side of the veil will take your hand. The Sidhe can break the veil wherever they desire. For mortals, there are access points everywhere. I have seen them, hidden at the bottom of lakes, where so many have drowned trying to find them, or buried deep inside mountain caves."

"Tell me about your captor, Vivienne," I said. As she told her story, it became as vivid in my mind as if I had lived it myself.

"Oh, he was tall and grand, a warrior from an ancient military aristocracy. His mother was a fairy who had mated with a human warrior centuries ago. I loved him and wanted to stay with him forever."

"Even after he kidnapped you and took you away from your home?"

"I had called him forth by the ritual. I went to him willingly, and, even if I had not, he was not to be resisted. Even if it had cost me my life, I would have been happy to sacrifice it."

I wondered what it was that had actually cost Vivienne her sanity. Had she gone mad and then began to fabricate that the fairy prince had kidnapped her? Or had she invented the story, and her growing belief in it had turned her mad?

"What was it that enthralled you so?" I asked.

"They drive mortals mad with pleasure, out of our minds with ecstasy," she said with an asp hiss. "Sometimes, they kill us! Not because they wish to, but because their bodies are fire and electricity, and mortals cannot tolerate it! The Sidhe love all that we love—feasting, fighting, warring, making love, music, and they love to seduce us into these pursuits. Humans go among them and return with their toes danced off, with their bodies drained of their very blood, with their minds a blank. The fairies do love us, but too often we cannot survive their intensity. When we die, they send their banshees to mourn our passing. Their cries fill the vault of heaven and shake the earth!"

"But you did survive," I said.

Leaning ever closer to me and looking around the room, Vivienne whispered, "I had a baby by him, a girl, I think, but I do not know what became of her."

I waited for her to elaborate, wondering if the insane were subject to Kate's method of letting information flow from the discomfort of silence. Vivienne went blank, as if something had wiped clean her mind. Her eyes rolled to the corners like lazy green marbles.

"Vivienne!" The sound of my voice snapped back her attention. "Please finish your story. Why did they take your baby?"

She began to play with her long hair, gathering it to one side and twisting it into a white swirl that hung down her shoulder. She looked like an elderly mermaid, if ever there was such a creature. "I offended the goddess. I was beautiful, and she was jealous. She told my lover to forsake me and she stole my baby away!"

She was quiet for a moment, but something begin to seethe inside her. She raised her arms and began scratching at the air in front of her. "He is right here, right here with me but he won't show himself. His world is all around us, I tell you. It is invisible to our eyes and silent to our ears, but it is right here!"

She looked at me with great desperation, and then grabbed my arms. "You can bring him to me! You must call to him and tell him where I am!" She let me go and paddled at the air, each stroke of her old arms more violent. I stood up, moving away from her. I did not think she could hurt me, but the sight of her was so pitiful. "I know you are here!" She screamed loudly, beating at the thin air with her hands.

Hurried footsteps came toward us. The two hall supervisors rushed in, each taking one of Vivienne's arms. She flailed, trying to get out of their grip. "I want my baby!" she yelled. "What have they done with my baby?"

"You had better leave now, madam," Mrs. Kranz said to me. Her voice was firm. "Shut the door and wait outside."

Vivienne's shawl had fallen off and I could see the old spotted flesh of her arms hanging off the bone. Her head was thrown back and she stared at the ceiling, limp in the arms of the two women, a trickle of tears sliding from the corner of each eye. "Good-bye Vivienne," I said timidly.

Her head snapped forward and she looked straight at me, fixing her eerie green stare upon me. "They will come for you and they will know you by your eyes."

Chapter Twelve

he next day, afraid that my encounter with Vivienne had upset me, John Seward called me to his office. I did not want to see him, but I did not know how I could refuse.

When I walked into the room, his eyes swiftly grazed my body, nibbling at every little detail, and then met mine with his signature look of concern. I told him everything that had happened with Vivienne, which he listened to with great focus and patience. "What I do not understand, Mina, is why the experience was so upsetting to you."

I had not said that it was upsetting, but apparently it was obvious in my demeanor and my voice. "I am a doctor, Mina, a doctor and a friend. Surely you know that you can tell me anything."

Seduced by the care in his voice, I found myself telling him bits of my own history—that when I was a child, I spoke to invisible people, to animals, and sometimes heard voices, and that my behavior had upset my parents.

"I still have strange dreams, John, dreams that I am an animal of sorts, and these dreams make me get out of bed and wander in my sleep. After these episodes, I sometimes imagine things, lingering images from my dreams. Sometimes I think I am being followed. It worries me. After

Vivienne's outburst, I started to wonder if I was glimpsing myself at her age."

He listened very carefully to what I had to say. Then he smiled at me as if I were a child confessing some petty crime that her father found endearing. "Dear, impressionable Mina, I did warn you that visiting the patients would be upsetting."

"I only wanted to help," I lied. I could not confess that my true motive had been to discover more about Lucy's death.

"The very idea that you might have anything in common with Vivienne! Let me set your mind at ease. Vivienne is what is known as an erotopath, a sexually preoccupied woman who becomes obsessed with one man, in this case, the lover who she recast in her imagination as the fairy prince." He grinned at me, waiting for me to smile back. "The erotopath generally becomes an annoying menace to the man, and he rejects her. The rejection drives the woman to nymphomania, which is a disorder in women who have abnormal sexual desires. It is a serious type of uterine hysteria. Do you see how drastically different that is from your innocent childhood fantasies and your dreams?"

I nodded, unable to admit that some of my dreams were not so innocent.

"Vivienne's family committed her because she had been randomly seducing men, causing them no end of shame, and eventually she had a child out of wedlock. To exonerate herself, she insisted that the father was a supernatural being."

"You must admit, she spins a good yarn," I said.

"The typical hysteric develops elaborate, far-fetched romantic histories for herself. Vivienne is not even her real name. Her name is Winifred," he said. He opened a tall cabinet, lifting a file and glancing at it. "Winifred Collins. Born 1818." He showed me the name and date before returning the file to the cabinet. "She identifies herself with Vivienne, the mythical sorceress who enchanted the sorcerer Merlin." Seward smiled wistfully. "A tale to interest a boy once enthralled by Arthurian legend but not much for a head doctor to go on."

"Poor old dear," I said.

"Vivienne is fortunate. Her family set up a trust for her care. Many girls like her are thrown out with their babies and have to earn a living on the streets."

"I am sorry to have disturbed a patient," I said. "That was not my intent."

"It was not your fault. The nymphomaniac loves to give vent to passion. I once saw a girl let rats eat her fingers, thinking that her lover was covering them with kisses. Some girls hurt themselves, lacerating their bodies and claiming they don't feel a thing. It's a sort of penance for what they have done."

"Penance?"

"Why, yes, they feel tremendous guilt over their promiscuity. Not all women are as noble and as good as you, Mina."

Crimson color spread across his cheeks. His eyes softened and his brisk professionalism disappeared, wiped away by something else, something tender. I knew that in that moment of vulnerability, I could extract the information I sought.

"John." I said his name softly, as if it were itself a question that must be answered. "We must talk about Lucy."

For what seemed an interminable amount of time, Seward said nothing, but studied my face. Though I remembered Kate's advice, I still felt compelled to explain myself. "I received a letter from her, written after I had left Whitby. She was excited about her engagement. Not six weeks later she was dead."

He sat in his chair and cupped his forehead in his hands, shaking his head back and forth as if the memory anguished him. This time, I let silence reign. Finally, he spoke. "There is no polite way to phrase it. Lucy suffered from erotomania—her obsession with Morris Quince. Quince's rejection drove her to hysteria, after which she could not be convinced of Arthur's love for her. Once she got it into her head that he had married her for her fortune, she had a complete breakdown. At the very the end, she was not so different from poor Vivienne."

"It's hard to believe that of our Lucy," I said. Yet I had seen the tendencies when I was in Whitby. Loving Morris Quince had made her seem mad and act as a madwoman acts; I had told her so myself.

"Lucy had all the causes that make females prone to hysteria: preoccupation with romance, high spirits, irregular menstruation, a delicate mother. She was also capricious and had abnormally strong sexual desires." He gestured toward his bookcases. "The symptoms are well documented."

"But hysteria is surely not fatal," I said. "Vivienne must be upward of seventy years of age."

"Lucy starved herself to death," he said. "Believe me, we tried every treatment. We tried to feed her through the tubes, but she regurgitated. We tried the water cure, which generally settles even the most extreme hysteric, but it only made Lucy worse. When she was on the brink of death, Dr. Von Helsinger even tried to give her blood transfusions to strengthen her."

"I must admit that when I apply your explanation of the disease to some of her behavior, she did fit the pattern." I was trying to make sense of it all and I wanted him to keep talking.

"Mina, I do believe you have the mind of a doctor." He beamed at me, and I hated myself for always needing to be the teacher's pet. Encouraged by my assimilation of his subject, he continued: "Consider how snugly Lucy fit the mold of the hysteric. Do you know what is their most ubiquitous symptom? They are cunning, the shrewdest liars known to man. Lucy carried on her affair with Morris by lying profusely to everyone, even you, her dearest friend."

"It is all true," I said. Hadn't she always been that way? The little girl who could fib her way out of every situation?

"I thought that the transfusions would regulate the menstrual cycle, which might have cured her. I am so sorry I couldn't save her."

Seward's eyes welled with tears. His face turned red, and he blinked, releasing a huge teardrop. "This is very unprofessional, Mina. I do apologize."

"Nonsense, John. We all loved her."

We sat for a long time in silence. Obedient to Kate's instruction, I did not speak, though the indescribable look of longing on his face disturbed me. "I thought I loved Lucy," he said. He walked around the desk and pulled a chair up next to me. "I thought that the fleeting attraction I had for Lucy might be love until I met a woman of such depth and beauty as to overwhelm me, mind and senses."

I waited, hoping against hope that he would reveal the name of someone with whom I was not acquainted.

"Have you not heard the deafening pounding of my heart when you are near? Please come to me, Mina, be with me. Your husband is an adulterer. The marriage remains unconsummated and is therefore not yet a legitimate marriage." He spoke quietly but firmly in contrast to his ardor of moments ago. "Moreover, you married him under duress."

"Did Jonathan tell you all this?"

"No, but Dr. Von Helsinger and I consult with each other about our patients."

Humiliation flushed and burned my face and neck. I wanted to contradict him, to prove him wrong, to produce some evidence of Jonathan's love for me. "My husband has been ill since our wedding. I brought him here so that you could help him. Doctor, have you forgotten your purpose?"

"Yes!" He threw his hands in the air. He pushed his chair aside, falling to his knees and grabbing a fistful of my skirt. "Yes, I have forgotten it. My love for you has wiped everything else out of my mind." He rested his head on my thigh, his hot cheek making its impression through my skirt. "I just want to stay here forever."

"Well, you mustn't," I said. "Please control yourself!"

He sighed, lifting himself up and sitting on the desk so that he was looking down at me. He straightened his shirt. "I know that what I am doing is outrageous, but I cannot apologize. Jonathan will never be the sort of husband you deserve."

"Is this what you and Dr. Von Helsinger have concluded?"

"No, but we have discussed the matter. Von Helsinger wants me to listen to his notes on the case, but I have not yet had the opportunity." He gestured toward the cylinders on a shelf next to the phonograph, neatly lined up and labeled.

"No man is perfect. I am trying to forgive him. Jonathan was not in his right mind when he was seduced in Styria."

"Do not be naïve. Men always like to imagine that they are helpless when in the thrall of a beautiful lover."

I lowered my head.

"I have upset you, when my fondest wish is for your happiness," he said. "No one will blame you for forsaking a man who has already forsaken you. I, on the other hand, would treasure you until one of us breathes the last."

I was so shaken that I thought it better to be silent.

"You are not running from me in horror, which I regard as a hopeful sign," he said. He took my hand again. "Come to me any time of day or night. I will inform the staff that we are working together, and that you are to have complete access to me. We will empty our minds to each other, and I will soon convince you that we are meant to be together."

I knew that I should chastise him for insulting a married woman, but here were more questions to be answered, and I believed that those answers could be found inside Seward's office. "You have stunned me, John," I said. "I must go collect myself." And I left the room.

. . .

That night I had a horrific dream. It began well enough, as they usually did. I was rolling on wet grass, letting it tickle me blade by blade, my limbs stretched out in ecstasy as I reached out into the night air—light, fresh, and skimming the surface of my body like gentle fingertips. Suddenly, I was jerked upward and imprisoned in arms that were foreign and mean. Angry arms. The lovely aromas on which I had been feasting disappeared, and I was thrown onto something hard, a floor perhaps. I was too frightened to open my eyes. I felt a lash across my back and I howled. Then came another slap, and I curled up like a snail to try to protect myself. A voice screamed at me: *Devil's imp, Satan's girl. Tell me the truth! Who are you, and what have you done with my daughter?* I started to suffocate, gasping for air, trying to reach out for help.

The next thing I knew, I was sitting up in bed, shivering and choking. I did not know where I was at first, but my eyes adjusted and I took in the environs of the room at the asylum with its canopy above and its dark panels of drapes enveloping the bed. I found that I could at last breathe and let out a heavy sigh. Jonathan lay beside me, holding a pillow against his body like a shield.

"You were screaming in your sleep," he said.

"What was I saying?"

He pulled farther away from me, clutching the pillow even tighter. "You were denying that you were the devil's child."

"You look frightened of me, Jonathan!" I said. "I am the one who has had the bad dream and needs comfort."

He tossed the pillow aside and put his arm around me. "Poor Mina. I am not frightened of *you*, but I am living with many fears. I have seen things and done things that must be expurgated from my psyche. That is what the doctor says. Then and only then will my soul be cleansed."

The next day Jonathan informed me that Dr. Von Helsinger thought it best if he slept in a separate room. "Only for a little while, Mina," he assured me. "I will soon be better." I wondered if this was part of a scheme between Seward and Von Helsinger to separate me from my husband. Would Seward have confessed his affections to Von Helsinger? I decided that it was time to talk to him myself. I sent him a note and waited for a reply, but received none. I had a queasy feeling in my stomach and could not look at my breakfast. As the morning wore on, I felt more and more agitated.

Since Seward had told his staff that I was to be given free access in the asylum, I no longer needed permission to walk the halls. One of the staff directed me to Von Helsinger's study, which hummed with the bass of male voices. I assumed that one of those was my husband's and I rapped lightly on the door before opening it.

To my great surprise, Arthur Holmwood—Lord Godalming— was pacing the room while Seward, Von Helsinger, and Jonathan sat in big leather chairs. Von Helsinger's pipe was clamped between his yellowing teeth, filling the air with a spicy aroma of nutmeg and cinnamon. Arthur's overcoat sat in a rumpled heap on the floor where presumably he had thrown it. His hat lay atop it on its side so that I could see the label of the expensive London hatter. He was pale as sand, and his blond hair was stringy. The men were startled to see me and rose out of their seats.

"Lord Godalming," I said, "what a surprise. What brings you here?" No one spoke, and I wondered if I my question had been a rude one. After all, Godalming was Seward's dearest friend. Arthur started to speak, when Seward shot him a warning look. But Arthur was in no condition to be contained.

"It's Lucy," he said, looking at me with mad eyes. "She is not dead."

"Now, Arthur," Seward said, "you don't want to upset Mrs. Harker." To me he said, "Perhaps you should let us handle this."

I was not about to leave. I walked further into the room and took a seat.

"What do you mean, Lucy is not dead?" I asked.

"She is not dead," he insisted. "I have seen her with my own eyes!"

Those eyes at this moment were bloodshot. He looked as if he had not slept or changed his clothes in days. Von Helsinger's pipe smoke was probably saving us from the smell of Arthur's rank-looking shirt.

"At first, she only came to me in my dreams," he said to me. The men were silent. "She was bloodied and horrible, in some unnatural state between life and death. She would not speak, but she stared at me as if she hated me, just as she did sometimes in the last days, when she was so ill. It got so that I was terrified to go to sleep at night, but I consoled myself with the fact that these were mere dreams. 'Holmwood, get hold of yourself,' I'd say. I restored my grip on reality, and for one night I did not see her, and I slept with ease. But for the past three nights, she has come to me again, staring at me in anger as blood drips from her eyes and her mouth, and gushes from her arms.

"Then, this morning, I awakened, safe in my bed. I rubbed my eyes, feeling relief that I had been dreaming. I took in a deep breath and sighed, but when I took my hands away from my eyes, she was standing at the foot of the bed, bloody, just as she was in the dream. She held her arms out to me. 'I want your blood, Arthur,' she said, hissing like the most toxic asp, her tongue long and ugly. She said, 'Do you not love your Lucy? Do you not want to give me more of your blood?'"

He turned his head away, looking into the fire, burning in the grate.

"Then what happened?" I was completely caught up in his story.

He did not look up. He spoke quietly. "I shut my eyes and screamed, and when I opened them again, she was gone."

Seward was staring at me with such intent that I wondered if my husband was going to notice. But Jonathan clutched the arms of his chair, his face whiter than Arthur's, his forehead pinched so tight that his eyebrows could not be distinguished from the furrows.

"Does Mrs. Harker need to be subjected to this, Arthur?" Seward asked.

Lord Godalming ignored his friend. He picked up two pieces of newspaper, waving them at me. "Lucy is alive, I tell you. I saw her, and so have others."

I scanned the two articles that described a "Bloofer Lady," who was luring the children of Hampstead away from their playgrounds, returning them hours later or the next day, with wounds at the neck and throat.

"The newspapers print fright stories like this every year as All Hallows Eve approaches merely to sell papers," I said. "This is naught to do with Lucy."

Lord Godalming turned to Von Helsinger as if he were about to spring on him. "You just said, before Mina came into the room, that there are women with unnatural powers over men and that they thrive on drinking blood! I believe that you turned Lucy into one of them with your strange treatments!"

Von Helsinger showed no reaction. Seward stood, putting his arm around his friend.

"Arthur, you must get hold of yourself," Seward said. "With all due respect to my colleague, I believe that you have been having nightmares, which would be a natural response to the death of your wife. I can help you to analyze these dreams and settle your mind, but you must calm down."

My husband interrupted. "I think we must excuse my wife."

"As I have already suggested," said Seward in his doctor's voice. Seward offered his hand to me to help me out of the chair. To his colleague, he said, "Ring the bell, please."

I did not take his proffered hand. Remaining in my seat, I said, "I will not be excluded. Lucy was my dearest friend."

"That is why you must leave, Mrs. Harker," Seward said. "All this talk of her, bloody and rising from the dead, is too upsetting."

"I am not upset," I insisted.

"Mina, let the men handle this." Jonathan was animated now, his eyes bright, the lines of worry in his face smoothed over.

Von Helsinger reached under his desk, tapping something with his foot, which created a loud buzz. A few seconds later, Mrs. Snead arrived. "Escort Mrs. Harker to wherever she would like to go," Seward said. He offered his hand again, and this time I took it. As I was leaving with Mrs. Snead, he mouthed the words, *Come to me*.

In the evening, 22 October 1890

At suppertime, Mrs. Snead brought me a tray of food with a note from Jonathan that I should dine alone in the room. Later still, he came to the room to change into heavy clothing.

"Where are you going?" I asked.

"I will tell you about it when I return," he said.

I questioned him about what had transpired after I had left Von Helsinger's office, but he would say no more, only that he was going somewhere with the men.

I had no idea how long they would be gone, but I wasted no time in asking Mrs. Snead to let me into Seward's office. "I want to make use of his medical library while he is gone. That way I can look through the volumes without disturbing him."

She let me into the office and lit the lamps before warily closing the door. Worried that she might reenter the room, I pulled a fat volume off the wall and opened it on the desk in front of me so that I might pretend to be reading.

Fortunately, I had convinced Headmistress a year before to purchase a phonograph to utilize in teaching elocution, for there was no better way to rid a girl of her coarse accent than to let her hear how she sounded to others. I looked through the cylinders on his shelf until I found the two that were labeled with my husband's name. I reached for the first and removed its cardboard cover, afraid of what it was going to reveal.

The cylinder was new, its waxy surface still nubby, whereas for economy's sake, Headmistress insisted that I use the same one over and over until its surface was smooth. I placed it in the machine and turned it on, praying that no one would hear. I supposed that I could tell Mrs. Snead that I had permission to listen to the doctors' recordings and face the consequences if she reported me to Seward.

Sitting at the desk, I poised my diary inside the larger volume so that I could take notes. Coughing to clear his throat, Von Helsinger began to speak. "Jonathan Harker, twenty-eight years of age. The patient suffered a severe case of brain fever in which he experienced erotic hallucinations and loss of memory. He was hospitalized and treated, with an extended period of rest in the town of Exeter. Symptoms of neurasthenia, melancholia, and listlessness persist. Upon occasion, he also exhibits paranoia, believing that women, in particular his wife, are in league with the devil. Reasons for this assumption will become clear."

My pen dropped from my hand, blotting ink on the few words I had already written. Von Helsinger's voice continued. "Harker claims that while in Styria, the niece of the Austrian count for whom he was conducting real estate transactions, seduced him. He describes the girl as more beautiful than the paintings of Mr. Rosetti, with flowing hair of gold and a naturally red, sensuous mouth. Harker engaged in sexual relations with her, and, in turn, with her and two other women, both described as raven-haired beauties with mesmerizing eyes, red lips, and glittering white skin. All three of the women were irresistible and exotic, and in his words, 'not pure like our English beauties.' The women performed what he called 'unspeakable and unholy acts,' exciting his 'most base instincts and desires.' He was unable to resist them and, in fact, searched them out in the Count's castle whenever they left him alone. After two weeks, he was no longer able to keep track of time. All three women were practiced in the arts of intercourse and fellation, which the patient had never experienced. Because of this, he awarded to these females magical powers.

"Even under hypnosis, he has had difficulty talking about aspects of the experience, so I asked him to write them down. Here is an excerpt of what he wrote:

Ursulina invited me to ride with her one morning. Never have I seen a person, male or female, gallop across difficult terrain with such reckless abandon. Her dazzling blond tresses danced in rhythm with the steed's long white tail as she galloped across the valley ahead of me; it was as if she were the goddess of dawn riding Pegasus. After exhausting me in the outdoors, she enchanted me in the castle by engaging my senses with feasting and music and dancing, and lulling me with wine, all the while slowly removing her clothing and mine, one agonizing piece at a time. Then she showed me the very meaning of pleasure with her hands, her lips, her mouth, and even her teeth. When she had me in her thrall, and when I was at my most vulnerable, she invited two of her demon sisters to join us. These creatures weaken a man's feeble will against temptation, thrilling him with every bliss-making act. Oh, they have secrets, sir, undreamt of secrets to bring a man to a state of incomprehensible enjoyment.

"Harker continues to have vivid dreams about the women, especially the one named Ursulina. He cannot release her from his mind, imagining that it is the girl herself who comes to him in his dreams and makes love to him. I proposed that nocturnal emission was a common experience for the male, but he insists that his experience is different. 'It is not an ordinary dream, doctor,' he says. 'It is as if she is possessing me.' He believes that he acted immorally by succumbing to the women, but he admits that at times, he has had to restrain himself from returning to Styria to look for them. Over this, he feels tremendous guilt."

Von Helsinger paused, breathing laboriously. I heard him shuffling papers and striking a match, presumably to reignite his pipe. My mind raced. How was I to compete with these seductresses of unearthly beauty and sexual prowess? I, who had kept myself pure so that I might marry a respectable man and, in turn, have his respect? Oh, the irony of having lost that man to degenerate women.

After a few little sucking noises and a deep exhalation, the doctor continued. "I had originally believed that Harker's sexual naïveté caused him to attribute supernatural elements to an orgiastic encounter. However, what he subsequently revealed leads me to ruminate on a different and more dramatic conclusion. He claims that at the height of ecstasy, which he described as a dark place where pleasure and pain cannot be distinguished, the women took turns breaking his flesh with their nails and teeth and extracting blood.

"I ask myself, is it possible that young Harker was in fact seduced by she demons? Without the factor of the blood taking, it would be presumed that the women were mere harlots, who can also drain the vital forces from a man and leave him in the confused and fevered state Harker describes. But if the blood taking is interpreted literally and not as a hallucination, it is possible that these were vampire women, the unnatural creatures of myth who achieve extended or eternal life by drinking the blood of others.

"I have long heard tales of bloodsucking female creatures and of the incubi who harbor them, in this case, the Austrian count. One of the symptoms of having being bitten by them is the craving it creates for reoccurrence, such as Harker describes. The brilliant minds of the ancient world wrote of these blood drinkers, trying to grapple with their powers. Men like Aristotle and Apuleius, and the historians Diodorus Siculus and Pausanias, wrote of their magic and mystery and the horror they wreaked upon mankind by the seduction of the innocent. They have gone by many names: lamia, witch, demon, succubus or incubus, sorcerer or sorceress. Lilith, the first wife of Adam, was one such fiend. Some believe that these creatures are descended from those who mated with the gods and Titans, creating a terrible hybrid that is neither human nor divine. Some say there exist those who were born mortal and made themselves immortal by taking the blood and vitality of other humans. These are the so-called undead.

"The writer who visits John Seward is full of such tales from the darker regions of Moldavia, Walachia, and the Kingdom of Hungary, places I have never been. He presents a good case for their existence. 'There can be no great smoke arise be there no fire, Dr. Von Helsinger,' he says. He is intrigued by my experiments with blood and in blood's mysterious powers as research for some horrific work of fiction he has in mind. I introduced him to Goethe's poem "The Bride of Corinth," about a female vampire, and to the "Vampirismus" of Hoffmann, for which he was most grateful. He has also gathered stories about the vampire from a compendium of medieval sources and folktales: the vampire lives on the blood of others, which he takes by night; he must sleep in a coffin filled with his native soil; he is active from dusk to just before dawn but sleeps during daylight hours; he is repelled by garlic and Christian symbols such as the Host, holy water, and the cross; he can be killed by a silver bullet or by a stake through the heart and decapitation; and he is able to assume the shape of certain animals with which his species identifies, such as wolves and bats. Fanciful and horrific stuff, most of which I have heard from folktales. But I have found that in researching the metaphysical, it is important to rekindle that part of the brain's imagination that one left behind in the nursery.

"Is it possible that these fiends or their hybrids, who have fascinated and occupied minds greater than mine, have always existed—biological misfits who have no link on Darwin's evolutionary chain? If so, I am curious to see if the males and females share the engendered traits in their human counterparts. If Harker was not hallucinating, and he was indeed seduced by supernatural women, whose behavior mirrors wanton human females, then the aforementioned hypothesis is correct.

"In conclusion, when I first began with Harker, I did not dream that his infirmity would reveal the exchange of blood as its possible source. What luck! Thus my lifelong devotion to delineating the essential elements and mysteries of blood is validated once more. One thing is certain: the blood is the life. Its qualities hold the secrets of life and death, of mortality and immortality. Did the ancients not offer human blood to the gods? Did they possess the knowledge that human blood somehow enhanced divine powers? It seems a contradiction, yes. But science is full of paradoxes.

"As for Harker, he is a male and strong, and the loss of blood seems to have been minimal. He does not require a transfusion. With time, he will fully recover. However, he is impotent with regard to his wife. I prescribed a series of visits to a brothel. As a customer paying for the services, he will be restored to the natural position of power over the female and his potency will return."

. . .

The phonograph stopped playing, and Von Helsinger's rough voice gave way to the ghostly moans of the institution wafting into the room. I put down the pen, letting the blood flow back into my hand after my furious scribbling, but Von Helsinger's words hit me like blows to the body. I had stopped breathing and now took a deep intake of air, hoping it would clear my head. What was this man doing advising his already adulterous patient to go to prostitutes? I could not decide what was more insane—that remedy for his ailment or the idea that he had been attacked by supernatural creatures, an idea encouraged by that redheaded menace who had stumbled into my life in Whitby. And even more baffling, Jonathan seemed to be living out the same erotic, blood-drinking experience that I had in my dream. Why were both of us being haunted?

I bent over, resting my head on my knees, hoping that I would not black out. Suddenly, I heard the door creak open, sending a fresh shiver up my spine. I looked up. Mrs. Snead was looking at me suspiciously. I sat up, blood rushing to my head. It took me a moment to speak. "Oh, I must have dozed off," I said.

Her strange, sideways glance was blank. She cast her eyes downward at the notes in my journal. "Are you done here, madam?" she asked. "I cannot leave my duty unless I lock up behind you."

The second cylinder sat untouched on the shelf. "Would it inconvenience you terribly if I stayed another thirty minutes?" I asked.

She agreed to return later and begrudgingly left the room, closing the door behind her. I waited for several interminable minutes before gathering the courage to reach for the cylinder. I slowly substituted it for the other, trying not to make one incriminating sound. I started the machine and reached for my pen. Von Helsinger cleared his throat and began speaking.

"We must remain skeptical of Harker's claims while entertaining the possibility that they are true, at least to a degree. The reality that he encountered vampire women is remote, but he might have fallen into a coven of self-proclaimed witches who take men's blood to use in magical spells. It would behoove me as a metaphysician and a man of science to travel to Styria and investigate the matter. Perhaps I shall do so in the spring. It would be interesting to see how the harpies, whether mortal or not, would react to a transfusion of male blood, if I could find a way to do such a thing. Perhaps young Harker might help with this. At the very least, I would like to procure samples of their blood to study.

"In the meanwhile, I am committed to remain God's warrior on a crusade to obliterate the evil brought upon the female by the sin of Eve. God created woman to be pure and naïve, but the sinners Lilith and Eve were not satisfied with His will and tainted their sex. If God had wanted woman to have knowledge, would He have forbidden her to pick from the tree? Yet today's woman would transform Europe into the new Gomorrah with her demands to turn nature upside down.

"I admire the work of Sir Francis Galton, but I do not believe that his theory of eugenics will have any impact. We will never be able to prevent the inferior classes from breeding. More realistic is to create a female that is a better breeding machine able to produce superior progeny. Once the transfusions are perfected, the female recipient will genetically assimilate the higher traits of the male—strength, courage, moral rectitude, rational thinking, even superior physical strength and health—and will thereby bring a healthier biological profile to the mating process. I believe that in the future, we will not only improve the quality of the female through the transference of superior male blood but also may create an überbeing, or even an immortal being—not the fiends of Harker's description but a noble, godlike creature.

"The transfusions must be perfected! Why some patients react to the transfused blood with high fever and shock I do not know. The young wife of Lord Godalming, a woman even more duplicitous than most, may have had blood that was inordinately female, which reacted badly to its opposite, that of strong and virile males. In the coming days, we will observe the effects of the infused blood on the other inmates. I predict that we will see miraculous improvements in the behavior of some of these hysterics.

"I hold to my theory that blood transference is the key to expedited human evolution. The female, strengthened by male blood, will be relieved of her biological and moral weaknesses, and from the union of two superior beings will come a race of supermen with the highest and purest of human qualities and the most desirable genetic characteristics."

Chapter Thirteen

With trembling fingers, I placed the cylinder back on the shelf. A few months ago, I could have blithely written Von Helsinger off as an eccentric, a mad scientist in a horror story, a Frankenstein who wished to compete with God as a creator. But too many strange things had happened in recent times. Any rules by which I could deem someone either mad or sane no longer applied.

Jonathan's experience with the women in Styria reminded me of some of the things that Vivienne had described. Yet Von Helsinger had not leapt to the conclusion that Jonathan was mad. Suddenly, I wanted to see her, to see if her stories held any further clues to these mysteries. But I had no idea if I could convince Mrs. Snead to give me access to a patient at this late hour.

I neatly packed up the volume I had opened and went to put it back on the shelf, but out of nowhere, thunder exploded in the sky, and I dropped the book on the floor. It fell upon the broad plank with an echoing thud. I stooped to pick it up, but the clock chimed half past the hour, and the noise made me drop it again. Frustrated, I fell to the floor and clutched the leather volume to my chest, which was how Mrs. Snead found me.

"Madam?" She came toward me, leaning over me. "Are you well?"

"I dropped a book, that is all. Mrs. Snead, I would like to see the patient Vivienne, the older woman with the long white hair," I said.

Mrs. Snead took a step away from me as if I had frightened her.

"I realize that the hour is late, but didn't Dr. Seward tell you to afford me access to what—"

"Madam, I am afraid you don't understand. It will always be too late to speak to that poor soul now. Vivienne is dead. She died earlier today."

"That is not possible!" I knew that by my reaction, I must have sounded mad, but the news stunned me. I had just visited with Vivienne, and though she was crazy, she was not physically ill.

Mrs. Snead stared just to the left of my cheek, as if she were addressing an invisible sprite on my shoulder. "She's dead, all right, poor old soul. She went into paroxysms this afternoon, shivering with fevers and chills and the like. I called the doctor out of his meeting with the older doctor and Lord Godalming and Mr. Harker. It was after you left the room, madam. By the time Dr. Seward arrived, she were gone. I believe he said it were a stroke, madam. 'She's out of her misery now, isn't she, Mrs. Snead?' That is what the doctor said. He was very sad."

This unexpected culmination to the day's bizarre events shattered my already fragile state of mind, and I started to cry. "Please tell me that you are lying, Mrs. Snead."

"Madam, I ain't lying. You can see the body if you like." She offered this with the ease with which she would offer a cup of tea. "'Twon't be carted off till morning. We use the cellar as the morgue."

I followed Mrs. Snead downstairs and outside to the rear of the house. A slanted rain struck us as I waited for her to disentangle the cellar key from her bulky ring. She opened the door, and we stepped into the wet, moldering air of a low-ceilinged brick room. A single torch cast light on a cot, covered with an old, graying sheet. Vivienne's long white hair fell over the side of the cot, hanging almost to the floor, like some lengthy dust ball that had gathered over the years.

We walked closer, and I noticed that the room was used as a wine cellar, walls lined with diamond-shaped wooden bins, many of which were filled with bottles—an odd juxtaposition to the lifeless body on the cot. Mrs. Snead approached the body, and I followed her, unsure why I had come. Without asking me, she pulled back the sheet, revealing Vivienne's face and chest. She looked as if she were asleep. Her eyes were closed, and the torchlight cast a warm glow on her face, making her seem lifelike and not pale like the dead. She wore a loose, unbuttoned night-dress, and I noticed a tiny drop of blood marring the sleeve. I did not want to ask Mrs. Snead's permission to lift the sleeve, nor did I think it proper to begin to undress the dead. Bracing myself, I took Vivienne's cold, stiff hand. Closing my eyes, I began to pray. "Our Father, Who art in Heaven, hallowed be Thy name." I opened my eyes slightly. Mrs. Snead's hands were in the prayer position at her chest and her eyes were shut tight. "Thy kingdom come, Thy will be done . . ." I continued to pray, eyes open, sliding Vivienne's sleeve higher up her arm until I saw what I suspected I'd see: a fresh wound at the inner elbow covered with a patch of blood-soaked gauze.

. . .

Jonathan returned to our room at midnight, his clothes and hair drenched, and carrying an indescribable scent—dirt, decay, and other odors I could not identify. He took off his coat and boots and dried his hair with a towel, rubbing furiously as if he was trying to scrub off his scalp. After a few moments of this, he dropped the towel, fell to his knees, and started pounding the floor.

"It's wrong, all wrong!" he cried. When he lifted his face, his cheeks were wet and his eyes wild. He started tearing off his clothes. "I have to get rid of these things," he said. "They carry the scent of death, Mina. I have seen it and smelled it."

He ripped off his shirt, tearing off a few of the buttons, which flew through the air and landed on the floor. His suspenders slid from his broad shoulders, and he fumbled wildly with the inlay of buttons beneath the flap of his pants. When he finished, they shimmied to the ground and he stepped out of them. He started to take off his underclothes when I realized that I had yet to see my husband naked.

I went to the wardrobe and opened it. "Would you like your sleeping shirt or your night suit?" When he was ill, he had favored woolen men's pajamas as advised by the doctors.

"Nightshirt," he said quietly.

I heard him stripping off his flannels as I removed the nightshirt from the drawer. When I turned around, he was naked but for his socks and garters, and I saw for the first time his lean physique, the triangle of nut-brown hair on his chest, his slim pelvis, and his penis, which jutted straight out from a thicket of dark pubic hair. An unexpected surge of desire shot through my body, and I cast my eyes downward in embarrassment, but they rested on his long thighs, and I felt the thrill of arousal once more. I had been trying to ignore how much I longed for him to touch me, but my reaction to seeing his body left me unable to deny it. Quickly, without meeting his eyes, I went to him with the nightshirt open at the neck, my hands inside it, ready to slip it over his head. He leaned forward, allowing me to do that, and then tucked his arms into the sleeves.

"I am going to put these clothes in the hall so that the laundress will pick them up at dawn," I said, bundling up the wet mass and holding my breath against the rank odor. I put the clothes outside the door and closed it behind me. When I turned around, Jonathan grabbed me into his arms. "I love you, Mina," he said.

Before I could respond, his lips were on mine and his tongue was inside my mouth, searing it with heat, probing, searching for something, some answer that I was not sure I could provide. He backed off a little but held me tight against him. "How sweet you taste, and how pure you are." He picked me up and carried me to the bed, laying me on the velvet duvet. He gathered my hair in his hand. "The first time I saw you, I knew that if my hand ever got hold of this thick black hair I would lose all control."

I was titillated by his words, but I had no experience with men's loss of control. The stranger who made love to me in my dreams was the one in control.

"You don't know how much I want to make love to you, Mina. Do you want me?"

"I do, Jonathan," I said. "I have longed for this."

"Let me see you. Let me see what you look like."

I pulled my nightdress up slowly, revealing my legs. "Go on," he said. His face was expressionless. I squirmed a little so that I could raise the gown even more, pulling it up to my neck, exposing everything. I could not tell by the look on his face whether he was pleased with me or not. His eyes scanned me as if he were taking inventory. "Beautiful," he said. "I knew that your skin would be finer than silk." He saw the heart with the key that he had given me before he had left for Styria and he touched it gently with his finger. "You still wear it? Even after what I did?"

"I have never taken if off," I said.

His finger snaked its way down my body to graze the wine-stained birthmark on my thigh. "But what is this?"

"It has always been there," I said.

"It has wings, like a butterfly," he said, tracing its outline. His trembling finger scoped the entire perimeter and then slid across my thigh. He put his hand over my sex and caressed it very gently, stirring me inside. He closed his eyes and slipped a finger into me. I felt him shiver. "Warm, so warm," he said. "Living flesh."

He opened his eyes and looked at me. "You have no idea what to do, do you?"

"What do you mean?" I asked. I assumed that my husband should kiss me and touch me. That his lips would linger on my neck and other tender places, and that he would put an erect organ inside me. I expected it to hurt. Was I supposed to be more knowledgeable than that?

"Nothing, dear Mina. You are innocent. Thank God you are innocent."

He gave me a weird little grin, and then he lay on top of me. He pulled up his nightshirt so that our skin connected and he kissed me again, slower and deeper and with less urgency than before. I started to melt into his kisses, pressing against his long, muscled frame, and spreading my legs. He took his hard penis in his hand and rubbed it against my opening a few times before slowly sliding it in. Unlike his finger, his organ felt as if it were scorching my flesh. I cried out, but he did not stop.

"Does it hurt, Mina?" he asked. "Tell me the truth."

"Yes, yes, it hurts," I said.

"If you are the right sort of woman, it is supposed to hurt," he said. "I'm sorry. I hate that I have to hurt you, but it makes me love you even more."

It does not hurt in my dreams, I wanted to say, but this was not a dream, and I knew from common gossip that the first time always hurt.

"I'm going to do it now, Mina," he whispered into my ear. "Try to relax." He thrust himself deeper into me, making the pain worse, so much that I thought we were doing something wrong. I found myself appalled at having to endure it. I pushed him away from me.

"Don't push me away. Prove that you love me. I don't want to hurt you, but I have to, at least at first," he said. He looked more desperate than aroused, his sorrow at causing me pain obliterating any excitement on his face. "The pain is a blessing, you'll see. You have to get past the pain so that we can have our babies. And we must have them. We must create life to counter all the death around us."

I wanted to ask him what he meant, but with his desperation, I did not think I would get a lucid answer. I took a deep breath and tried to let my body go limp. "Good, Mina. Do not resist me." He started moving again, and I could feel him get longer and harder inside me. He lifted himself slightly to one side and looked down so that he could watch the thing go in and out of me, as if he had to see it to guide it. He slowed for a few merciful moments, sliding it in and out with great care and fascination.

Suddenly, it began to feel different, better, less hurtful, and almost like pleasure. I stopped panting and let my thighs relax, allowing him deeper access into me. I recognized the same pleasure I had experienced in my dreams, and I caught a glimpse of what lovemaking could be between us after I grew accustomed to having him inside me. But soon, he started moving faster again, and the pain returned. Then he cried out with a force that would have indicated that he was in greater pain than I. With one great propelling thrust, he finished, and I realized that it was over. He let out a deep sigh, buried his face in my hair that was strewn across the pillow.

He rolled off me and onto his back. He would not look at me. He stared up at the canopy. I could see his face because we had not turned out the lamps. I pulled my nightdress down around me.

"Am I so inadequate compared to your previous experiences?" I asked. I was angry and humiliated but still afraid that I had spoken a truth and that he would confirm it.

"Dear God, no. Is that what you think? No, Mina, it is something far more sinister." His brows twitched and then tightened in an anguished grimace. "We went to Lucy's crypt." He closed his eyes again. "Godalming did not believe that Lucy was dead."

My stomach turned, and I thought I was going to be sick. I sat up, drawing my knees up to my chest and covering myself with the velvet duvet.

Jonathan turned his desperate eyes on me again. "It was Von Helsinger's idea. He is very persuasive. He is a follower of Mesmer. He will tell you so himself. He can hypnotize a person to do his will!"

"What did he say to you and the others to make you do this thing?"

"After you left the room, Von Helsinger suggested all the blood that Lucy had received in transfusions may be bringing her back to life."

I went back to that awful moment when the men ejected me from their cabal. "Why did you demand that I leave the room? Was this gruesome scheme in its planning stage before I came in?"

"No. But when I heard Godalming describe Lucy standing over his bed, I—" He stopped talking and tried to collect himself. He spoke slowly, his mouth forming the words carefully. "Mina, for many weeks now, I have felt haunted by the women I—encountered—in Styria. I did not want to speak of it in front of you. At times, I suspected that you were one of them. Von Helsinger calls it paranoia. Forgive me. Now that we are truly man and wife and I have seen your innocence, I realize that I have been suffering from madness."

He hung his head, and I noticed that the white streak in his hair had grown wider. "Von Helsinger said that visiting the crypt might enable me to leave my fantasies, if indeed they were fantasies, behind me. 'Who knows, Harker?' he said. 'Perhaps an entire world previously relegated to fantasia is opening up to us few explorers. We must investigate. You may be a modern-day Perseus who will find and slay the Medusa!' He was wrong. I am no hero but a prisoner of fresh terrors."

I was furious that Von Helsinger had drafted my husband, a man with a tenuous hold on health and sanity, into this grim exploration to appease the doctor's own fascination with the bizarre. "Tell me what happened."

"I cannot," he said. "You are too good."

"Unburden yourself, Jonathan. Speak of it, and then we will learn day by day to forget it."

Encouraged by my words, he began to spill out the horrific details of the evening. Godalming's coachman had taken them to a street near Highgate Cemetery that was known for houses of ill repute. They intimated that they would be spending the evening in one of them, and agreed to meet him at midnight. Lit only by the soft radiance of the moon, they entered the cemetery, making their way straight to the Circle of Lebanon. "As we walked down the path to the vaults, I heard birds screeching from that mighty tree that sits atop the circle of tombs. I knew that it was a bad omen, that we were violating something sacred. I asked them to reconsider before disturbing a consecrated tomb. Seward would have turned around with me, but the others' wills were too strong. I suppose that I wanted to prove to myself too that Lucy was dead and that Godalming had been hallucinating. I thought if a man like him was letting madness get inside his head, then it would not be so shameful for me to have succumbed to it too."

With a hammer and chisel borrowed from Lindenwood's toolshed, they opened the marble door to the crypt. "Godalming took it upon himself to open the coffin. Von Helsinger stood over him, encouraging him like an avid instructor. Removing the screws took an interminable amount of time. I was cold and sweating at the same time, which reminded me of having brain fever, and I feared that I might collapse. Finally, Godalming removed the last of the screws and lifted the lid." He paused, and I waited for him to continue.

"It grieves me to have to describe it, but this is the condition we shall all find ourselves in after we are shut away in our coffins. Nature is cruel." His eyes gleamed with a mixture of wonder and revulsion. "Her skin was pale, the color of ice when it is so cold it turns blue. Her lips were an unnatural scarlet, a stain by the embalmer's hand. Patches of skin had burst open, as if the body were attempting to turn itself inside out."

Jonathan recoiled at the memory. "I could have sworn that Von Helsinger was disappointed that Lucy was there in the coffin. I think he truly believed—wanted to believe—that the blood had brought her back to life. I could hold back no longer and I said to Godalming, 'Are you satisfied, sir?'"

He stopped again, recalling the moment. His face flushed with anger. "Godalming looked me dead in the eye and he said, 'No, Harker, I am not satisfied.' He took a leather sheath from his sack and retracted from it a knife. The blade must have been nine inches long and sharp enough to slay a large animal. Instinctively, I put my hands up. I thought it was me he was going to stab with it. But Seward stepped in front of me. He said in that calm, dispassionate voice of his, 'Arthur, I have seen you use that knife to cut a fish from a line. What are you going to do with it now?'

"Godalming laughed at him and said, 'What's the matter, John? Don't you want me to rid you of Harker? Isn't he the obstacle to your fondest desire?'"

Jonathan waited for me to respond. "Yes, Jonathan, I am aware that Dr. Seward has some feeling for me. I assure you that it is neither welcomed nor returned."

"Has he made overtures to you?"

"No, nothing like that," I lied. "When we met in Whitby, he needed someone in whom to invest his disappointed passion for Lucy. Arthur teased him about it one evening at dinner."

"There was no sense of jesting in the crypt. Godalming ignored Seward and turned to the coffin. He lifted the knife high above his head, and with something like a cry to battle, he thrust it into the chest of the corpse. 'Now I defy you to come ask for your money, little bitch!' That is what he said, Mina."

Life has its moments of great clarity. They usually come retrospectively and rarely at a convenient time. At that moment, I knew to the core of my being that Arthur had married Lucy for her money and had had her committed, and perhaps even killed, so that he might keep it. Dazzled by his title and his charms, Mrs. Westenra had played straight into his hands.

"We must pack our things and leave this place in the morning," Jonathan said. "I am sorry for what happened to Lucy, but we cannot help her now. That is up to God and God alone."

At that moment, I put aside all thoughts of vindicating Lucy, of pleasing Kate with my discoveries, of saving any more women like Vivienne from Von Helsinger's treatments—of anything at all but Jonathan and me saving ourselves. We threw our belongings into a valise, leaving behind the odorous clothing he had worn that night. We planned to announce our departure first thing in the morning and we agreed to brook no arguments for our continued stay. Jonathan and I slept that night holding each other, our arms encircled. We were, at last, a family.

When I woke up the next morning, Jonathan was not in the room. I supposed that he had gone to Von Helsinger to announce our imminent departure. I dressed in the clothing I had laid out the night before. At eight o'clock, Mrs. Snead came to the door with the announcement that my husband would like to see me in Dr. Von Helsinger's study. I asked her to send someone up for our luggage. "I have not been informed of your departure, madam," she said.

I assured her that we were leaving immediately.

When I entered Von Helsinger's office, Jonathan and the two doctors were standing over the desk, staring at a newspaper. Jonathan glared at me with hostility. "You almost had me in your thrall," he said.

Seward put his hand on Jonathan's arm. "Let me handle this." He turned to me. "Mrs. Harker, were you actually planning to leave the asylum this morning?" His eyes completed his thought: *So you do not love me after all.*

"My husband decided it was time to go home," I said, deferring the blame.

He picked up the newspaper and handed it to me. There, on the front page, was my own image, staring back at me. The photograph of Kate in mourning attire holding the ghostly baby was side by side with the photograph of me with the mysterious stranger hovering next to me. The headline read: CLAIRVOYANTS EXPOSED IN FRAUD SCHEME by Jacob Henry and Kate Reed.

"Now deny that you are one of them." Jonathan seethed.

I tossed the paper aside dismissively. "Did you gentlemen not read the article? I accompanied my friends on their mission to expose these frauds. This is but a photographic trick, Jonathan. I don't know what you are upset about." The room was thick with tension and with the smoke that churned from Von Helsinger's pipe, which was turning my empty stomach acrid. I waited for someone to break the cold silence and to draw away the attention of the three men who were eyeing me suspiciously.

"Are you going to deny that you know this man?" Jonathan yelled at me, and I cowered at the ferocity of his voice. I could not speak because the truth was elusive. No I did not know the man. But at the same time he was no stranger to me.

"Mrs. Harker, I think it is in your best interest to tell the truth," Seward said. "Have you had secret relations with the Count? Do you have some secret history with him that you hid from your husband?"

"With the Count?" I asked. "Who is the Count?"

Jonathan threw his hands up in frustration and then reached them out to me, forming a noose around which I knew he would like to put my neck. "Stop pretending that you are innocent. What an actress you are, Mina! What a performance of guileless virginity you put on last night! When the truth is that you are one of his she devils, undoubtedly practiced in every sordid act."

My face was on fire with mortification, blood burning over it like an army marauding across a continent. I put my cold hands to my hot cheeks, hiding my face, hoping to make sense of what he was saying.

"Mrs. Harker, do you deny that you know the Styrian count?" Seward's voice was cool and steady.

Jonathan picked up the paper, pointing to the ghostly figure beside me. "You were in conspiracy with him all along! That is how he found me. You sent me to my ruin! Why, Mina? Was it all in the name of evil?"

"The man in the photograph is the Austrian count?" I felt as if someone had just scrambled a puzzle that I had been working on for a long time, sending its pieces scattering to the wind.

"Enough of this pretense!" The vein slashing the length of Jonathan's forehead was a vivid purple. Tense muscles ran along the sides of his neck like two columns. He smashed his fist on the desk so hard that I jumped. I believe that if the two doctors had not been in the room, he would have attacked and killed me. "Admit what you have done, Mina. Admit once and for all who and what you really are."

Von Helsinger spoke for the first time. "Mrs. Harker, do you deny that you have ever seen this man before?"

What could I say? "I have seen him, but I do not know him," I said. I was too baffled and far too afraid to try to be clever. How could this be the man Jonathan had gone to see in Styria? "I have no idea how he inserted himself into the photograph. He was not in the room. Ask Kate Reed."

"Who is this Kate Reed?" Von Helsinger asked.

Jonathan spoke before I could answer. "Kate Reed is a brazen creature who has been trying to corrupt Mina for years."

I could not contain my tears anymore. I broke down, sobbing, and for a while, they let me cry. No one spoke, but the tension in the air was palpable. I made a decision. I thought that if I confessed everything I had been trying to hide—the inexplicable mysteries I had been trying to solve on my own—that someone, anyone, would help me to clarify them. "I do not know this man, but he follows me," I began.

"That's better Mrs. Harker. You are among friends here. Tell us everything," Seward said. The velvety words flowing from his mouth caressed my nerves. "We are doctors. We can help you." He addressed Jonathan. "Are you willing to listen to your wife's side of this story?" Jonathan nodded. The men took seats, and I asked for a cup of tea from a pot sitting on a tea cart by the small stove. Omitting details too graphic or sexual in nature, I told them of the night I found myself on the riverbank after sleepwalking. I told them of the rude man's attack and of the way that the mysterious stranger rescued me.

"This is the first I have heard of any of this," Jonathan said. "Why didn't you tell me?"

"I was afraid to upset you. I thought I had done something wrong, but I had no control over what happened. I was afraid you wouldn't believe me."

He did not answer, so I continued, relating my experiences in Whitby, about the storm and shipwreck, and how I saw the Count, or thought I saw him, at the abbey. I even admitted that I had received a note from that same person giving me Jonathan's whereabouts. "If you are his victim, then so am I," I said to Jonathan. "I have invited none of this."

Von Helsinger put down his pipe. "Mrs. Harker, the female always feigns innocence when seducing the male. It would be better for you if you would admit your weakness for this man. Then we might be able to help you."

I started to protest, but Jonathan stopped me. "You told me that you found out from my uncle that I was in the hospital."

"I did not know how to explain it to you otherwise. I am sorry. You were in no condition to hear another's bizarre tale." I started to cry, and Seward handed me a handkerchief. "I had no rational explanation for how he knew where you were, but if he is, in fact, the Count, then of course he knew where you were. But how he knows me, I do not know."

Seward had been taking notes as I spoke. He continued writing, while the other two men looked at me dubiously. Finally, Seward spoke. "Mrs. Harker, I have listened carefully to your story. I must say, it appears to me that you are obsessed with this man, or the *idea* of this man, who you say follows you around, saving you and giving you information, entering your dreams, and appearing out of thin air in Whitby to seduce you. You have given this phantom of your own creation extraordinary powers."

"I did not create him!" I said. "He is there—there in the picture!"

Seward put his hand up to stop me from continuing. "But moments ago you claimed it was a photographic trick. Can you not make up your mind?" He turned to my husband. "Mr. Harker—Jon—let us be sensible. It is very easy for one person to resemble another in a photograph. May I submit to you that the gentleman in the newspaper photograph merely looks like the Count? Might you at least entertain that possibility?"

Jonathan nodded slowly, dubiously. "Yes, that is possible, though the resemblance is remarkable."

"May I suggest to you that because you were so disturbed to see your wife's picture in the newspaper with another man, and because you associate all recent bad experiences with the Austrian count, that you are imagining that it is he? I can see how this figure in the photograph might resemble many people. The image is rather blurred, is it not?"

"That is possible," Jonathan said carefully, considering the idea. He examined the photograph again. "Yes, it is a blurry image, especially the face." I saw that Jonathan was capable of making peace with an explanation that posited that I was insane.

"Now everyone, please try to follow my analysis, especially you, Jon. I have seen hundreds of women suffering from various forms of sexual hysteria, and I know the symptoms and patterns all too well. Could it be that when Mrs. Harker saw the image of the handsome gentleman in the photograph, which this article proves was achieved with a photographic trick, she fell in love with that image? Already she was prone to sleepwalking and hallucinatory dreams. You were away on business, and so she began to transfer her feelings for you onto this phantom, which she associates with the gentleman who interrupted the attack on her at the riverbank. In Whitby, caught up in Lucy's obsession with Morris Quince, she felt deprived of romance herself and so escalated her fantasy about this man. She began to have dreams about him, dreams of an erotic and fantastic nature."

Seward looked at me with accusing eyes, but I was paralyzed by the direction of his analysis.

"As the obsession escalated, Mrs. Harker began to imagine that the man was following her, in love with her, appearing wherever and whenever she required him to take part in her fantasy. She even imagined that he sent her a letter about your whereabouts in Austria. And now, Mr. Hawkins, the true sender of that note, is most inconveniently deceased, so that we cannot ask him about the matter." Seward shook his head sadly.

I wanted to argue with him that the Count was in fact doing the things I claimed, but how could I be certain? The more I insisted, the more I would sound insane, or that was my reasoning at the time.

"Mrs. Harker, you know what I am about to say, do you not?"

I shook my head.

"Yours is a typical case of erotomania." Seward turned to Jonathan. "If not treated, the patient progresses into nymphomaniacal behavior. Mrs. Harker knows this is true because she is familiar with certain cases in this very institution."

"And what is nymphomaniacal behavior?" Jonathan asked.

"The indiscriminate seduction of men, which would prove to be humiliating to both of you. Fortunately, there is treatment available."

My body went cold. "No, I do not need treatment. I am not ill! I am not the patient here!" I remembered how Lucy's emotional response to the suggestion of treatment in Whitby gave Seward the confirmation of hysteria he sought, so I tried to calm myself. "Can we not discuss this rationally? I am in perfect health. I have had bad dreams, that is all. Dr. Seward, you, yourself, confirmed this just days ago. Why do you now think I am ill?"

"I did not know the extent of your condition, Mrs. Harker. You were not honest with me," he said, and then he added, "not honest about many things." He crossed his arms in recrimination. "You remember what I said about lying and cunning being symptoms of the sexual hysteric? I held you above that, but I now see that I was wrong. You came to me for help. You advised me of your imaginings, but you did not give me the whole truth, and I misdiagnosed you. I am the physician, and I should have seen through your carefully constructed version of reality, but you must let me make it up to you by treating you."

He turned to Jonathan. "You see, of all animals, woman has the most acute faculties, which are exalted by the influence of their reproductive organs. They are most sensitive creatures, easily susceptible to hysteria. The female body conspires with the female mind. We must be compassionate toward them and try to help them, or the spinning of fantastical tales and hallucinations escalate out of control."

"Mina, you must submit to treatment," Jonathan said. "You asked me to come here for evaluation, and I did as you asked. Now it is your turn to accommodate my wishes."

"Do you want this phantom lover of your imagination to haunt you for the rest of your days, Mrs. Harker?" Seward asked.

My only hope lay with my husband. "Jonathan, please do not let them treat me. Their treatments killed Lucy. They force-fed her and gave her fatal blood transfusions and she died!" I tried not to sound desperate. My mind raced for something to say to get out of the situation—anything to free me from being entrapped in this place—but I was too frightened to think. I was, in fact, the antithesis of the cunning liar of Seward's description. I felt utterly hopeless to affect my situation. Even Lucy, the great liar who had been manipulating people since her childhood, had not been able to escape Seward's diagnosis and treatment. What hope had I?

Seward easily rebuked me. "Lady Godalming refused food, made herself weak, and contracted a fever. You know all this, or rather, your rational mind knows this, but your disorder is causing your mind to distort the facts." He turned to Von Helsinger. "Is that not correct?"

Von Helsinger turned his palm up and shrugged as if to say *of course.* "The manifestations of Lady Godalming's disease were the same as Mrs. Harker's. Obsession, imagining the object of desire is in love with her, insisting that she is love's victim, et cetera. It is a common female illness, born of the weakness of the female mind, which I believe has a strong genetic component. I have devoted my life's work to finding a solution."

"Jon, do we have your permission to treat Mrs. Harker?" Seward maintained treacherous calm.

Jonathan picked up the newspaper again and stared at the photograph. "Now that I reexamine it, I see that could be a ghostly image that resembles the Count. I am sorry that I caused a sensation this morning, but I had such a fright when I saw him, or what I thought was him, with my wife. But it is all for the best. God has been at work here, using this situation to expose Mina's problem."

"Very well said, sir." Seward opened his black bag, extracting a hypodermic kit, similar to the one Mr. Hawkins's doctor had used.

"No!" I protested. "I do not need medication!" The more I talked, the more I sounded like Lucy. I forced myself to be quiet, but when I saw Seward come toward me with the needle, I started to scream.

Dr. Von Helsinger rang the bell beneath his desk, while Jonathan came to me, wrapping his arms around me. "Just let them help you, Mina. Soon, it will all be better," he said. Seward stood in front of me holding the long, loaded syringe in his hand, needle pointing to the sky. Mrs. Kranz and Mrs. Vogt came through the door.

"We will be admitting Mrs. Harker this morning as a patient," Seward said. "Make all the preparations to begin the water cure immediately."

"What is the water cure?" My heart was racing as Jonathan gave way to the two women, who each took one of my arms. I was astonished at how strong they were, how able they were to subdue my efforts to resist.

"It will relax you. It will expunge all the bad humors from your blood that cause nervous debility, and it will give you peace," Seward said as I squirmed beneath the grip of the two women. "Mrs. Harker, please do not resist. You don't want me to hurt you."

The room went silent but for the sound of Von Helsinger sucking on his pipe, and my silken sleeve being pushed above my elbow.

. . .

The drug swept through the current of my veins, carrying with it some numbing agent that caused the tension in my muscles to vanish, rapidly giving way to a loss of interest in rebellion. My arguments and logic for self-preservation dissipated like so much smoke, disintegrating into the air like the fumes from Von Helsinger's pipe. Waves of apathy rolled through my torso, limbs, and loins, and I was vaguely aware of being carried, of being undressed, of lying alone on a soft bed, of caresses, and of murmurs of comfort breathed into my ear. And then, of nothingness—the sheer relief of nonexistence.

My next awareness was of cold—bitter freezing, arctic cold—enveloping me, as if I had been buried in a tomb of ice. At first, I thought I was a child again. I remembered being sick with chills and thinking that I would die from it. Horrible feelings and images came to me—of being baptized, submerged, and drowned; hands holding me under cold water as I struggled to rise. But as I opened my eyes, I saw two women I did not recognize standing above me. My arms were pinned against my body, which was swaddled tight in a freezing-cold sheet. "Where am I?" I asked through trembling lips. I thought that I had died and gone—where? To the antithesis of hell?

"You are in the water treatment room, dearie," said one of the women.

I could take in only minuscule amounts of dank air with each breath, but enough to recognize the acrid odor of chemicals. I could not move my head enough to see what was being done to my body, but I felt the scratch of stiff, cold muslin against my skin.

"Help me," I managed to get out. "I am so cold."

"We are helping you, dearie. You are taking the water cure. It will do you a world of good." The woman who spoke did not look at me, but I could see the saggy wattle beneath her grizzled chin move as she talked in a singsong voice that was not at all personal or friendly. "Now be a good girl. You needn't do a thing but lie there. We have to do all the work."

I could not believe that they were going to leave me to freeze to death, but both walked away. I heard their bottoms hit chairs, each woman sighing as if she had just exhausted herself by troubling with me. I murmured over and over, moaning, crying for help through my chattering teeth. A few times I bit my tongue, which made me cry. A warm tear fell down my face, one drop of hot liquid in this frigid sea of cold. But no matter how many sounds I made, or how much I pleaded, they ignored me, even once or twice shushing me.

I heard one of the women rise and leave the room, and before long, I heard what I thought was the clattering of knitting needles. I lay shivering, trying to warm my lips with my tongue, which had gone cold too. I was lying on some sort of hard metal slab. The room had a low ceiling of white tile with black grout. I do not know how much time had passed, maybe an hour or more, when my natural body temperature began to rise enough to take a slight bit of chill out of the muslin wrap. I thought that this would signal that the treatment was over. I heard the woman stand up and walk not toward me, to free me, as I had hoped, but to the other side of the room, where I heard the cranking of a pump and of water flowing from a tap.

The next thing I knew, she was standing over me, pouring freezing water over my body. I could not move at all, but my body tried on instinct to escape, bouncing and flailing inside the sheet. This time I screamed and then screamed again, the sound of my shrieks echoing in the room. I thought that surely the sheer loudness would bring someone to my rescue, but my pitiful cries were lost in the pervasive moans that filled the rooms and halls of the asylum. Mine was nothing special, just another anonymous cry of suffering.

Another hour or so passed the same way. The woman had a psychic instinct for the very moment when my body had begun to warm, and at those moments, she dumped more cold water on my already frigid form. I shivered so hard that sometimes I lost consciousness but not for any decent length of time during which I might escape my misery. Finally, I heard the other woman come back into the room, and the two of them began to unwrap the horrible cloth from my body. If I had had the strength, I would have thanked them. My body was rigid and cramped, and I anticipated being wrapped in a warm robe or blanket and told that my treatment was complete. Instead the two women lifted me, one by the shoulders and the other by the hips, and without warning plunged me into a tub of ice water, colder even than the sheet that had bound me. The shock took my breath away. Blackness rose up before me, but I did not faint. The full force of the cold hit every part of me at once, and I began to fight the hands that held me down.

"Oh, dearie, why do you act this way?" The one who spoke pushed my head under the water, and it filled my nose and mouth. I felt myself choking, gulping and drowning with every swallow, the big hands on my neck keeping me down in what would surely be my watery grave. I have done this before, I thought. I knew all too well this feeling of insidious cold water taking me over.

They pulled me out of the water and into the chilly air of the room, which made gooseflesh over every inch of my body. I was shivering hard again and weak in the knees. One of them held me up while the other wrapped me in a blanket. Together, they carried me to a chair, holding me beneath my armpits, while my numb feet dragged on the wet, tiled floor. They sat me down, and I keeled over to one side. One of the women caught me before I slid off the seat and onto the floor, while the other brought a tray with a huge pitcher of water and a glass.

"Water on the inside is as important as the water on the outside," she said. She poured a glass of water and tried to hand it to me, but I could not lift my arm to take it. She held it to my lips, pouring the cold, unwanted liquid into my mouth. I tried to swallow, but I did not have the strength, and it dribbled out the sides of my mouth and down my neck. "Come now, you must drink the pitcher," she said.

I was still shaking from the cold bath and did not see how I could down all that water. The small bit that was traveling to my stomach was making me sick. I had eaten nothing since early the night before, but my empty insides were churning. I shook my head: I could not drink any more. The woman holding the glass let out an aggravated sigh. "It's no use to disobey, miss. We cannot let you out of the room until you drink it."

"If I drink it, I can go?" I managed to choke out the words. I was still chilled through to the marrow and would have agreed to do anything to get out of the room and back into warmth of some kind.

"Yes, so be a good girlie." The full glass came toward me, and together, she and I held it to my lips as I drank down the water. I am not sure how I got through the next six glasses, but I did, fighting nausea and remembering that with every sip, I was closer to getting out of that room. It must have taken me the better part of an hour to gag all of it down, but I did it, and when I finished, I waited for release. They pulled me up out of the chair and took the blanket off me, leaving me naked and cold. Rather than head for the door, they directed me deeper into the room, where they opened a metal door and pushed me inside. I heard a cranking noise, and then water rushing through pipes. Suddenly, it came out of a spigot over my head and poured all over me, icy cold again, scaring me so that I threw myself against the side of the stall. But I could not escape.

One of the women yelled out, "Be a good girlie, now, it's just ten minutes."

I screamed and beat the walls of the stall for the duration of the shower. I could not believe that any person had survived this treatment. When I could take it no longer, I started to count out loud, sixty, fifty-nine, fifty-eight, and so on, but nothing seemed to make the time pass fast enough. I was well beyond the point of anything I thought I could endure, and yet I was still alive. Finally, I fell to the cold floor of the stall, letting the frigid water pour over me.

After they released me from the cold shower, they did not bring me back into a warm room but sat me down and forced another pitcher of water into me. I do not know how long it took. I was utterly delirious and convinced that I would never again be dry, never be able to leave that torture chamber, never again wear warm clothes and sit in front of a fireplace with a cup of tea. Just as I was drinking the final glass, I started to remember people I knew who were outside this establishment, people who might help me—Kate, Jacob, Headmistress, even the mysterious stranger. Had I been hallucinating on the banks of the river when he pulled the attacker off me? I had one moment of hopefulness, remembering that rescue.

On the heels of that fleeting moment of hope, the blanket was ripped away, and I discovered that the finale was yet to come. The two women hoisted up my limp, naked body, and plunged me once again into a fresh tub of icy water.

. . .

When I regained consciousness, I was lying in a bed. Intoxicated by the small and fragile pleasure of being warm, my first thought was that

I was safe. The warmth of the bed lulled me. My body felt weak, as if the substance that willed my muscles to move had been drained from it. As soon as I remembered where I was and what had been done to me, my thoughts turned to methods of escape. I opened my eyes. The single window in the room had two heavy iron bars. The halls were never without attendants, and guards manned the gates. A further and more insurmountable deterrent was that I did not have the strength to move.

I dozed for a while and awoke to the smooth hush of Seward's voice. "See? She is as peaceful as a lamb, like a sleeping angel." His words came slowly, like thick syrup from a bottle.

"The water cure purifies the blood of some of its undesirable elements." Von Helsinger's guttural notes chimed in. "It is the perfect treatment in preparation for the transfusion; otherwise, the fresh blood has too much to fight against."

Hoping that my reaction did not show on my face, I fought the urge to open my eyes. I wanted to hear what they would say next.

"I must say, the water treatment brings more peace and tranquility to the female than any narcotic I have ever used," Seward said.

The men spoke in shaded tones, trying not to wake me.

"She is very still," Jonathan whispered. "I do not like that she is so pale."

"Harker, I want you to go to your room and rest. We are going to need your blood for the second transfusion," Von Helsinger said.

I raced, mouselike, through the tunnels of my mind for something that I could say, an argument that would convince them to let me walk, unscathed, out of the room, and out of the institution. I tried to peek through the tiny slits between my eyelids without alerting them that I was awake. I saw Von Helsinger nod to Seward, who held a syringe in his hand. I shut my eyes tight but heard his footsteps approach the bed. He took my arm in his hand, turning it palm up. My eyes darted open.

"No!" I was so weak that the word came out as a whimper. I tried again, but it was as if I were in a dream where I was trying to run but could not move.

"Don't hurt her!" Jonathan said, pulling Seward's arm away. His face, along with the rest of the room, was hazy to me, but I could tell he was concerned and perhaps would forbid them to proceed.

"Do not worry, young Harker," Von Helsinger said. "We are going to pump her full of brave men's blood. That is the best thing on earth when a woman is in trouble. Your wife will be cured of her ills and, with the superior blood, will bear you strong children. That is what you want, is it not?"

"Even the most benign medical procedures can be disturbing to the layman," Seward said. "We will send for you when we're ready."

Jonathan came to the bed and kissed my forehead. "You are going to get better, Mina. The doctors are going to make you well again."

I reached up with whatever strength I had and clutched at his shirt, but I did not have the strength to hold it. "Do not let them," I whispered, my words slurred.

Jonathan's brown eyes, soft with concern, were searching mine. "What did you say?"

"Lucy." I whispered her name as best I could. The syllables dripped slowly from my numb lips.

"I believe that she is calling for Lucy," Jonathan said to Seward.

Seward tried to move Jonathan aside. "She is hallucinating. Best to let her stay drowsy."

Jonathan gripped the doctor's arm. "Lucy died here. You must promise me that you won't let that happen to Mina. I must have your guarantee."

Oh steadfast reader, how many times do we revisit the past and wish that we had made different choices? Even at that moment, when I was virtually unconscious, I rued my decision to spare Jonathan the worst details of what the doctors had done to Lucy because I had feared that their gruesome aspects might impede his recovery. Why had I not given him her letters to read for himself? I believed that in protecting him, I was acting in his higher interest; little did I know that I was possibly signing my own death warrant.

"Lady Godalming was given the blood as a last resort to save her from acute anemia. Your wife is physically strong. With the blood, she will also gain strength of mind," Von Helsinger said. "But the donor of blood must also be in a state of relaxation to achieve a beneficial result. Perhaps the blood of Lord Godalming failed to save his wife because he was in an excitable state at the time."

"No wonder he is having nightmares," Jonathan said thoughtfully. "He believes that he failed his wife. That will not happen here, sirs."

"I will take good care of her," Seward said. "You can trust me."

"I do trust you," Jonathan said. After all, who had stepped in front of Godalming as he wielded his fishing knife at Jonathan in Lucy's crypt? Of course Jonathan would trust Seward.

Jonathan leaned over me and took my limp hand. "Good-bye, Mina, darling," he said, with a little catch in his throat. He kissed my hand and then squeezed it tight before turning away. I tried to speak again, but he receded from me, and I heard his footsteps as he walked away.

Von Helsinger closed the door behind him and stood over the bed. "Now be a good little miss," he said. Seward held my arm while Von Helsinger stroked it up and down. He put his monocle to his eye and examined me. "Such lovely skin, like a little baby's." He looked up and down my body, moving the neckline of my nightdress aside and slipping his hand inside, putting it over my chest. Then he cupped it under my left breast. "But she is not a little baby after all." He left his hand on my breast for a long while, looking up to the ceiling. Finally he moved it away. "The heart rate is good," he said. "You may give the injection now."

Seward took my arm in his hand. I tried to jerk it away, but he said, "No one will hurt you if you do not resist." With brawny fingers, Von Helsinger held my arm in place while Seward slowly traced the lines of my veins from shoulder to wrist and back with his finger. "What a fine and delicate network," he said as his finger slid the length of my inner arm, making me squirm. "As if a master painter has been here with his brush." He caressed the sensitive skin near the top of my underarm. "I think you like that," he said, smiling.

"This is good!" Von Helsinger said enthusiastically. "She is getting more receptive to the blood."

Seward retraced the line of my vein back down my arm, stopping at my inner elbow, gently teasing the crease. "Here, I think," he said, and he brought the needle to that place and stuck it in my vein.

I felt the sting of the injection and the burn of the medicine as it flooded my arm. He rubbed the spot where the needle went in and then put his hand on my face, caressing my cheek. "Sweet Mina," he said with a wry laugh. Von Helsinger said something to Seward in German, and the younger doctor laughed and answered him back in that language.

The room around me faded; I was rapidly losing consciousness. I wanted to stop the doctors, but I was completely incapacitated and the medication made it easier to give into my fate. Floating into that darkness, I felt less and less attached to the idea of escape. I thought that perhaps I should pray, but I could not summon the mental energy to do so. Strangely, the words of a hymn came to me, one I'd sung at the last service I had attended in Exeter. I recalled the resonant pipe organ filling the cathedral, vibrating the nave.

> You, Christ, are the king of glory
> The eternal Son of the Father
> When you took our flesh to set us free
> You humbly chose the Virgin's womb.
> You overcame the sting of death
> And opened the kingdom of heaven to all believers
> You are seated at God's right hand in glory . . .

The image that the hymn brought to my mind was neither Christ nor heaven but my savior, standing on the banks of the river with his arms outstretched, inviting me to go to him. What a fool I had been. How I wish that I had known that the danger ahead lay not in his arms but in stubbornly clinging to the life of safety and security that I wanted with Jonathan. What exquisite gifts had my dream lover offered me that I would never know?

I saw his face in my mind's eye, and I imagined staring into his feral blue eyes, dark as twilight. I wanted to sink into them, to melt into the escape that they promised. My mind was now like a stage where my dreams of the mysterious stranger were played again—his voice, his touch, his kisses, and his blood-draining bite. I was in a somnolent state, in which the line between reality and hallucination was easily blurred, my mind alternating between the sweet sensations of my imagination and the faint sounds in the room—the tinkling glass and metal as Seward and Von Helsinger prepared for the procedure, words muttered between them in German, and the low, ambient hum of the asylum's inmates.

All of a sudden, I felt a shift in the room, as if someone had made a surprise entrance, but through hazy eyes, I saw that the door was still closed. Von Helsinger's alarmed voice barked exclamatory words to Seward in German, and Seward responded with a strange cry. I wanted to slip back into my reverie, but then something crashed to the floor, as if one of the doctors had dropped a thing made of glass. I opened my eyes again and in my dreamy state, I thought I saw a thick mist seeping through the shuttered window. Confused, wondering if this was part of a dream, I blinked my eyes and looked again. The two doctors—eyes wide with astonishment—stood frozen, watching the vapor as it swirled before them, growing in luminescence and intensity. Before our eyes, the numinous particles began to sculpt into a form, and I thought that perhaps an angel had come to save me.

Slowly the thing took shape. It was not an angel but a shimmering coat of silver fur, which gradually molded itself over great muscled haunches, its outer ends elongating into a bestial tail and head. My dream world collided with my reality as I watched the wolf dog I had seen in Whitby growl at Von Helsinger, backing him against a wall and baring his teeth at the incredulous doctor. Von Helsinger pressed himself against the wall, yelling something in German, and the beast lunged at him, pinning him with its thick paws. The treacherous canines were not an inch from Von Helsinger's face. Seward tried to get to the door, but the wolf dog turned around and, with preternatural speed, leapt on him from behind, sinking its teeth into the doctor's back. Seward cried out in anguish as he pulled away, leaving some of his flesh in the animal's mouth. Von Helsinger pushed Seward through the door, but before he could escape, the animal swiped at his face and neck, leaving sharp claw marks from cheek to throat. With a howl of agony, Von Helsinger grabbed his face and fell through the door after Seward, slamming it shut.

I lay in bed paralyzed. The wolf dog jumped on the bed, straddling me, staring at me with its vivid indigo eyes. The last thing I remember seeing in that room was his huge incisors above my face, red and dripping with Seward's blood.

Part Six

LONDON

AND AT SEA

Chapter Fourteen

I woke up under thick velvet covers in a vast bed. Truly, it was like floating on a sea of feathers. I had no idea where I was. I remembered traveling, my body jostled as I lay on what felt like leather. In my stupor, I had wondered if I had died, and the jostling was from my hearse as it rolled toward my grave. If I was dead, I had pondered, then why did my thoughts rattle on? After that, I floated into a long, dreamless repose.

Now I opened my eyes. The room was dark, though weak autumnal light filtered in through arched windows high on the walls, illuminating the room's rich aubergine brocade wallpaper. Its color cast a soft violet haze that floated through the bedroom, twinkling the huge diamond-shaped crystals that dropped from two immense, many-tiered silver chandeliers. They were larger than any I had ever seen, things out of a palace or a fairy tale. An imposing, heavily carved wardrobe, which looked as if it had been in place since the early fifteenth century, faced the bed where I lay. Beside it on the wall hung a large bronze shield with an iron French cross at its center, crowned by a gilded fleur-de-lis with a dazzling gemstone in the middle of the petal. Large portraits of nude ladies, odalisques that looked as if an Italian master—Titian, perhaps?— had painted them graced the adjacent wall. A heavy crystal vase of white long-stemmed roses sat on a table at the bedside, their petals tight, but their sweet perfume filling the air, mingling with the aroma of fresh baked bread.

I ran my hands down my body. I was not in my own nightdress but in a pale green gown of fine quality damask silk with a triangular neckline and long, full sleeves that cupped my wrists, draping white lace over my hands to the fingers. I had never seen such a rich garment. I imagined it was something that the queen's daughters would have worn.

I heard a door open, and it startled me. I pulled the covers to my neck.

"Ah, she is awake."

It was the voice. His quick footsteps approached the bed, and he soon stood over me. His presence was different this time. He was more solid and real, more like a man—a human—than in all the previous times he had come to me. He looked anchored inside his body, which let me know that I was not dreaming or hallucinating. At least it did not feel that way. Still, his skin was slightly more luminous than that of an average person, and I wondered if it was noticeable enough to attract the attention of those who passed him on the street. He sat next to me and put out his hand, and I put mine into it. His body did not seem to have a temperature. I realize that is difficult to imagine, but while his hand was a perfectly formed male hand, it was neither warm nor cold, but beyond those things. It was concrete, but it had a subtle and peculiar vibratory quality, like the tremor of a violin string.

He put his fingers over my pulse at the wrist, and then leaned into me, inhaling my scent at the neck. I felt little shivers inside me, remembering the dream in which he bit into me and tasted me. But he soon withdrew.

"The medication is still in your blood, but you are recovering well. You are very strong, Mina. Very strong." His full crimson lips formed a little smile. "Do you like the bed? You have been asleep for two days."

"I do like it," I said, my voice crackling with the first words of the day. "It is the most luxurious bed I have ever slept in."

"It once belonged to Pope Innocent, though he was anything but. Ironic that you are lying in it now."

"Do you think I am not innocent?" I cannot say that I wasn't afraid of him; yet there was something between us that made it seem as if we were simply picking up a conversation where we had last left it.

"No, you are innocent, but the pope was not. He knew that he was dying, and he tried to save his life by transfusing the blood of healthy young boys into his sick body. They died, of course, and so did he. If the doctor had given you his blood, you would have died."

"Is that why you came to me? To save me once again?"

"I came because you called me," he said.

I was about to dispute this, but I remembered that when I was drifting into unconsciousness, it was he who came into my mind most strongly.

"How do you know that I would have died?" I asked.

"Because I can smell your blood and the blood of the others, including your husband's, and I can tell by the fragrance which blood will not mix well. It is inexplicable to you, I realize. But if you accept the Gift, you will understand."

"What Gift?"

"The Gift you have rejected for the better part of a millennium," he said. "But that is for another day. You are hungry. Your stomach is terribly empty."

He produced a wide silver tray with wrought handles that was piled with sliced bread, grapes, apricots, oranges, apples, cheeses, and a goblet of red wine, and put it on the bed.

"Wine?" I asked. I wanted a cup of tea.

"Your blood needs its elements. Drink at least some of it." He sat on the bed next to me. "You must eat now. You will need your strength."

At that moment, the pungent aroma of the cheeses, the sharp citrus of sliced oranges, and the yeasty smell of the bread overrode both my fear and my curiosity. I wanted to dive into the food like a hungry dockworker. With great discipline, I picked up a silver knife and spread soft butter across a slice of the warm bread and then daintily cut a piece of dark cheddar cheese. The food tasted exquisite, and I tried to chew slowly, as he was taking in my every move. We sat in silence for a while as I ate my fill and let the wine relax me.

"Where am I?" I finally asked.

"You are in the mansion that I purchased for us in London, the one your fiancé found and helped me to buy," he said with the slightest touch of a smile. "One does not live for seven hundred years without developing a keen sense of irony."

I imagined how shocked Jonathan must have been to see my picture in the newspaper with the man who left him to be ravished by his nieces. It almost made me forgive him his violent reaction.

"I am very confused. I do not understand—well, any of this—but I do not even understand how you know me," I said.

"In this particular life trajectory, you have a very obstinate memory. It is difficult sometimes to remain patient with you." His eyes turned a chilly blue, and he got up off the bed, turning his back to me. "But then, it always has been so," he said with an air of resignation. "That is why I am taking you to Ireland. We are going to go to the place where we first met, and then you will begin to remember."

The Count opened both doors of the heavily carved medieval wardrobe revealing dresses of many colors and fabrics. "I have selected for you clothing for every occasion, but I suggest you dress simply. Ireland is a poor and hostile country. You do not want to appear as a haughty Englishwoman flaunting her wealth."

"I have no wealth," I protested. "And I am not going to Ireland!"

"You are wrong on both counts. You will find first that you do, indeed, have wealth and second that you are going to Ireland. Select the things you would like to take on our journey," he said. "I will have them packed for you. As a courtesy to you, I brought my staff from Paris to run this house. I happen to know that you speak French. We leave this evening for Southampton and we will sail in the morning. I have purchased a small luxury steamer for the trip. Will you please be ready in an hour?"

I see that you are unaccustomed to being told no, I thought but did not say. Something in me wanted to challenge this creature that was both regal and feral.

He read my thoughts as clearly as if I had said them aloud. "Not accustomed to being told no? You have told me no hundreds of times." His eyes flared bright and angry. I knew that he could easily hurt me—kill me—if he wished. But if he were going to do that, I would prefer that he do it here, rather than on a boat in the middle of the Irish Sea.

"What would happen if I decided not to go?" I asked, trying to test where I stood with him. He had once said he was my servant and my master, but I saw nothing of the servant.

He took two steps back, and I felt the anger he had hurled at me moments before recede. He shrugged. "The choice is yours. The doors to the mansion are open. Walk through them anytime you like."

His sharp change of tone disarmed me. I could not think of anything to say that would not sound like a schoolgirl fumbling for words.

"I would enjoy watching you dress, but there will be time for that later. I sense that you require some privacy." He gave me a perfunctory bow. "One hour. Please be ready." And then he left me alone in the room.

At sea, the next day

The vessel he had purchased had fifty first-class staterooms designed to transport one hundred people and considerable cargo, but besides the crew, we were the only passengers. I was given my own quarters, luxurious and small. I opened the wardrobe, which smelled of sweet sachet. Everything in my trunk—from undergarments to nightdresses to gowns to jewelry—had already been unpacked and hung or folded with supreme precision and care. French soaps, lotions, and powders populated the drawers of the vanity, and a vase of white lilies sat on its top. I sat on the narrow bed, looking out through the round porthole to sea, and marveling that three days prior, I had been in an asylum being tortured with the water cure. But was this voyage going to prove any less dangerous? I must have been lulled into a shallow sleep by the undulation of the sea when I heard a rap at the cabin door. A steward was delivering a note advising me that dinner would be served at eight.

I had seen renderings in *The Woman's World* of elegant, bejeweled ladies with gentlemen in ties and tails, dining in the new transatlantic luxury liners, but I did not know the protocol on this mysterious ship. I selected a simple but graceful gown with a sage-colored organza overdress and a seed-pearl choker, hoping that I had chosen well, and I swept my hair up with long, pearl-dotted pins from a small ivory box on the vanity. I checked my appearance in the mirror and then opened the door to find that the steward waited in the hall to escort me.

The centerpiece of the dining room was an atrium of etched glass surrounded by exquisite plaster crown molding patterned with vine roses. Classical columns held up the lower portions of the paneled ceiling. The room would have seated one hundred at its stately mahogany tables, but we were the only diners. Bowls of fruit and big vases of hothouse violet-blue hydrangeas covered the room's sideboards. In one corner, a pianist softly played a sonata on a grand piano.

"Do you like the music, or would you prefer to dine in silence?" the Count asked, standing up to greet me as I entered the room. He sat at the head of a table wearing evening clothes, much like those in which I had first seen him on the riverbank.

Another steward rushed over to help me into a chair adjacent to the Count. The steward exchanged a few words with the Count in a language I did not understand, bowed, and hurried away.

"The music is lovely," I said.

"Chopin. Such talent. A pity that he died so young."

I was woefully ignorant of serious music, an aspect of my education that Headmistress had ignored. "How did he die?" I asked.

"The doctors thought it was some disease of the lungs, but it was exacerbated by his taste for, shall we say, the wrong sort of woman." He smiled. "Or rather, their taste for him."

I had arrived in the dining room with a litany of questions, but the soft light from his luminous face and his incalculable eyes that were devouring me erased them all. I thought of Kate's advice to be silent so that the words of another might come forth, and I tried to relax, but I felt fidgety under his gaze.

"I knew that the dress would match your eyes, or that your eyes would change their color to match the dress," he said. "And do not worry. All your questions will be answered in due time. That is why we are making this trip."

Waiters began to appear with tureens of soup, platters of fish and meat, and bowls of vegetables. Another with a huge gold tasting spoon hanging like a necklace at his chest showed the Count a bottle of wine, which he approved, and when opened, sniffed the cork, and then nodded so that a glass could be poured for me. He ordered the waiters to put everything on the table and retreat to the rear of the room. "I will serve her," he said. "Tell me what you would like, Mina."

I opened my mouth to speak, but he put a finger to my lips. "Not that way. Tell me with your thoughts."

Without looking at the food, I directed my attention by scent to the tureen of turtle soup, whose aroma I recognized from my first dinner at the asylum. "Yes, good," the Count said, ladling out a small bowlful for me. "What else?"

I relished the aromas of the white fish with wine and capers, the lamb with mint sauce, and the carrots, but rejected the turnips, which I had eaten for so many years at Miss Hadley's that I had come to abhor them. My repulsion made him laugh, and he signaled for a waiter to take the bowl away. He finished serving the food and sat in his chair with an empty plate in front of him. "Bon appétit," he said to me.

"You are not eating?" I asked.

"When I am fully living in the body, which I am now, I do feed it, but not tonight," he said. Seeing my confusion, he added, "I will explain all in time, Mina, but I know your appetites as surely as I know my own, and I know that you are dying to eat but wondering how you might do so politely when your dinner companion is not eating with you. You must forget your training for the moment and enjoy yourself."

Unlike other times when I seemed to frustrate him, now he seemed utterly amused by me. I obeyed him, taking the first bite of food, and, finding it delicious, I proceeded to eat while he watched.

I finished one glass of wine, which made me more relaxed, even blithe. "You seem to know me exceedingly well, Count, while I know you very little, or at least, I do not remember knowing you, as you say that I do. May I please ask you exactly who and what you are?"

"Exactly? At this moment in time, I am Count Vladimir Drakulya. Some twenty years ago, I reclaimed a Carinthian estate and title in Styria that was rightfully mine through an ancestor. He was given them hundreds of years ago by the King of Hungary and inducted into the Sacred Order of the Dragon for his role in assassinating a certain Turkish sultan. Of course, the ancestor is myself, but you are the only person alive with that knowledge."

As outrageous as his claim was, he spoke with the sort of certainty that made me believe him. "I feel as if I have entered some sort of magical kingdom," I said. "Forgive me if I do not know how to respond."

"Respond any way you like, Mina. I must admit that I have been surprised at the way that you have allowed politeness and formality to suppress your higher nature. But that will change," he said. "You *have* entered a magical kingdom, but it is the realm in which you have existed before, the realm in which you belong."

"Are you speaking of the hallucinations I had as a child?" I asked. "I remember that in one of them, you came to me."

"Oh yes, and not just once, though that is all that you seem to recall. I have been aware of you since you reentered the earthly plane. It took me some time to find you. You had come back to the place where we first met—the stormy west coast of Ireland—and I took it as an omen from you that you were going to be receptive to me and to all that I have been offering you. Once I found you, I saw that you had been incarnated with powerful gifts and that they frightened you and those around you. That is when I decided to watch over you and protect you. I did not want to wait another lifetime for you to come back to me. I would merely wait for you to grow up. Though you were not, by any means, defenseless, you believed that you were. It amounts to the same thing."

"But how did you find me? How did you even know that it was me you were looking for? I must have been just a baby." Some part of me understood that he was telling the truth, but none of it made sense.

"We are physically and psychically attuned, you and I. Everything that exists in this material world also exists on the other side of the veil. On the etheric plane, you and I are eternally united. You have read the philosopher Plato?"

"No," I said. "I have not read philosophy."

"You must do so sometime. What he said of the twin souls is not far from accurate. We are twin souls, so to speak. You know this, but it frightens you."

He poured me another glass of wine. "Drink it," he said.

I was not accustomed to having more than one small glass, but I liked the soft and careless way it made me feel. I took a long sip and swallowed it. He leaned over toward me, putting his fingers under my chin. He grazed my lips with his nose and then with his own lips, first gently, and then taking them into his mouth and biting them one at a time. He put his big hand around my neck, covering my throat, terrifying me with the power he had to wrap those fingers tight and suffocate me, but exciting me because I knew that he would not do it. There was too much that he wanted from me, and I did not know yet exactly what it was. He kissed me with an open mouth, my lips subsumed by his. His tongue found mine, and he pulled it into his mouth.

As soon as he felt my enthrallment, he pulled away from me so that I was looking into his eyes, and I understood in that moment why he called himself my master. His eyes were intense and fathomless, an eternity of deep blue, like the sea at twilight, and they left me without a will of my own.

"I want you to suck my tongue," he said. "Taste me." He put the length of it into my mouth, and I obeyed him, latching on to it. I was surprised at how much it thrilled me, and for a long time, I nursed at his tongue as if I expected it to feed me. His lips and his tongue—and his entire being—hummed with a subtle but indelible current. I felt that I could stay there forever, feeding on his tongue, but he broke it off, pulling back, his hand still on my throat.

"Does that feel familiar?" he asked.

"No, I have never felt anything like that before," I said, disappointed that he had stopped and wanting more.

I was still catching my breath, yet wanting him back inside my mouth where I could taste him again. What had he tasted like? Salt, iron, spice—like nature itself. But his mood had changed, and I could tell that he was not going to invite me to do it again, at least not now. I could not imagine how to collect myself, which he apparently knew. "Tea will help," he said, at which point one of the waiters appeared pushing a tea cart.

"I did not hear or see you call for the tea," I said.

"My staff have been long with me. Their training is rigorous."

I wanted him to kiss and touch me again, and at the same time I wanted to ask him more questions, when I realized that I had no idea what to call him.

"You may call me whatever you like," he said, addressing my unspoken words. "In time, I hope that you will call me by the term of endearment that you have always used."

"And what is that?" I asked.

"You have said it in many languages, but it is always the same." He put his hand around the back of my head, bringing my ear to his lips. "My love," he whispered.

. . .

"Are you human?" I asked. We were in the ship's small library, where we retreated after dinner. He gestured for me to take a seat in a big stuffed chair covered in a Turkish carpet.

He shrugged, turning his back to me. He lit a pile of herbs whose smoke filled the air with a heady mixture of flowers, spices, and vanilla. "I know how keen your senses are, Mina. We must feed them a variety of delights," he said. He poured topaz-tinted brandy into a heavy crystal glass and handed it to me. He sat on the divan opposite me.

"Why do you not want me to sit beside you?" I asked. I thought I was beginning to have inklings of what passed through his mind, as he could read mine, and I knew that he had a purpose in relegating me to the chair.

"I must tell you about myself, but if I am sitting next to you, your scent will overcome me, and then I will overwhelm you, and you will still be ignorant of me and afraid." He sighed a heavy sigh, stretching his long legs out in front of him.

"I began life as a human. But I have transcended the human condition and am an immortal. At least that is what I believe, as I no longer age, and no one has been able to destroy me. But who or what is truly immortal? I cannot be certain."

"I want to know everything about you, and about us," I said. "Have we always known each other?"

"No, not always. Shall I tell you about my life before we met?" he asked.

"Your life before you came to me when I was a child? Or before you took me away from the asylum?"

"My life before we met seven hundred years ago." He got up and poured a brandy for himself. He put his nose deep into the glass, but he did not taste it. He sat down again.

"I was born in the Pyrenees in the southwest of France in the time of the king known as the Lionheart and into a distant branch of his family. Those were the days of the Crusades to the Holy Land. As a young man, I trained as a warrior, and when I came of age, I entered the service of a French nobleman, the Viscount of Poitou, a relation, who was raising an army to help King Richard reclaim the city of Jerusalem after it fell to the Saracen commander Saladin. The Viscount of Poitou was known for his bravery in battle, and eager young knights and vassals flocked to his cause when he came to recruit us. While King Richard set off for the Holy Land through Sicily, the Viscount of Poitou marched through France and eastward through the Rhineland, the Kingdom of Hungary, the Slavic countries, and on through Greece, recruiting a huge army before we crossed the Hellespont and entered Byzantium.

"In the evenings, by campfire, a time when men love to tell tales of conquest, our leader enthralled us with the story of how he courted and captured a fairy queen and made her his lover and wife. At first, some of us scoffed at him. We had heard old nurses and midwives tell these kinds of tales to charm and frighten us. Yet he convinced us that his story was true. 'I was hunting in the forest one day,' he said, 'when I shot an arrow at a fleeting form. It was a careless, quickly delivered shot, for the deer seemed to come out of nowhere. I shot blindly, and my arrow hit a tree. When I went to retrieve it, the animal was standing beside the arrow, staring at me with insolent eyes. I could not believe the boldness of the creature. It seemed to defy me.'

"The Viscount of Poitou was as intrigued by a challenge as any man alive, and so he nocked another arrow and aimed straight at the deer, which then took off with great alacrity into a thicket."

The Count smiled at the memory. "Hunting stories captured our young imaginations. I can still see the rapt faces sitting round that fire. I remember it exactly as he told it, for he told it more than once, and always in the same manner. He said, 'The little beast ran into a part of the forest through which no path had ever been cleared, and I chased it, scrambling through bush and brush, which ripped at my new cloak and angered me, for I have always been proud of the elegance of my costume. Soon I was in a small clearing, which had an eerie, chilly atmosphere, as if the surrounding forest had thus far protected it from both sunlight and human entry. I knew instantly that I had entered an enchanted place.

In its midst was an enormous tree with a massive trunk that had bowed over—either by its own weight or by the winds that howled through that part of the country—and now slithered along the ground like a long-snouted dragon. It bore no leaves, and its bark was thick and gnarly like the scales of that reptile. I was out of breath, but I could hear movement, and so I drew my bow and aimed in the direction of the rustling leaves. Suddenly, from out of the thicket came, not the deer but a beautiful naked woman with golden hair so long that it protected her modesty. Her eyes were like none I had ever seen—dark, wild, and green, as if they too were a product of this magical forest.'"

The Count paused. "You can imagine how he had us young men in his thrall."

"An old woman in the asylum told me the story of magical women who enchanted men," I said. "I thought she was mad. Yet I have seen you as both wolf and man, and so I must believe you, as you believed the French nobleman."

He smiled. "Shall I continue?"

"I would like that," I said.

"The viscount told us in great detail how he and the mysterious woman coupled, first on the forest floor and then in every curve of that serpentine tree, leaving him so fatigued and spent that he fell into a deep sleep. When he awakened, he found himself in his lover's kingdom, and that is where he learned the history of her tribe."

The Count stopped speaking. "Are you tired, Mina? Do you want to go to sleep?"

"No, I am not tired," I said. The room had grown chilly, but I was as eager as a child to hear the rest of the story.

"I do not want to strain your credulity," he said. I thought he was teasing me, but I could not be sure. He opened a cabinet, producing a thick wool throw, which he put over me. Then he sat down and continued.

"The viscount learned that his fairy lover and her tribe were descendants of the angels who left heaven, but not because they were expelled by God. That, he said, was a lie told by priests. These angels were powerful creators in their own right and enchanted by human life. After observing humans for millennia, they craved all that physical life offered—touch, sound, scent, the heat and desire that comes with the flow of blood through the veins, and the taste of food and of wine. Sensuality is an abstract quality in the spirit realm, so they came to earth to experience all the senses. The angels thought humans to be magnificent creatures, and they longed for their companionship and their adulation. With their power to shift their shapes, the angels made themselves into physical beings and selected humans who were the most likely to give them children. With their superior intelligence and supernatural gifts, they were irresistible to the mortals.

"Now, all this happened thousands of years before man began to record his history. The fairy queen who seduced the viscount was a descendant of those first couplings between angels and humans. She claimed that some of the offspring of the angels were mortals but some were immortal. As with any two creatures mating, the outcome is not guaranteed, no matter how careful one is in the selection of a partner. But the viscount's wife was an immortal, and from his union with her came three daughters—beautiful, magical creatures—who went to live with their mother's tribe in Ireland.

"After hearing his story, all the young knights wanted to go on a quest to find immortal lovers, but the viscount explained to us that even if we did find them, some of us would be driven mad and some of us would die. 'Their bodies emit a strange power,' he warned. 'No one can predict its effect on a mortal.'

"Naturally, each of us wanted to prove that we were as strong and virile as the Viscount of Poitou. So full of bravado were we that the more he tried to warn us, the more we desired to journey to these mystical lands and test our manhood."

"Did you turn around and go looking for the fairy creatures?" I asked. I was anxious to hear more about them, and this time, not from a madwoman.

"As curious as we were, our honor would never permit desertion. The enchanted women would be our reward for our service.

"The viscount assured us that in battle, we had the protection of both the Church and the fairy queen, and so when we faced the enemy, we fought fearlessly—viciously, in fact. We were as close a band of brothers as has ever existed, and it tore us apart when one of us succumbed, either in battle or to one of the epidemics that infiltrated our camps. We began to inquire about special herbs and tonics and spells that we had heard of that would make us invincible; and with these inquiries, we attracted the attention of a sect of warrior monks, who began to reveal to us their mysteries.

"These monks believed that through the daily transubstantiation of wafer and wine into the body and blood of Christ, magical powers were conferred upon them—powers that could be used over our enemies, who were instruments of Satan. 'We use the very power of Satan to defeat his disciples,' they claimed. They invited us to take part in a forbidden ceremony, a Requiem Mass, said not for the dead but for our living enemies. We gathered in secret at midnight before the day of battle, and we prayed with great fervor for the souls of our enemies, who we strongly envisioned as already vanquished and dead. At first, it was eerie to imagine the living as dead, and moreover to pray to God to take their souls. But we left these ceremonies elated, and the next day, we fought with uncommon ferocity, slaying greater numbers of our enemies than we thought possible. Whether or not the Black Masses were the reason for our victories, they gave us the faith to go into battle with the certainty that we would win. And win we did. We became a renowned fighting force, and our loyalty to one another grew with every victory.

"As our success grew, so did our ambitions. The monks believed that they had discovered what we were looking for—not just invincibility but immortality. They said that the Christ himself had given us the key when he said, 'Except ye eat the flesh of the Son of man, and drink his blood, ye have no life in you.' These words, as you may know, are from the Gospel of John, and the monks believed in their literal interpretation, that drinking blood was the secret to life everlasting.

"Some of us were appalled at the idea, but at the time, monks were the keepers of all the world's knowledge and knew things that no one else knew. They said that in ancient times, it was known that the blood housed the soul. Supplicants of warriors and heroes like Theseus and Achilles poured blood into the soil of their graves to give them strength. With this blood, the heroes rose from the dead to fight alongside them in battle. The monks told us other stories to support these ideas: the goddess Athena gave Asclepius the power to heal by giving him the blood of the Gorgon. The Roman gladiators drank the blood of their kill, both animal and human, to absorb the strength of the enemy. The berserkers, the savage warriors of Odin who tore their opponents apart, ripping through their jugulars with bare teeth and eviscerating them without the aid of weaponry, got their power by drinking animal blood. The maenads, the original followers of Dionysus, drank both wine and blood in their rituals, sacrificing animals and sometimes a human in their frenzies. The monks said that blood consumption and blood sacrifice were as old as time, and that was why Jesus made himself a human sacrifice, giving us His blood to drink. They also warned us that drinking the blood of another can cause illness, even death, for blood carries humors both good and bad. But we were men who faced death every day. For us, drinking blood would be just another test of our strength.

"We young men desperately wanted to join the ranks of the eternal heroes. We formed a secret brotherhood and vowed that we would not rest until we discovered the key to immortality. Despite the risks, we began to drink blood as part of our ritual to prepare for battle—the blood of animals, the blood of our enemies—and eventually, we shared our own blood with one another."

He paused. "You must sleep. Your body is still recovering from the treatment at the asylum, and some of the medication is still in your blood." He reached his hand out to me. "Please come and sit beside me."

I did as he requested. He took my hand and put his fingers to the inside of my wrist. "As I thought. Your pulse is not what it should be right now. Your energy centers were weakened by what they did to you."

"How do you know these things?" I asked, remembering what he had done to my pulse points in my dream, and I felt a hot, crimson flush across my face.

"I was not always a warrior. I have also been a doctor," he said, placing my hand back in my lap. "And by the way, it was not a dream, Mina."

I was astonished that he had read my thought so quickly. It was both thrilling and terrifying to be so vulnerable to another. There was nowhere to hide. It was like being perennially naked. "It had to be a dream. It happened in my sleep," I said.

"It happened in another realm, one in which I have visited you many times. And do not worry. As you grow stronger, you will be able to efficaciously hide your thoughts from me. I do not look forward to that day, but it will come. Now to bed."

"I do not want to go to bed," I said. "I want to hear the rest of the story."

"That will take a very long time," he said. "I would prefer if you would rest. You will need your strength in Ireland. It is not a kind climate at this time of year."

I had been listening to the rain beat down on the ship as we sailed. I wanted him to lie next to me so that I could fall asleep safely beside him. "Will you sleep as well?"

"Not tonight," he said. "Sometimes I sleep for long periods of time, years at a time, and sometimes I do not sleep at all. If I am bored, if I do not admire the ways and customs of an era, if my physical body is wounded or fatigued, I go into a deep sleep, an altered state during which the body is preserved. You would call it hibernation or a very long trance. I have entered this state before when you broke my spirit with your rejection. When I reenter the world, it has inevitably changed."

"I do not think I can sleep. I will lie awake thinking of you and of all that you have told me," I said. There was no use in lying to him.

"Then I will put you to sleep myself," he said.

Before I could object, he swooped me into his arms, carrying me out of the library and down the stairs to my quarters, kissing me lightly on the face and lips along the way. I wrapped my arms around his neck, wishing for the journey to never end, relishing the strange and electric touch of his lips, and marveling at their power to ignite all the small cells of my body.

He opened the door to my cabin. The mysterious staff that had unpacked my things had been inside, lighting low lamps and laying out a satin nightdress. He put me down, standing me in front of the mirror, and he stood behind me. As I watched our reflections, he reached around, unbuttoning the front of my dress and slipping it off my shoulders. He ran his lips along one side of my neck. "The scent of you is as familiar to me as my own."

I shivered, which I know he felt. Nibbling my ear, he slowly pulled the pearl pins out of my hair until he removed the last of them, and the tresses tumbled down upon my shoulders. He grasped my hair in his hand, tugging so that I could not move my head. "I once told you long ago that you were like a wild horse that I would control by its mane." I pictured him as he was in my dream, pulling my hair as he bit into my neck. I held my breath, hoping that he would do it again, right now, and resurrect that strange ecstasy.

"You are not strong enough for that, Mina," he said, reading me. He released my hair, and it fell down my back.

He unlaced my corset and pulled it apart, loosening it, and letting it fall to the floor. I stepped out of the clothes, and he knelt in front of me, sliding his hands up my legs and rolling down my garters. He sat me on the bed while he unlaced my shoes and removed them. Then, one at a time, he slowly glided my stockings down my legs, making all the hair on my body bristle with excitement. With his fingers, he caressed the bottoms of my feet, and then sank his lips into one of the arches, and then the other, and I moaned.

"You have always loved your pleasure, Mina. It is no different this time, despite the armor you have put around yourself."

Holding my hands, he pulled me up, putting the nightdress over my head and then smoothing it along my body until it fell fluttering at my feet. He swooped me up in his arms again and laid me on the bed.

"There is another way to taste you," he said. He pulled my gown up and slid his hand up my thigh, parting my legs as it reached my private place. With one fingertip, he separated the lips. "How often have I worshipped at this altar."

I closed my eyes to enjoy the pleasure, slipping into dreamy arousal. *Do not look away from me.*

I opened my eyes again, and he locked them to his. When he looked at me this way, I had no will. *Modesty has no place between us. Do you understand?*

"I do," I said. I was his to do with whatever he wished.

Spread your legs wider for me.

I did as he said, and his hands pushed them far apart, while his mouth sucked and tasted me. I wanted to scream with pleasure, but my voice was choked inside me and I could not breathe. My mouth was locked open and my head thrown back as I reached for something I could not name. His tongue snaked its way into me, and it seemed to expand there, electrifying my insides, and then he pulled it out and carpeted the whole of my opening. I felt his lips lock onto my flesh, and he took as much of me as he could inside his mouth, sucking there as I had earlier sucked his tongue. I started to rock with pleasure, just as the sea rocked beneath us, but he grabbed my thighs in his viselike grip so that I could not move at all. I was on the threshold of some kind of ecstasy but afraid that he would bite into me in that most vulnerable of places. I wanted him to do whatever he pleased, for I anticipated that anything he did would bring unimaginable thrills. But I also held the memory of his wolf dog blood-drenched fangs, and it was impossible to know if he would tire of giving pleasure and choose evisceration.

I waited for the shock and pain of his wound, but instead, he pulled away, leaving me panting and desiring him to resume. As much as I was afraid of what he would do to me, I was more afraid for him to stop. The inside of me throbbed with violent contractions, searching for something to hold in its grip.

"Though it would please me to do it, I am not going to taste your blood," he said. "But I will give you what you want. What do you want?"

He knew exactly what I wanted.

"Yes, but I want to hear the melody of the words as you say it aloud," he said.

"I want you to fill me up, as you did in my dream," I said, surprised to hear this request come from my mouth. "I want to feel the whole of you inside me."

He wasn't even touching me now. Suddenly, it felt as if he had left the room. Had he disappeared? I looked around. All was dark but for a bluish orb of moonlight coming through the porthole.

"Where are you? Please don't go away. Please don't leave me," I shouted.

Not ever?

"No, not ever," I said. I could feel him in the room again, even if I could not see him. I was so relieved that he had not left me, but I needed to see him again, to believe that he was real to me and that all this was not a dream.

It's not a dream, Mina.

If it's not a dream, then touch me.

I waited. I took a deep breath, but before I could completely exhale, I felt a mad rush of heat, and he was between my legs again, and like some kind of eel or lamprey, he had sucked me into his mouth as if he was consuming all of me. I felt completely electrified, though I recognized that he was not moving but letting me feel the power of his being, the force of his vibration, for that is the only way I can describe it. He was flooding me with some sort of furious energy, like the gods of old who created storms by their whispers. He sent this power straight into the dark cavity of my sex, where it swirled and expanded, and then shot up my spine and into my head. At that moment, both ends of me exploded with staggering pleasure, as if my body had been ripped in half and my skull cracked wide-open, letting in the heavens. For a long moment, I felt nothing but elation.

Welcome home, Mina.

I heard the strum of the rain as it began to fall again on the sea. He pulled the covers over me, and I sailed on the rhythm of the waves into my dreams.

. . .

I awakened alone the next morning to dark skies, a turbulent sea, and a chilly cabin. I tried to get out of bed, but the churning waters tossed me right back. I sat up and looked out the porthole when a wave came crashing against the glass with enough velocity to send me on my back again.

I managed to stand up. A mysterious valet had been in my cabin and picked up last night's discarded clothing and replaced it with a fresh dress, undergarments, stockings, and shoes, which I put on despite the efforts of the sea to knock me off my feet. In a box on the vanity, I found a bracelet made of ten black onyx snakes in figure-eight patterns, inlaid with ivory and diamonds and outlined in gold. The centerpiece was an exquisite angel's face, which covered a watch face. The time was noon. I put the dial to my ear, listening to the precision of its ticking and imagining my heart beating at the same steady rate.

I am waiting for you.

As soon as I heard his voice, I saw in my mind's eye the lounge where he sat. I was able to walk directly to it by following some internal navigation that I understood now would always lead me to him. It was a small room with a fire burning. Breakfast and tea were laid out and waiting for me. He stood as I walked into the room. His very presence almost knocked the wind out of me. Light entered the room from small etched-glass windows, emphasizing his effulgent skin and his chiseled face, and last night's pleasures rushed back to me.

Suddenly, a blinding ray of light shot through the glass, creating strange prisms in the room. In that instant, I saw him, not as he was or as he had been last night, but as a different man in strange surroundings. He was younger, fiercer, and less ethereal, with a thick, dark beard and dress from another time and another place—an ermine-trimmed scarlet cape, a bright white tunic, a red cross slashed across the chest, a low-slung belt of gold. His eyes were a brighter blue, and they stared at me from a face desperate with either rage or love or desire or all those things. Feeling faint, I grabbed onto the doorframe for support, and I closed my eyes. When I opened them again, he was standing in the same place, as if what I had just seen had not happened at all.

"You are famished," he said. "Sit down and have something to eat."

The aroma of bacon and of the sugary confections neatly laid out on silver platters overwhelmed me, and I came into the room and loaded a plate with the sweet and savory treats.

"Exposure to my frequency leaves one very hungry," he said. "You will find that."

"Frequency?" I asked, spreading cream over a scone, savoring the delicious blend of flavors in my mouth.

"Every being has a frequency, a certain vibration. A scientist would call it electromagnetism. The electromagnetism of my being is greater than that of a mortal. That is why being in my presence, or in the presence of any immortal, depletes one's own life forces."

"Is that what happened to Jonathan in Styria?" I asked. As soon as I mentioned his name, my voice started to shake.

"Yes," he said implacably.

After he had abandoned me to the doctors, I did not want to care about Jonathan. Of course he had had the shock of his life seeing me in the photograph with the Count. And perhaps he believed Seward and thought that by allowing the doctors to treat me, they were curing me. One thing was certain: if not for the Count's obsession with me, Jonathan would still be the man he was when I met him, and perhaps he and I would have been happy together.

"Jonathan was innocent until you brought him into your world, and now he may never recover," I said. I chewed a rasher of bacon and waited for him to elaborate on what had happened to Jonathan in Styria, but the Count was silent. Had I really expected this prodigious being to explain himself as if he were an ordinary man?

"He was never innocent," he said. "He might have left Styria after we concluded our business, but he wanted Ursulina from the moment he saw her. He chose to remain at the castle, just as you chose to stay with me. I invited you to leave my home in London. Instead, you laid out the clothes you selected for the trip and came with me on this voyage."

I had no rebuttal to this.

"Mina, all of your life, since you were a child, you called out to me in ways that you do not yet acknowledge. I had vowed to reveal myself to you after you reached your twenty-first birthday, but that was when Jonathan Harker appeared; and in a short time, it became obvious that you were determined to marry and settle into a life of convention."

"I did not call out to you. I was not aware of your existence," I said.

"You do not call out with your voice but with the hum of your desire. Think of us as musical instruments that vibrate with the same note. A note is struck, and it is heard by the note that must answer it."

He sighed. "I will try to explain it to you. I was able to involve Harker in my affairs because he desired such a commission. I left him with Ursulina because that is what he wanted. This is what the religious among you call free will. They are accurate about its existence. The doctrine governs all human behavior."

"Why did you leave him in Styria? Was it to come to me in Whitby?"

"Frankly, I thought that, like most of the humans who succumbed to her, Harker would perish. He is a stronger rival than I anticipated." He laughed a very bitter, human laugh. "I chartered the *Valkyrie* to come to you and persuade you to travel with me to London. But the ship's crew discovered that my cargo contained gold and other priceless treasures. The fools attempted to murder me and steal my belongings. I regret that they did this because I had to kill them while keeping their captain alive long enough to bring the boat to safety but not long enough to tell what he had seen."

I shuddered remembering the sight of the dead captain tied to his ship, his bloody corpse battered by the rain and the sea.

"I know what you are thinking. You are not responsible for his death, or for the deaths of the crew. Human greed is to blame. I had to come for you, Mina. Your longing was intense. I answered your call. It is against my very being to resist."

"And the creatures who seduced my husband? Did he call out to them?"

I have already explained this to you.

His impatience with me was the same sort that I sometimes experienced with my students when they refused to grasp the truth.

"Dr. Von Helsinger called them vampire women, the undead— monsters who made themselves immortal by draining the blood of their prey. Is that what they are?" I asked. *Is that what you are?*

"The creature that he imagines is but a ghoul that represents men's fears. But the stories of the immortal blood drinkers are not fantasy."

He must have read my confusion because he continued. "The German doctor misunderstands. It is not the blood draining that weakens and kills the prey but the exposure to our power. My being carries an electrical current similar to that of a lightning rod. You know this because you have felt it. When we interact with the body of a human— call it making love if you wish—even though this current brings great pleasure, it acts as a kind of electrocution. Over time, the mortal's energy is depleted. Depending upon the weakness of the human, they may either get sick or in extreme cases go mad or die. It is nothing to do with draining the blood, unless one takes too much of it. The men who gave your friend Lucy their blood—did they die? No, they poured pints of their own blood into her but it did not affect them. I have never killed anyone by draining their blood, unless I meant to kill them anyway."

"Is that what I have done by calling you to me? Have I signed my own death warrant? Will I go mad? Will I die?" I felt locked into my fate with him, but I still feared it.

"You are not like your husband and other mortals. At a juncture of history, the blood of the immortals entered your bloodline, introducing certain powers. Within that blood is the key to immortality, to being able to live within a body but to also exist without it, to walk on both sides of the veil in worlds seen and unseen. They say that at one time, it was a common trait, but over the millennia, humans have lost the ability."

Jonathan had explained to me the science of how humans evolved with certain traits but not others. "Perhaps, if one is to believe the theories of Mr. Darwin, the trait was not advantageous to humankind," I said.

"I have spent centuries studying science, medicine, philosophy, metaphysics, and the occult. I believe that it is a natural step in the evolutionary process, a step toward the merging of the mortal and the immortal. Eventually, the veil between the worlds will shatter. The warrior monks believed that Jesus was trying to teach this when He rose from the dead and ascended into the unseen world. But the knowledge was buried by the Church, which wanted power over its members and so kept true knowledge from them."

Everything you are saying is against everything I have been taught to believe.

"You should have no trouble believing. You and others like you have a seventh sense, something beyond telepathy. Within you is the ability to fully integrate the body with eternal consciousness, to fuse flesh with spirit. If you do not embrace your gifts, they will forever be a plague to you, Mina. And I do mean forever."

Part Seven

IRELAND

Chapter Fifteen

The black cliffs along the Irish coast sliced perpendicular lines into the sea, where watery tendrils sucked at the colossal jet walls with ferocity. The sun shone brightly upon the sea, but its rays did nothing to calm the water's turbulence. The farther north we sailed, the more the landscape became austere and unforgiving. Black stone flags began to jut like tentacles into the ocean from the mainland. The gray-green waters merged on the horizon with purple-tinged skies, and the winds shimmied the waves into prancing white peaks.

We watched the winds whipping the water from the glass-enclosed promenade deck of the steamer, where the Count wrapped me in a fur blanket against the chilly afternoon. About an hour before twilight, the steamer dropped its anchor off Sligo Harbor, where two rowboats met us to take us to shore. The sea spray left us wet, and me very cold, but a carriage and coachman greeted us to take us to the castle.

For the last two days of the voyage, the Count had insisted that I rest. Not once did he touch me as he had on the first evening, though I am sure that he read my thoughts and knew that I craved it. Sometimes he dined with me, and at other times, he left me to myself, sending broths and potions in the evenings that would help me sleep. He insisted that

I had to gather my strength for the days ahead. He would not even continue the story of his early life but promised that he would tell me the rest of it at the appropriate time once we were in Ireland. He often pressed his fingers to my pulse and listened to my body's rhythms. Sometimes, he would say, "Good, good." Sometimes he would frown and send me to bed. I yearned for him to come to my cabin with me, or to allow me into the quarters were he slept, but he refused on the grounds that I must have uninterrupted sleep. A silent and dutiful staff saw to my every need, often while remaining invisible. I was never certain who had been in my cabin while I slept, taking care of my clothing and preparing fresh dress for the following day, or who left the trays of nuts, fruits, and tea to refresh me upon waking from naps.

We rode now in the dark, the countryside vaguely lit by the carriage lamps. A light mist had drifted in from the sea, and I saw only shadows and silhouettes as the Count pointed out sights and landmarks.

"There is the great mountain Benbulbin. It sits on the earth like an anvil, and when it rains, the deep rivulets run with water as if the mountain is shedding tears."

"I barely see its outline," I said, squinting to see what he described.

"Ah, I forget that you do not see what I see. But you will, Mina, and you will be amazed at the secret beauty of the night," he said.

"There is the castle. Do you see it on the promontory at the top of the hill?"

The monstrous stone structure, with a tall, thick watchtower, lorded over the headland, the walls slit by long, thin bars of yellow light emanating from its windows. The carriage began the long climb up the hill, where we gazed over the dark and glossy moonlit sea. At the top of the hill, we were turning onto the long curved lane that led to the castle, when I glimpsed its massive entryway lit by torches. As we came closer, I saw more clearly its two huge, turreted wings with long, tall windows, united by a great stone façade.

A tall, thin woman in a plain black dress with a swirl of gray and black hair piled on top of her head greeted us as we alighted from the carriage. "My lord," she said with a low curtsy to the Count.

The Count nodded politely. "We are delighted to be in your care, madam," he said, introducing her as Mrs. O'Dowd. She was not old, perhaps younger than Headmistress, and though her frame was bony, she had very correct posture, and her sallow skin was unlined. "This lady is from the clan of the fiercest warlords in Ireland," he said, which brought a pleased look to her face, and I wondered if she was one of the Count's kind and had been alive since the early days of her tribe's existence.

Awed by the sheer size of the castle, I let the Count take my elbow and guide me. Refreshments awaited us in the grand reception hall, where a roaring fire burned in a hearth as tall as a man. Immense animal heads crowned the room—big-toothed bears, elk, and an animal with jagged, tiered antlers that I could not identify. A tripaneled stained-glass window with English kings and imposing crests presided over the wide staircase that curved around on either side of the well and disappeared into the upper stories of the castle.

I wanted to run about the rooms like a little girl and investigate this wondrous place, but Mrs. O'Dowd took my cloak and gestured for me to sit on the divan in front of the fire, where she poured me a cup of tea. She neither poured any for the Count nor offered it to him. "Shall I serve the young lady some food?" She did not address me, but asked the Count, who nodded his head. She selected an assortment of sandwiches and fruit, placed it before me, and then left the room.

I ate while the Count told me some of the castle's history, how it had originally been built in the last years of the twelfth century by a French knight who abandoned it some years later. "It went to ruin and was rebuilt again in the era of Cromwell, and modernized about fifty years ago by its present owner."

I was curious to know more of this mysterious owner, but the Count said that he had another story he would prefer to tell me. He took me by the hand through the castle to a parlor at its rear. I could not see much of the room in the dark except the glimmer of its chandeliers and the large gilded mirrors on the walls. From a bay window, in the distance, I saw a vine-covered ruin sitting beside a moonlit lake. Something inside me stirred. I felt dizzy, faint. I leaned against him.

"Do you recognize it, Mina?"

"I do not, and yet it is familiar."

"Come," he said, taking my hand. He opened a door that led outside. The temperature had dropped, and the night was cold. He put his arms around me. "You will be warm," he said.

He picked me up and started to walk toward the ruin and the lake. In moments, he was no longer walking, nor was he flying, but we were moving at a rapid pace, as if gliding on an invisible track. I held my breath as the landscape sped by me and the castle drifted away. In another moment, time collapsed, and we blasted through a window of sorts and were inside the ruin.

He put me down, and I held on to him while I caught my breath. "As your body adapts to mine, it will get used to that sort of travel," he said. The room was very dark, but enough moonlight came through a big hole in the roof to illuminate its outline. It was a small room, bare but for some big logs that sat beside an abandoned hearth. The Count picked up a few and stacked them inside. He closed his eyes and held his hands over the logs. His long fingers, stretched out in front of him, seemed to pulsate and glow. Somewhere in the distance, an owl screeched, and wings fluttered madly in a tree, but I was too spellbound by his powerful shape in the moonlight to move or to utter a sound. He stood motionless until the glow in his hands intensified. I heard crackling noises coming from the logs, and suddenly, his hands ceased to glow, but flames started to shoot up in the fireplace, first in one place and then in another, until the hearth was dancing with fire.

He took off his cloak and laid it on the floor for me to sit on. He smiled at my astonished face. "It is not difficult to summon a fire spirit," he said. "I have seen you do it."

As soon as I sat down, the room started to spin around me. He knelt beside me, putting his arm around my shoulders.

"I feel sick," I said. My stomach was upset, and I thought I would throw up the food I had just eaten. He put his hand on my stomach. "Just breathe, Mina." I did as he said. "You are not accustomed to rapid travel." His hand grew warm as it sat over my belly, dissipating the uncomfortable feeling. "This room carries memories, and, as with any human life, not all that we shared here was good. Yet so much of it was glorious."

"What happened here?" I asked.

"We lived here. You and I, together, long, long ago."

"I do not remember anything, and yet the place has an effect on me."

"As it would, because the memories are still here," he said. "All time occurs at once, Mina. I have shown you that. In a place that exists just beyond a thin membrane that you cannot see, you and I are still living that life here together."

"I don't understand," I said. My eyes welled with tears and I clenched my fists in frustration. "I want to understand but I cannot. This is all too much for me." A few months ago, all I had wanted was a simple church wedding, a little home in Pimlico, and a baby. Now he was calling upon me to apprehend the secrets of the universe.

He pulled me close to him and pressed his lips against my forehead, soothing me. "It has taken me centuries to understand it myself. I expect too much of you. You are probably still in shock from what happened at the asylum. Perhaps I should have waited until you were stronger to bring you here."

"I wanted a life that was secure and simple," I said. "I yearned for it, and now it is all gone, and I must comprehend things that are beyond me."

"You cannot have that life because that is not who you are, Mina. You must be who you are, not who you wish to be."

He took my face in his hands and looked into my eyes, once again mesmerizing me, melting away my frustration and making me want only him—to understand him, to be a part of his world. "You asked me last night to tell you more of the story of my life before you and I met. I want you to know everything—everything in my life that drove me to you. It will help you to understand who you are—who you are at the very core of your being—and why you and I are here together at this moment in time."

He took his hands from my face and sat back, one knee raised, his arm resting on it, his elegant hand dangling. For a moment, he looked like an ordinary man, but he moved his face, and the firelight caught his skin, exposing his radiance and highlighting his fiercely strong cheekbones. "How we have arrived here is a long story." He seemed to be breathing in the room's memories. I had to draw my attention away from his beauty to listen to the words as he began to speak.

"After a time with the Lionheart's army, we fought and won major battles against the Saracens at Acre and Joppa, battles that went down in history and are still talked about today. By this time, we had become savage fighters. Our forbidden prayers and dark rituals seemed to have the magic that we had hoped for, and we believed more than ever that we were invincible. Our reputation spread through the land, not only for our courage but also for our preternatural strength and daring.

"Now we were joined by a band of mercenary warriors—murderers, really—known in the lands of the Saracens as the Assassins, for hire by anyone who could pay the price. The Assassins had been terrorizing the Christian pilgrims by the hundreds on their way to the Holy Land, raping them, robbing them of everything including their clothing, and leaving them for dead. The Assassins entered the service of the Lionheart, who paid them to protect the pilgrims rather than destroy them. They were a fearsome group of men, animalistic, and yet also practitioners of mysticism. Though we considered them sinister and uncivilized, in fact, we shared many of their characteristics as well as their obsessions, and they fascinated us.

"We heard rumors that in the dead of night, the Assassins practiced forbidden rituals, ancient secrets to awaken dark powers that would give them invincibility and immortality. We made it known to them that we too were a secret band with similar obsessions, and soon, we were communicating with them. We found that they made blood sacrifices to a heathen goddess of warriors called Kali by the mystics of India, who drained the blood of her enemies into a bowl and drank it. On Tuesday eves, they ate a substance called hashish, which made the real world disappear, and made sacrifices to this goddess. They claimed that she gave them the power to stop both time and death. They invited us to join them in this and in the ritual magic they practiced, which they called the path of the left hand. They taught us the seven hidden centers of the body, where power is stored and through which the life force may enter. In the rituals, we meditated on those hidden seats of power, and we were taught to stimulate the lowest and most powerful center in the genitalia, on ourselves and on each other, which brought ecstasy and climax. We learned to take in more energy and light with each ecstatic climax; and in time, our mental and physical powers grew stronger. We found that meditating on an event would influence it to happen or direct its unfolding. We believed that we had growing dominion over exterior forces as well as over our own beings.

"Later, when some of these things were revealed, the Church proclaimed our practices satanic, but it was not the devil we worshipped. We devoutly believed in the word of Christ. The monks had taught us that the Holy Grail—the very promise of Jesus—was nothing short of immortality. We believed that Jesus confirmed this with His words and with the blood ceremony that He made the centerpiece of worship.

"We were anxious to test our new powers in battle, but King Richard was more anxious for peace, and he signed a treaty with Saladin. That was the second day of September in the year of Our Lord 1192. Some of our members set off on a separate quest to find the sacred vessel carrying the immortal blood of Christ, which they believed still existed. Others went to Aquitaine and other parts of France and claimed the lands that were due them for their service.

"But a small group of us had never forgotten the stories of the

Viscount of Poitou and the daughters that he had from his union with the fairy queen. Intrigued with the idea of cavorting with immortals, we requested and received large grants of land in Ireland. Before I left him, the viscount came to me and warned me again of the danger of my quest. 'You are like a son to me, so I must tell you something that I do not admit to other men, and that is the deep sorrow that comes with abandonment by an immortal lover. They cannot help themselves; it is in their nature to love and to leave. They tire of mortal life with its illnesses and vulnerabilities. As we grow older, they tire of us and they leave. But to the one who is left behind, all is dark. That is why I have buried my grief and loneliness in war. Once lost, nothing can replace the divine pleasures they gave. Few are those who have the privilege of their love, but the loss of them is unendurable.'

"Because I was inexperienced in the ways of love, his words did not affect me. He saw that I would not be deterred, so he gave me his blessing and charged me with finding his youngest daughter. 'She is special and dear to me,' he said. 'Of the three, she is the most likely to be human. She seemed to have a deeply human heart.' He gave me a token to take to her, something precious that her mother had given to him for protection before he left France. I thanked him, and I took it with me. The next day, I set off with my cohorts for that foreign land."

He stopped talking and stared into the fire.

"And did you find her?" I asked. Surely he was not finished with the story. He did not answer me, and I grew impatient. *Did you find her?*

He slipped his hand into a pocket and pulled out something wrapped in a linen handkerchief. He handed it to me, and I was surprised at the weight of it—heavy and substantial. I untied the piece of string that held the package together and carefully unfolded the linen, revealing a silver Celtic cross inlaid with a mosaic of dozens of stones—amethysts, tourmalines, emeralds, and rubies. I stared at it, entranced by its glimmering beauty. The gems flickered and pranced in the firelight.

I put the cross to my heart and fell into his chest, and the world around me disappeared.

31 October 1193

My sister and I help each other dress in the black robes we have made for the ceremony to honor the Raven goddess who rules over the night, the moon, and its mysteries; who flies over battlefields protecting her beloved ones and destroying their enemies. The dresses are thick and heavy because it will be frigid cold this evening under the full ice-white moon. We cross the panels over our breasts and then tie them tight around our bodies with silver sashes. Our long hair—mine, midnight black and hers, dark copper—spills down our backs in thick waves, offering extra protection against the cold and the wind that whispers incessantly through our valley. This is the evening of the year when the invisible barrier between the two worlds falls and the deities reveal themselves to their faithful; a time when mortals and immortals may take delight in one another, a time when mortals are rewarded not only by the fruits of their labors in the fields but by the immortal ones as they bestow favor. This is the eve when the fairy mounds open and the riotous, pleasure-seeking Sidhe cavort with their chosen ones who live on the earthly plane. On this evening, mortal men too are restless. Knights and kings prowl the land, hoping to attract the Raven Lady, who bestows victories in battle upon her lovers, or one of her ladies, who will pray to the goddess for them, or a Sidhe woman who will give them both pleasure and protection.

We douse our necks with rose water because we know that the immortal princes who tonight may rise and come to us are attracted to the scent. My sister is betrothed to one of them, and tonight, she hopes that I will attract another so that we may remain together. The sweet fragrance fills my senses until I am dizzy with it. I am known to hear and smell and taste beyond what others do, even my sister, who is skilled in sorcery. We have made thick diadems of crimson roses to place on our heads. Careful not to prick ourselves on the thorns, we crown each other, and then slide our arms into the black gloves we have made with long talons at the fingers, turning our beautiful white hands into lethal weapons.

We slip out into the night and walk along the stream, following its babbling path until we are in the sacred grove, hidden from the sight of men, where the others have already lit two great bonfires. They sit in a circle, an unkindness of ravens, each draped to the lengths of their fingers in black, the elders hooded and the maidens crowned with flowers. Some of the women wear wide ruffs of black feathers that cover their necks and chests; and our leader, the high priestess, wears a tall, feathered hood, reminiscent of the hooded raven that represents our Divine Lady. They are passing around a bowl, an infusion of magic purple moonflower seeds that we have nurtured all year in our secret garden. Every year, foolish ones with no knowledge, curious about the tales they have heard of our powers, die from eating the poisonous blue and white moonflowers that grow wild. Little do they know of our sacred garden and the herbs and flowers that we cultivate for our brews.

My sister and I join the circle of women and take our share of the bitter broth, made palatable with herbs and honey so that we can drink enough to lose our heads to the goddess. The bonfires, pyramids of peat and timber and flame, fueled and tended by two priestesses, grow taller, casting ghostly shadows on the majestic trees that shelter the grove. Three women beat goatskin drums, and we pass the bowl around again while the winds pick up, whipping and whirling the fires, the flames spitting up toward the heavens. I look up and see a swirl of stars twinkling in the sky. The silver moon hangs lightly in night's dark gloss, and the women begin to chant:

> Come, goddess of the crossroads,
> The One who goes to and fro in the night
> With torch in her left hand and sword in the right,
> Enemy of the daylight, friend of darkness,
> Who rejoices when wolves howl and warm blood is spilt,
> Who walks among the phantoms and tombs,
> Whose thirst is for blood and who strikes fear into hearts mortal.
> Draw down the powers of the moon
> And cast your auspicious eye upon us.

With the fires blazing at pinnacle heights, we stand one by one and walk nine times around the fires to honor the priestesses of times past, preparing to walk between the flames that will purify our souls and make us worthy recipients of the goddess's grace and power. I am behind my sister, who is older than I and has stronger magic and goes first in all things to protect me. I have never done this before, but I am unafraid because the broth has made me bold. The flames are calling to me, and I want to feel their scorching heat on my ivory-white skin, because I know that tonight I am invincible. The women walk between the bonfires, dancing to the rhythm of the drummers, twirling in the places where the flames meet, defying the fire to work its power. We know that the goddess gives us immunity and we can therefore be unafraid.

My sister turns to me before she enters the flames and whispers, "If you wish for it, you will see the face of your beloved in the fire." I give her an encouraging smile and start swaying, throwing my shoulders from side to side as she walks straight between the blazes, her red-gold hair indistinguishable from the flames, her long, black-clad arms twirling above her head, her talons reaching into the night sky. I wait for her signal and then join her in the fire dance, walking fearlessly ahead until our bodies meet. Face-to-face, we grind against each other, heads thrown back as if we are offering our faces to the flames in sacrifice. I feel the crushing heat, so hot that I cannot breathe, but I remember what I am supposed to do, and I hold the image of the Raven Lady foremost in my mind as my sister and I dance together between the fires. She is the first to leave, looking me straight in the eye before she dances away to safety. I know that it is my duty to stay in the center, and I spin and spin, holding my arms above me in prayer as I let the flames lick my body.

From somewhere in the distance, I hear—no, I feel beneath my feet—hooves treading gently upon the earth, but because of my acute hearing, it sounds to my mind like rumbling. I know that a group of riders has approached, though they move stealthily. In my mind's eye, or in the very flames, I have a vision of them as they dismount, tying their animals to trees, and creeping toward us, and I wonder if the Sidhe warriors have risen from the underworld. Over the cackle and roar of the fire, I hear them moving through the brush and see them standing behind the trees now, watching us. I feel eyes—intense, blue, curious eyes—upon me, and it breaks my trance.

Now I feel the flames on me and I throw my body out of the fire and into the arms of my sister, who is waiting to catch me. She pats my hair, and I can smell that the fire has scorched it. She holds me in her arms, and I am dizzy from the heat and the dance and the broth. I close my eyes, but I hear the other women start to scream, and when I open them, I see you—the owner of those curious blue eyes—standing in the grove and staring at me. You stand alone, but others, perhaps a dozen warriors, soon emerge from the thicket where they too have been watching us, and they flank you. You and your men wear heavy riding cloaks, some trimmed in fur, all of a more luxurious kind than what we are accustomed to seeing, and I can tell by the reaction of the other women that none of us is sure whether you are mortal or from the other side of the veil.

You are clearly their leader, and you hold my gaze and walk toward me very slowly. As you approach, I catch your scent—the musk and sweat of human male. The others stay behind, and they seem uncertain of what you are going to do. None of you have weapons, or if you do, they are not drawn. You come straight up to me, and the flames light up your features—enormous deep-set eyes beneath a strong, almost feral brow, your cheekbones rising up as if to meet your eyes. Your red lips defy the beard that surrounds them and protrude in a sensuous pout. Though you hair is long, I can see that it is clean, and that your curls have been combed in recent days. Beneath your coat, the flames highlight a low-slung belt of gold, something that looks as if you stole it from a god.

The high priestess does not like your boldness, not in her sacred grove, and she begins the chant of the raven, a loud, croaking caw, shrill against the silence of the night. The others join her, their cries escalating as you come closer to me. The women begin to move toward me with their arms outstretched, fierce shrieks coming from their wide mouths. Though I am staring only at you, I can see my sisters in my mind's eye with their teeth bared to you and to your men, who are slowly receding in the face of the priestesses' threats.

The women form a half circle around me to protect me, showing teeth and claws and chanting in a taunting chorus of tocks and cackles. Unflinching, you stand right in front of me, looking down at me, and I am trembling. I try to stand tall and regal to let you know that I am filled with the grace and protection of the Raven Lady. You watch me intently, unblinking, for a good long while, and then you drop to your knees.

With this unexpected move, the women stop their cries. "Princess of the night, I have come to offer myself to you," you say in French, the language of my homeland. "Come with me." I am trying to look inside you, to foresee your intentions—lust, rape, or ransom—but your beauty clouds my sight.

"Why should I go with you, stranger?" I ask, though I am thrilled by the candor of your request and the desire and enthrallment in your eyes.

"Because I am yours, whether you wish it or not. You enchanted me, with your eyes that hold the light of the moon within them, and your starlit skin that defies fire. Come with me, my lady, and I will give you all that I have."

I am gazing at you, weighing your flattery, when, from somewhere in the night, we hear the cries of a raven. Everyone looks around to see who is entering the grove. Suddenly, out of the night sky, a wide pair of black wings is soaring above us. The large bird penetrates the sacred space with its strident cries. In the moonlight, I can see its long, thick ruff of feathers and its spiky talons, as it swoops and soars above me.

"She is warning us," the high priestess says.

In the distance, I hear hooves beating the earth, unmistakably coming our way, but louder this time than the approach of you and your men. This band on horseback comes not in stealth but announcing its arrival with music—tinkling chimes, pipes, and cymbals—drifting in on the wind, which picks up force and grows stronger, sweeping through the grove. "Someone approaches," I say.

"I hear them," my sister says. "It is the Sidhe." I can feel her exhilaration rise at the thought of seeing the fairy prince with whom she is in love.

The women grow excited, but I know what this means for you, who are still in front of me on your knees. "Go!" I tell you. "Get your men out of here."

You stand, but you do not leave, though your men are calling out to you. None of them wants to do battle with the Sidhe warriors, but you do not move, and I wonder if this is the real challenge you have come for.

"Come with me." You try to take my hand, but recoil when you feel the talons on my glove. There is something in me that wants to go with you, but my sister is yelling at you to go away. She reads my mind and knows that you are tempting me.

"Are you mad?" she asks me. She and I have discussed that mating with a fairy prince will deepen my powers and carry on our mother's lineage. Tonight would be that opportunity. "Go away before they find you here," she says to you. "My sister is not for you. Leave!"

"Not without her," you say, reaching into the neckline of your tunic, and I wonder if you are going to produce a weapon and try to take me by force.

"You are wasting time," I tell you. I do not know you, but I do not want to see you slain by the Sidhe. "It could cost you your life and the lives of your companions."

But you are not listening to me. You wrestle with your garment, pulling out a bejeweled cross that hangs on a leather thong. My anger rises at the sight of it. I grab the leather, clutching it around your neck so that I am choking you. Your eyes pop out and your face turns red. You are surprised to be attacked this way by a woman. "That belongs to my mother," I say, hissing at you, pulling your face closer to mine. "You stole it from her." My sister and I are exchanging thoughts and we arrive at the same conclusions—you are just another mortal who spied my mother in the woods; just another whom she has taken for a lover and cast aside, and you, vengeful, stole her cross. "Damned is the man who steals from the Sidhe," my sister tells him, looking him up and down. Suddenly, though, she bursts out laughing. I look to see what she is laughing at, and I am amused to see that even though I mean to choke you, being this close to me has given you an erection.

"Your father sent me," you say. "He told me to find you and give it to you."

Now it is my turn to be shocked. I release you so that you can catch your breath. I have not seen my father in years but know from my inner sight that he left Aquitaine to fight in the Holy Wars. I do not know where he is, but I know that he is alive. But the cacophony of the Sidhe is upon us. The drumbeat of their galloping horses, the sharp barking of the dogs that accompany them everywhere, and their music that sounds strangely like the color silver grow louder and louder, and we can hear them singing one of their rowdy songs as they come in pursuit of pleasure with us.

I have to make a decision. My heart is telling me to follow the man in front of me, the man who my father anointed to seek me out and give me this gift. But in the grove, the authority belongs to the high priestess. Reading my thoughts, she waves her feather-covered wand at us. "Go with him," she says. "And hurry."

Spurred on by the approach of the fairies, your men have readied their horses.

One of them doubles up with another so that I can ride his horse, a moon-white stallion with a long mane. Before you help me mount, you pull the claw gloves off my hands, so that I can ride, and throw them into the bushes. As we start to ride away, the Sidhe warriors leap into the grove on their horses, slipping through the trees and the brush as if they did not exist, lighting up the dark space with their celestial glow. Glimpsing the dazzling Sidhe, with their radiant skin, bronze colored hair, and shimmering green mantles, I have a moment of regret, wondering what might have been.

But there is no time for wistfulness. You come behind me and kick my horse hard, making him bolt away. Ahead of us, your men fly through the night, and we follow. The animals know the terrain and gallop down the path so that the landscape is a blur. My head is still clouded by the moonflower broth, so I close my eyes and make myself one with the steed until I can no longer feel my own body but have melted into his. I feel his animal strength infusing my body with his power, and his with mine, and when I open my eyes again, it is to look up at the stars, which swirl above in a greenish glow.

After a time, we approach a stone castle guarded by men in the torchlit watchtower and surrounded by a deep ditch. One of the riders calls out to them, and they lower the bridge so that we can enter. Inside the gate, you, my blue-eyed captor, help me off my horse, and I fall into your arms, where it feels as familiar as if I have done this one thousand times and will do it one thousand times more. Someone lets us inside, and we pass through a large room with men sitting round a fire, who look at us as if this is just another ordinary sight. You carry me through a torchlit hall and into a bare room with a tall hearth and iron bars slashing the two windows high in the walls.

You place me on a mattress on the floor covered in furs near the hearth, and I yelp in pain as a thorn in the back of my crown pierces my scalp. Gently, you remove the crown and kiss my wound. But as you toss the crown aside, another thorn tears your finger, making a slit in the skin that soon fills with red. We are both startled at the sight, but I take your finger into my mouth and suck some of the blood, savoring its fresh taste and your salty iron flavor.

I want to show you my magic, so I when I have had my fill of tasting you and of watching your desire rise, I take your finger out of my mouth and show you the cut again. Then concentrating deeply, I run the tip of my tongue along the incision very slowly, first once, and then a few more times, sliding my tongue sensuously along the cut. In my mind's eye I see you watching me in wonder, those gemstone eyes of yours sparkling with arousal.

When I stop, I show you that the wound is closed and the skin, unbroken.

I thought that you would be awed by my magic, but, instead, without a word, your lips are on mine. Your hands have untied my silver sash and are inside my robes, grasping greedily at my body. I feel your raw, human hunger and I answer it. It is not my first time making love with a mortal. I love the body heat that comes with palpable human desire, and the scent and taste of flesh and blood. Earth time collapses, and we enter a timeless space, kissing with great care, exploring every inch of our lips, tongues, faces, and necks. You discard your braies and hose and you pull up my dress to look at my body, touching the wine-red mark on my thigh, tracing its winglike shape with your finger.

"The mark of the Sidhe." Some ignorant men think it the mark of the devil, and I hope that you are not one of them. But your look tells me that you are feeling something else, something closer to wonder. Because I am infatuated with you, I cannot read you as clearly as I would like.

"Why are you not living with the Sidhe?" you ask.

"My human side enjoys earthly pleasure," I say, and it is true. I like the solid beat of a human heart, the aroma of roasting meat, and the delicate tickling of rain on my face. "I am not like my mother who loves mortals but wearies of them. I have a different nature, and I am still trying to discover it."

"Are you immortal?"

"Perhaps," I say. "I can extend my life by spending time in the Sidhe kingdom. But whether I am forever, I do not know."

At this moment, my Sidhe blood is taking over as I inhale your scent. That small taste of your blood has aroused me, and I want to drink more, but I do not want to weaken you or kill you. My mother would be angry with me for these feelings. She hates me to question my nature.

"You have endangered yourself by bringing me here," I say. I am looking at your bare legs, and they draw me like a magnet. I push them apart, my fingers slowly creeping up the length of your thighs as I lick my lips, anticipating the thrill of tasting you. Your eyes are wide now, straining to see what I will do to you, but I have paralyzed you with my touch. Without warning, I bring my mouth to the muscle at the innermost part of your thigh, surrounding the flesh with my lips, teasing, licking, kissing, and nibbling, first one side of the groin and then the other. You open your legs wider, making yourself vulnerable to me. You let me take more of your inner thigh into my mouth, so that my cheek rests on your sac, and I fondle it very gently with one hand while the other holds your bare, tense buttock. You close your eyes and moan with pleasure and anticipation. But I use that moment of weakness to break your skin with my teeth and bite into your tender flesh, taking what I want from you while you cry out in ecstasy and surprise. When I am done, you are panting and glowing with your own sweat.

But unlike some of the others I have been with, you quickly recover. "You are not ordinary," I say.

"I am accustomed to danger and practiced in the ways of mysticism. Even if I were not, a night with you would be worth my life," you say.

I fold my arms around you and pull you toward me, taking your lips and tongue into my mouth. You kiss me back with ferocity, and I see that you have not been weakened by me. Indeed, your erect penis is stabbing at me, looking for entry, and I realize that indeed you are a mortal like no other. The taste of your tongue pleases me, and I want to bite your lip, but I refrain, instead wrapping my legs around you to invite all of you to come into me. You enter me slowly, a man familiar with women's pleasure. I wait for you to thrust hard into me so that I can meet your passion, but you barely move, and your body trembles. I remember that I do not feel like an ordinary woman to you, and you must grow accustomed to the hum of my body. You hold my hips tight against your pelvis as if you are trying to consume me. I feel you steady your breathing and your heartbeat as if you are preparing for battle, and, reading your memories, I have flashes of the kind of warrior you are—fierce and unfazed by your enemies. When you are ready, you pace yourself, moving in and out of me rhythmically until you reach the end of your control and explode inside me in a series of frantic thrusts. I wait while you recover your senses, and then you whisper into my ear, "I want to drink from you."

I push your shoulders back so I can look you in the face. "You do not know what you ask," I say. Few humans know the secrets of the blood, and I wonder where you have obtained such knowledge.

You look as if I have insulted your manly pride. "I have drunk the blood of others and have only grown stronger." Your blue eyes are angry and indignant.

"But I carry the blood of the Sidhe. You may grow stronger, but you may also weaken and die. There is no way to tell. Even the soothsayers and seers have failed to predict who will die from our blood, or even from making love to us."

"I can only stay with you if I am one of your kind. Otherwise, you will tire of me."

I know there is truth in what you are saying. I often reflect on the cruelty of mortal life, how all things of beauty fade into decay and death. Looking at you, I cannot bear the thought of your degeneration, of the daily pain of watching your skin and muscles shrivel, your spine bend, and the fire fade from your eyes. This could happen to me too, if I give into my mortal heritage, but I have the refuge of my mother's kingdom to keep me young. You must be reading my thoughts because you take me by the shoulders. "Lady, I am not afraid. Test my strength. If I am too weak, I deserve to die."

I have enough magic in me to open a place at the base of my throat with a light touch of my fingernail, an incision just big enough for your mouth. I let it fill with the red substance that is my blood. It is brighter than mortal blood, the color of cranberries, and more luminous, and I see that this surprises you. Without giving you a chance to change your mind, I press your head to my throat and let you drink.

Chapter Sixteen

31 October 1890

Every nerve in my body was on fire as I felt him pierce my skin and sink into the tender flesh at the base of my neck. I threw my head back and held him close to me, a fistful of his hair in my grip. His hand was between my legs, fingers inside me, making me reach for a climax, while his mouth brought something close to agony, but it was nothing I wanted to stop. I surrendered all of myself to him. His mouth kept pace with his hand, and when he felt my insides tighten around his fingers, he bit harder into my neck. The world went blurry, and I was afraid that I was going to die; but in the moment, it seemed better to let this wild passion be the wave I would ride out of this world and into the next one. Even if all were darkness after this, it did not matter, for what could compare?

He let me writhe under his touch until the final shudder, when my body went limp in his arms. "Ah, Mina, the taste of you," he said, holding me to his chest and stroking my hair.

We lay by the blazing hearth for a while, until the cold of the stone beneath us seeped through his cloak and into my bones, and I began to feel the pain from the wound in my neck. It throbbed and burned, competing in intensity with the heat of the flames of the fire. Drops of my blood were on his shirt.

"I know that it hurts you. Close the wound," he said.

I put my hand over it and felt the torn flesh and the lazy ooze of blood.

You know how to do it. You have done it before.

Yes, but how? How to unite the magical woman I was in the past with the ordinary Mina in this body—this drained, throbbing, bleeding, and very human body? It seemed impossible.

He placed a fingertip on my forehead at the temple and made a tiny circle, soothing me. I closed my eyes, until the dark emptiness behind my lids was replaced with a mental image of the wound. Words long forgotten, words stifled for centuries, rose from their grave and sounded in my mind: *Divine Lady, I am parched with thirst for your power. Bring me to the Lake of Recollection, where I can drink its cool waters and recall my source. Let me bathe in the Lake of Memory, so that I may remember all that you are, and all that I am.*

My hands began to heat and electrify, and I placed the left one over the wound. *Power of the Raven, be mine! Take my pain, close my wound, and let it offend me no more.*

The heat from my hand met the burning sensation in the wound, and it felt as if I were setting myself on fire. My hand seared the lesion, and I did not know if I was further injuring myself or not. But some knowing inside me made me keep my hand over the gash. In my mind's eye, my flesh bubbled and frothed, like something that rose to the top in a boiling kettle. It was more painful than the original insult to my tissue, and I was tempted to stop before I seared my neck. Maybe my former powers were forever lost to me.

Do not stop now. Trust.

In time the pain began to subside, and my hands went from scorching hot to warm. I put my finger where the wound had been, but it was gone and the area was smooth. I searched for evidence of the gash, but the skin on my neck and throat was flawlessly intact.

I sat up, and he sat with me, arms around me. We said nothing for a long while but simply held each other. I stared into the flames as they resurrected images and memories from my first days with him in this very room so many lifetimes ago. There is no explanation for love; no spoken words compare with its silent exhilaration. If that was true of the ordinary love between two mortals—if love is ever ordinary—then it was truer of a love that has contorted itself into different bodies in different eras over the centuries.

Finally, I had to ask, "How was it that you, a mortal, lived on eternally, and I, a daughter of the Sidhe, died a mortal death?"

"It was your choice," he said, looking away from me. "I could not force you to choose eternal life, though I did try."

"What would make me choose a life away from you, my love? I cannot imagine it."

"My love," he said, repeating my words. "I have waited a very long time to hear it roll from your lips again so effortlessly." Then his expression turned to sadness. "The rest of that story is not a happy one," he said.

"Then I do not want to hear it," I said. "Let us forget the past—all our pasts, whatever they were—and let us bind to each other again in the here and now, and let us make it forever. I never want to be apart from you again."

I expected a declaration of love, but he put two fingers on the pulse in my wrist, and then on my neck. "How do you feel? Are you dizzy or nauseous?"

No, I am not sick, I am exhilarated and on fire with love for you, and I want to drink from you and be with you forever.

"Yes, I know that," he said dispassionately. "But I must gauge your physical response to what has happened. It is the rare human who could experience both returning to a past event and losing blood at the same time without severely weakening the body."

"Did we actually go back in time?" I had experienced the return to the past with every physical sensation, but that was the way in dreams too.

He opened his hand, palm up. "The past is right here for those who know how to access it. Yes, we returned to it together. It was not a dream or hallucination, and that is why I could not restrain myself. When you opened yourself to me, the veil dropped, and we were caught between the two worlds. When we returned to the present time, I was still taking your blood, and I could not stop. I did not intend for that to happen, but our desire for each other was too intense. We must be certain that I did no harm."

"How could you think that you have done me harm? You have opened up the world to me. You asked me to remember who I am, and who we are together, and now I do remember. Nothing else matters now."

"Let us go back to the castle," he said. "It is crucial that you stay warm and rest."

I want to take your blood into my veins. I want to be your blood lover and live with you forever.

"This moment is seven hundred years in the making, Mina. We must be very careful. You are still quite mortal."

Suddenly, an overpowering hunger struck me. I felt restless to the core. My legs and arms began to quiver, and a void opened up inside me that I had to fill or go mad. I did not know what I desired, what nourishment could possibly quell this odd starvation. My body yearned for something, and I could only imagine that it was for him. *I am starving for you. Let me feast on you.*

He did not respond but observed me as a doctor would, as John Seward had done. He took my pulse again. "Mrs. O'Dowd will have food prepared when we arrive."

. . .

In the dining room, jumpy flames from the iron candelabra on the table made flickering shadows on the walls. I sat down to a lavish meal of Irish stew, boiled salad with beets, celery, potatoes doused in cream sauce, haddock and rice, and a long cheeseboard piled with pungent varieties and tasty rolls. I ate with fiendish voraciousness, and slowly, my hunger subsided and my nerves calmed.

We said little. The Count watched me eat, refilling my wineglass as I emptied it. "Much better," he said, pronouncing on my condition.

Why did you stop me?

"It is not a decision to be made lightly," he said. "There are consequences along the path to eternal existence."

"You said that I have the blood of the immortals, and that you have been trying to convince me for hundreds of years to accept eternal life with you. But when I agreed to begin it—thirsted for it, in fact—you would not allow it." The food had calmed me, but I was still angry that he was able to control me. He had evoked something wild inside me, some feral part of me that eschewed danger and lived to perform feats of magic, and yet he stifled me.

"There is more that you need to know."

"I know all that I need to know about you, if that is what you mean. And I know all that I need to know about myself. I do not care what happened seven hundred years ago after we sealed our love. I no longer care what happened seven days ago, for that matter. The past is dead, my love. I only care about the present and the future."

The Count looked at me as if I wearied him. "Let us see if you still feel the same way tomorrow."

"I feel more alive now than I have ever felt in this lifetime," I said. I pushed away from the table and went to him and sat in his lap. He hugged me to him, letting me rest my head on his shoulder. "If we can visit the past, my love, can we not change it? I want to return to the past and change whatever I did that separated us for all this time."

I heard him laugh to himself. *How many times have I tried to do just that?* "If it were possible, I would have already done it, Mina. I would not have stopped revisiting the day of your decision until I changed your mind. I'm afraid that the gift of visiting the past is all that we have. We can revisit it, but only as it happened."

"Like actors on the stage who must obey the lines that are already written," I said, for that is what it felt like to me. "I inhabited my former body, but I did not control it."

"And yet our powers are ever evolving," he said. "We may discover in the future that we are able to do things that now seem impossible."

Why did I decide to live as a mortal?

"Slowly, my love, slowly. Impatience will not serve you in this process."

. . .

I woke the next day in the afternoon and tried to get out of bed, but my fatigue was great, and I was unable to combat it. Every time I rose, exhaustion came over me, and I retreated to the bed, where I took a light meal and some tea. The Count watched me with concern. I could tell that he had not expected me to respond this way to the loss of blood and the rekindling of my powers. He had been so sure that I would be able to make the gradual transition out of mortal life, but my overwhelming need for rest troubled him. He had the kitchen prepare strong, meat- and bone-based broths for me, which he watched me drink to the last drops. In the evening, he made me take a mulled wine spiced with something that he said would relax me.

"I do not need a sedative," I said. "I can barely keep myself awake."

"There is a difference between a fatigued body and a relaxed body," he said. And so I drank it and slept for fourteen hours.

With one more lengthy sleep, I was able to rise in the afternoon, though a queasy feeling invaded my stomach and would not go away despite three cups of ginger tea and some toast. But a tepid yellow sun shone through the clouds for the first time since we had arrived, and it inspired me to dress.

I could not find the Count anywhere. I sought Mrs. O'Dowd, finding her in the kitchen. I asked her if she knew his whereabouts, but she shrugged. "I do not, madam," she said. I waited for her to speculate as to where he might be, but she was as silent as a stone. I sensed that she knew many things about him, perhaps more than I knew at this point, but I also saw that she was not about to reveal them to me. She was solicitous toward me, but by the way that she curtly answered my questions, she seemed either amused by me or suspicious of me, and I wondered if I was not the first female guest the Count had taken to this castle.

"Mrs. O'Dowd, I would like to try to find out if I have any living relatives in the county," I said, trying to establish a connection with her so that she might give me some information about my family. I explained that my mother had been an only child, and I did not know anything about my father's family. I ran the only family names I remembered past her, but she claimed not to be familiar with any of them. She was very formal with me despite my attempts to approach her in a friendly manner. I asked her to arrange for me to have a carriage and coachman. I wanted to pass by my old home and I also wanted to find my mother's grave. "You may try the old cemetery at Drumcliffe," she said. "That is where many are buried."

She looked at me coldly, and I stared back into her eyes, when, in my own mind's eye, I had a vision of her as a much younger woman in this very room bent over the long, pine worktable hatcheted with knife marks, with the Count's mouth on her lips and neck. He looked exactly as he looked today, whereas she looked perhaps forty years younger. I almost swooned with the sight of it, after which she looked at me with even greater suspicion. "I am fine, Mrs. O'Dowd," I said quickly, even before she asked me. "I took a sedative that has had a lasting effect on me, that is all."

"I understand the effect very well," she said in a very knowing tone. "You needn't explain anything to me. Do excuse me while I arrange for your carriage."

. . .

By the time the coachman brought me to the cemetery and helped me out of the carriage, the sun had dropped and the light had grown dimmer. An ancient stone watchtower flanked the cemetery, casting a long shadow over some of the gravestones, and an Irish High Cross that must have sat there for one thousand years, marked by its great circle at the center and decorated with biblical scenes, lorded over the entrance.

A Gothic-style church with an inviting wooden door recessed in a massive arch was attached to the cemetery. I wanted to have a look inside, but knew that I must take advantage of the ever-diminishing daylight.

I asked the coachman to wait by the carriage and I began to walk the rows between the headstones, searching for familiar names, especially those of my parents, Maeve and James Murray. I had nothing else to go on but that my grandmother's name was Una. Moss, fungus, and wear from the passage of time obscured many of the stones' inscriptions. I did not find any tombs bearing the name Murray, though it was common enough in the area. I was about to leave the cemetery when I saw a name and date that seemed strikingly familiar: Winifred Collins, 1818–1847. Where had I seen it before?

I closed my eyes, resting my hand on the headstone. The wind picked up, sending a languid chill across my face, as if it had intentionally stopped to caress me. I remembered the name written on John Seward's patient file. *Winifred Collins: Born 1818.* Vivienne? But she had died in 1890 in London. A sickening feeling swept through my stomach, but I quickly told myself that it could not possibly be the same person.

What were the chances that two female children with the same name had been born in the same year in Sligo County? On the other hand, Vivienne had not said that she was from Sligo. Perhaps this was just a coincidence after all. Though Winifred was not a common name, Ireland was rife with families named Collins.

Poor Vivienne. I tried to banish my last image of her from my mind, dead by the hands of the doctors and their unnecessary, fatal experiments. If the doctors had had their way, I would be lying in the cellar next to her on another cot, covered by a sheet and waiting for burial. I did not like to think about her, either dead or alive, with her mad eyes that were the same color as mine. I remembered how her outlandish stories had captivated me. Now I had relived them the other night in my vision, or whatever that was, with myself as the central character. Had I been correct when I told John Seward that when I looked at Vivienne, I saw my future? Was I, in fact, as mad as she? The experience of two nights ago had been as real to me as any waking moment I could remember, but now I had to wonder if Vivienne had planted those ideas in my mind, and they had taken hold, transforming into an experience that I re-created and called my own.

I sat down on the grave of Winifred Collins, whoever she was, and put my head in my hands. I wished that I could be more rational, more sleuthlike in assembling all the information I had gathered with all that I had experienced to construct some semblance of reality that made sense to me. I needed a firm identity that I could hold on to, but as things were, that identity was in constant flux, and growing ever more sensa-tional.

Feeling disturbed, and with more questions than answers coursing through my mind, I walked slowly back to the carriage and gave the coachman the location of the cottage where I had lived for the first seven years of my life. Perhaps I would find something there—anything at all—to help me sort out what was happening to me. "Ah, yes, off the old Circuit Road," he said confidently, and put me inside the coach.

We drove down a country road lined with barren trees that I remem-bered from my childhood. I used to think that the jumble of scraggly branches cradled at the tops of their trunks were giant birds' nests. Cross-ing a stone bridge that straddled a narrow, rushing river, we turned away from the sun, driving past old cottages hobbled with neglect—fallen chim-neys, overgrowths of reedy grass. When we reached our destination, I saw that my parents' house had fared no better. Weeds filled the garden where I had played, and windows and doors were crudely boarded up so that I could neither enter nor see inside.

I walked around to the back of the house and sat alone on the steps, feeling discouraged and rootless. I did not know exactly what I was look-ing for, but I had hoped to discover some connection with my past. I thought I could hear the current of the river charging over the big black stones I had seen in its midst as we had crossed the bridge. Or perhaps it was just the sound of the wind whipping through the valley. I contemplated taking a walk to the river while I still had a bit of daylight. I stood up and turned around.

"Mina, Mina, Wilhelmina, hair as black as night!"

I heard girls' voices singing as if they were standing next to me, but no one was there. I knew those voices, had heard them before.

"Mina, Mina, Wilhelmina, eyes so green and bright!"

The voices were encircling me now, frightening me. I swirled around to try to see who or what was singing, and I stumbled backward. I tried to break the fall with my hands, but I kept falling and falling until darkness enveloped me, and only then did I hit the ground.

. . .

I laugh and spin, singing with my friends. I am giving a tea party for them, I know, because I see the little cups and saucers on the play table with low benches where I sit every day and play with my toys. My dress is of plain forest green wool, but the other girls are wearing beautiful tunics the colors of gems—ruby dresses with sapphire mantles and dappled with jewels that dance before me like little insects on fire. My hair is dark as a crow, but theirs is red and gold and even longer than mine. A ray of sun slashes through the turbulent Irish sky, and I see that my friends' perfect skin shimmers in the sun, making them almost translucent. We all hold hands and sing songs, dancing in circles until I am dizzy. "Mina, Mina, Wilhelmina!" They sing my name again and again, making me feel giddy and special. I fall to the ground laughing. My three friends laugh at me, holding out their hands to lift me up, trying to get me to dance, but I am too tired to join them. While I am lying on my back, catching my breath, they drain all the tea from the cups on the little table and then they disappear. Suddenly, my mother's face is above me, and I ask her where they have gone, and her look turns dark and angry. "You were alone in the garden, Mina. Why must you always cause mischief? You know that your father does not like it when you invent these stories. Why cannot you be a truthful little girl?"

"I am a truthful girl," I insist. I have seen the girls and held their hands in

mine and listened as they sang my name with their beautiful, high voices. I do not lie, and I do not understand why the adults insist that I do.

"Go kneel in the corner until your father comes home," she says.

She drags me in the house, and I kneel with my face to the wall, my stomach turning sick because I know that when my father comes home I will get a spanking. The light outside changes and it is dark and I am still kneeling and it is very painful. My mother finally tells me to get up and eat my supper. My father is still not home. My mother's frown is a fixture now. Over a lumpy stew, she tells me that it is my fault; my witchery is keeping my father away. "This house will be without a man if you do not change your ways," she says.

. . .

The past faded away. I realized that I was curled up like a baby in the garden, my stomach still upset from the memory. I was cold and cramped, and I did not know what to do with myself. I stayed there for a while, waiting to see if the voices of the girls would come back, but all was silent except the distant sound of the river. I sat up, thinking that a walk to its banks might be what I needed to clear my mind. Perhaps the sight of the rushing water would sweep away my bad memories.

Luckily, I had worn a thick woolen skirt and calf-length leather boots against the unforgiving coastal weather, and I set out through a half-cleared path that I had trodden as a child. My skirt caught on thistle, and as I bent down to free it, I saw that a small red fox—a female, I somehow knew beyond doubt—was staring at me as if asking whether I was lost. I found myself telling her that I knew my way, and she turned and skittered into the brush, waving good-bye with her bushy tail. Beech and oak trees, some with broken branches and misshapen trunks, covered the glen leading to the river. The sun's glow had faded almost to dusk, and I hurried so that I would not be trying to find my way back in the dark.

Tall grass lined the banks of the river. The current was even mightier up close than it had looked from the bridge. The water leapt over the black rocks chaotically, angrily, spilling its white froth as it raced to the mouth where it would be set free into the sea. I walked closer to the river's edge until water splashed my skirt. I took off one of my gloves and reached out to put my hand in the water. Its bracing coldness shocked me, and I withdrew my hand, but I saw a strange reflection in the water, as if two people were standing behind me and I was watching their shadows on the current. I heard men's angry voices and something like a howl. I turned around. The same strange feeling of falling came over me, and I shut my eyes, but did not like what I saw in my mind's eye—two bodies intertwined beside the river, two men fully clothed, grappling with each other, hitting and punching. Shivering violently as if I were wet— as if I were in the midst of the water treatment again—I opened my eyes.

The Count was sitting on the ground next to me. My teeth were chattering and my eyes wet. Tears came running down my face—but from what cause, I did not know. He put his arms around me, and I sank into him. His wool coat was thick and scratchy, and I burrowed into his chest.

Do you remember?

I do not want to remember.

You must, Mina.

Images that I did not want to see and sounds that I did not want to hear came back to me: the sickening thud of a punch; a preternaturally strong hand upon a neck, gasping, choking; a body gone limp and disappearing into the water. "No, no, no!" I screamed, beating my fists against his chest until the futility of it overtook me and I let my arms drop helplessly and looked up at him. "Why?" I asked. "Why did you do it?"

"For seven long and painful years, I watched you and I did not interfere," he said. "You were born with tremendous powers. You were unlike any mortal child I have ever seen, and you suffered for it. You were just a small thing, even for your age, and I used to take the form of animals and visit you so that I could watch over you and protect you. Sometimes we talked, sometimes at this very spot. But whenever you told your mother that you had had a conversation with a fox or a hare, she got very angry with you.

"Your father was suspicious of you from birth, but he did not panic until he saw you change shape. I think you remember the night. Your mother tried to convince him that he had been drinking and was imagining things, but he knew better. He wanted a confession from you that you were in league with some sort of evil entity, so he tied you to your bed for two days and starved you. But, of course, you could not tell him what he wanted to hear.

"He decided that you were a changeling—that the fairies had taken his real child away. He wanted to throw you on the fire to see if you would burn like a human child, for it is said that changelings do not burn. I did not have to interfere because your mother was able to stop him. She insisted that they consult a wise woman, which was against everything he believed in. The old woman told them that you were a fairy-struck child and that he must take you to the river every morning before dawn for seven days. If he dipped you twice in the water, calling upon the Blessed Trinity and all the saints to heal you, it would chase the magic out of you. After two days of this, you contracted pneumonia and almost died."

"Dear God, the water cure!" I said. "It *had* been done to me before." The feeling of drowning, of being held down against my will in frigid water, had been all too familiar.

The Count continued. "Despite that you were on the verge of death, he was determined to do it again. Though your skin and lips were blue and you could barely take a breath, he wrapped you in a blanket and carried you to the water. I could read your body and knew that it would mean certain death if he proceeded. I tried to speak to him, but he would not listen. He told me to stay out of his business. 'I do not know you, stranger,' he said. He thought that I was one of the Sidhe come to rescue his own. He strode right past me with you in his arms and put you down by the side of the river. He was going to bathe you in its waters again. I asked him to stop, but he did not."

He did not have to finish his story, for I remembered it all—the two men fighting, one delivering the fatal blow and the other floating away down the river. "I carried you back to the house. Your mother never knew how you got home, which made her all the more afraid of you. I wiped your memory of the entire experience, which was easy to do because you were young and impressionable, and you had a fever at that time that made it difficult for you to distinguish between real and imagined events. His body was found that evening downriver."

I rocked back and forth, holding my arms around my chest as if I were trying to prevent my body from shattering into little pieces. "Why did he hate me so?"

"Your father knew about your grandmother and the shame she had brought upon the family. He did not want that to happen to him."

"What do you know about my grandmother?" I asked. "My mother would never tell me anything about her, just that if I was not careful, I would end up just like her."

"You met your grandmother, though you did not know it at the time. But you were enchanted with her stories."

He waited for the truth to dawn on me.

Vivienne?

"No, that cannot be," I said, growing more upset at the idea of a madwoman being my grandmother. "My grandmother's name was Una. Why are you telling me this? Why do you continue to fill my head with things that will make me go mad?" I got up to run away, but I did not get ten paces before he was standing in front of me, and he caught me in his arms and held me tight. I wanted to take shelter in his strength, but at this moment, he was the bearer of information that I was sure was going to make me go insane. He read my thoughts, of course.

"You cannot hide from the truth, Mina. Anytime you try to argue with truth, you will lose. Anytime you try to evade it or run away from it, it will find you down the road. Now sit down and just try to listen."

Though I had not run but a few steps, my heart raced, and blood swirled around in my head, tightening into a band of pressure. I wanted to escape, but I felt too sick and too afraid to move. We sat down together on a big gray rock that I remembered standing on as a little girl to watch the flow of the river.

"Growing up, Vivienne was called Una, which means 'unity' in the old language. 'Winifred' is the Anglicized version of the name. She was very rebellious against her rigid father, intrigued with the old religions, and also very lustful. The family was racked with shame over her pregnancy, which came after she had slept with many of the local men. No one was certain who the father was, not even Una herself. Una's own father, your great-grandfather, decided that the best thing to do was to send her away for good, but publicly they declared her dead and buried her. Your mother's grandfather was Anglo-Irish and had considerable holdings at one time. He took your mother away from Una and raised her. He also paid for Una's care."

"His trust paid for my schooling and comes to me still," I said, wondering how I would have reacted to Vivienne if I had known the truth.

"No, it was I who did that. Your great-grandfather was furious that your mother ran away with a Catholic not of her class. When he died, she inherited nothing. I set up the trust as if it were from the old man. I kept the stipend small so that no one would be suspicious or try to lay their hands on the money."

"You paid for me to attend Miss Hadley's School for all those years?"

"It seemed the safest environment for you, considering the circumstances," he said. "I could not take you from your mother. You were a child. You were terrified enough as it was."

I was trying to reconcile all that Vivienne had told me with what I had now experienced myself. "But Vivienne's stories about the fairies? Was she mad?" Of course, the question I really wanted to ask was, am I mad?

"Una had heard the stories of the Sidhe all her life and adopted them as her own. But she heard them from those who had actually experienced these things."

Whereas I?

"Who do you think told Una those stories?" He waited for me to hazard a guess, but I could not venture one.

"Her own grandmother, who was very powerful. The Gift often skips several generations until it manifests again. And though it skipped Una, as much as she desired it, it has manifested again in you."

"This is too much for me to apprehend," I said. I slid off the rock and sat on my heels, trying to absorb all that I had learned and all that he told me. "My great-grandfather locked his daughter away, and my own father would have killed me? What sort of family is this?"

"Your father feared you. And so you spent years fearing yourself."

I do not know if it was the shock of the truth, or the relief of finally knowing all, but I crumpled to the ground and began to cry again. He let me sob for a little while, and then he took me in his arms and raised my tear-streaked face. But I was not ready to be appeased. "What about Mrs. O'Dowd? Have you been watching over her since her childhood? Did you have to murder someone in her family too?"

He smiled at me with the benevolence of a saint. "Are you jealous, Mina? You were not even born at the time of our brief liaison."

I felt foolish. Had I expected him to be faithful to me for seven centuries? When, apparently, for a good deal of that time, I was dead?

"I have had other female companions, but you are the only one I have wanted to go through time with. I have endured your interminable cycles of birth and aging and death and rebirth; and every time, it has cost me a piece of my soul. I want you forever, but I wanted you to know the truth of what happened—the truth about your family history, and about my history—before you made a choice."

"It is difficult to contain all this in my mind," I said.

"You must give up the very act of analysis. You have a gift that is greater than the conscious, rational mind. It is the key to unlocking all mystery, and it is the very thing that you always try to deny."

I had spent my life denying my gifts because they were frightening to me and to others, and trying to find a place in the orderly, rational world. But the rational world—the world of my father, of the asylum doctors, of all those from whom the Count had kept me safe—was where my nemeses existed. Despite how difficult it was to hear the things he was telling me, he was not the one to fear.

The sun had gone down, leaving us in the steel gray November dusk. "There is one more thing that I do not know, my love," I said. "I do not know why I would ever have chosen a life without you."

"At the time, you had your reasons. I did not agree with them, and I tried everything to change your mind."

"You are my refuge, my sanctuary from everything that would harm me. We won't part again, will we?"

He stood and offered me his hand. "I want to show you something," he said. "There is a place near here for which you once had great fondness."

I started to walk toward the carriage, but he stopped me. "If we take the carriage, we will miss twilight time."

He picked me up in his arms and started walking back toward the house. But soon, his feet were off the ground and we were moving at great speed, so fast that the landscape whizzed by me in a blur of browns and greens. I was exhilarated and afraid. I had experienced this once before with him, but not at this speed and not for this lengthy a distance. We seemed to be following the river, the wind whooshing past my ears. Beyond was the great glassy dark of the sea, and behind us, the outlines of a mountain range. It looked as if we were going to collide into the side of one of the tall cliffs, when we suddenly were standing inside one of its alcoves that overlooked the bay.

My heart was pounding from the elation of flying, but I was thankful to have my feet on something solid. The alcove was dark and not very deep. I turned around to look at the sea, but panicked when I saw that my feet were on the precipice. I cried out, losing my balance and falling forward, when his arm caught me from behind and pulled me to safety. I fell back against him, looking over the bay. On one side, the gilded moon, brilliant though days past its fullness, hung over the water, while on the west side, the sun's orb had almost sunken into the sea, and the last violet mist of daylight was fading into darkness.

He wrapped his arms tight around my waist and put his lips to my ear. "Have you forgotten this place?"

I closed my eyes, and in my mind's eye, I saw us lying on a blanket of fur in the little cave, a cube of peat burning in the corner, lighting up the craggy dome. "Of course I remember it. This was our secret place, our eagle's perch. This is where we came to be alone and to stay dry when the rains poured outside."

"Yes. Do you remember what we used to do?" He put his hands on my temples. *It is still happening, right here in this very place. We are still here making love. We never left.*

I let myself rest against him, willing my mind to go blank. Then I saw myself on top of him, looking down at his face while I rode him, his blue eyes watery with pleasure and made translucent by the light of the fire burning in the deep end of the alcove. My hair was long enough to cover the length of my torso, and he moved it aside so that he could see my body. In my memory, I saw his younger face—eager and innocent— as he tossed his neck aside, baring it to me.

Do it now.

I ran my finger along his tender nape, making an incision in the skin, which burst with crimson color, drawing my lips to it.

He interrupted my memory now with his lips on my neck, kissing it gently, taking my flesh between his teeth, not breaking the skin but igniting every nerve in my body. I turned around to face him, knowing that he had read my mind and revisited the memory too. Wordlessly, he opened the collar of his shirt and exposed his neck and throat to me. His tendons and muscles were prominent, like sculpted ivory, and inviting. Together, with our thoughts, we opened the skin, and the cut filled with a peculiar pool of red—brighter than ordinary human blood, and glimmering. He was perfectly still, and I knew that he could not encourage, nor could he force. I had to do this entirely of my own volition.

I covered the wound with my lips, taking in his essence, and it assaulted my senses. The blood flowed into my mouth, and, like the rest of his being, it hummed with a life of its own that was palpable to my lips and tongue as I took in more of it. At first it was a challenge to get enough of it, but I sucked harder, letting the stream fill my mouth and slowly slither down my throat. I kept my lips tight on his skin; and he pressed my head into his neck, encouraging me. At one moment, I began to feel weak from the hard work of getting the blood from his vein, but I continued, sucking like a baby at its mother's breast. Something inside me drove me on—desperation to have him in me, to make him part of me, to have his blood mingling with mine, and this time, forever. I imagined it coming into my body and integrating with all that I was. I drank furiously, oblivious to him and to all things outside of what my lips were doing. I was in the thrall of taking him this way, feeling unleashed, as if I could go on forever, when he pulled my hair, detaching me and snapping my head back so that he could look at my face.

I tried to free myself so that I could go back for more, but he held my hair firmly in his grip. His shirt was torn and the skin on his neck broken. A trickle of blood leaked out of the corner of the wound. He passed the two fingers he always used to take my pulse over the wound, closing it and sealing my source.

At sea, 15 November 1890

From the moment that I took his blood, until days later when we left Ireland, he did not let me out of his sight. He treated me like a baby, bathing and dressing me himself, bringing me my food, feeling my pulses, listening to my heartbeat, and giving me potions to drink. I did not welcome this pampering. My energy was so high that my ears buzzed. Something had ignited inside me, something that I did not know how to quell, and I tried to get him to let me drink from him again.

"Too much could poison you. We must be careful."

"I have been careful all my life," I said, hearing a new strength in my voice. His blood was animating my body, heating me up from the inside and infusing me with an unfamiliar vigor.

At those times, he held me close, not to demonstrate his love but to contain me. "We must proceed slowly, Mina. Let us see how your body responds."

"How is it supposed to respond?" I asked.

"Responses vary. Some humans become very ill; some die. You were born with the Gift, so we know that you will survive, though you may experience some very unpleasant symptoms. On the other hand, you may not. We will observe you to gauge whether your powers are intensifying. If you take sick, then it means that we have moved too quickly."

"How long before I become immortal?" I asked.

"You are getting ahead of yourself. It will take a long time to tell whether or not you are aging. You must be patient."

"I do not want to be patient. Now that we are together, I want to gobble up life with you. I want to go everywhere and experience everything, all that life holds for us."

He laughed at my enthusiasm. "My love, I am confident that we will have forever. Believe me, there is no rush anymore. One needn't 'gobble' life if one has an eternity to explore its mysteries and to experience its pleasures."

We set sail for Southampton on a glum Saturday afternoon, standing in the steamer's glass promenade silently bidding good-bye to the land where we had first met. Black smoke sat like a wide-brimmed hat atop the great mountain that presided over the green-blanketed county. We glided out of the harbor and into the sea, where from our vantage point, barren stone slabs stood like sentinels guarding the coastline from the wind-whipped breakers. As the Irish coast receded, we looked ahead to the silver-gray ocean that had begun to shimmer with rain.

We intended to close the mansion in London and travel the world. The Count wanted to show me the lands where we had spent lifetimes together. He said that we had lived and loved in many countries—England, Ireland, Italy, France, but he would only tantalize me with snippets of information. "You said that the past was dead to you and that you only cared for the present and the future," he reminded me.

"But now I want to remember," I had replied. "I want to recapture the time we have lost."

"There is no such thing as recapturing lost time. But much of it will come back to you when we return to these places, as you saw happen in Ireland. I hope that it will be a joyous discovery for you, Mina." He added with a rueful smile, "I will try to avoid the locations of our past discontent."

"At some point, I will remember all of it," I said. "But past hardships are inconsequential now that we are together again."

As Ireland receded into the mist, the rain, and the waves, he wrapped me in a blanket, and we lay on lounge chairs inside the promenade. "I have been thinking, Mina. There is so much of the world that I want to show you, so many places that I traveled in the years that I was alone—India, China, Arabia, Egypt, Russia. It would take lifetimes for me to tell you about my adventures. Let us go there, and let it all unfold before you. Only then will you truly know me as I am today."

"I want to know everything," I said. "Though now that I have you inside me, I feel that I know you like I know myself."

"I have been a merchant, a soldier, a diplomat, a physician, a scholar, and many other things. I have served princes, kings, warlords, and usurpers; and I have also, at times, served no one but myself," he said. "I have known thousands of people, and have had numerous alliances and intimacies, but my heart was a place of desolation until now."

"But we have been together before," I said. "We have spent decades together."

"Yes, but it was never for forever, and I was always painfully aware of that fact. I always knew that sooner or later, I would lose you to one of the causes of mortal extinction. At least now, you have made the choice to try to be with me forever."

"You will never have to be alone again, my love," I said, wondering what would have made me choose life without him. But we had agreed not to discuss it, at least not yet. "I am strong and determined. We must never be apart again."

In the first few days of the voyage, I noticed that my senses were gradually heightening. My night vision became sharper and my hearing more acute. The sensation was strange and not always pleasant. The pots and utensils used by the kitchen staff clanged loudly in my ears even when I was on the other side of the vessel. One of the servants stirred sugar into a cup of tea, and the sound of the spoon against the fine bone china irritated me and gave me a headache.

My olfactory sense too was dramatically affected. The smells of the ship were often intolerable to me. From the timber scent of the hull's planks, to the polish on the finely wrought woodwork in the interior, to the ropes on deck and the oil used to maintain the machinery—scents I had once found fresh and exotic—were now abhorrent to me. Even the musky sweet tar that filled the plank's seams was sickening to me. The cozy parlor and library now carried a fusty air, and I smelled evidence of mold everywhere, which turned my stomach.

By the third day at sea, I began to turn my face away from the look and the aroma of food. Though the table was set three times daily with many varieties of dishes, I had lost my appetite and only wanted tea and toast. The Count did not say that he was worried, but reading his thoughts, I learned that I should not be losing my taste for food, at least not yet. In the evenings, my senses calmed and my nausea subsided, and I lay on the big bed in his cabin, listening as he regaled me with stories of his life. Though he fascinated me more than ever, and I could no longer imagine life without him, the passion I had for him, the physical craving for his touch, was nowhere present. While he did not sleep at all, I often dozed off in the middle of a story, and he would carry me to my own bed, where I slept long hours.

After days of this, I awoke to fierce nausea. I rushed to the basin to vomit, but it did not calm my stomach. I had not been seasick on the last trip, though the waters on the return trip were rougher. But today the weather was clear and the sea rocked us gently. I sat on the bed, wondering if I did not have this ability to assimilate his blood after all and if I was being poisoned by it, just as the blood of their donors had poisoned Lucy and Vivienne. I was pondering the irony of this when the Count, hearing my thoughts, came to my quarters to allay my fears.

"It does so happen that some have a toxic reaction to the blood of my kind. I did not anticipate that it would happen to you," he said.

It will not be fatal.

I heard his words in my mind, but they sounded less like a statement and more like a command to the gods, more a wish than a certainty. His uncertainty frightened me. Was I, in fact, going to die?

He must have felt my moment of terror. "I will not leave you again," he said. "I wanted to let you sleep uninterrupted, but from now on, I will stay by your side through the nights."

I was grateful for this; I was afraid and did not want to be left alone. But I also wondered if he would always be able to read each and every one of my thoughts. Would I never have the privacy of my own mind again?

This too he heard, and smiled. "As I have previously explained, as you develop your powers, you will be able to shield your thoughts from me," he said. "After all, it is a woman's prerogative to dissemble with her lover."

"I have nothing to hide from you," I said. It was true. I had spent my life dissembling before others, hiding my secrets, denying my abilities, and feigning demureness. Why would I hide from the one who had shown me my true nature?

"Good. Then allow me to examine you thoroughly," he said. I lay on the bed and he took my pulse, scrutinized my tongue, felt me for fever, and listened to my heartbeat. He put his hands on my diaphragm and asked me to breathe deeply and to exhale. Then he lowered his hands, cupped my pelvis, and closed his eyes. I watched his face as he concentrated. I imagined that he had been a superb physician and I wanted to know more about the time he spent studying and practicing the medical arts. I was about to ask him to tell me about those days when I saw his face begin to change. The serene and objective air of the physician gave way to a shadowy expression. His hands began to quake beyond the normal hum and vibration, and he pressed me harder. A strained look came over his face as if he had to work to control himself. I felt the atmosphere in the room change. The little path of light streaming in from the porthole dimmed, and I could no longer see the details in his face but felt a roar building inside him.

"Damn the gods," he said, hissing the words.

"What is it?" My voice sounded timid and weak. Had he detected a violent illness inside me? He did not answer me but kept his hands firmly on my body. Dark thoughts skirmished in my mind, making it impossible for me to have any clarity about what he was thinking or seeing. Perhaps the fluid that ran through his veins was slowly poisoning me. No matter that in other lifetimes, the blood of the immortals had coursed though my body; in this life, I was a mere mortal, and I could die from the exposure. And by his quivering hands and the palpable ire rising up in him, I knew that he felt responsible.

How could it be that after the wild invigoration I had felt upon taking his blood that I was now weakening so rapidly? I had once wondered if the Count was my savior or my destroyer. Now I feared that I had the answer.

He opened his eyes and looked at me, but instead of sadness or self-recrimination, his expression was full of scorn. "Damn the gods and damn you," he said. He stood over me for a brief moment, looking as if he had to restrain himself from committing violence, and then he walked briskly out the door.

I rolled myself off the bed and stood up. Though I was dizzy, I waited until it passed, and I slipped into a dress and shoes, and left the cabin to look for him. Was he angry with me or with himself? I had taken his blood of my own volition, even after he exposed the truth of having killed my father to protect me. I was his willing accomplice every step of the way. I was responsible for my own fate, and I wanted to assure him that I was aware of it.

The unpredictable weather at sea had shifted and the water had become turbulent again, throwing me from one side to the other of the hall as I searched for him. I grabbed onto a rail, remembering that I did not have to look with my eyes so much as with my mind. I closed my eyes and brought his face into my mind's eye to locate him. At once, I felt commotion and turmoil more vivid than the sea's turbulence, and I knew that it was emanating from him. Slowly, I let the feeling direct my footsteps, guiding me toward him, bracing myself along the hallway as I walked. I went up the stairs to the glass promenade, where I saw him through the window, standing on the deck in the rain and looking out to sea. The steamer rolled in the violent green waves, but he stood as still as stone.

With no care for my condition or for the pouring rain, I ran outside onto the deck. He sensed me coming and turned to look at me. Anguish and ferocity glared from his rain-streaked face. The vessel's bow plunged deep into a wave, throwing me into his arms. I wrapped myself around him, desperate at the thought of losing his love. I yelled over the roar of the sea and the pounding of the rain. "We knew that there were no guarantees, my love. I do not care if I die tonight. This short time with you is worth my life and more."

He grabbed my arms and held me away from him. Even though the boat rocked madly, his grip was steady. He looked so angry that I thought he would throw me overboard and be done with me. How had I disappointed him so with something that was out of my control?

"Get inside before you hurt yourself," he said. He was so full of rage that I could feel it in every cell of my body.

"Not without you," I said. "Never again will I be without you."

"Mina, don't play the fool. You are not being poisoned and you are not going to die. You are pregnant."

The words came from his lips with such force and precision that though I was shocked to hear them, there was no mistaking what he had said. Before I could respond, he said, "It's a boy. A very human boy. It is strong and healthy, and it is Jonathan Harker's son."

The rain beat down on our faces, and the sea tossed the vessel about at its will, but the Count's stance was firm, and he held my arms so tightly that we did not sway with the ship. I had no words to speak so I just stood there in his grip, letting the rain pound the words into my head. An enormous wave splashed over the deck, spraying spume over us. For one brief instant, I caught a look on his face that made me wonder if he was going to let it wash the two of us overboard and into the sea, where life would have ended for me and the child. Instead, with his preternatural speed, he moved us in a split second back inside the promenade.

"Why did you not just let the sea take us?" I asked, trembling in his arms.

"I considered it." He let go of me and stepped back. "I will leave you now. The staff is at your service."

"Please do not leave me like this," I said. "I do not think I can live without you."

"Damn you, Mina. Damn you and damn your womb." He said this with a frostiness that chilled my already shivering body. I felt him put a shield around himself, cutting me off from his thoughts and his feelings. And then he literally disappeared from my sight, and I was overtaken with a profound loneliness.

I ran to my quarters, throwing the wet clothes off me as quickly as I could. Even with the shocking news and the Count's bitter response, I was frantic to get warm so that no harm came to my baby. I got into the bed under two blankets and wrapped my arms around my abdomen to protect the small, vulnerable thing growing inside me, and trying to absorb the new development and its ramifications. Though he was angry, I knew that the Count would not harm either the baby or me. Perhaps after he pondered the matter, he would want to resume our love affair. That was all that I wanted, but on the other hand, even if he wanted me to stay with him, would it be morally right—or lawful, for that matter— to deprive Jonathan of his child? I belonged to my lover, body and soul. Surely it was our destiny to remain together forever. But could I reconcile that destiny with the condition of being pregnant with another man's baby?

Fear gripped me and sadness weighed on my heart. Some part of me wanted to rejoice at the miraculous gift of being pregnant, yet this miracle was rapidly reshaping my world in ways that I could not control. Questions rose up to confront me, and I could answer none of them. What if I had harmed the child by taking my lover's blood so early in my pregnancy? The Count had said that the baby was human, but did that mean that the child would be mortal? The fetus had had exposure to the Count; was it the breed of mortal who could survive the intensity?

What if Jonathan found out about the child and tried to take him away from me? With the cooperation of the doctors, he could easily portray me to the authorities as an escapee from an asylum for the insane, unfit for the duties of motherhood. But with the Count's protection—if I still had that—and my newfound powers—if they were indeed intensifying—was I above all that?

I had no answers. The new life I thought I had forged was shattering into tiny crystal shards and disappearing into the atmosphere. Thoughts of my son's welfare quickly subsumed yesterday's fantasies of endless travel and adventure and eternal love. I did not know if the Count would leave me, and I was completely unprepared to be left on my own with a child. What would I do? Kate thought that I had the potential to work as a journalist, but no newspaper—no employer, for that matter—would hire a pregnant woman. Perhaps I could see Headmistress about returning to my teaching position. But how would I explain being an abandoned expectant mother? As much as I had been Headmistress's pet, realistically, she would not consider a pregnant woman in need of work to be a suitable example to her students, whose parents were paying to train their daughters to attract financially advantageous marriage partners. As far as I could see, I was soon to be alone and penniless. My only source of income was the stipend that I had been receiving since the age of seven. And why would the Count continue that? None of the skills I had so scrupulously absorbed in Miss Hadley's School for Young Ladies of Accomplishment was going to help me now.

I let the day and evening pass, fitfully ruminating on these irreconcilable thoughts. After a night of little sleep, I decided to try to talk to the Count. He had completely shut me out of his consciousness so that I could not read his thoughts or emotions, or feel him anywhere around me. Though I had no idea what to expect from him, I sent him a note by the steward, explaining that I wanted to seek his advice. I thought this was the best approach. No matter how much wisdom and supernatural ability he had acquired over the centuries, he was still a man and susceptible to a woman's helplessness.

In the same precise script that I recognized from the note he had written to me in Whitby, he sent a reply for me to meet him in the library. Though I felt dreadful, I dressed with care. My hands shook as I rolled my stockings up my legs. My skin was cold and clammy, yet perspiration covered my armpits and burst out on my temples. I did not want to let him see me feeling or looking so pathetic, even though he had access to my thoughts and undoubtedly knew the state I was in.

I sat in a chair to compose myself and to remind myself that no matter what my circumstances, I was not powerless. Months ago, before he had announced himself to me, the Count had asked me to remember who I was, and he had been successful in helping me to do that. Somewhere in my essential being, I was still the woman who had given *him* the gift of immortality, the mystical priestess who had enchanted him and for whom he had waited long centuries. I closed my eyes, and in my mind's eye, I wrapped myself in a celestial cloak of gold, letting it tingle as it caressed the length of my body, calming me and constructing a shield of protection around me and my unborn child. I could not recall where I had first learned to do this, but I knew that I had done it many times in the past to shroud my intentions, to arm myself with additional power, and to guard myself from harmful things. As the shimmering light surrounded me, I remembered a truism that I had always known: no woman need let a man know the contents of her mind. I certainly learned that from Headmistress, but I was positive that I had also known it from somewhere deep in my past. Our mystery was our power. It was an elemental certainty unchanged through the ages. Though my stomach was still slightly unsettled, I felt alive and rejuvenated. I checked my appearance in the mirror, threw a paisley shawl with incarnadine silk lining around my shoulders, and went to face him.

. . .

He was in the room, staring at the bookshelves, when I walked in, and I was pleased to see that my shield had worked. I had surprised him.

"You wanted to see me?" he asked as if responding to a request from a stranger.

"I want to know what is going to happen to me, to us."

"By 'us' you mean you and the baby?"

"I also mean you and me," I said, trying to emulate his impersonal tone.

"Why are you asking me? Are you not aware by now that we create our own destinies? Is this baby not what you want? What you wanted since you met Jonathan Harker?" He said that name with such disdain that it made me cringe. He must have thought that I wanted to go back to Jonathan, when I had barely considered it a possibility.

"How do you know that the child is a boy? And human? How do you know that the fetus is not on the path to immortality like its mother?"

He seemed utterly exasperated with me. "He carries the vibration of Jonathan Harker, which I know very well. The fetus has Harker's frequency rather than yours, which is sharper and more intense. That is because of your immortal heritage, which you will have no use for now."

"What do you mean? How do you know that?" I had come to him feeling powerful, but he was quickly deflating me.

"Because I have lived your past so many times that I can predict your future. You are incapable of change, Mina. Do you think this is the first time you have done something like this? No, you have destroyed our love time and again with your foolish choices."

His voice was low and steady, but the words themselves had some kind of force attached to them that made me quiver.

"I do not know what you mean," I said, hugging myself. "I did not choose to be pregnant."

For a moment, his eyes flickered, turning pale and then dark again. "Your human tendencies are tedious, Mina. They have always been so. At your level of evolution, you should be weary of feigning helplessness, when you are a master at creating and attracting the very things you most desire. Every time you come close to reclaiming your power, you do something to sabotage it."

"You are wrong," I said. His words confused and offended me. I did not see how I had asked for any of the things that had happened to me, including my reunion with him. "I have barely thought of Jonathan, or anything else but making a life with you, since you took me from the asylum. I have wanted you and nothing but you. I took your blood so that nothing would ever come between us again. I did not ask for this." I put my hands to my face, not wanting him to see my confusion.

"I am sure that this is what you truly believe, at least at this moment. But it frustrates me that you refuse to look deeper into your memory, where you would see what happened in the first cycle of our lives together."

A feeling of dread began to creep over me. I knew that I was about to hear something that I would have preferred never to hear again, and I knew that I could not stop him from telling me.

"After we met, you very quickly got with child. Surely you can imagine that having revisited our time together. It was a joyous time, but because I was just beginning my transition, and because your father was a human, the child was mortal."

I did not know what he would say next, only that I did not want to hear it. I waited for him to speak, but he was silent. He looked at me with the smallest hint of sadness.

"*Nous l'avons appelé Raymond.*"

When I heard the name of the baby in the language that we used in those days, I felt my body go weak.

Ah, tu te souviens.

"I do not remember, and I do not wish to remember," I said. But I had begun to remember, not facts or faces but the feeling of that lifetime and of this experience that he was going to force me to relive.

"You give me no choice but to remind you. Otherwise, you will not understand my ire at this present situation," he said. "I am not a cruel man, but I can only endure so much, even at my advanced state of development. I must continue, Mina. Do you understand?"

I nodded. Whatever he would say had happened in another lifetime and to another woman. How much could it hurt me now?

I suppose that he heard that thought because he answered it with a bitter smile.

On verra. We shall see.

He continued: "Raymond was born healthy and strong. He resembled your father, and we had every hope that he would be as strapping as that great warrior, who, after all, had withstood mating with a fairy queen. We believed that with time, and with our guidance, our son would make the transition to immortality. But when he was three years old, a plague swept through the land, and he contracted it. Even with your superior knowledge of herbs and cures, you were not able to save him. You could not live with that, and so after one year of despair and self-recrimination, you tricked your sister into revealing the ingredients for a deadly potion that would kill one who had the blood of the immortals, and you drank it. You did not give me the option of taking it with you."

"And you?"

"I was already powerful when we met. Your blood flowing through me was apparently the last component I required to live on eternally, or at least for as long as I have."

What good is this gift of immortality if it forces us to sit by helplessly watching those we love die?

Those had been my words; they had tumbled from my own lips, and

I could hear their echo. I started to shake, doubling over, trying to hold back the tears. I wrapped my arms around my belly as if to protect the mortal child inside, so that I would not lose him too.

The Count, on the other hand, was unmoved. "Forgive me if I cannot share your grief, Mina. I lived it for many years, while you, with your selfish actions, escaped it rather quickly. At this point, it has been completely wrung from me. And do forgive me if I seem a little angry with both myself and with you at finding us once again faced with a similar challenge."

He stood in front of me and took my hands in his, exposing my face and defying my anguish with his eyes. "Mina, what do you want?" Each word felt like a blow to me. I had come here to ask him what I should—must—do, but he was not going to give me any instruction or direction or offer comfort.

"No, I will not offer you comfort. I have offered you comfort and every other sort of gift over many lifetimes, and I have found no reward in it. It is up to you now to decide your path."

What do you want?

The words were even more deafening and insistent than when he had uttered them aloud. I shut my eyes against him and reminded myself that I had power in this situation.

"Yes, Mina, that is what I have been trying to tell you. You have *all* the power in this situation, so please do not play the victim with me." A modicum of feeling crept into his voice, though I am certain that he would have preferred to hide it.

Remember who you are, remember who you are. I repeated this over and over again. I wanted to be wise enough to know exactly what to do, but I could not access whatever knowledge I needed, particularly with him staring at me and denying my vulnerability. I closed my eyes, drawing my invisible golden cloak around me until I felt it caressing my body, buoying me.

"You cannot shut me out," he said, but the mere fact that he had to say it aloud made me think that, with effort, I could shield my thoughts from him and divorce myself from his influence so that I could think. I opened my eyes to see that he was searching my face with the same curiosity of any man.

"Until yesterday, I wanted nothing but you," I said. "But what I want is no longer as significant as what I must do for the child. I was an unusual child, a misfit rejected by my own parents. Now you tell me that though you and I are of the immortals, my son is mortal and carries the blood and the frequency of his father. What will that make him?"

He was much quicker to know my own mind than I was. He dropped my hands. "You want to tell Harker about his child. Is that correct?"

"I do not want to, but I believe that I must," I said.

There was one moment when I felt at peace for having discerned and confessed what I felt that I must do, one moment when I believed that he understood my plight and would help me through it. But in the next instant, I saw in his face that that was not to be.

"Well, then, let us make haste," he said angrily. "We do not want to keep you from him. Let us settle this business once and for all."

He glared at me for an interminable amount of time, but even with my new confidence, I could not read him. I could feel his anger, but, because of his greater power and because he wished it so, his thoughts were his own and not to be shared.

Without the Count uttering a word, a steward appeared with two heavy cloaks, handed them to the Count, and then left the room. The Count wrapped one around himself and tossed the other to me. I felt energy swirl around him, some force that he seemed to gather at his command. I could not see it, but I could feel it as surely as I could feel my own body, and it threw me off balance as I tried to put the cloak around me. The room and its furnishings went blurry as time seemed to speed up. In a whirl of movements, he had wrapped the cape around me and wrapped me in his arms. My body went limp, overpowered by his greater force—not any physical strength he was using but the very power of his being, that great stream of energy that he had summoned from somewhere deep in the universe.

Quickly I succumbed to the excitement of being in this strange, overwhelming aura. I wondered if this mad energy would be harmful to the baby, and in a split second heard him answer with a resounding *no*. It seemed as if the walls were falling away for us, and soon we were gliding through the promenade deck, moving faster and faster toward the glass doors, which burst open in front of us. A frigid blast of sea air hit my face, but we were soon above the water out of range of its white crests and its spray. The rain had stopped, but the winds were still fierce. He flew us so fast through the air that we were not hit by the air current but somehow slinked through it. I could hear the blustery gales around us, but we slid through them like thread through a needle's eye. I clung to him, watching the gradations of gray—the sky, the sea—blend together as we sped along going faster and faster until the blur of land appeared in the distance.

Part Eight

LONDON

Chapter Seventeen

The doors to the mansion flew open, letting us into the reception hall. No one was present, but the house was warm and light glowed from the lamps. The Count threw off his cape and flung it on the floor. "You will find that a warm bath is drawn for you and a gown laid out. Please be dressed by midnight, and I will take you to see your Jonathan. In the interim, as always, the staff is at your service."

Nothing in his demeanor invited questions, and, besides, he disappeared, so I did as he said, entering a steamy bath scented with lavender, and tried to let the water suppress my anxiety. I had no idea how he had arranged this midnight meeting with Jonathan, but I trusted, perhaps foolishly, that he would not let any harm come to me. Jonathan, for his part, would surely not want any harm to come to me once he knew that I carried his child, even if he was certain now that I was another of the creatures he had learned to fear. I did not welcome this mission, but I also did not think that I should keep the pregnancy from the child's father, if only because the boy would grow up and discover his true identity, and surely hate me for it.

The Count sent a French girl, Odette, with a tray of food, which I devoured. I suspected that my powers were heightening because this time, despite my pregnancy, flying with the Count had not exhausted me. Could I be pregnant with a mortal child and transforming all at the same time?

I sat at the vanity and watched in the mirror as Odette swept my hair into a sophisticated twist with pinned curls at the crown, held together by bejeweled ornaments. She dressed me in a glistening emerald green taffeta gown with a matching cloak. I watched myself being transformed in the mirror, astonished at my stylish appearance. I could not imagine why the Count had selected such an extravagant and devastatingly flattering outfit for a meeting with my husband. Was he trying to get Jonathan to take me off his hands?

Tiny gems were sewn into the binding of the neckline, throwing light onto my face, which Odette tinted with barely discernible rouge on my cheeks and lips. Thinking of the baby, I had asked her not to lace the corset ribbons too tight. Still, the bodice lifted my breasts high on my chest and made my already small waist look even more narrow. Two puckered seams ran horizontally down the length of the skirt, giving my hips the curve of a mermaid. When she finished dressing me, we both admired her handiwork in the mirror. Before I left the room, she handed me a matching mask that turned up at the ends into cats' eyes and had a long ebony handle.

The Count tried not to show any pleasure with the way I looked as he helped me into the carriage. We did not speak, and I tried to keep my mind blank so that he could not read my thoughts. He wore a simple black satin half mask so that his face was inscrutable. I tried to fathom the sort of gathering that demanded formal dress, which Jonathan would also be attending. I could not even imagine that Jonathan would agree to be in the presence of the Count. I could stand the suspense no longer and asked, "Is Jonathan aware that we are coming?"

To which he replied, "In a manner of speaking."

Why won't you talk to me?

No sooner had I thought it than he answered me wearily. "What can I possibly say that you do not already know? All decisions to be made are yours. I will not interfere, Mina. I have paid the price of interfering in your life before and I will not do it again." He turned away from me and looked out the window.

I paid little attention to where we were going, though I was looking out the opposite window. I became vaguely aware that we were driving through Mayfair when the Count tapped on the window with his walking stick, and the coachman turned onto a narrow street and stopped. The Count exited the carriage first and helped me out. He took my arm—not lovingly and not roughly but indifferently—and led me down an alley that opened into a small square, in the center of which was a garden. Though it was late autumn, the trees retained their green finery, and heady flower bushes bloomed. I wanted to stop to examine a gaudy pink peony poking through the garden's spiky wrought-iron fence—a miracle in November—but the Count pulled me on impatiently.

The square was dark but for soft light coming from the windows of a three-story white Georgian mansion. We walked up the steps to an imposing portico supported by four grand Corinthian columns. He lifted a gargantuan bronze knocker with the face of an imperial lion and then smacked it down. The door opened, and we entered the foyer, a room with marble floors and a sweeping staircase with glinting rails of white and gold. Two butlers greeted us, one taking our wraps, and the other giving us long flutes of champagne.

We entered a ballroom where a small orchestra was playing a waltz for masked dancers who filled the center of the floor with a swirl of color and motion. The masks they wore were varied and ranged from simple to severe—masks with jesters' bells, hawks' beaks, delicate gold wings, shiny jewels. Some had crests of feathers, and some gentlemen wore full face masks of silver or gold. An enchanting glow filled the room, but I could not find the source of light. A fire blazed in the hearth, but the great chandeliers above were unlit. Gradually, it dawned on me that the light came from the creatures in attendance, the dancers themselves, who were luminous like the Count—not enough to disturb the eye but enough to dazzle.

"Where are we? Who is hosting this gathering?" I asked. My eyes scanned the room for Jonathan, but I saw no one who resembled him. Could he be behind one of the eerie metallic masks?

"There is no host," he said. "Let's see, how shall I explain this to you? This is a collective hallucination of mass desire. We and everyone else here have had a part in its design. Many of my kind are here among us. They have come to mingle with one another, and some have brought the mortals with whom they are currently fascinated."

He took my arm, leading me past the twirling dancers and through a labyrinthine series of rooms, littered with couples intertwined in the darkness. I saw flashes of naked skin, arms twisted around bodies like serpents, booted legs spread in the air like wings, and one bare-chested lady swinging on a velvet-roped seat hanging from the tall ceiling. In one room, a woman with hair piled high atop her head played a piano, her crinoline covering the bench, while a man in a powdered wig turned the page of music for her. With the masks and the music and the champagne, which quickly went to my head, I could not tell who was mortal and who was not.

The Count read my thoughts. "Everyone has come seeking answers to questions and the fulfillment of desires. You want to see Jonathan. He has his own reasons for being here. All is arranged."

He opened double doors to a room and invited me to enter first. In this room, the candles were lit. It took me a moment for my eyes to adjust to the flickering light, but the scene before me came all too quickly into sharp focus. Three lavish gowns were strewn across a chaise—two white ones, and one of scarlet that slashed across the other two making a cross. Jonathan was lying supine on a huge bed covered in plush red velvet. Straddling him, riding him like some sort of animal, was a blond woman in a red corset that I knew must be Ursulina. Her voluptuous, scarlet lips were curled and her mouth wide-open while she took her pleasure. Two dark-haired women lay on either side of Jonathan, kissing and caressing him and each other. His eyes were shut tight, his mouth open, and his face shining with rapture as each of the women sucked the fingers of his hands. Ursulina's head was thrown backward, exposing her long ivory white neck.

I thought I would run away in horror, but I forced myself to watch. I saw the Count watching me through his mask with great interest. The foursome on the bed did not seem to notice me, and I wondered if this vision was real. As I watched the blond succubus writhe on top of the father of my child, rage suddenly rose inside me, taking me over and igniting some primitive sense of rivalry. I was possessed by fury and I wanted to punish her for all that she was doing and all that she had done.

I focused my intent on that pristine white neck of hers until I felt I could puncture the skin. Making a crescent in the air with my finger, I slowly and carefully made a big slash at the base of her throat. Her head popped up straight, and our eyes met, hers wide with surprise, and then seething with anger. With no time passing, I flew through the air, and my lips were on her with such force that I threw her off Jonathan, pinning her arms to the bed while I sucked in her strange-tasting blood. It was tart, like a bitter fruit that one cannot stop eating despite the astringent taste and the way it makes the mouth pucker. I heard myself grunt with pleasure while the others tried to pry me from her. The Count yelled at them in a language I did not understand, and they backed off. I was electrified with the thrill of vanquishing her in this way, eager to drain her until she was inert.

But soon I felt her gather her strength. Stronger than me, she flipped us over, dislodging me from her neck, which was bleeding a rivulet of shimmering rubies down her chest. I could feel her try to close the wound with her mind, but with each mental stitch she made, I reopened it. The tug-of-war went on, with me reopening the wound each time she closed it, my excitement growing as I watched it bleed its unnaturally red stream. Our fingers were linked, and she pushed my hands toward the bed, while I pushed against her. In my mind's eye, I saw her flying backward away from me, hitting the heavy wrought-iron headboard, and falling into her sisters' arms. With that image strong inside me, I pushed with all my might and powered her off me. The Count grabbed me, and, before

I could attack her again, he had me by the waist and was taking me away. Ursulina, still pressed against the headboard, was hissing at me like a serpent woman. Jonathan and the other two female creatures cowered together, looking like some profane triptych. His face was full of terror.

Tell him, the Count's voice demanded. *Tell him, or I will tell him.*

"You are going to be a father, Jonathan," I said. "It's a boy." I freed myself from the Count's grasp, and together we walked out of the room.

. . .

I caught a glimpse of myself in a full-length gilded mirror as we walked through the ballroom. I looked taller, stronger, my already correct posture now exhibiting a strength that gave me a statuesque potency. I felt as if people were moving aside to make way for me, admiring me and fearing me as I glided through the crowd. As we left the mansion, a force gathering inside me erased every thought and consequence of what I had done.

This is who you are, Mina. It is undeniable now.

The Count knew that I was elated and could not be confined in a carriage, so he sent the coach away and walked with me down London's smoky gaslit streets. Soon enough, though, the rapture began to wear off, and I started to think again, wondering if I might have hurt my baby by what I had done. The Count put one arm around my shoulder and rested his other hand on my abdomen. "I do not think that you have harmed it or altered it," he said. "Despite your formidable display this evening, the child still carries the frequency and vibration of the father. It is unchanged."

"Jonathan is too weak to be a father," I said.

Indeed. He is too weak to be the father of your child.

"Too weak because you left him to be the victim of those creatures," I said.

"You are not so different from those *creatures*," he said. He had removed his mask, and I saw the little ironic smile that crept over his face.

We walked through Shepherd Market, where a few dim lights shone weakly through the windows above the closed shops. It was a cold evening, but I did not feel the temperature. The Count kept his arm around me as we walked up Half Moon Street and on to Piccadilly, where we crossed the street and walked into the park.

"Those women—what are they? Did they begin as mortals?" I asked. His comment that I was not unlike them disturbed me. If I developed my powers, would I start preying upon the innocent?

"No, they did not. But in your original lifetime, neither did you. You would know them as the daughters of Lilith. They are enchantresses who live separate from men until they wish to seduce them. Some call them lamia. They are unruly and wanton beings, and they are able to take many different forms—swans, seals, snakes, and sometimes women with serpents' tales."

I had a vague notion of Lilith from artists' paintings and biblical tales. "I remember the name Lilith from Von Helsinger's notes. He had speculated about whether she might still exist."

"The doctor was correct in a way," the Count said. "Everything that once was still exists in one form or another. Lilith was one of the angels who, with Lucifer, called themselves into physical existence through their desire for life on earth. She first appeared in the midst of a wild tempest, and the humans who witnessed it called her the Lady of the Storm. Her beauty struck the mortal men who saw her. They fought savagely for her attention, shedding blood and betraying one another. Eventually, they turned the blame on Lilith herself for enticing them, and they began to demonize her, which made her turn angry and vengeful.

"By this time, she had given birth to many daughters; and together, they began to haunt those who feared and hated them, coming to them at night and sucking away their energy and their blood. They began to take revenge wherever they could, seducing the strongest of men to get their stock and then discarding them. If one of their lovers took a mortal wife, they invaded his home at night and drank the blood of his children."

His words stopped me cold. *They will try to do that to my child.* I cringed at the vengeful acts I had invited by attacking that creature. How would

I protect my child if he were fully human with none of my powers? They would easily do to him what they had done to his father. Or worse.

"The lamia live by their own code," the Count said. "Men have called the fate on themselves by their own desires."

"It seems to me that you arranged Jonathan's fate. He is only human. You left him to be ruined by your women."

"That is correct: he is only human. You are so much more."

"And my child?" I asked.

"As you fear, the child will be in danger, but I will protect him. After all, he is yours too."

. . .

The next day, plagued by curiosity, I went to look for the mansion where the masked ball had taken place, but I could not find it. I retraced the carriage ride onto the narrow street where the coachman had let us out, and then found the alley that led to the square, but neither the house nor the square was there. In fact, the alley dead-ended into the back of an ugly brown brick hospital.

After that, I gave up trying to solve any of the mysteries in my life. The Count and I loved each other, and if he accepted my child and could protect it against the creatures that might do it harm, then I would stay with him. I did not want to remain in London where I would daily see shadows of my former life. I could never face the people I had known without explaining something of what had happened. Kate Reed was probably still waiting for my information to write an article about the scandalous treatment of women in the asylum. Headmistress was undoubtedly contacting people who knew me to find out how I was adjusting to married life. Somehow, I thought that word would get out that I had fallen in love with a mysterious foreigner and left my husband soon after the wedding, and that would be the end of my existence in this city.

I did not want to go to the Count's estate in Styria, the site of Jonathan's fall. We decided that we would live quietly in the London mansion until the Count's staff could ready one of his country estates in

France. Then we would move our household there well in advance of the birth. He assured me that the French midwives were superb, and that the estate would be a wonderful place for my son to spend his early years. "You have lived there before, Mina, and when you see it, you will know that you are once again home," he said.

"Was it a good life?" I asked.

"One of the very best," he said.

After the blood-drinking incident with Ursulina, we watched my body for signs of change. Though my senses were keener than ever before, the only other changes we observed were the effects of pregnancy. I was happy to simply be that—a woman expecting a baby—and I was not anxious to use my power or my magic for fear that it might harm the fetus, though I knew that the resurrection of those gifts had permanently emboldened me. The Count acted as my physician and metaphysician, checking my human vital signs twice a day, and also reading my frequency for evidence of the transformation. He believed that the pregnancy had interrupted the process, or slowed the pace of it, in order to accommodate the creation of another being. As he had warned, this was a highly unpredictable game with no rules. "The body knows what it is doing, Mina," he said. "The fetus is strong. Let us be satisfied with that for the present."

In early December, snow cast an austere white hand over the city. I spent my days taking advantage of the Count's magnificent library, which contained leather-bound volumes collected over the centuries. Sometimes at night, we took walks in the parks, where, between the snow and my new superior night vision, I saw as well as if it were daytime. Birds, animals, branches, all were clearly revealed to me by moonlight, and it was thrilling to watch night's performances, largely invisible to the naked human eye, in all its vivid wonder. Some evenings, we read together by lamplight, or talked of plans for the immediate future. We did not speculate on eternity. I did know that I had at least this lifetime ahead of me, and I started to teach myself to play the piano. One day, a beautiful baroque harp appeared in the parlor, and, strumming the strings, I fell in love with its resonant sound, and melodies that I must have played in some long-lost lifetime came back to me with ease. I also imagined that it soothed my little one when I played a simple lullaby on either instrument.

One cold winter afternoon, two weeks into Advent, on the sort of gray London day when the sky begins to darken before daylight had taken hold, we were sitting in the library, when the Count looked up from his newspaper. "Someone is coming," he said. He stood up, letting the newspaper flutter to the floor. Nothing had disturbed our serenity in weeks, and I did not like the alarmed look on his face. He walked toward the door and then stopped. I noticed that he had made a fist, which rested by his side. He turned and looked at me. "It's Harker. And another man."

As soon as he said it, I could feel the essence of Jonathan coming toward me. I felt him so vividly that I could hear the creak of the gate as he gingerly opened it and the snow crunching beneath his feet as he walked to our door. I could also feel that he was not alone. His companion felt familiar, but I could not put an identity to him. This was a new sensation for me; thus far I had been able to feel only the vibration of the Count. But now I could feel Jonathan's essence—his being, his core, that hum that identified him as who he was—as if he were standing next to me. As soon as I was fully aware of him, something deep inside me—perhaps it was my baby talking to me—knew that I had to hear what he had come to tell me.

"Let me speak with him in the parlor," I said.

"I do not like it," the Count replied. He closed his eyes for a moment and stuck his nose into the air. "They carry the scent of danger, and the one who is with Harker is very strong." He did not have to tell me that he was surprised by Jonathan's courage in coming here.

"I can protect myself," I said, knowing intuitively that the danger was not directed at me. "Perhaps it is Jonathan who is in danger. He might be coming here for help."

He is not your responsibility, Mina.

"That is where we disagree. If not for me, and hence, if not for you, Jonathan would be living a perfectly normal and happy life."

We stood, staring at each other for a while, until he knew that I was not going to change my mind.

I will be watching. And then he left the room.

I opened the door myself before Jonathan had a chance to use the knocker. Standing at the portal with him was Morris Quince. Both men wore heavy, dark coats against the December chill, and their shoulders were hunched, either from the cold or from the anxiety of the visit. Quince looked larger and more chiseled than I had remembered. His strong jawline was set with a new ferocity. Jonathan had lost the haunted and defensive look he had worn on his face since his days in Styria. His eyes were clear and his face determined.

I invited them to come into the parlor, but they hesitated. "We would like you to come with us," Jonathan said. "Mr. Quince would like to talk to you."

"Please come in," I said, knowing what the Count's reaction would be if I left with them.

"Is he here?" Jonathan asked, trying to peer inside. Before I could answer, he said, "I have no care for my own safety, Mina. I will face him if necessary. But I do not want to put you in danger. Or the baby," he added. "Things are happening that you should know about."

"We will all be safe, I assure you," I said, though seeing Morris Quince brought back the memories of his abandonment of Lucy and her subsequent death, and I could not be sure that I would not try to kill him.

The men exchanged looks to reassure each other and then followed me inside to the parlor. No one sat down. Morris Quince began to speak immediately. "I can only imagine your opinion of me, Miss Mina. I know that you think I callously left Lucy last summer, but I assure you that I did not."

I did not respond, but sat down, waiting for him to explain himself. Jonathan hesitantly sat in a chair opposite me, but Quince continued to pace while he talked. He poured out his story, explaining that he had left Lucy in Whitby only so that he could hurry home to reconcile with his family and tell them that he intended to come into the family business and to marry. "I had begun to realize that I was not much of a painter after all," he said, shaking his head with what looked like regret. "When I read that nonsense in the paper about Lucy being attacked, I saw the terrible stress our relationship was putting on her. I rushed to see her, but her mother told me that she was ill and could not see anyone. I thought that I was making her sick—sick with passion and longing, which made me aware that it was time for drastic action. I wanted to move the mother aside and go to Lucy, but Mrs. Westenra already despised me enough, so I left a letter with her that she promised to give to Lucy. I also sent a letter to Arthur, informing him that Lucy and I loved each other and intended to marry, and that as a gentleman, he must not press the issue of their marriage.

"When I arrived in America, I sent Lucy a telegram telling her to wait for me. I wrote her a letter every day, and, after weeks of not hearing back, I returned to London to find out that she had married Arthur and had died."

His face was full of self-recrimination. "I am a wretched man. I never should have left her, but I did not want her to be treated as a runaway bride. My family would have thought less of her. She was too good for that. Instead, I killed her."

As he spoke, I listened with the sorry knowledge that everything he said was true. Guilt flooded me, competing with sadness for mastery of me. "I had a hand in it too, Mr. Quince," I said. Would I ever be able to forgive myself for encouraging Lucy into the arms of Holmwood? "I was convinced that you were a scoundrel and tried my best to convince Lucy of the same. If it is any consolation, she never doubted your love."

The clock chimed four o'clock, and Jonathan stood up and looked out the parlor window. "I am sorry to interrupt, but there is a matter of some urgency that we must discuss," he said. "There is not much time."

"I have spoken my piece, and you have my gratitude for listening to me," Quince said. "If you don't mind, I will go outside to smoke." He turned to Jonathan and added that he would keep watch.

I was about to ask Jonathan what he might have meant, but he spoke first. "Mina, you must leave this house immediately." His voice was grave.

"What are you trying to tell me, Jonathan?" I asked. He was terribly nervous, and I realized the risk he was taking in coming here to talk to me.

"Just listen to me, Mina. Listen, and judge me later. We've no time for that now. We must get away from here."

"I will decide what I must and must not do," I said. How dare he come here, trying to command me like a husband? "Are you trying to recapture me for another of Von Helsinger's experiments? Do you have any idea what I endured, with your consent, in that asylum? They would have killed me if they had gone through with their plans."

"I will spend the rest of my life atoning, if you will just hear me out. I was in shock after what happened—seeing you in the photograph with the man who had orchestrated my ruin and believing that you were in league with him. The doctors assured me that they would help you. I did not know what else to do. My mind was muddled from all that I had experienced. This world, Mina"—he gestured around the room—"this world—the Count's world, Ursulina's world—that you now inhabit is not my world! And now you tell me that I am going to have a son and he is going to be raised in this world?"

I saw the frustration and helplessness in his eyes. "After I left you to have the transfusion, I sat in the parlor, worried about what was going to happen to you and wondering if you were to meet Lucy's fate. I was about to return to the room to stop them, or at least question them further, when Seward and Von Helsinger came running into the parlor. They were bleeding and screaming that a wild beast had attacked them. We gathered weapons and we went back into the room, where the window had been ripped from its frame, the thick iron bars that no man could have possibly removed had been torn asunder, and your bed was empty.

"Not knowing what else to do, and believing that it was not safe to be alone, I remained at the asylum. I wanted to call the authorities and report you missing, but Von Helsinger said that the matter was beyond anything that the police could comprehend. He was right, of course. I lost all hope and spent weeks lying in bed, disillusioned and certain that I was suffering from a madness from which I would never return. When Ursulina came for me that night, offering pleasures that would relieve my anguish, I did not resist."

Like a bolt of lightning, the sure knowledge that the Count had arranged the entire affair struck me. I knew beyond a doubt that it was true, that he bade the lamia to seduce Jonathan yet again, so that I would see him as unfit to be a father to his child. I felt manipulated by him, and I started to feel angry.

Love is not a game played fairly, Mina.

He was listening to every word. I could not hide from him, so I made up my mind to speak plainly to Jonathan regardless. "I hold you blameless for that," I said. "You were the victim of forces beyond your control. But are you not afraid of me after what you saw me do to Ursulina?"

He almost smiled, not the boyish grin I had so loved in our innocent past but a more mature, knowing smile. "With all that I have seen, I too have changed. I have thought of little else but you and the child in the weeks since I saw you. I do not think that I am worthy of it yet, but I do want to be a father. I will do whatever I must do to strengthen myself for that task. I wish for that, Mina. Despite what you may think, I have never stopped loving you or wanting the life we dreamed that we would one day have together."

I could not say to him that I had the same feelings. Nothing would equal my attachment to the Count, but the third party growing inside me had to be considered, and some of my affection for Jonathan endured despite all that had transpired.

"I am no longer the docile woman you used to know," I said. "And I do not ever intend to return to being her."

"Yes, Mina, I have seen ample evidence of that." The sardonic tone in his voice was new, but with it came a new level of understanding, a new depth that had not previously been there. "But nor am I the same man. Perhaps we will not have the life we had imagined, but we might have some new and wondrous version of it." In that moment, he looked hopeful, and I saw a shadow of the man I had once loved.

"You do not have to answer me now, but I must get you away from here. Terrible things are going to happen. After the extraordinary way that the Count took you from the asylum, Von Helsinger became convinced that he was indeed a vampire and that he must be vanquished. I do not know what the Count's fascination with you is, or yours with him, but I do not want to see you hurt. Von Helsinger has done his research and has discovered the means to destroy him—a bullet of silver through the heart. He is coming here at sundown with Seward and Godalming, who is a collector of weapons and an expert shot. They are going to confront him and kill him."

"Their efforts will be fruitless," I said. "He cannot be destroyed."

"Von Helsinger believes otherwise. They will be here soon. Please come away from this place. Let the others do as they may. For once, let us save ourselves." He was pleading now.

"Von Helsinger is mad, and Seward is his disciple, but why would Lord Godalming involve himself in such a plot?" I asked.

"It is my fault. They questioned me rigorously about the Count and his business in London. Von Helsinger assured me that I must spare no detail, so I disclosed that the Count had filled fifty crates with his treasures, including a large amount of gold, and transported them to England on the *Valkyrie*. They believe that the gold is stored here."

"And Godalming intends to lay his hands on it?" I asked.

"Yes! It is an undocumented fortune. The Count has vast holdings under many different names, but the gold is part of his secret trove. No one knows of it, and no one will know if it is missing."

The Count's laughter cackled in my mind as he listened to Jonathan reveal their plans. *Greedy fools.* I thought of the doomed captain and crew of the *Valkyrie*, and wondered if the Count would do the same to this group, trying their luck as novice buccaneers.

"Are you going to take your share of the loot?" I asked him. "Is that your true purpose here?"

"I could not convince the others to abandon their plan, so let us leave them to it. The Count can summon the powers of hell to defend himself. I care only about you and the child. There will be violence here. It is no place for a woman, not even one with your astounding abilities."

Jonathan tried to take my hand, but I pulled it away.

You know who you are now, Mina. You cannot go back.

The Count's voice sounded deafeningly in my head. He was correct: How could I possibly return to ordinary human life after what we had experienced together? Yet how could I tell Jonathan that his child was going to be raised by another—the supernatural being who had laid waste to the life that he and I had hoped to live?

Mina, what do you want?

I could feel the Count pulling at me, drawing me to him, sending out his powerful energy to recapture me. I felt surrounded by it, wrapped in the invisible blanket of his devotion and eternally connected to him as I would never again be to another. If he had been present in the room, I might have fallen directly into his arms and never left him again. In the instant that I had that thought, he felt my vulnerability, and he was standing between Jonathan and me. Jonathan jumped back, almost tripping over a table and stumbling before he regained his balance.

"How nice of you to visit, Harker."

Jonathan planted both feet firmly on the ground. "I did not come here to see you," he said.

"I am aware of your purpose, as I have always been aware of your every desire, no matter how subtle," the Count replied. "I have been explaining to Mina that there are no accidents in the world, that no living being is seduced into an entanglement that he did not invite with his innermost desires. Would you agree with my estimation?"

Rather than shrink with fear or shame, as I thought he might, Jonathan considered what the Count said, as if he had been presented with an interesting new scientific theory. "I do agree, and that is why

I have come. I have had ample opportunity to contemplate my deepest wishes, and they are to be a father to my child and a husband to my wife."

"I have never stood in your way," the Count said. "And I will not do so now. Mina is free to do as she chooses."

The men turned to me for a decision, but I was roiling in the wild torrent of their colliding desires. I tried to shield myself from both of them so that I could hear my own thoughts and feel my own emotions, but their opposing energies were tearing me apart. I could not look at either of them, but in my mind's eye, I envisioned my possible lives. As much as I belonged to the Count and did not want to leave, the little being that had invaded my body, temporarily taking possession of me, had to be considered.

Was this every mother's dilemma—to be caught between her own desires and the welfare of her child? I had just rediscovered my true nature and was beginning to explore my gifts. Would I now have to forsake all that for a life of convention?

Make your choice, Mina. I will not interfere.

"Mina, what do you want?" Jonathan asked.

Suddenly, I knew. "I want my child to be safe. I want him to be healthy and happy and to have the loving family that I did not have when I was a child. That is what I want. That is what I must care about. Not your wills and desires or mine. Just the child." Somewhere in my soul, I was still the woman who would take her own life in despair over not being able to save her son. That was as much an essential part of my nature as my gifts. Perhaps that was woman's true gift—to be able to obliterate her own desires and choose for a child. Jonathan was right; I could not raise our mortal son in the Count's world.

As soon as I resigned myself to that reality, relief overtook me, and I knew that the sacrifice I was making would not be in vain. The Count did not even look surprised, but quickly met my decision with a decision of his own.

And so it is again.

He retracted his energy from me, drawing it back into himself. His withdrawal opened up a void in my being and I thought I would crumple from the loss of him. I had not realized how much we had become a part of each other until he took himself away from me. I felt as if my own heart were being ripped from my chest. Jonathan had no conscious idea of what was transpiring, but he must have perceived my sudden weakness because he put his arm around my waist as if to catch me.

I could not move. Jonathan took my hand and started to lead me toward the door. But at that moment, Morris Quince came barreling through the foyer, bringing in the scent of cigarette smoke and an even more distinct sense of urgency and danger.

"They are here," he said to Jonathan. He visibly recoiled as his eyes took in the Count, who was suddenly emitting an air of menace.

"Let them come," he said, as if the idea intrigued him.

We heard footsteps coming toward the front door, and we saw it slowly open. Godalming entered first, a pistol in his hand, followed by John Seward and Von Helsinger, whose face bore long scars from the swipe of the wolf dog's treacherous nails.

"Morris?" Both Seward and Godalming looked astonished to see Quince, but only Seward spoke. "Morris, what the hell are you doing here?"

Von Helsinger's attention was on Jonathan. "Harker, you have betrayed us to the monster!" he said. He turned to Seward. "I told you not to trust him. He was bitten. His loyalty is with the creatures!"

Seward looked at me. "We should have expected it. They are a family of betrayers."

I cannot say that the appearance of the two doctors did not frighten me. The fear that they could capture me and once again inflict their cruelty in the name of science and medicine came rushing in. I had to remind myself that now I had power against them. "Whoever touches me will pay the price," I said. The two men looked fearfully at the Count, unaware that it was I who would happily kill either one of them if provoked.

No one seemed to know what to do until Morris Quince looked at Godalming and at the pistol and without hesitation leapt on him, knocking him backward into the other men and onto the marble floor. Oblivious to anyone else or to the gun that Godalming still held, Quince started punching him in the face.

The two doctors were unprepared for the appearance of this new enemy, and they both shrank back. Seward yelled at Quince to stop. "You have no idea what you are interfering with, Morris. Get out of here!" He tried to grab Quince from behind, but the larger man did not budge. Godalming struck Morris in the temple with the gun, but Morris did not seem to feel it. He continued to straddle Godalming, delivering his blows until the gun, still in Arthur's hand, was pointed at Seward. The doctor saw that the barrel was directed at his face and he cowered.

Von Helsinger was pressed against the door, his big black grasshopper eyes darting between the fight and the Count. Jonathan moved to enter the fray, I suppose, to help break it up. But the Count held him back. "This is not your affair, Harker."

"It is my affair. I'm taking Mina out of here," Jonathan said, reaching for my arm, but the Count stopped him, seemingly by just putting a hand on his shoulder. "Not yet," the Count said. I saw Jonathan's arm and shoulder flinch under the Count's touch and knew that he must be using his intense energy to detain him.

One must know when to interfere in the course of human events.

Though he had removed his essence from me, I still heard his bitter words inside my mind, and I knew that they were directed at me with the intent to let me know that I had wounded him yet again.

But I was afraid to take my attention off the fight. Quince was seething and out of control. "This is for Lucy," he said, delivering one blow after the next. Clearly the stronger man, his fury magnified his power. Seward kept circling the two men on the ground, trying to find an opportunity to grab Quince, but his arms were swinging too wildly for anyone to get close.

My eyes followed the barrel of the gun as Quince's blows sent it pointing all over the room. Arthur's finger was on the trigger, and I was afraid he would fire it and hit someone. The barrel swung with the force of the punches, making targets of each one of us. I was amazed at how Arthur was able to retain his grip on it.

Morris Quince pulled back his huge fist preparing for the coup de grâce. He swung, punching Arthur hard across the face, connecting with a sickening whack. The gun flew out of Arthur's hand, sliding across the marble, and landing at Von Helsinger's feet. The doctor quickly picked it up.

Morris did not look up, but continued to pummel Arthur.

"Morris, you're going to kill him," Seward said, standing back but using his doctor voice. "Do not do this. You will regret it."

I turned to the Count. "Please stop him," I said. I hated Arthur for what he had done, but I did not want to watch a man die. *Please*. I begged him with my mind, with my eyes, with all my feeling, because I knew that he was the only one who had the power to stop the brawl. He looked at me impassably, doing nothing.

It is not my affair, nor is it yours. Many faces are at work here. Do not interfere.

The Count turned away and looked at Von Helsinger, who held the gun in his quivering hands. I thought he would use it to whack Quince on the head and save Godalming, but instead, he sidestepped the two fighting men and pointed the gun at the Count. The doctor's hands were shaking as he slowly pulled back the hammer, unsure what he was doing. It looked as if the effort of drawing it backward was more than he had anticipated, and he had to use both thumbs. The barrel of the gun wavered in the air, pointed at everyone and no one.

"Get out of the way, Harker," he yelled. "Give me a clear shot at the demon!"

Look at me, Mina. Look at me.

I did not want to take my eyes off Von Helsinger, but I felt the Count demanding that I meet his eyes.

I looked at him, and he gave me an almost indiscernible smile. In that instant, I heard the gun explode. Jonathan put his arms around my waist and pulled me aside. I did not see who or what the bullet hit, but, as the deafening noise echoed off the marble floors, sounding through the foyer, Quince stopped hitting Arthur and jumped to his feet.

Von Helsinger was shaking, his big eyes bulging. A puff of smoke hung over the barrel. The Count's great sapphire eyes were gleaming, brighter than I had ever seen them.

"It is not over, Mina," he said to me. "It is never going to be over."

Eternity is ours.

The bullet had punctured his chest, but it had not exploded with blood. Rather, a white vapor began to pour out of the wound. The expression on his face did not change, and he held me with his eyes. Slowly, his body began to fade, like a painting that has muted over time, only this was happening before our very eyes. The color drained out of him until he turned pearlescent and increasingly more transparent, the way he had looked in the Gummlers' photograph. Particle by particle, his shimmering essence transformed into the fine white mist that I had seen creep through the asylum window. Then, without a trace, he evaporated into the air, joining with some invisible web of things.

Everyone was quiet, watching the miracle in astonishment. For what seemed like a long time, no one moved or spoke, too awestruck by what we had just witnessed. Despite the agenda the men had come with, both Seward and Von Helsinger were moved to wonder. Von Helsinger muttered something in German, and Seward replied, "Amen."

We stood as tense as statues, staring at the space that the Count's body had once occupied. Everyone was afraid to move. Morris was the first to let out a deep breath, which reminded the rest of us to breathe. Von Helsinger dropped his gun hand to his side, his arm still shaking. I could hear everyone begin to take breaths. Just as everyone began to exhale, Arthur grabbed the pistol out of the quivering hand of Dr. Von Helsinger and pointed it at Morris. Without hesitation, he shot him in the heart.

Morris dropped to his knees, a look of shock on his face. Godalming kept his gun pointed at his victim's chest as the other man fell. Morris held out his arms in surrender, and I thought that Arthur was going to fire again, but he did not. He just continued to point the gun at Morris, and by the time the rest of that man's body crumpled to the ground, his eyes were closed and his once powerful form, lifeless.

John Seward raced to Morris, ripping open his vest and shirt to get to the wound, oblivious to the blood that gushed out of his chest. He tore the shirt apart, exposing the wound, a garish hole marring the perfection of Morris's youthful body.

"Dear God," Seward said, and I felt his helplessness.

"If you can remove the bullet, I will close the wound," I said.

The men looked at me, wondering what I meant, but Jonathan said, "She is capable of it. I have seen it."

Seward put his hand to Morris's neck, but then his back slumped in defeat. "Can she raise the dead too?" he asked.

I knew that it was too late. Morris's life was over the moment the bullet penetrated the heart. Arthur had shot to kill.

"You will never get away with this," I said to Arthur, ignoring the gun in his hand. I knew he would not turn it on me.

His face was swollen beyond recognition. His eyes looked like little red pinpricks inside the puffy sockets. He had lost his front teeth to Morris's punches. Bruises were beginning to form below his eyes. In a few hours, his countenance would be as hideous as his character. I suspected that his cheekbone was broken, and his grimace twisted to one side.

"Everyone present saw that I was attacked by a man who was obsessed with my late wife," he said calmly. "And if you choose to disagree, let me remind you that you are an escapee from a mental asylum and hardly a credible witness." He gestured to the men. "And the rest of you are accomplices, are you not?" Neither Von Helsinger nor Seward responded, but Jonathan said, "I am taking Mina out of here."

Jonathan took my arm, but I shook him off. I began to feel my fury rise, the same savage vehemence that had set me on Ursulina. Jonathan must have been aware of what was happening because he stepped back, giving me room. I felt the surge inside me gathering strength, filling me with the excitement of taking revenge. I envisioned myself flying through the air and landing on the murderer, attaching my teeth to his neck and sucking the essence from him until he was dead. I saw it all happen in my mind's eye. I would not make the incision neatly as I had done with the lamia. No, this time, I would do it savagely with my teeth, tearing into him like an animal, causing him the most severe pain possible. Revenge for Lucy. Revenge for Morris.

Without any effort, my body propelled itself toward him. I did not feel myself moving, but found myself with my legs wrapped around him, suctioned to his body, his hair in my fist, and my hand jerking his head back, exposing his long white neck. His hair felt oily and thin, and he smelled like sweat and gunpowder, nauseating to my stomach, but I would not let that stop me. I heard the gun drop from his hand and onto the floor.

"Help me," Arthur cried out, his voice strained because I had jerked his neck back so far.

Out of the corner of my eye, I saw Von Helsinger stoop to pick up the gun, when Jonathan's boot stepped on his big, meaty hand, and the doctor cried out in pain. "Do what you must, Mina," Jonathan said.

In as savage a moment as I have ever experienced, I sank my teeth deep into Arthur's neck. I am certain that all the men were yelling, but I was too focused on my task to give them my attention. Hissing and growling like a wild beast, I did not merely take his blood from one wound, but made a network of incisions on his neck, tearing the flesh each time, causing him fresh agony. I would have drained him to death, but I could not bear the taste or scent of him—acrid, like vinegar left too long on a poultice.

I backed off him and left him slumped and bleeding on the floor. I coughed, spitting the taste of him out of my mouth. I wiped my lips clean and I turned to Seward, who was pale and in shock, clutching a table as if that inert piece of wood could save him. "Your turn, John. You wanted me, and now you are going to have me."

Before he could move, I sped across the room and had my hand around his neck and his body pinned against the wall. Looking into his gray eyes and remembering what he had done to me, I was overtaken with an urge to kill. My teeth were touching his skin when the door flew open, and a strong, cold wind blew through the room. I felt it swirl around me, caressing my face and body, and chilling me to the bone. With it came a haunting sound, a woman's voice keening a funereal lament. Lonesome and sorrowful, the cry filled the room, and I knew either intuitively or from a long-distant memory that it was the song of the banshee.

I released Seward from my grip, but he remained backed up against the wall, whether more afraid of me or of whatever had entered the room, I did not know. I looked about for the source of the screeching wind, but saw nothing. The song grew louder and louder to the point of intolerable, and I wondered if the Count had unleashed some malevolent force upon us. The men were trying to dodge the presence as it circled and encircled them, toying with them. The volume continued to grow, coming from no one and no direction, escalating until its weeping and wailing was unendurable. The very room was shaking with it, and I put my hands over my ears and noticed that everyone else had done the same.

All of us were hugging ourselves now, shivering. Arthur was still slumped on the floor, bleeding and in a daze. The air around him began to shimmer, forming the familiar shape of a young woman. I watched Arthur's face contort with horror as he realized who was standing before him. Her long blond hair was loose and hanging almost to her knees, and layers of white and gold energy draped about her like a diaphanous gown.

Arthur screamed, cowering against the wall, sliding to his knees, his bruised eyes staring up at her in terror. I could not see her face, but from the horror in Arthur's eyes and the revulsion of the other two men, and from the hideous wailing that seemed to originate in her ghostly being but penetrated into every crevice of the room, I am sure that she appeared as her husband had once described—vengeful and angry, eyes dripping with blood like one of the Furies. She did not attack Arthur but dropped to the floor, draping herself over Morris's corpse, her gossamer gown spreading like wings until he was entirely covered. She continued to howl with such intensity that I thought the sound would permanently deafen us.

Jonathan grabbed me by the hand and pulled me toward the door, but I resisted him.

"The baby, Mina. You must think of the baby," he said, yelling over Lucy's preternatural cries, which were reverberating so furiously in the very core of my body that I had to wonder if indeed the child might be harmed by it. He put his hand on my stomach as if to emphasize his point, and I let him pull me away from the horrific scene, my eyes riveted to it until he slammed the door behind us.

"Our business here is done," he said with finality. We looked each other in the eye, and there was a silent understanding between us. Hand in hand, we walked away from the mansion and into the muted twilit evening.

Epilogue

ear reader, my tale is not yet done. I fear that more blood is on my hands. Early in the year 1891, Kate Reed and I wrote a story exposing the doctors at Lindenwood for administering blood transfusions that killed at least two patients. Authorities began an investigation after the story was published, but before evidence could be gathered, John Seward committed suicide, and Dr. Von Helsinger disappeared, possibly going back to Germany. Kate and I visited the asylum with a lunacy commissioner, and Mrs. Snead told us that the night before, a red-haired man with a bump on his forehead came for the doctor and drove him away. I suppose that together they concocted the far-fetched tale with which some of you are already familiar.

Soon after our story was published, Kate got pregnant by Jacob, who married her, left the newspaper business, and became a partner in her father's textile company. Kate's editor fired her, claiming that no respectable man would employ a pregnant woman. I see Kate often; our sons are the same age, though her daughter is five years old and mine is still an infant. Kate continues to attend meetings of organizations that are fighting for women's equality. For myself, I am still relieved to not have the responsibility of voting, but I suspect that my daughter and her generation will feel different. It was Kate who showed me the newspaper announcement that Lord Godalming was engaged to another heiress, though I have heard that he is thin and pale, that his health is not good, and that he has a recurring problem with insomnia.

Perhaps of all of us, Headmistress came to the most surprising and happiest end. As Kate predicted, Miss Hadley's School for Young Ladies of Accomplishment closed its doors as wider doors of education opened to girls. At the age of sixty-five, Headmistress finally used the skills she had taught to other females for almost fifty years and married a handsome, widowed grandfather five years her junior.

Though I do muse on what might have been, I do not regret my decision to stay with Jonathan. He and I do not bring up the past, but our exploits with the immortals opened up a world of infinite sensuousness, which we continue to explore with each other and enjoy. Jonathan no longer has the youthful exuberance that had drawn me to him, but I recognize that I am largely responsible for its loss. On the other hand, he is a well-respected solicitor and a loving father.

Our son, Morris, is a sanguine child. As a baby, he nursed furiously—almost violently—but since that time, he has proven to be a happy little boy. Our daughter, Lucy, is just a baby, and I am not sure what sort of temperament she will develop. My labor with her was shockingly easy. She came out of me without a cry, and when the midwife lifted her up, she stared back at me with my own green eyes. "Look at this," the midwife said, pointing to the wine-colored stain on her thigh. "She has the exact same birthmark as her mother."

As for me, I have evidence that I still have my powers, and that if I desired, I could develop them. I often hear others' thoughts, which is not as interesting as it sounds, for with the exception of children, most minds are cluttered with the mundane. I cannot say that I crave blood, though I look forward to a time when I will drink it again—and this I will do, though I cannot say when. Once while Jonathan and I were making love, he was at the height of arousal and encouraged me to take his blood. Though it brought both of us ecstasy, it later made him feel weak and ill, so I have not done it again.

When people see me, they always comment that I have not changed in many years, but I am only just approaching my thirtieth birthday. We shall see what the future brings.

A few weeks after the death of Morris Quince, Jonathan went into his office to discover that the title to the Count's London mansion had been transferred to my name, along with a substantial endowment for its upkeep. The Count's staff had disappeared, so I hired my own minimal one. We do not live there—we are more comfortable in our home in Pimlico—but I visit it often by myself, reading the Count's books or lying in the big bed in which I found myself after he had rescued me from the asylum. It is in these two rooms that I most feel his presence. He has not come to me since the day he vanished, but I am aware of him, though I cannot locate him in time or space. Yet I know that he still exists somewhere, and, as he said before he vanished, it is not finished between us.

I have no idea what happened after Jonathan and I left the mansion on that last evening. By the time I took possession of the house, it had been long cleared and tidied, looking exactly as if the Count still lived there. No one was charged with a crime, and, undoubtedly owing to Godalming's name and connections, there were no newspaper reports, nor was there a public scandal of any sort. Morris's body was to be sent back to his family in New York but was lost at sea in a shipwreck and never recovered. My heart bleeds for his parents, and if I ever find myself in America, I will pay them a visit and tell them what a heroic man their son was.

I do not know what will become of the red-haired writer's story. Despite its sensational tone and its gripping narrative, it has failed to sell many copies or capture critical acclaim. Like almost all works of fiction, I am sure that it will be read by a few, and in the coming years, all copies not thrown out with the rubbish or lost in fires or other disasters will rot in musty libraries until the shelves are purged to make way for newer and more relevant stories. But I have said my piece and corrected the record so that in the future, my children, should they ever come to associate their parents with that work of fiction, will know the truth.

My dear Mina, why are men so noble when we women are so little worthy of them?"

"A brave man's blood is the best thing on this earth when a woman is in trouble."

Bram Stoker wrote these lines and many like them in his novel *Dracula* without a trace of irony. Today, the text is often read as a cautionary tale against the unbridling of female sexuality at the end of the nineteenth century. In this vein, I wanted to turn the original story inside out and expose its underbelly or its "subconscious mind," by illuminating the cultural fears, as well as the rich brew of myths and lore, that went into Stoker's creation.

At the time *Dracula* was written, while some women were taking to the streets for emancipation, the majority clung feverishly to Victorian ideals of purity and piety, which were considered the norm. I chose to portray Dr. Seward's asylum as it would have been—not with an insect-eating madman but full of female patients incarcerated for what we today would consider normal sexual appetites. My portraits of the asylum's cases are largely taken from original late-nineteenth-century physicians' notes in the archives of Bethlem Royal Hospital, once known as Bedlam. (The obvious exceptions are Von Helsinger's experiment to improve the female sex through the transfusion of male blood, and the inference that Lucy and Vivienne died of hemolytic reactions from receiving incompatible blood types.)

I experienced two extraordinary coincidences in conducting my research. I had set the place of Mina's birth as Sligo before I discovered that Stoker's mother was born there and had raised her son on its ghost stories and folklore. Secondly, I had fabricated the character of a journalist who had been Mina's school chum and named her Julia Reed long before I read in Stoker's notes that he had toyed with including a character named Kate Reed who was to be Mina's friend. Stoker's original setting for Dracula's home was Styria, and I decided to use that location, if only to remind vampire fans that the Count's Transylvanian origin was Stoker's invention, and that he entertained other possibilities.

The vampire that sprang from Bram Stoker's mind has subsequently spawned hundreds of variations. I wanted to illuminate the historical and mythological sources for the creature that so ignited my childhood imagination, while revisiting the lost landscape of female magical power that clearly informed Stoker's tale and shaped vampire lore. My fond hope is that both readers and the eternal essence of Mr. Stoker, whom I revere for his ingenious work, will take the book in the spirit of fun and adventure in which it was written.

Acknowledgments

I'd like to thank not only those who helped with this novel but everyone who continues to make my literary life possible. At Doubleday, Bill Thomas and Alison Callahan gave me room to venture into new territory, and Alison, with her sure hand, keen instincts, and collaborative spirit, wrestled with and for me in its creation. I appreciate the genuine enthusiasm and creative thinking of Todd Doughty and Adrienne Sparks, and also of Russell Perrault and Lisa Weinert at Vintage/Anchor. I thank creative director John Fontana for giving me beautiful books; Nora Reichard for her patience and diligence; and the support I receive from everyone on the staffs. I am blessed to call Doubleday and Vintage/Anchor my publishers.

Amy Williams in New York, and Jennie Frankel and Nicole Clemens in Los Angeles, are not only representatives but creative partners and loyal friends. I would be lost without this triumvirate of dynamic women.

In London, Katie Hickman opened up her home, family, and community of friends to me and made many things possible. Caroline Kellett-Fraysse has been a true companion in the search for all things esoteric. On that side of the pond longtime friends Virginia Field, Elaine Sperber, and Nick Manzi keep me royally entertained and keep my spirits high.

For fifteen years, Bruce Feiler ("Council of Bruce") has listened to my ambitions and concerns and has put his considerable energy into helping me shape my writing life and career. Michael Katz is always willing to support in every way. Beverly Keel injects razor sharp humor and warmth when I need it most. C. W. Gortner is the compassionate listener and collaborative friend on the other end of the phone. My brother, Richard, reads everything I write with enthusiasm, a red pen, and a Jesuit education. My mom and stepfather alienate strangers and friends by shamelessly promoting me.

In Los Angeles, I depend upon eternal optimists Vince Jordan and Jayne McKay for long, soulful conversations, and the more cynical humor of Keith Fox, purveyor of excellent food and wine, and provider of airline tickets to exotic locations. My daughter, Olivia, has the true spirit of a Muse, and continues to inspire and inform my characters. For her tremendous bravery and her resilience, it is to her that I dedicate this novel.

Printed in the United States
by Baker & Taylor Publisher Services